JACK'S FRIEND, MONDAY, ON THE ISLAND OF LIMBI.

"Mole's wives abused him in the choicest terms of their language."

JACK HARKAWAY

After Schooldays;

HIS ADVENTURES AFLOAT AND ASHORE.

BEAUTIFULLY ILLUSTRATED.

LONDON:
PUBLISHING OFFICE, 173, FLEET STREET.
MDCCCLXXIII.

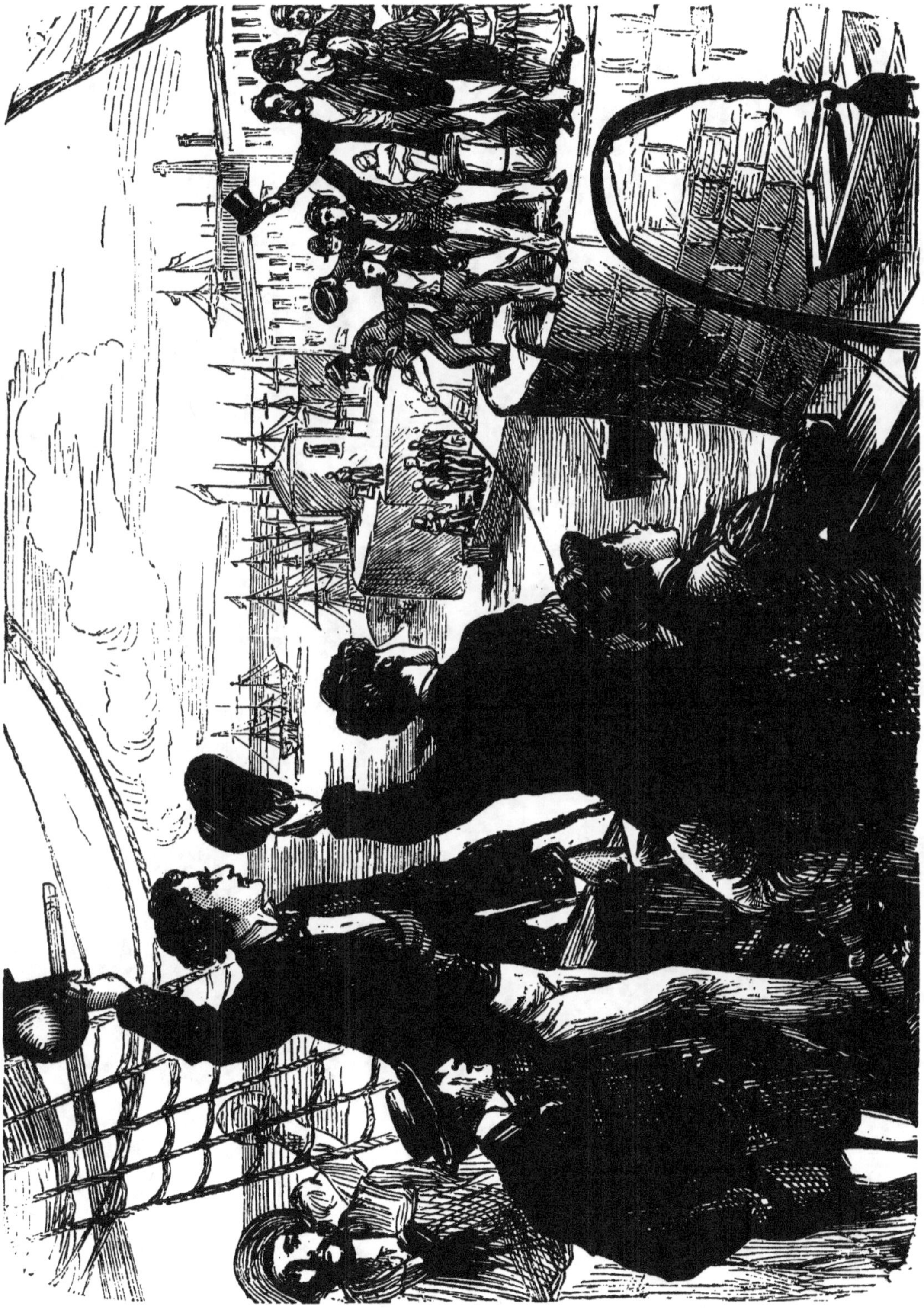

"LET'S GIVE 'IM A CHEER,' SAID JACK HARKAWAY."

JACK HARKAWAY AFTER SCHOOLDAYS.

His Adventures Afloat and Ashore.

BEING A SEQUEL TO "JACK HARKAWAY'S SCHOOLDAYS."

CHAPTER I.

GETTING ON BOARD.

"COME on, Dick. Here's the ship," exclaimed Jack

"All right! I'm close behind," answered Harvey.

It was eleven o'clock in the morning, and the tide served in about an hour, so that the ship "Fairy" would have to start on her outward voyage in a short time.

The two friends had come down by rail from Fenchurch Street to Blackwall, where the ship was laying.

Most of their kit had been sent on board the day before, by an outfitter in one of the tortuous streets in the neighbourhood.

But they had brought a lot of things down with them from London, with which the thoughtful care of their parents had provided them.

Jack's father and mother, Mr. and Mrs. Bedington, and Harvey's mother, accompanied them to Blackwall, but having been on board twice before, the ladies did not care to go again, in the bustle and confusion of sailing, for they knew they would only be in the way.

Mr. Bedington had escorted the ladies to a private room in the famous Brunswick Hotel, promising to go and see the boys on board, and return to them when the ship went out of the dock, and stand with them on the pier to wave a handkerchief and wish them a last good bye.

Both Dick and his friend were groaning beneath a weight of parcels, and they with difficulty ascended the ladder at the ship's side.

The "Fairy" was a vessel of 1,000 tons burden, and as trimly built and neat a craft as any lover of the sea could wish to sail in.

No one took any notice of the boys as they went on board.

Everybody was bustling about, appearing to do something.

All was confusion.

The boys knew their way about pretty well, for they had been on board three times before, and they proceeded below.

Going aft, Jack descended the companion, and Harvey said—

"Where shall I put the things?"

"Chuck 'em down here. Stow 'em anywhere for the present," replied Jack, pointing to a corner near his bunk.

There was a tall, surly-looking young fellow standing by, smoking a short pipe.

He was in his shirt, and his sleeves were turned up, as if he had been at work.

Looking at Jack, he said—

"Are you one of the new hands?"

"Yes," replied Jack, returning his stare.

"Oh! I've heard about you, and as I'm an old sailor and have made two voyages, you'll have to knock under to me. Don't you think you're going to chuck things about here just as you please. Ask my permission next time."

"Next week," said Jack.

"What do you mean?" said the other.

"What I say. I'm a remarkably plain spoken sort of a chap, but very simple. I'm so easily imposed upon; I was such a fool when I was at school that they sent me to sea to sharpen me up a bit."

"You look it."

"May I ask who you are when you're at home?" continued Jack, with a stupid air, but giving Harvey a sly wink at the same time.

"That's no business of yours. I'm senior midshipman on board this ship, and my name's Wren."

"Thank you. Do you live far from here?"

"What's that to you?"

"I was thinking what a pleasure your poor father and mother must have lost in not coming to see you off. Do tell me where you live. I feel quite interested in you—I do indeed."

"I live at St. Mary's," replied Wren.

"Where's that?"

"Axe," said the senior midshipman, turning away with a grin, and adding— "That's Whitechapel for ask and find out. You're not such a fool as you want to make yourself out; and, perhaps, you're clever enough to understand that we know a thing or two more than you land-lubbers."

"I have heard of St. Mary Axe. It is somewhere in the City, I believe," answered Jack. "Thank you very kindly for the information. It has taken a great weight off my mind. I feel better."

Wren stared at him as if he could not quite make him out.

Presently Jack said—

"In the boot and shoe trade?"

"What do you mean?" cried Wren, angrily.

"Ah, I see; fried fish and taters line, perhaps," continued Jack, with an innocent look.

"Come, you shut up, youngster," exclaimed Wren. "If I have any more of your cheek, I'll give you something which will knock you off your sea legs for a fortnight or more. My father's a merchant, and had ships of his own once."

"You don't say so," exclaimed Jack, in apparent astonishment. "I wouldn't have said anything if I'd known you'd been a merchant's son. Did your father really have ship's once?"

"Yes."

"All his own?"

"Of course."

"Oh, my! fancy being the son of a swell who had his own ships! Were they ships like this?"

"Merchant ships," answered Wren.

"Great big ships! Well, I never! I'll always ask your permission before I do anything in future. Dick."

"Well?" said Harvey.

"Take your cap off. He's had his own ships—at least his father had, and he lives in the parish of St. Mary Axe."

"No we don't. We live at Dalston."

"I thought you said——"

"That was only chaff. I see I shall have to teach you a thing or two. You don't seem to be over sharp, after all," said Wren, with a patronizing smile.

"I was pretty well when I came on board, thank you," answered Jack. "It was the ships that did it."

Harvey was laughing so hard that he had to turn round, and pretend to arrange the parcels to prevent Wren seeing him.

"Don't," he whispered in a plaintive tone to Jack. "I shall be ill. I'm bursting now."

"Burst then," replied Jack. "I haven't done with him yet."

"What have you got there?" asked Wren, pointing to the parcels.

"Literature," replied Jack.

"What?"

"Something to improve the mind in one bundle, and the rest's prayer-books."

"Go on," said Wren, dubiously; "you wouldn't bring half-a-ton of prayer-books on board."

"Yes, we did. They're all for the heathen when we get to China. I promised my mother I'd give them to the poor creatures."

"I thought it was something good to eat, and as you're sure to be sea-sick, I and Sinclair would have eaten it for you, and saved you the trouble."

"You're very kind. I wish it wasn't prayer-books now. But, if I may venture to inquire, who's Sinclair?" answered Jack.

"He's the other midshipman."

"Is his father a merchant, too?"

"Something of that sort."

"And has he got ships?"

"Shut up about ships, you fool. I

hate a fellow who's an ass," cried Wren, angrily. "I shall have to lick you into shape with a rope's end, as the showman said to the young bear."

"What did the young bear say?" inquired Jack, pretending not to hear.

"It wasn't the bear; it was the showman."

"What did he say?"

Wren looked round for a bit of rope to give him a practical exemplification of what he meant, but not finding any, he simply said—"Shut up," and puffed away at his pipe.

"We'll drop the showman and the bear, and the ships," continued Jack, "and we'll talk about Sinclair. Is he a nice sort of messmate?"

"Very."

"Like you?"

"There's much of a muchness about us. We're rough and ready, and have made more than one voyage together."

"He must be nice if he's at all like you," said Jack, adding thoughtfully— "But I don't think I shall like him so well as I do you, because his father never had ships. Is there anyone else in our cabin?"

"We had six midshipmen last voyage, but only Sinclair and myself are left."

"How's that?"

"Between you and me and the foretop mainsail," answered Wren, "the captain is not all he looks, and he generally can't get fellows to make more than the single run out and home with him."

"Whew?" whistled Jack.

"I thought Captain Cuttle such a nice man," remarked Harvey.

"So did I; and so did lots of fellows. You don't find him out before you've sailed under him."

"How does he get men?" asked Jack.

"Oh, he hangs about schools and picks up boys, and spins them yarns, and all that," replied Wren.

"Why do you stop?" said Harvey.

"Oh, I'm all right. I'm well in with the owners, and Cuttle knows he must not say much to me, or——"

"What?"

"Well, I won't blab, but I could say more about Silas Cuttle than he'd like you or any one else to hear. I'm cock of this walk, and if there's any dispute which is referred to the captain, you may lay your life he'll back me up through thick and thin. Is that good enough for you?"

"It's gratifying," replied Jack, "when you come to consider that you've shipped for a good five or six months' voyage."

Wren grinned rather savagely.

"I generally let all the youngster know I'm master because it saves a deal of trouble. Sinclair and I are palls, but he daren't say much to me. We shall, I expect, have five midshipmen as they call them, though you're only apprentices perhaps. There's myself, Sinclair, you two, and another land crab.

"What are you?" asked Jack.

"Well, of course I'm only an apprentice if you come to that. I had a premium paid with me, but I expect to be third mate soon. There are real midshipmen in the royal navy, and it sounds well to call us so; that's how it is."

"I'm astonished at what you say about Captain Cuttle," Jack observed, dropping his jocular air and becoming serious.

"You'll be more astonished before you've sailed far," replied Wren, with a grin. "You'll have something to put in your log, my hearty."

"What's that?" exclaimed a voice behind him.

"Oh, it's you, S'clair," said Wren, abbreviating his friend's name. "Glad to see you on board. Thought you'd join at Gravesend."

"So I should have done," replied Sinclair, a short, ugly, shock-headed boy who didn't know how to pronounce his "h's" "only I spent all my money last night in Ratcliff 'ighway, and found it would be no bottle, as they say, to go in for another spree down the river. 'Ard up, my boy."

"I beg your pardon," exclaimed Jack. "You've dropped something.

"What's that, my sea griffin?" answered Sinclair.

"Only a letter or two."

"What?"

"One of those things belonging to the alphabet," continued Jack. "The letter H, I mean. 'Twas whispered in Heaven and mutttered somewhere else, while echo caught faintly the sound as it fell. Don't you know the riddle? But I suppose you don't. You'd spell horse with an O."

"I'll give you something to say O for if you don't mind. Look out for squalls. You're a green hand and must pay your footing," said Sinclair, angrily.

"Plenty of time," answered Jack. "I'm going on deck. Step out Dick."

The boys trotted away, and Sinclair, who looked as if he had not had an hour's sleep all night, and had drank more than his shock head could stand, said to Wren—

"That's a nice pup, any way."

"So I begin to think," answered Wren, "though I'm not quite up to his rig yet."

"Have you talked to him?"

"Yes. He's either a great fool or else he's been kidding me."

"Perhaps a bit of both. Never mind, wait till we're fairly in the Channel, and we'll cob him within an inch of his life."

"That's as certain as that we shall spend Christmas in the tropics," answered Wren. "He says he's got prayer-books here. I think it's grub. Let's overhaul his locker."

"Steer ahead," replied Sinclair.

And the two old tars approached the corner in which Jack and Harvey had deposited their little parcels, and began to look at them curiously.

CHAPTER II.

DROPPING DOWN THE RIVER.

ON deck Jack found his father. Mr. Bedington was looking round for him with a puzzled air, as if he did not quite understand the bustle and confusion which reigned everywhere.

"Oh, here you are, John," he exclaimed, "I expected you would come and meet me."

"I'm bound to turn up like a bad penny," exclaimed Jack.

"I don't think this is the time for such remarks," replied his father. "You have bade your mother farewell, and she is now in great grief at losing you. Remember that you are going away for a year at least, and that your friends are very anxious about your conduct and welfare."

"My dear father," said Jack, "will you kindly remember that I have heard all that before, and that I have promised to be as good a boy as I can?"

Mr. Bedington looked grave.

"Do you feel no sorrow at parting from me?" he said.

"I want to see the world."

"Then you don't feel anything. You are hardened," Mr. Bedington replied, with a painful intonation.

"I did not mean that," Jack answered, quickly, noticing the change in his father's voice. "I only love four people in the world. They are my mother, yourself, little Emily, and Dick Harvey."

"Well, well. I only speak for your good, as you ought to know by this time. I say that you are going away from us. I should like to see you show your sense of the separation."

"I'll cry, if it would please you," Jack said.

"There you are again. This perpetual levity gives me great uneasiness. You are like—like—what shall I say?"

"A trough full of dough with some yeast put in it, always rising," Jack suggested.

Mr. Bedington could not help smiling.

"I hope your jocular temperament will not involve you in serious disturbance with your future comrades," he said. "In the captain I have the utmost confidence."

"Have you?" said Jack. "That's more than I have, since——"

He paused, thinking it scarcely worth while to arouse his father's suspicion, when he had only heard a hint from Wren, which might or might not be well founded.

"Since when?" repeated his father.

"I did not mean anything. One of the fellows below does not speak well of him; that is all," he replied.

"Perhaps he has given his captain displeasure, and Mr. Cuttle has rightly reproved or punished him for it. Boys are rarely if ever satisfied with those who are placed over them. I should not listen, if I were you, to such idle tales. Endeavour, my boy, to do your duty, and if you know you are right, you may defy the world."

"But suppose," said Jack, "that you are not one of those beautiful boys you read of in story books, and cannot always do your duty; what then?"

"Then you must take the consequences."

"I'm ready," answered Jack, in a good humoured voice, "and can't say more than I have said; and that is, I will do the best I can, and that I am very—very sorry to leave you and my mother, who ever since I thought about you have been as kind as it was possible for anybody to be."

"We have tried to be so, and it is now by your own wish, not ours, that you are going to sea. So, whatever result your venture has, you must not blame us," replied Mr. Bedington.

"I shall never do that. I'm big enough now to go on my own hook," replied Jack.

Mr. Bedington looked at him affectionately.

"Recollect one thing, Jack," he said.

"What's that, father?"

"You're my son, and the heir to a fine property."

"I am as likely to forget the latter as not, but the former, I shall never, never let slip out of my mind," replied Jack, warmly.

Mr. Bedington pressed his hand, and a voice exclaimed loudly—

"Any more for the shore? Now then, any more for the shore?"

"You're off, Jack," said his father. "Good-bye, and good luck go with you!"

"Never fear for me, father; I'm like a cat; I always tumble on my legs," answered Jack.

"You won't worry yourself, if you think of the home you've left and the kind friends?"

"Don't fret; I'll make new ones."

"Any more for the shore?" cried the voice a second time.

A sad expression stole over Mr. Bedington's countenance.

He was sorry at parting with Jack, more sorry than Jack was, if the truth must be told.

Captain Cuttle came up at that moment with his cheery smile, and his frank, open countenance, which certainly belied the character that the senior midshipman had given him.

"Never trust faces," was a maxim Jack had heard, and he looked doubtingly upon his future captain.

"I'd rather have Crawcour and old Mole to deal with," he thought.

"Now, sir; going ashore?" cried Captain Cuttle.

"Ah, captain, how do you do?" replied Mr. Bedington.

"Oh, it's you, sir. Now lad, bustle about. Glad to see you," answered Captain Cuttle, with a bland look and an oily smile, which he could put on when the occasion required it.

"You'll see to my boy?"

"He's right enough with me," answered Captain Cuttle. "Lord love 'em! I treat all my youngsters as if they were my own children. Sorry I didn't see you before. We've had half-a-dozen of champagne in the cabin, and I should have been proud of your company. Must wet the anchor, as the saying is."

Captain Cuttle caught sight of Jack again.

"Step aft, my lad," he continued; "you're in the way here."

Jack thought he detected a dangerous gleam in those sly grey eyes which he had never seen before.

"Good-bye, father," he said.

"Good-bye, Jack, and God bless you!" answered Mr. Bedington.

Jack went aft, as his captain had ordered him, showing his appreciation of the golden rule of obedience to orders at an early stage of his career.

In a short time all those who were for the shore had gone, except one or two who had made up their minds to accompany their friends as far as Gravesend, where the ship was to lay to for the night, and where they could travel back without any difficulty, as the "Fairy" had to take on board a passenger at the last-named place, and look out for fresh hands to supply such of her crew as might be missing at the last moment.

It is not an unusual thing for a captain, when the roll is called over, to find several seamen absent.

Either they have been too drunk to sail, or they have changed their minds after signing articles, and the deficiency has to be made up by the crimps at Gravesend, as a ship cannot go to sea short-handed.

The gates of the dock were opened, and the "Fairy" sailed out.

Jack and Harvey posted themselves in an advantageous position, to catch a last glimpse of their friends as they went through the cut leading from the dock to the river.

"I wish I were like you, Jack," said Harvey, with a sigh.

"Why?" asked Jack.

"My father can't come to see me off, and I think he's rather glad I'm going. We've such a lot at home. He's only a clerk in the City, you know, and it comes hard upon him to have to keep half a dozen of us. How he paid the premium for me here I don't know."

"Keep up your pecker, old boy," replied Jack. "We'll make our fortunes in the East, and then we'll come back and astonish them."

"Look!" cried Harvey.

"Where?"

"On the pier. I can see your father and mother, and my mother. There they are, standing on the edge almost, to see us off into the river."

"Let's give 'em a cheer," said Jack Harkaway.

"Right you are," replied Harvey.

The lads took off their caps, and gave a ringing cheer, which Mr. Bedington answered from the shore.

"Hurrah! hurrah! hurrah!"

The beautiful vessel glided slowly into the river with sails set.

Soon the stream caught her, and, aided by wind and tide, she dropped down the river.

Mrs. Harvey turned away and hid her face, as her tears fell fast, and Mrs. Bedington who had made her acquaintance, tried to comfort her.

Harvey saw this, and he, too, began to cry.

"Dick," said Jack, "this won't do—blubbering."

"I can't help it. Mother's looking so cut up," replied Harvey.

"You're a man now and a sailor. It won't do to cry. Look at me," said Jack.

Harvey did look at him.

"Why," said he, "your eyes are as wet as mine; you're crying too."

"So I am old fellow. I was only humbugging you. After all, we're only boys, and we can't help feeling it," answered Jack, in a hoarse voice.

But in spite of their emotion, they kept the old pier in sight, and waved their hats, though the figures standing upon it were indistinct, and the only things they could make out clearly were the mud-begrimed bank of the Thames' low-lying shore.

"Come!" exclaimed a voice at Jack's elbow, "we've had enough of that. No snuffling; you'll find something to do."

It was Captain Cuttle who spoke.

The men were getting into their places and attending to their duty in a stupid sort of way, looking as if they had not revived from the night they had made of it before sailing.

The officers, however, were sober, and they saw that the necessary work was done somehow or other.

"Touch your cap when you are spoken to," continued the captain.

"I didn't know we were on board a man-of-war, sir," replied Jack, with his usual impudence.

"Never mind whether we are or not. I'll have dicipline maintained on board my ship; touch your cap," said the captain.

Jack did so, and the captain went amidships.

"That's a taste of what we got to expect," observed Jack.

"Yes," said Harvey; "he's beginning early."

"Rather. I think all that Wren told us isn't far from the truth."

They turned round with a sigh, and unexpectedly met an old foe.

"Hunston!" exclaimed Jack, astonished.

"Yes, my boy, it's me, as you truly remark, alive and kicking," replied Hunston, senior.

"I heard that one of Dr. Begbie's boys was coming, but I didn't think it was you!" cried Jack.

"Or you would not have shipped, eh?"

"Perhaps not."

"You see, we're destined to meet, and we'd best be friends; shake hands."

"I shan't. I don't want to be friends with you, because I know what your friendship means, and how treacherous you are," replied Jack.

"All right, my hearty, please yourself. It won't break my heart," said Hunston.

And he walked away with his hands in his pockets.

"Fancy that beast, Hunston, being on board," said Harvey, as he looked after him, blankly.

"I wish I'd known it, that I do," added Jack. "It seems to me we are to have more annoyances on board ship than we ever bargained for."

"THANK YOU FOR COMING TO SEE ME," SAID JACK."

"It can't be helped, unless we cut and run at Gravesend."

"I shan't do that; I'll stand to my guns."

"What you do, I'll do," replied Harvey, looking at his friend with confidence, "though I can't help saying I almost wish we were back again at Crawcour's."

"Don't turn tail at the start, Dick," said Jack, with a reproachful glance.

"I'm not turning tail, but I don't like Hunston being on board, and I don't like what I've seen of the captain, or what Wren said of him."

"They can't eat us or skin us. We shall be right enough. Don't funk," replied Jack. "Still it is funny Hunston should be here. I thought we had done with him for ever. I've licked him and can do so again, and he won't play any tricks with us, though he may be a better sailor, as he's been to sea before. If I'm afraid of anyone, it's——"

"Wren?" said Harvey.

"No, the captain."

The boys hung over the side, and looked in a melancholy manner at the river, which was running down in a muddy stream to the sea.

CHAPTER III.

TAKING IN A PASSENGER.

BEING a sailing-ship, and the wind not being very strong, the "Fairy" did not make very quick progress, relying almost entirely upon the tide.

She was heavily laden, and bound for Canton, in China.

There was accommodation for a few passengers, though she was not a passenger ship, but merely a trader.

New hands, like Jack and Harvey, were not molested by anyone, and did very much as they liked for the first day.

When the pier faded away, and the friends they had left behind were but dim specks, and then entirely shut out as they rounded a reach in the river, the boys turned to go below.

"We'll put things a bit straight," said Jack, "and indulge ourselves with a glass of currant wine and a slice of cake."

Not being in the habit of looking down on the deck, he did not see a coil of rope, over which he tripped, pitching into a tub of water, and getting up slightly wet, while the sailors laughed loudly.

"What cheer, my hearty?" exclaimed an old salt.

"I've had enough cheering," answered Jack. "I've been cheering till I'm hoarse."

At this the sailors laughed again, and to avoid their ridicule, Jack was glad to descend the ladder.

But he was in such a hurry to get below that his foot slipped.

He lost his hold, and rolled along the deck till he was brought up by a kick from Wren.

"I say!" he cried. "That's a nice way of coming below. You're not obliged to do it all of a lump."

"I couldn't help it," replied Jack, rubbing himself with a dismal expression.

To his surprise, Wren and Sinclair were eating various delicacies, which, at the moment, he did not suspect belonged to himself.

"You might ask a fellow to join you," he said.

"So we will. Help yourself," answered Wren.

Jack did so, and Harvey joined in when he came up.

Cake, oranges, and currant wine vanished like lightning.

Presently Wren and Sinclair were called for, and stuffing their mouths and pockets full of anything they could lay their hands upon, they went away.

"That was generous of them," said Harvey.

"Very," answered Jack. "It's more than I expected. Wren does not seem such a bad sort after all. Now let's put our things away."

"They'll be safe enough. The fellows won't bag our grub as they've got some of their own."

"I'd rather have them in my chest, though," replied Jack.

He turned round to open the packages, and to his disgust, found that they were all empty.

"Hallo!" he exclaimed.

"What's up, now?" asked Harvey.

"Bless their eyes," replied Jack; "they've been and gone and done it."

"Done what?"

"Why, we've been drinking our own wine and eating our own stuff. That's a good joke. Wren said we had something to learn, and it looks like it, rather. First of all I go and tumble over a rope and douse myself in a tub of dirty water, then I roll down the ladder, and now I find they've stolen a march upon us, and eaten our prog. We certainly have got something to learn, and must keep our weather eye open, Dick."

"It looks like it," answered Harvey. "But it's no use crying over spilt milk; let's go and look about us a bit."

Concealing his mortification as well as he could, he led the way on deck again.

Being on board ship was very different to being on shore.

They were continually in the way, and were pushed about from place to place, and once very nearly fell into the hold, as the hatch was not down yet.

At last they got into the steward's cabin, where the first mate, Thompson, was taking a sip of brandy with Smith the steward.

"Well, youngsters," said the mate, "how do you like the ship?"

"The ship's right enough," answered Jack. "It's the people on board I don't quite understand."

"You'll drop into your places in a day or two, and find everything go on like a piece of machinery," answered Thompson.

"When shall we get to sea?"

"We shall be in the Channel to-morrow. To-night we lay to off Gravesend to take in a passenger."

"Who is he?"

"I don't know his name, but he's going out to Canton in a hurry. An uncle has died and left him a tea garden in China, and he's going to look after his property," answered Thompson. "I heard he's been a schoolmaster, or something of that sort."

"I thought we'd done with schoolmasters," said Jack. "We've had enough of that sort of cattle."

"He can polish you up in your A B C when you've nothing else to do," answered Thompson, with a laugh.

Jack did not quite agree with this prospect, but consoled himself with the thought, that as the schoolmaster was a passenger, he should not come much in contact with him.

When they reached Gravesend, it was fully expected that the ship would drop anchor.

But the captain, finding his crew answered to their names, and that he had only to take a passenger on board at Gravesend, contented himself with taking in sail and making a signal for the boat to come alongside.

As the passenger was waiting with his luggage in a boat, the rowers soon put off and came alongside the "Fairy."

The luggage was quickly hoisted on deck, and the passenger, who was reported to have been a schoolmaster, and to have had a tea garden left him near Canton by the sudden death of a relative, followed his luggage.

The boat dropped behind.

All sail was set, and the "Fairy" continued her way down the Thames.

Suddenly the passenger caught sight of Jack's face.

"Stop the ship! stop the ship!" he exclaimed. "I'll get out! Stop the ship!"

Attracted by his frantic gestures, the captain approached.

"What's the matter, sir?" he inquired.

"Stop the ship, I say! I'll get out!" continued the passenger, with increased vociferation.

Captain Cuttle regarded him curiously. Was he mad?

CHAPTER IV.

THE STOWAWAY.

"STOP the ship!" repeated Captain Cuttle. "What does the man mean?"

"I'll get out, I say. Let me out," persisted the passenger.

"Do you think you're in an omnibus? You won't have any chance of getting out until the pilot leaves, and then you'll have to pay a good price for being landed at Deal, and forfeit your passage. What's the matter with the ship? The owners sent me a telegram, saying you'd taken your passage at the last moment, and I was to pick you up at Gravesend. Have you forgotten anything important?"

"It isn't that," groaned the passenger. "It's Jack Harkaway. If I'd known he was on board this ship, I wouldn't have sailed in her."

"It's too late to give her a wide birth now," said the captain. "But what harm can one of my midshipmen do to you?"

"You don't know him as well as I do. Something dreadful will befall the ship. I know it will. We shall never get to our destination."

"What have you had to do with him?"

"I was his tutor. My name's Mole. I was Mr. Crawcour's senior master, and if anybody knows anything about Harkaway I'm the man. Little did I suspect that I was going to fall into a trap when I took my passage in the 'Fairy,' 1,000 tons register, A 1, at Lloyd's, seven years. Oh, dear me! This was a prospect I did not bargain for, when I hastily determined to leave my native land, on the occasion of my eccentric uncle's sudden death, and his demise to me by will of an extensive tea garden in China, near Canton."

Captain Cuttle looked at Mr. Mole, and then at Jack.

The latter tapped his forehead with his finger significantly.

"Oh, it's like that, is it?" said the captain, in a low voice.

"Been so on and off some time, sir," replied Jack, raising his hand to his cap respectfully.

"Cranky, eh?"

"Touched in the upper story, sir. Got a tile off as we say. I don't believe he's got any tea garden at all. It's a delusion. He said he was the Prince of Wales once, and wanted us to call him Albert Edward the First."

"All right. Leave him to me."

Jack saluted Captain Cuttle again, and went forward, where Harvey was waiting for him.

"Is that Mole?" asked Harvey.

"Yes."

"Our Mole?"

"Yes. Crawcour's Mole. He's the school-master who's had a tea garden left him by his uncle," answered Jack. "Isn't it funny that he should come to sail in this ship?"

"Rather," ejaculated Dick.

It certainly was curious that Mr. Mole should have selected this particular ship to sail in.

An eccentric uncle of his, from whom he had long had expectations, had settled years ago in China, and hearing of his death from his solicitor, Mr. Mole determined to go at once to Canton.

He was left sole heir of his wealth, and being tired of drudgery in a school, he resolved that he would travel to China and look after his newly-acquired property.

Seeing by an advertisement in a paper that the "Fairy" was the first ship to sail for China, he took leave of his friends and booked his passage.

When he found that Jack was on board he became alarmed lest he should play him some tricks, and render his passage uncomfortable.

Captain Cuttle however allayed his fears.

"I'm master here, sir," he exclaimed, "and I make every one do as I please. My midshipmen are supposed to be young gentlemen, and if they don't behave like gentlemen, I'll skin them alive."

It was a fact, in spite of what Wren had said, that all the boys were midshipmen, and not apprentices.

They had paid a premium which was to be repaid them in the shape of wages, and they could leave the ship when their voyage was done, whereas had they been apprentices, the captain could have made them serve until their time was up.

In their cabin, in which they messed together, were bunks on each side, and in these they slept.

The ship soon got into the Channel, and the pilot left her.

Then she went gaily on her voyage, favoured by winds that promised to make her passage a quick one.

Jack and Harvey were down with sea sickness as soon as they got past the Nore.

Hunston, Wren, and Sinclair, laughed at them heartily, and told them they would be all right in a day or two.

It was early in the morning when Captain Cuttle was startled by the apparition of a pale and timid-looking lad, who approached him on the after deck.

He could scarcely stand, owing to the motion of the waves, and looked very miserable.

"Who are you, sir?" demanded the captain, sternly.

"A stowaway," answered the boy.

"Have you dared to come aboard my ship under false pretences?" thundered the captain.

"I thought I might, sir."

"What's your name and where do you come from?"

"My name's Maple, sir, and I come from Mr. Crawcour's school."

"Maple!" repeated the captain, adding, "who put you up to this?"

Maple hesitated.

"Out with it."

"Hunston did, sir. I always liked him, and thought the sea would suit me. I knew my parents would not let me come, and so Hunston brought me down with him and smuggled me on board. He told me just now it was time to speak, but I feel so ill that——"

Here Maple felt sick, and rushed to the side of the ship.

"Pass the word for Mr. Hunston," exclaimed Captain Cuttle.

Hunston came up looking anxious.

"So you've been accessory to getting that useless worm on board, have you?" continued Captain Cuttle.

"It was his wish, and——"

"Take that," replied the captain, dealing him a blow in his face, which sent him rolling over the deck.

Hunston got up half stunned.

"I'll have it out of you," cried the captain, furiously. "You don't play your games with me for nothing. Out of my sight, and some of you take that boy below."

Captain Cuttle was showing himself now in his true colours.

Hunston did not reproach Maple.

He was glad to have him on board, because he knew, where Maple was, he should have a sneak and a toady always at hand.

But he vowed vengeance against the captain, and bided his time for an opportunity.

In a few days the fresh hands were well enough to come on deck and do their duty, which Jack soon learnt.

Maple and Harvey were slower.

Jack liked the life of a sailor, but Maple found out that he had made a mistake, for if there was any dirty work to be done, such as swabbing the deck, it was by common consent given to him; even his friend, Hunston, did not stand by him.

"You don't seem so lively," remarked Hunston, with a sneer, to Jack one morning, at breakfast, as Jack was munching a ship's biscuit, and drinking his tea.

Jack made him no answer.

"Captain Cuttle isn't Crawcour. Old Cuttle is one too many for you," continued Hunston.

"Wait a bit," replied Jack. "I've hardly had time to look around me."

The only two passengers were Mr. Mole, and a naturalist named Blader, who was sent out by some scientific society to make explorations in the Indian Archipelago.

Mr. Blader had with him a favourite monkey in a cage, which stood in the saloon.

Jack had had his eyes on Jocko for some time, and one day slipping into the saloon, unfastened the monkey, and put on his head a paper cap, on which he had written, in large letters, "Captain Cuttle."

Then he turned the monkey up in the captain's cabin.

Jack had scarcely had time to get on deck before he heard a smash, at which he grinned, for he knew the mischievous creature would jump from place to place, and smash everything breakable he came across.

The captain did not go below for half-an-hour, being a great drinker, which in some respects accounted for his ill-temper and savage disposition. He imbibed little glasses of spirits at short intervals.

Smacking his lips at the prospect of a dram, he opened his cabin door.

The place was in a state of horrible confusion.

A case of bottles was knocked down, brandy, rum, and gin, saturated the carpet, glasses were broken, his swinging looking-glass smashed, and many things that he prized lying in a heap irretrievably damaged.

Looking up for the author of the mischief, he espied the monkey.

"Who has done this?" he gasped.

Jocko nodded his head, and the captain read on his absurd-looking paper cap—"Captain Cuttle."

Seizing a chair, he darted at the monkey intending to brain him.

The creature was too quick for him.

Jumping on his shoulder, he gave him a claw in the face, and, darting past him, made for the deck, followed by the irascible captain.

The monkey jumped and frisked about the deck, delighted at his newly-found freedom.

When the sailors saw him, and read on the cap "Captain Cuttle," they grinned and watched its antics with glee, which increased when they beheld the skipper following him.

In vain the captain chased the monkey from ship's end to ship's end.

He could not catch him.

"I'll shoot the brute," he cried.

Going below for a pistol, the sailors awaited the sequel with impatience, though they laughed long and loud when the skipper's back was turned.

It was a capital joke to them, for none of them really liked the commander of the "Fairy."

Mr. Blader was walking arm in arm with Mr. Mole as he inquired the cause of the commotion.

"Bless me! it's my monkey," he exclaimed.

When he saw the inscription on the cap he could not refrain from smiling.

Jocko gibed, and chattered, and danced about the shrouds in a frolicsome manner.

Captain Cuttle now appeared again, armed with a single-barrelled pistol.

The monkey recognised him as his enemy, and dexterously leaping towards him, seized his cap, and ran up the shrouds with it.

"The fiend take him!" exclaimed the captain.

He levelled his pistol.

"What are you about to do? That is my monkey, Captain Cuttle," cried Mr. Blader, who really liked his pet.

"Stand on one side, sir. The beast has made a wreck of my cabin, and by Heaven I'll shoot him," replied the captain.

"I protest that you will do nothing of the sort," answered Mr. Blader.

He ran to the shrouds, and called the monkey.

"Jocko—Jocko!"

The creature at once came to him, and nestled in his arms affectionately.

"I will make good any damage he may have done," continued the naturalist. "Reflect, sir, that the monkey could not have got loose of his own accord, and ornamented this cap with the absurd device it bears."

"Let him go, or I'll shoot you," cried the captain, angrily.

"I shall not do so," replied Mr. Blader, firmly, who was a quiet, middle-aged man. "I shall protect my animal, and if you fire, I take this ship company to bear witness that my blood will be on your head, and you will be guilty of murder in the eye of the law."

Mad with rage, Captain Cuttle pulled the trigger and fired.

CHAPTER V.

LASHED TO THE MASTHEAD RIGGING.

AN old seaman, whose name was Slocum, happened to be standing near the captain.

Seeing his murderous intention plainly displayed in his face, he kept his eye upon him.

Directly his finger pressed the trigger, Slocum dashed his arm up.

The ball flew harmlessly through the rigging.

Finding his attempt to shoot either the monkey or its owner frustrated Captain Cuttle diverted his wrath upon Slocum.

"What the blazes do you mean by spoiling my shot?" he cried, still more furious than ever.

"Duty, cap'en," replied the sailor, touching his hat, respectfully.

"Duty to whom? Not to me."

Slocum pointed to the sky.

"There's one up aloft, and he's a skipper we owe a duty to. We've no right to take the life we can't give back," he said.

"Get out, you canting cur," exclaimed Captain Cuttle. "I'll have no mutinous dogs on board my ship."

With that he gave him a blow on the forehead, which caused him to fall bleeding on the deck.

The blow was a severe one, as it had been dealt with the butt end of the heavy pistol.

"Shame!" rose to the lips of the men.

But they were afraid to speak openly.

Some of them had sailed under Captain Cuttle before, and his character was well known in the merchant service.

So tyrannical was his conduct, that one ship which he had commanded came to be called the "Hell afloat."

Mr. Blader had hurried below with his monkey, and replaced him in his cage.

He took off the paper cap.

It was a sort of ordinary fool's cap, in which something had been wrapped.

In his hurry Jack had omitted to notice one thing.

This was of the utmost importance.

The paper had contained some article which his mother had bought for him at a shop, and on it was written, in a small, running hand—

"Master John Harkaway Bedington."

Taking this in his hand, Mr. Blader ran up on deck.

He was just in time to see Slocum stagger forward, bleeding from the forehead, and supported by two of his shipmates.

"Look here, sir!" he exclaimed, handing the captain the paper.

Captain Cuttle took it and saw only his own name.

Thinking Mr. Blader wanted to add insult to injury, he crumpled it up in his hand.

"It's a fool's cap, and would fit you," he said.

"Stay; read the address on it, and you may find out the culprit," Mr. Blader hastened to exclaim.

The captain did so. His face darkened and he looked more repulsive than before.

"One of my youngsters,' he muttered; "I had his character with him."

"Have you any one on board of the name of Harkaway Bedington?" continued Mr. Blader; "if so, the presumption is that he must be the culprit, though it does not follow absolutely that he is. Some one else may have used the paper, though it has his name attached to it."

"It's Harkaway safe enough. Don't stand jabbering there; we don't want any sea-lawyers here," said the captain.

"Captain Cuttle, as a passenger, I demand to be treated with proper respect and——"

"You've got the run of the ship—take it."

"You attempted my life, but, being of a forgiving disposition, I am inclined to look over that; yet if this course of conduct is persisted in, I shall be compelled to lay the matter before the proper authorities," replied Mr. Blader.

Captain Cuttle pushed him impatiently on one side, and went to where Jack was standing with Harvey.

Jack saw his fist clenched, and, remembering what he had done to Hunston, which had been a good deal talked about in the midshipmen's mess, retreated so as to avoid a sudden blow.

"What did you dress that infernal monkey up for, and turn him loose in my cabin, eh?" vociferated Captain Cuttle.

"How do you know it was I?" asked Jack.

"Look at the cap you gave him. It's got your name inside. You did it. No lies."

"To the masthead! Away with you, and stay there till you have my permission to come down, which won't be yet awhile."

Jack made his way to the mainmast, and put his foot in the shrouds.

"Captain Cuttle," he said.

"What now?" said the captain, turning round sharply.

"You'll send my dinner up," continued Jack.

The captain made a run at Jack, and would have sent him up the rigging by the help of his foot, quicker than he might have liked, had not Jack already taken the precaution to go up the shrouds and remove himself out of harm's way.

"Monkey meat is all you'll have," he said, looking up at Jack.

Jack took out his watch.

"How long am I to stay here?" he said. "It's a fine airy situation, but it's possible to have too much of a good thing."

"You'll stop there until this time to-morrow, and that will teach you to play tricks upon me again. So no more of your palaver, my lad."

"By what authority do you act?" asked Jack.

"Say another word, my boy, and I'll put you in irons, by the living Jingo," cried the captain, who was beside himself with rage.

Jack slowly ascended the rigging and reached the top.

Jack looked down, and having a bit of wood in his pocket, threw it at Hunston and hit him on the nose.

Hunston looked round wonderingly, but could not discover where the missile came from.

From the top, Jack ascended to the cross-trees, and sat there for a time very contentedly, but the pangs of hunger began to assail him, and his watch told him that the midshipmen's mess was being served.

"I'll have a cut at the salt junk any-how," he muttered.

With that he began to descend, and to the astonishment of his comrades, entered the cabin as they were just commencing dinner.

"Has he let you off?" exclaimed Wren.

"Not he. I've let myself off," replied Jack. "The air up there has made me so sharp-set that I could eat a shoal of whales."

"Cut in then," replied Wren. "It's your own look-out, and I'm not one to crab you."

Jack soon fell to and made an excellent dinner.

He chatted gaily, and recounted what he had done to the monkey, making them all laugh.

"You'd better get up again before the captain sees you," suggested Wren, who was not a bad-hearted fellow at all. "He is not a man to be trifled with, as you have already found out, I daresay; but he has already got his knife into you for what you have done, and you'd better keep his swivel eyes off you if you can."

"One more chunk," said Jack, eyeing the beef affectionately.

While he was finishing his dinner, Hunston and Maple went on deck.

"Here is an opportunity not to be lost," said Maple.

"How?" asked Hunston.

"Let me go and tell the captain where Harkaway is and what he's doing, and I shall get into his favour, and Jack will get into a row."

"Go ahead then," replied Hunston. "I've no love for him, and he's treated me none so well since we've been on board together, that I should care for him."

Maple went into the captain's cabin, and found him at dinner with Mr. Mole and Mr. Blader. With the latter he had made up the difference by apologising for his hastiness, and the naturalist being of a forgiving disposition, as he had said, shook hands with him.

"What do you want, youngster?" asked Captain Cuttle.

"One of my former pupils," interposed Mr. Mole. "A very good boy. It is a pleasure to sail with so many old friends, more especially as Harkaway has let me alone."

"Please captain," said Maple, in his

sneaking way; "I have come to inform you of a circumstance of which I think you ought not to be ignorant."

"Very good!" exclaimed Mr. Mole, rubbing his hands, "very good, indeed."

"Mutiny in the ship, eh?" asked the captain.

"Not so bad as that; but it's disobedience of orders," answered Maple.

"I'll tell you once for all, that I don't care for talebearers; but I'll listen to you," said the captain, in his blunt way.

"Harkaway has come down from aloft to have his dinner, and he's at it now."

"Is he?" said the captain, grinding his teeth.

"I hope you'll remember it was I who told you, sir," said Maple, thinking he had made a favourable impression.

"Take that," cried the captain, jumping up from his chair, and dealing him a box on the ears. "That's all the thanks you'll get from me for telling tales."

Maple ran away, and the captain followed him on deck.

Mr. Blader ran after him, saying—

"Do not be hasty, I beg, Captain Cuttle. Perhaps the poor lad Harkaway has been sufficiently punished for a harmless joke."

"Harmless! That's your opinion. Leave him to me, and mind your own business."

Mr. Blader fell back.

Calling a tall, stalwart seaman to his side, the captain exclaimed—

"Take Mr. Harkaway, the midshipman under punishment, who has disobeyed orders by coming down from the masthead, and who is now in the midshipmen's berth, and lash him to the topmast-rigging. Be off and look sharp."

The sailor, whose name was Davage,

went on his errand, and met Jack coming up the hatchway.

"You've got to come along with me, sir," he said.

"Where?" asked Jack.

"To be lashed to the rigging."

"All right," answered Jack, coolly. "It will save me the trouble of sitting on the cross-trees."

Davage took a coil of rope, and, preceded by Jack, went up the rigging.

When they came to the topmast, he tied him up tightly so that it was impossible for him to extricate himself.

"Very sorry, sir," he said. "But it's the captain's orders."

"I'm all right; don't flurry your fat," replied Jack. "But Captain Cuttle may take his davy I'll be even with him for this."

"You'd have the ship's company with you, sir," said Davage.

The sailor descended to the deck, and Jack was left alone in his glory.

In the heavens the sun was shining brightly, and the wind whistled melodiously through the cordage.

For a time Jack did not mind it, but after an hour had elapsed, his position began to get painful.

"I suppose it's my fault," he said to himself. "But it is not pleasant. I've been deceived in old Cuttle. He's a humbug. Crawcour was a lamb compared to him. I wish I hadn't let the monkey loose. I wish I hadn't gone to sea. What a fool I was!"

The day declined, and Jack's position became every hour more and more irksome.

There did not seem any prospect of release.

"Perhaps Dick will come up to me," he muttered, as he thought of Harvey.

CHAPTER VI.

THE CAPTAIN'S SECRET.

WARILY passed the evening.

The pain which Jack had hitherto suffered increased to positive agony as the ropes with which he was lashed to the rigging chafed his limbs.

Had not Davage mercifully made the strain come round his body, and under

the arms, his condition would have been worse.

To bodily pain were added hunger and thirst, the latter especially, for the salt beef he had eaten at dinner time made him long for a good draught of sweet water.

To his parched throat, even the salt sea appeared enticing, and he longed to be able to shake himself free from the galling cords, and plunge into the waves which leaped and danced at his feet.

There was a gleam of comfort when he remembered that it was Harvey's watch.

About twelve, as near as he could guess, for he could not look at his watch, he heard some one coming up the rigging.

It was Harvey.

"Thank you for coming to see me," said Jack, in a faint voice.

"I've come to do more, if you like to risk it," answered Harvey.

"What's that?"

"Cut you down. All the fellows in the ship say it's too bad to keep you tied up here the best part of the day and all night too. Are you not stiff?"

"Rather," replied Jack; "but I think I shall be able to get down. The circulation in my limbs is all right. Davage didn't lash my wrists and ankles."

"Cuttle turned in tight, I think, and won't come on deck till the morning. Thompson, the first mate, is on deck, and he told me if I liked to go up and speak to you, he shouldn't see me."

"Thompson's a brick," said Jack. "Under the circumstances, I'll come down, Dick, and chance it. I'm that dry, I could dip my beak into a puddle of road water; and my head aches fit to split."

"I should think it did; you had a tidy sun on you for some time."

As he spoke, Harvey cut away the lashings, and threw them into the sea.

It was lucky he supported Jack with one arm, for the latter had overrated his strength, and it was some few minutes before he could recover himself sufficiently to trust himself off the trees.

At length he reached the deck, and crawled along in the shadow to the main hatch, and so reached the midshipmen's mess.

His first care was to quench his thirst. Then he looked around him.

Wren, Sinclair, Hunston, and Maple were fast asleep, and only a faint light came in through the portholes.

Wren was tossing about in an uneasy, restless manner, as if indulging in the luxury of a private nightmare.

"What is he saying?" Jack muttered, as he heard him talk in his sleep.

"He wouldn't masthead me," said Wren, speaking thickly and excitedly at intervals. "I'd call him Captain Scuttle, as I did once before."

"Captain Scuttle!" repeated Jack, listening intently. "There is something in this."

For a brief space Wren was silent.

"Didn't I see him with my own eyes bore holes in the bottom of the 'Polar Star?' She was lost off Newfoundland. Foundered in a fog. Ha! ha! Crew saved in the boats, and reached St John's. The Mercantile Marine Insurance Company wouldn't have paid the damage if they'd known what I know. Cuttle or Scuttle, he mustn't talk to me."

Jack drank in every word of this revelation, after which Wren was silent.

The sleeping boy had probably been contrasting his position with Jack's during his waking hours, and the result was a dwelling of the mind, upon what often occupied it, while asleep.

"That's the captain's secret, is it?" Jack said to himself. "A pretty villain Captain Cuttle is. I see now why Wren isn't afraid of him. Wait a bit."

Jack turned in, "all standing," as he phrased it—that is, with all his clothes on, and slept very well till morning.

His messmates were astonished to see him.

"I didn't know they'd let you run about loose again," said Wren.

"You don't know everything," replied Jack.

"How did you like it?" asked Sinclair.

"Oh, stunning; lovely sky and beautiful prospect."

Jack had scarcely finished his breakfast when he was sent for to the captain's cabin as he had expected.

Captain Cuttle had been on deck, and discovered that the prisoner was not in his proper position.

He made inquiries without any result, and sent for the offender.

He was alone when Jack entered, and glared at him fiercely.

"Is there going to be a fight between you and me to see who is to conquer, my lad," exclaimed he.

"Yes, Captain Scuttle," replied Jack.

"Captain WHAT?" roared the skipper.

"I beg your pardon," said Jack. "Being aloft so long has made me rather stupid. I meant Cuttle. It was gazing at the Polar Star that confused me."

The captain looked keenly at him, as if

he would read his soul in its innermost depths.

For a moment he could not make out whether he was speaking by design or from accident, and Jack's perfectly cool and offhand manner rendered his task all the more difficult.

"Aren't you afraid of me?" he asked, presently.

"No. I knew you wouldn't do anything more to me."

"Why not?"

"A little bird told me so," answered Jack.

"Wren. You mean Wren," exclaimed the captain, losing his presence of mind. "You've been talking to Wren."

"He was only spinning me a yarn, sir," replied Jack, "about being wrecked off Newfoundland. The ship foundered in a convenient spot, went down in a fog, which fogged everybody, even the Mercantile Marine Insurance."

Captain Cuttle went up to Jack, and put his hand on his shoulder, grasping it till he hurt the flesh.

He was very white now, and he spoke with an intensity of feeling that showed he was in earnest.

"Keep your tongue between your teeth, lad," he exclaimed, "if you want to save your life."

"My life!" repeated Jack, who was rather alarmed at the skipper's tone and manner.

"Aye, your life. Never dare to talk to me again as you have to-day. There was one about your own age—but no matter. Wren had best look to it. The one I was about to speak of *fell overboard during the night !*"

Jack's flesh crept with horror.

"Go. I have said enough for a sensible lad like you. Don't provoke me too far!" exclaimed the captain.

Jack moved towards the door.

"I suppose, sir, I needn't go star-gazing any more?" he said.

The captain flung a boot at him, and he retired precipitately.

Jack had gained his point, but at what a cost!

He had incurred the hostility and suspicion of the captain, who was a violent and vindictive man.

He did not stick at trifles, or he would not have fired at Mr. Blader as he did, when Slocum so providentially spoilt his aim at the cost of a broken head.

The horribly mysterious hint which the captain had thrown out ran in Jack's mind.

It was easy enough for a strong and determined man to throw a boy overboard on a dark night.

So he resolved not to irritate the captain beyond the latter's power of endurance.

How he kept his resolution, we shall see presently.

He had conquered in the first fight, and was so far master of the situation.

CHAPTER VII.

WREN DISAPPEARS.

AFTER the interview that Jack had with the captain, he began to grow afraid of him.

Captain Cuttle was not the amiable person he had appeared to be, and his true character was showing itself day by day.

Though Jack appeared to have got the best of it, the captain was evidently not a man to forget.

His mysterious hint about the midshipman who fell overboard because he dared to talk about what he knew, alarmed Jack.

He took Harvey into his confidence.

"It won't do, Dick, to play with our captain," he said.

"Why?" asked Harvey.

"Because he wouldn't mind murdering a fellow."

Harvey laughed.

"Draw it mild, Jack," he said. "We are living in a civilised age, and with all the men on board he would scarcely like to risk getting his neck in a noose."

"Suppose I fell overboard."

"That would be your fault."

"Ah, but suppose I was pushed over on a dark night, when no one was looking, and only the wind heard my cries for help."

"JACK PERCEIVED HIS ADVANTAGE—IT WAS NOW OR NEVER."

"What do you mean?" asked Harvey, curiously.

"I scarcely know myself. But I'll tell you what I have learnt. When Wren was asleep the other night, he talked wildly about our captain scuttling the 'Polar Star,' to get the insurance money. Scuttling means boring holes in her bottom, so that she may sink. Wren sailed in the 'Polar Star,' and I hinted to Captain Cuttle something about it."

"You did!"

"Yes, and that is why I was let off. But at the same time, the captain told me that one of his midshipmen 'fell overboard,' because he couldn't keep his tongue between his teeth. I believe it will be Wren's turn next, because Captain Cuttle thinks he has been chatting to me. I shall be very careful what I say this voyage, and when we get to Canton I shall cut and run, and hide till the 'Fairy' has started homewards, and then ship in some other vessel. I'm not going to risk the return voyage with such a skipper, if, please God, I last out this journey."

"Here is Wren," said Harvey. "He don't look as if he funked much."

"Well, my young true blue!" said Wren, approaching Jack. "You got out of your little scrape better than I expected. Old Cuttle doesn't generally let fellows off; I couldn't have done it better myself."

"You've got a hold over him," said Jack.

"So I said; but neither you nor anyone else knows what that is, nor are you likely to."

"Come here," said Jack.

Wren approached, and Jack whispered in his ear—

"It's something about the 'Polar Star,' isn't it, and Captain Scuttle?"

"How did you know that?" asked Wren, much astonished.

"Captain told me. We're like brothers," replied Jack. "By the way, who was the midshipman who fell overboard?"

Wren turned deadly pale.

"Did he tell you that, too?" he said.

"If he hadn't how should I know it all?" answered Jack. "You didn't, did you?"

"It would have been as much as my life is worth to have done so," replied Wren. "If Cuttle let on about what only he and I knew, since Damer's death, he must be going off his nut."

"He was tight," Jack said; "and I caught him in the humour. How did Damer die?"

"Damer was the only friend I had on earth, and he was drowned one night in a gale of wind. What's the use of your asking me a lot of questions, when you know all about it?"

"Foul play?"

"Of course. But I won't be pumped; take my advice, and keep your mouth shut, or else you'll follow Damer," said Wren.

"Perhaps you'll go first," replied Jack.

"Not I," said Wren; "I don't go and clack about. I'm too wide awake for that, so sheer off, my hearty, and keep the chain up, or else——"

He broke off abruptly, and pointed to the sea with a significant air.

"Food for fishes, eh?" said Jack, coolly.

"And no mistake," replied Wren, as he slouched off with his hands in his pockets.

"A lively prospect," Jack remarked to Harvey.

"For goodness sake, Jack, don't be rash; take his advice and shut up," Harvey replied. "There is danger, I can see it now. Captain Cuttle——"

"Scuttle, you mean?"

"No, I don't. I wouldn't whisper such a word, lest he might hear it, and wipe me out as—as he did Damer."

Harvey sank his voice to a low tone as he uttered the last words, and looked around him cautiously.

There was no one near.

"I've concluded one thing," Jack said, "and that is, I'd better subside for the present, though I should like to wake old Mole up."

"You'll have plenty of opportunities," replied Harvey.

Jack was prudent enough not to offend Captain Cuttle in any way.

He remarked that he treated Wren with marked coldness, and although Wren could not guess the reason, Jack knew it well enough.

The captain thought Wren had betrayed his secret, and distrusted him accordingly.

The ship made a good voyage as far as the Cape, when they encountered stormy weather.

Jack was in his bunk one night, when

the weather was more than usually boisterous, and the noise made by the gale that was raging woke him up.

It was Wren's watch.

He could hear the steady pacing of his footsteps on deck, every now and then, as he passed overhead.

Suddenly he heard other footsteps, and he fancied there was the sound of a scuffle, and then a despairing shriek came up from the sea.

Jack sprang up and looked out of a porthole.

Was he dreaming, or did he for a moment see a wan, white, hopeless face rise to the surface, and then fall rapidly astern?

"I could swear that was Wren's face," Jack said to himself.

He would have gone on deck and cried "Man overboard!" but he was afraid to do so. He might be mistaken. If he raised a false alarm he would be bullied on all hands, and he knew enough of seafaring to be sure that no boat could live in such a storm.

If, indeed, Wren was overboard, he was lost without the possibility of hope.

Trembling in every limb Jack turned over and tried to go to sleep, without avail.

He could not get the horrid sight out of his eyes.

The apparition, if apparition it was, haunted him.

Towards morning he fell into an uneasy slumber, but did not say anything to his messmates, being too much afraid of the captain to do so.

At breakfast time Wren was missing from the mess, and on inquiries being made, nothing could be heard of him.

The man at the wheel had seen him at midnight, but not afterwards.

As the sea was running heavily at the time, and the decks were repeatedly washed by huge waves, it was supposed he had been swept overboard. Jack had his suspicions to the contrary.

So had Harvey.

And looking mournfully at one another, they asked whose turn it would be next.

Jack had not the remotest doubt that Wren had been thrown overboard by the captain in the storm.

He was most circumspect in his conduct afterwards for fear of arousing the resentment of Captain Cuttle, which had been slumbering for some time.

"Poor Wren," said Jack to Harvey, "if I had not spoken, he would have been alive still."

"You didn't mean anything," replied Harvey.

"God knows I didn't," said Jack; "I had no particular cause to like the fellow, but I did not think he would come to an end like this."

The captain did not seem much concerned at what had happened.

He spoke a few words to his midshipmen, and concluded by saying, as he looked steadily at Jack, "You must all of you be careful. The best sailors are liable to accidents, and what has unfortunately occurred to poor Wren might be the fate of any of you."

The ship, however, went on her way, and, as Jack was very civil and well behaved, and took care when on deck at night to look about him, to prevent a surprise, he was alive and well, when the ship, leaving the Indian Ocean, passed through the straights of Malacca, on her way to the China Seas.

The old seaman, Slocum, who had been knocked down by the captain for stating his ideas of duty, had taken a great fancy to Jack, and taught him many things he would not otherwise have learnt.

The first mate also gave him lessons in navigation, and Mr. Mole induced him to read with him in his leisure hours.

So it will be seen that Jack, through fear of his life, which he thought the captain would not hesitate to take if he offended him, was making very fair progress, and behaving very well.

After Wren's loss, Sinclair, Jack and Harvey became friends, and Hunston and Maple were left to themselves.

Everyone was glad at reaching the Eastern Archipelago, for it was an indication that their voyage was drawing to a close.

Hunston who was profoundly ignorant on almost all points, was holding an argument with Sinclair one morning at mess about the position of Singapore, at which place the ship was to touch.

"I tell you," said Hunston, "that Singapore is one of our settlements in the West Indies."

Sinclair laughed.

"I'll refer it to Harkaway," said Sinclair, who came down in his shirt-sleeves to have his breakfast, for the heat was fearful.

"You've made two mistakes in one sentence," replied Jack, "for Singapore is a free-state, and can't be called one of our settlements, exactly; and we are in the East, not the West Indies."

"It doesn't matter," exclaimed Hunston, annoyed; "I thank goodness I don't know much about these things."

"Then you thank goodness for your ignorance," said Jack laughing.

"Suppose I do; what then?"

"Oh, nothing much; only you've a great deal to be thankful for," Jack retorted, with a gravity that made the others laugh still louder.

Hunston held his tongue, for he was no match for Jack when the latter began to chaff him.

At Singapore some cargo was delivered, and Mr. Blader, the naturalist, went on shore to see if he could purchase anything for his collection.

He came back just before the vessel started again, with a large box, which he had placed in his cabin.

There were holes in the top, as if it was intended to give air to some living thing.

Jack saw it come on board and his curiosity was strongly excited.

"Dick, what's in that box of old Blader, do you think?" he asked, as the anchor was being weighed.

"Can't guess. A hippopotamus perhaps," replied Harvey.

"Hippopotamus my eye," exclaimed Jack. "Will you help me to find out?"

"Like a bird."

"When?"

"After the 'uproar is over' my pippin," said Harvey, meaning when they were fairly under weigh.

CHAPTER VIII.

WHAT WAS IN THE BOX.

As soon as they could get away from their duties, Jack and Harvey stole downstairs into the passengers' cabin.

It was deserted.

By applying his eye to one of the holes in the box, Jack got a view of what was inside.

He sprang up with a cry.

"What is it?" asked Harvey.

"My eye!" exclaimed Jack; "I never saw such a thing in my life. It's a snake as thick round as a man's thigh."

"Perhaps it's stuffed."

"You're stuffed," said Jack derisively. "What are the holes for if it isn't alive?"

"What does old Blader want with a thing like that on board? I wonder the captain allows it."

"The skipper, I expect, doesn't know anything about it. Suppose we let it out. Won't there be a dust up!"

"Oh, Jack!" said Harvey, lost in admiration of this brilliant idea.

The snake was a python of the largest size.

Fully fifteen feet long, and wide in proportion. It had been presented to the naturalist by a gentlemen who had lately returned from a long journey to Cambodia, and it had been caught while gorged by the natives of Bankok.

Mr. Blader intended to drown it, by suspending the box in the sea by ropes, and then to put it in alcohol to preserve it; but as the ship sailed early, he had not had time yet to put his plan in execution.

The lid was fastened securely with a padlock, though it was easy to undo it by taking out one of the staples.

This Jack proceeded to do.

"I'll go and tell Mole," said Jack, "that someone wants to see him in the cabin. Won't it be a lark?"

"Suppose the beast eats him," suggested Harvey.

"He's a fool if he does, for Mole's so tough he's sure to disagree with him."

"It'll be all up with Mole's tea garden."

"Mind he doesn't collar you, Dick," said Jack, "the staple will be out directly."

"I say, don't funk a fellow into fits,"

replied Harvey, getting further off. "I've read of those big snakes—pythons they call them—and they're not poisonous. Their dodge is to fix their fangs in your leg, and then twist their coils round you, which they do as quickly as the lash of a whip twines round a post. Your bones crack, and it's all U P with you in half-a-jiffey."

"There isn't much of you, Dick," said Jack, pausing a moment in wrenching out the staple with his pocket knife; "suppose you let him have you. "It'll be a nice whet to his appetite, like half-a-dozen of oysters before dinner."

"Thank you," answered Harvey, "you're very kind. Show me the way first."

"Next week," said Jack, grinning.

"Won't you?"

"Not much," replied Jack; "I'm not tired of my life yet. His snakeship doesn't gobble me up if I know it."

"What'll the captain say?"

"I'll chance that."

Suddenly the staple came out with a run, and Jack, who was pulling hard at it rolled over on his back.

Harvey made for the door, like a startled hare.

The snake, astonished at his unexpected freedom, raised his ugly head and glared savagely at Jack, who picked himself up and retreated to a safe distance.

"Morning, governor," he said, nodding his head. "How do you find yourself?"

The python's only reply to this was to uncoil himself and glide out of the box on to the floor.

Jack was astonished at his prodigious size; he did not think he was half so big or formidable, and was rather sorry he'd let him out.

"He's a nice sort of customer to meet on a dark night," he muttered.

Retreating to the deck, whither Harvey had retired before him, he looked round for his friend and found him perched upon the monkey-rail, leaning his back against the mizen-rigging.

Mr. Mole was on deck, attired in a Chinese bagu, or loose blouse, a pair of canvas shoes and a large sun hat, which he had bought at Singapore, as being seasonable.

"Well, Jack," exclaimed Mr. Mole, "now you can sing 'I'm afloat' once more."

"I know that; I could sing the tune the old cow died of if I wanted to," replied Jack. "I'm not in a singing humour. But I shouldn't mind reading one of the Odes, if you've a Horace handy, sir."

Jack knew he hadn't, and would have to go down into the cabin for one.

Certainly, my boy. I am always ready to instruct the mind of youth. Ingenuous youth, as we used to say at my esteemed friend, Mr. Crawcour's."

"Rather a change, sir, in going to China, and larruping niggers," said Jack.

"I shall behave humanely to my labourers. Larruping, as you term it, is not a part of my programme."

"Chain them up, sir," Jack replied, thinking of the treatment he once received at Mr. Crawcour's. Mr. Mole smiled, and said he would go for the Horace.

Harvey came down and exclaimed, "I see Mole's gone."

"Hold your row. He'll come up quicker than he went if the snake doesn't cop him," rejoined Jack.

The two boys, breathless with impatience, awaited the result of Mr. Mole's journey.

Presently there was a noise as of some one scampering up the companion, and Mr. Mole reached the top, uttering dismal cries.

"Oh! Lord help me! Oh, Lord! Oh, Lord! He made a snap at my canvas shoe! It's awful," exclaimed the schoolmaster.

Captain Cuttle and Mr. Blader were walking together, and they came to Mr. Mole to inquire the cause of his fright.

"What's the shindy?" asked the captain, in his blunt way; "anyone would think you'd seen Old Nick."

"Worse, sir; worse, a thousand times," answered Mr. Mole.

"What's worse? the ghost of your grandmother?"

Mr. Mole's knees shook and knocked together, while he was obliged to lean upon the naturalist for support.

"There's a serpent in the cabin," he muttered, "as big as a horse, and as wide round as a young donkey. Oh, Lord! It made a dive at my canvas shoe, as if it was going to begin to eat me, legs first."

"A serpent on board my ship? I never heard of such a thing. That's a sort of merchandize I didn't bargain for," said Captain Cuttle. "You must be dreaming. It's the brandy-and-water you've had. Delirium tremens often makes men feel snakes in their boots, and you said he was at your canvas shoe."

"Why, it must be my python," remarked Mr. Blader, alarmed.

"Your python!" said the captain, "are you going to see snakes, too?"

"It's a fact. I had an enormous snake given me yesterday," answered the naturalist, "and brought him on board, intending to preserve him as a unique specimen."

"I wish you'd have told me," Captain Cuttle said, with a look of annoyance. "These reptiles are not easy to kill."

"How he got loose puzzles me, but I suppose his huge strength enabled him to force the staple. It is really very thoughtless of me, and I am very sorry Mr. Mole should have been so much alarmed."

Dick Harvey and Jack overheard this conversation with much glee.

"It was touch and go with Mole," whispered Harvey.

"Yes—and blow me tight," replied Jack, in the same tone, "if they won't have all their work cut out for them to kill him."

The captain reflected for a moment, and came to the conclusion that something ought to be done to get rid of the snake.

"It won't do to let the critter have the run of the ship," he said. "Here, you Harkaway, go to the carpenter, and get a hatchet."

"Right, sir," said Jack, running off for that purpose.

"I believe," remarked Mr. Blader, "that you may fire at a snake, and put a ball in his body without doing him much harm. What is necessary is to break his back, or cut him in half."

"Exactly—and that's what you'd better do," said Captain Cuttle.

"I!" cried the naturalist, aghast.

"Yes—the boy will be here with a hatchet for you directly. It's your snake. You were responsible for his coming on board, and you've got to kill him."

"Suppose I decline the honour," observed Mr. Blader, who did not seem to like the task assigned him at all."

Jack now arrived with the axe, and said, as he handed it to Mr. Mole—

"Go in and win, sir. St. George and the Dragon for ever. You can do it, sir."

"My dear young friend, I will have nothing to do with reptiles," answered Mr. Mole, declining to take the axe. "Rather than encounter the dreadful eyes of that awful monster again, I would be—a—be keelhauled."

"It won't harm you, sir. He's as tame as a kitten," continued Jack.

"Look here, my lad," exclaimed the captain, with a malicious look. "You're very fast in giving other people advice. If the thing is to be done as easily as you say, why don't you do it?"

"I shouldn't mind," replied Jack, speaking almost before he thought of the effect of his words.

"That's right—take the axe and go down into the cabin—kill that snake, and then we shall know what sort of stuff you're made of."

Jack hesitated and hung back.

The terrible risk he would run in an encounter of this kind, flashed across his mind, and he was more than half inclined to back out of it.

The mocking laughter of the captain rang in his ear.

"Ha! ha! You're all smoke and no fire," he cried, in derision. "Go about your business, my lad, and another time don't try and get credit for that courage which you do not possess."

"I didn't say I wouldn't do it," replied Jack, growing pale. "Give me the axe, sir. I'll have a shy at him, if he were as big as the mainmast. If he should swallow me, I suppose you'll come down and rip him up to let me out."

The captain laughed, and handed Jack the axe, which he took with a hand that trembled a little.

Removing his jacket, he stood in his shirt sleeves, which he tucked up, and shaking hands with Harvey, said, in a low tone—

"Good bye, Dick. It's odds on the worm chawing me up. I wonder how it will feel inside."

Harvey could not help wondering at the spirits his friend possessed at such a moment, but though Jack indulged in chaff, he was in reality in a dreadful fright.

However, the captain, who was his enemy had dared him to the encounter, and he resolved to do the best he could.

The "worm," as he playfully called the python, was no contemptible antagonist for a boy of his age, and the odds were against him as he had truly said.

Mr. Blader and Mr. Mole both remonstrated with the captain, about letting Jack embark in such an enterprise.

"Isn't it cowardly to let a boy do such a thing with the almost certainty of being killed," said Mr. Blader, "when there are men about?"

"You're welcome to go and do it yourself as I said before," said the captain. "One thing I know, and that is, I shan't."

This retort compelled Mr. Blader to be silent.

"If it wasn't for my tea garden and my prospects, and a certain rheumatic affection in my legs, which has just come on," said Mr. Mole. "I would go and despatch the serpent myself."

Captain Cuttle turned contemptuously from them.

"Ready, sir," said Jack, preparing to descend the ladder.

"Wish you luck, lad," replied the captain, who could not withhold his admiration of Jack's courage.

The men, learning what was going to take place, all crowded aft, and some of them ventured so far as to go down the companion, and look in at the cabin door.

It was a moment of unparalleled anxiety and expectation.

CHAPTER IX

THE STORM.

WHEN Jack got into the cabin the python was gliding about the carpet and seemed to have the appearance of being astonished at finding himself where he was.

Directly he saw Jack he recognised an enemy, and coiled himself np, raising his head high out of the midst of his huge coil.

His red jaws were wide open, and his eyes shone like live coals.

For an instant Jack felt his blood freeze in his veins, and it is not to be wondered at, considering that he had undertaken a task at which men presumably brave, held back, and were afraid.

As a fact, the bravest men are always ready to own to a sensation of fear. It is their will that carries them through.

The snake realised, as it were, instinctively, that one of the two must die on that spot.

Jack approached him, and the python darted at his foot, hoping to fasten his fangs in his boot. Now Jack could understand what Mr. Mole had meant by saying that it made a dive at his canvas shoe.

"Good morning!" said Jack, under his breath, as he started back with the agility of a chamois hunter, "you didn't do it that time, my beauty; and you are a beauty, after a fashion. I hope you'll have a pain in your stomach if you swallow me, for then I shall know what's going on outside."

Again the snake darted at him and again he stepped back.

Noticing that it was necessary for the creature to recoil after each spring, Jack ran in, just as he had sprung, and dealt him a blow with the axe.

Instead of falling across the snake and breaking its back, it only cut into the side, making a deep incision, from which the dark blood welled up.

The springing and dodging continued with more rapidity than before, and Jack jumped up and down with the activity of a harlequin, and the perspiration rolled down him.

"It's hot work," he thought, "I've heard of a bear dancing on hot plates, but I doubt if it's worse than this. By Jove! that was a shave. Look out, old fellow. Now I've got you."

The python's jaws came within an inch of his foot, but Jack perceived his advantage. It was now or never, and he flung himself upon the snake, dealing him a cut about fifteen inches behind his head, which severed it from the body, except about an inch on the other side.

As he coiled up this part fell over, and

in his dying agony he fastened his teeth in his own coils.

"That's the finisher," Jack cried in triumph as he dealt him another blow nearer the head, which rolled on the floor.

Drawing his knife, he stuck it into the brain, and armed with the ghastly trophy, ran out of the cabin.

The men made way for him, and a hearty cheer broke out. Such a cheer as only Englishmen, in their admiration of manly courage, can give.

Captain Cuttle patted him on the back, and said—"You're a fine fellow, my boy, and an honour to the ship's company."

Jack tried to speak, but he could not.

The reaction came, and sitting down on a bale of goods, he burst into tears, letting the head fall at his feet.

No one but himself knew what he had suffered in the few minutes that were occupied in his fight with the python.

He seemed to have lived a lifetime.

Some men were set to work to swab up the blood, and throw the loathsome reptile's body overboard.

The captain took Jack into his own cabin and gave him some cordial out of a case bottle.

"Thank you, sir," said Jack as he drank the dram.

"You're a lad after my own heart," said Captain Cuttle, filling the glass a second time, and adding—"Drink it up. It won't hurt you. It will steady your nerves after what you've gone through. You and I must be friends, so don't make any more allusions to what that foolish and unfortunate fellow Wren told you. I have watched you narrowly lately, and I see you can keep your tongue quiet. I'm not the man to stand falsehoods being spread about me, and if you are discreet, we shall pull together. If not—well, I need not say any more to a boy of your intelligence."

He gave Jack his hand, and the lad shuddered as he took it, for he felt sure that Captain Cuttle knew more about Wren's death than he chose to say.

However, he made a virtue of necessity, and disguising his real feelings, left the cabin high in his captain's favour.

This adventure made Jack quite a hero. He had all along been a favourite with the crew; now they looked up to him with admiring eyes as well as looks of affection.

This is always the reward paid by men to true courage.

Among those who congratulated him was Harvey.

"I wouldn't have done it," said Harvey, "if the owner had given me the ship and its cargo. How did you feel while you were about it?"

"Oh, jolly enough," replied Jack; "when I saw what the beggar's tactics were, I knew I was bound to have him."

"Everybody admired your pluck."

"Perhaps we shall have worse than that to go through before we get home," replied Jack, who did not like being praised.

He spoke at random, but there was more truth in the casual remark, as they were soon to find out, than either he or Harvey imagined.

For many a night afterwards Jack woke up in his sleep with a start, fancying he saw a snake coiling round him.

The "Fairy" went on her course up the China Sea, and at last encountered very rough weather.

A storm arose and came upon her suddenly.

She rolled about for some hours, and one of her masts went overboard—a terrific sea swept her deck, carrying over the side two seamen, and disabling her rudder, and washing away the binnacle. It was night.

With all Captain Cuttle's faults, and they were not a few, as we have seen, he was a good sailor.

The storms, in those latitudes are, however, so sudden and so fierce, that even a Thorough seaman cannot at all times prevent disasters.

About midnight a leak was reported.

The "Fairy" was drifting about on the waves, tossed hither and thither—rudderless and helpless!

Captain Cuttle was out of his reckoning.

By a reference to the chart he imagined that at the time the storm came on they were in about 4 deg. N. latitude, by 109 deg. W. longitude.

This would place them between two groups of islands in the Indian Archipelago.

These were the Anambas and the Natuna isles.

The latter islands were about 120 geographical miles from Sarawak, in Borneo, and about 200 miles from Singapore.

Reports stated that the natives of these islands were wild and savage.

The sailors spun yarns about head hunters or cannibals, and the boys listened with wrapt attention.

It was probable that the ship would be wrecked, or indeed, that she might founder and go down in mid-ocean.

When the captain realised the desperate condition of his vessel, he strained every nerve to save her.

Relays of hands were kept all night at the pumps, and in the morning the dismasted ship rode water-logged, the sport of the wind, which blew steadily towards the Natunas.

Jack and Harvey worked like slaves.

The only skuklers were Hunston and Maple, who, thoroughly cowed and frightened, did not dare to speak a word.

Captain Cuttle, however, made them take their turn at the pumps, and saw that they did their fair share of work.

The approach of morning was a relief, for the storm had subsided somewhat.

Still the tempest had done damage which was irreparable.

A complete wreck—the once buoyant and beautiful ship "Fairy" was at the mercy of the wind and waves.

"Here's a pretty kettle of fish," said Jack to Harvey, as he went below to snatch a morsel of food, after being at work all night.

"What will become of us?" asked Harvey, dolefully.

"If we escape being food for fishes we shall make prime joints for the cannibals. There will be hot boiled Harvey, and cold roast Hunston, while jugged Maple will grace the festive board of the chief of the savages," answered Jack.

"I wish," said Hunston, "that if you must joke at such a time as this, you wouldn't do it at my expense."

"Why not, old cock?" asked Jack, dipping a weevilly biscuit in his tea.

"Oh, if that's all, you'd better do the other thing."

"What's that?"

"Lump it," answered Jack, carelessly adding to Maple, "Have a weevil?"

Maple shook his head, and Jack threw the little insect—which often enough will creep into ship's biscuits—in his eye.

"Oh!" said Maple, "you must be a beast to throw a weevil into a man's eye."

"Call yourself a man! That's what you never were, and never will be," said Jack. "Wait till we land among the savages; you shall be my chief slave."

"Yours!" said Maple. "Perhaps you'll be one yourself."

"No, I shan't. I shall make love to the king's daughter."

"Suppose she likes me best," said Maple, extracting the weevil from his eye, and blinking over it like an old owl in an ivy bush.

"What!" said Jack, derisively, "a woman like you. That's coming it too strong. I tell you I shall marry the king's daughter, and you shall be my chief slave, while I'll have Hunston artistically tattooed in various parts of his ugly body every morning before breakfast, for my amusement."

A dark form appeared in the doorway. It was Captain Cuttle.

"No joking if you please, my lads," he said; "it's past a joke now. The water's gaining on us. Our only chance, as we can't stop the leak is to drift to shore. Who'll go aloft and keep a look-out for the land?"

"I will, sir," replied Jack.

The captain gave him a telescope, and he went aloft with alacrity, and taking his bearings, kept a sharp look-out.

These words, the first gloomy ones that the captain had given utterance to, struck a chill to all.

In a few hours their position had become desperate.

CHAPTER X.

LAND AHEAD.

AT the masthead, Jack amused himself with whistling the tune of the "King of the Canibal Islands."

He rather liked the idea of being wrecked. There was novelty in it, and it would be something to talk about when he reached home again, if ever he did.

Still he was as anxious as any of the ship's company to sight land, and strained his eyes, with the aid of the glass, to distinguish the slightest speck.

Hours passed and he saw nothing.

Another night like that of the last would settle the fate of the "Fairy."

Already the crew were worn out with the fatigue of pumping, and want of sleep.

To set them an example, Captain Cuttle had himself taken a turn with the men and contributed his share to their united exertions.

It was weary work for Jack to look out hour after hour upon that dreary expanse of water.

On all sides of him was the pathless sea, stretching as far as the eye could reach, like a vast prairie, undulating and objectless.

Presently he saw a speck, which turned out to be a bird, which he regarded to be a good sign, and a herald of the approach of land.

When Noah sent the dove out of the ark and it returned, having no place to set its foot, he knew that no land was near.

Jack pulled a biscuit out of his pocket and munched it, wondering what little Emily would say if she saw him in his present position.

All at once he beheld something through the glass that looked like a dark cloud.

In time it grew more distinct, and he clearly defined a ridge of rocks.

Joyfully he sang out "Land ahead!" and the cry was taken up by all, who saw in the announcement a gleam of hope.

Captain Cuttle and the first mate, Mr. Thompson, immediately reconnoitred through their glasses, and their practised eyes confirmed Jack's declaration.

They conferred together.

"I fear there is no chance of saving the ship," said Captain Cuttle.

"I can see none, sir," replied the mate. "She is hopelessly waterlogged, and we can't expect to keep her afloat any length of time, pump as hard as we may. What shore, sir, do you reckon we are nearing?"

"Some of the islands west of Sarawak. I don't believe they are named on the map. There is a group called the Natunas; I should think we are nearing one of them," answered the captain.

"It's a bad job; but after all our lives are the first care. We have done our duty to the owner. Some would have abandoned the ship this morning and taken to the boats."

"We may save some of the cargo, if we run upon a reef."

"I doubt it, sir. If we strike we shall go to pieces, and it will be the devil take the hindmost," replied Thompson.

"How is the glass?"

"Rising, sir."

"More wind, eh?"

"I can feel it coming," answered the mate.

Captain Cuttle's face, already clouded with anxiety, assumed a deeper hue still of dark care.

"Well," he said; "keep the hands at it. We are in the hands of Heaven. If the worst comes to the worst, we must take to the boats, that's all about it. To stay on board, and be driven on a lee-bound shore if the wind rises again, will be worse than madness."

"Sheer suicide, sir," said Thompson.

The effect of the storm upon Mr. Mole was very marked. He made friends with the steward and procured more than one bottle of brandy, which he drank to keep his sprits up.

With an unsteady gait he entered the midshipmen's mess.

"My dear boys," he said, "this is a time of peril, and I trust that you are all prepared to do your duty—for what says the song upon this point, my dear boys ? It says—bother me if I know what it does say. That's funny, isn't it ?"

And Mr. Mole sat down on a locker, and began to laugh.

"I say, Jack," whispered Harvey, "Mole's a little bit on."

"On!" replied Jack; "I should say he was a good bit gone—half-seas over."

"We can't offer you a glass of grog, sir, for we've had none served out to our mess to-day," continued Harvey aloud.

"Grog, my dear boys. What is grog ?" asked Mr. Mole, with a vacant stare.

"Generally rum and water on board ship," replied Jack. "I like it two parts rum and one water—none of your three water grog for me."

"I was about to observe, Harkaway, when you interrupted me with your usual impulsiveness, that grog is a vanity in which I never indulge; a glass of sherry and a biscuit satisfy my moderate desires. What says the song about biscuits ?"

"I really don't know, sir," replied Jack.

"No more do I; fac' is my mem'ry is not so perfect as I could wish. Time was when I had a flute and could calm the savage breast with melody."

"I've got a concertina," said Harvey.

"Keep it," answered Mr. Mole, waving his hand with dignity. "At such a time as this concertinas are sinful. We are on the eve of a shipwreck—savages loom in the distance—all hands are pumping. I myself would have taken a turn at the pumps, if—if—the rheumatism in my lower limbs had not suddenly attacked me."

"What says the song to rheumatism, sir ?" asked Jack.

"My dear boy, I am unaware that any song has been written upon so dismal a subject. If, however, I am mistaken, I shall be glad to sit corrected," said Mr. Mole. "Consider, however, the perils we have gone through, how sublimely the waves rolled, and——"

"How beautifully they smashed the rudder and swept away the binnacle," put in Jack.

Mr. Mole smiled, and took from his pocket a big bottle, which he raised to his lips. It was labelled "brandy."

"Fair dues, sir," replied Jack.

"What do you mean by that phrase ?

It is foreign to my comprehension," replied Mr. Mole.

"Give us a drink, that's all, sir. I've been on the look-out, and want a drop of something."

"Take it; take it all. It's nothing but vanity," answered Mr. Mole, handing him the bottle. "Had it not been at the urgent solicitation of the steward, who is a good and likewise a humane man, I should not have provided myself with this cordial.

"Take it Harkaway, but—and this I must impress upon you—drink not too deep; remember that your humble servant, Isaac Mole, has spirits to keep up as well as you, and this is a trying time."

"So it is, sir," said Jack, taking a pull and handing the bottle to Harvey, with, "Take a swig, Dick ?"

"Don't mind if I do," replied Harvey, adding, as he looked at Mr. Mole, "here's luck, sir."

"Luck, my dear boy ! What is luck ? —what says the song to luck ?" answered Mr. Mole. "Here, hand back that bottle, I see the form of Hunston in the doorway, and truly he is an imbiber; a bibber as the Scripture hath it, a bibber of wine, and, truth to tell, anything else he can lay his hands on. I demand back my bottle. Thank you; truly the flesh is weak."

A long gurgle followed this remark, and Mr. Mole stretched himself at full length on the locker.

The bottle presently fell from his hand empty, and the worthy possessor of a tea garden in China, left him by the death of his uncle, snored.

Hunston only put his head in at the cabin door.

"Been at it again. Sorry for his tea garden he speaks of," he exclaimed, pointing to Mr. Mole.

"If you want to know, you can ask him," said Jack.

"All right. I only came to tell you that the position of the ship is considered so desperate that orders have been given to man the boats."

"Go on," said Jack, "you're chaffing."

"Perhaps I am, and perhaps I'm not," answered Hunston.

"Well, it isn't a thing to chaff about."

"Did I say it was ?"

Maple was just behind Hunston, and he said in a whisper—

"What do you want to tell them anything about it for ?"

"JACK SHOUTED, AND MADE SIGNALS; BUT IN VAIN"

"They'd be drowned if——"

"Would that be any loss? didn't he cheek you just now as he always does?" interrupted Maple, who was of the same vindictive and sneaking disposition as when he was at Mr. Crawcour's.

"I don't care twopence for either of them," replied Hunston, "you know that as well as I do."

"Let them alone then."

Jack began to think that there might be something in what Hunston had said.

"Look here old man, if I'm wanted on deck," he cried, "I'll come, but I haven't had a wink of sleep all night. I've been turn on and turn off hard at the pumps for twelve hours, and I'm very tired. I want to have a pitch somewhere for an hour or two."

"Have it then," said Hunston.

"No. Were you in earnest or not about the boats being manned?"

Hunston hesitated.

"Say No," whispered Maple, "and if they stop here, they'll be left on board. You know Captain Cuttle told us to go and get all hands up from below. Do as I tell you. What do you care for Harkaway? He has no power over you, has he?"

"Not he," replied Hunston, adding in a louder tone, "it was only my humbug. The ship's right enough."

"Is it!" said Jack; "then don't you joke like that again, or I'll lick you with a rope's end, Mr. Hunston; I don't like such chaff. We may all be in Heaven in a few hour's time, for what you know."

"You won't be there," said Maple, peeping over Hunston's shoulders.

"You mean I shan't meet you there," cried Jack, shying a biscuit at Maple, which hit him on the ear, and made it tingle till he howled again.

Hunston and Maple went away, and shut the door of the cabin.

The key was on the outside, and it caught Maple's attention.

"Lock them in," he exclaimed.

"What?" said Hunston.

"Keep them in the cabin, and then we shall be sure of not being worried any more by them, because they'll go down with the ship. You heard the captain say she could not live much longer in this sea. The wind is as bad as it was last night, and threatens to get worse."

Hunston caught at the idea, and turned the key in the lock as noiselessly as possible.

What Maple had stated was the truth.

Captain Cuttle and Mr. Thompson, the first mate, had determined to abandon the ship.

She was fully covered by insurance, and rather than risk being wrecked on the unknown—to them—shores of the Natuna Islands, and cast amongst the unhospitable and savage natives, they decided to take to the boats.

The boats were launched with great difficulty, as the sea ran very high, and with wind and tide there was danger of their being stove in.

Hunston and Maple made haste to get up the companion.

They had not ascended more than five steps before the vessel shipped a heavy sea, which ran in a volume down the hatch, and, striking the boys, hurled them backwards.

Stunned and bleeding, they lay on the deck deprived of sense or motion.

CHAPTER XI.

WRECKED.

THE first boat, containing the captain and several of the crew, had been successfully launched, and cleared the ship.

But the second was not so fortunate.

In it were the first and second mate and the remainder of the crew.

A wave dashed it against the side of the ship. It heeled over, filled, and turned bottom up.

Dreadful cries ascended to Heaven. Wretched men struggled for a brief space in the water, and then all was still.

Hearing the cries, Jack looked out of the porthole and saw his shipmates drowning.

"Dick!" he cried, in alarm, "they have taken to the boats. The ship's launch is stove in. Hunston wasn't chaffing after all."

He rushed to the door of the cabin only to find it fastened, and made frantic efforts to open it.

"We're fastened in," he cried. "Hunston must have done this."

Pale with rage and fear, he increased his endeavours to force a way out, which he at last succeeded in doing, by the help of his thick boots.

He literally kicked his way out.

Hunston and Maple were just recovering their senses.

Shaking the former, Jack said, "What is the meaning of this?"

With a vacant stare Hunston looked sullenly at him, but made no answer.

Rushing on deck, Jack saw the boat in which the captain was gradually growing smaller as distance separated it from the doomed ship.

He shouted himself hoarse, and made signals, but without avail. His shipmates could not have come back to his rescue if they had been desirous of doing so.

At such a time all the selfishness in a man's nature comes to the surface.

The ship was deserted.

With a tremor of the heart Jack realised the fact, and he gazed dismally at the pieces of the broken boat, which were tossing about in wanton sport by the wild waves.

Hunston and Maple were caught in their own trap.

Sent below to bring up any who might be unaware of Captain Cuttle's intention to abandon the ship, they had endeavoured to seal the fate of Jack, Harvey and Mr. Mole.

The wave which knocked them insensible at the foot of the companion ladder was proper retribution and now they were destined to share those dangers to which they would have condemned their messmates.

Harvey, who had followed Jack, stood by his side sharing his fears and blank looks.

Cast away, as it were, in the middle of an almost unknown sea, in a waterlogged vessel, which even then was a wreck, their prospect was indeed miserable.

"Go down below Dick, and shy a bucket of water over Mole," said Jack, "and bring him into the captain's cabin. We must hold a council, and see what is to be done."

Harvey, obeyed orders with alacrity, and succeeded, after thoroughly dousing Mr. Mole, in rousing that gentleman to a sense of his position.

He was about to apply his lips again to the brandy bottle, but Harvey threw it on the floor and broke it.

"This is not a time for drinking, sir," he exclaimed; "we are left to ourselves, and the ship is sinking."

"Bless me! where is the captain?" exclaimed Mr. Mole. "I will go and remonstrate with him."

He staggered into the captain's cabin, where he saw Jack sitting at a table, Hunston and Maple were standing sheepishly before him.

"What is this I hear, Harkaway?" asked Mr. Mole.

"We five are the only souls on board this ship," answered Jack; "and as someone must take the lead, I have made myself captain. If anyone refuses to obey my orders, I will shoot him with one of Captain Cuttle's pistols."

He placed one before him as he spoke.

"Very improper conduct of the captain to leave me here," remarked Mr. Mole. "I am a passenger and the proprietor of a tea garden in China. My life is too precious to be entrusted to a parcel of boys."

"Mr. Mole," replied Jack, sternly, "understand that in the face of our common danger——"

"Uncommon danger," hazarded Mr. Mole.

"Our positions are reversed," continued Jack, not heeding his interruption, "and please God, I will take successful command of this ship and run her ashore somewhere. The cargo is chiefly cotton goods, and I hope she will float. If you must behave like an old woman instead of a man go to bed."

"Harkaway," cried Mr. Mole, with drunken gravity. "This language to me is unseemly. It was I who taught your young ideas how to shoot. Talking of shooting reminds me that pistols are dangerous. Remove that pistol—you will not? Very well; a time will come. You called me an old woman—I shall not forget you. Mr. Crawcour shall hear of this."

"He thinks he's back again at Pomona House," said Harvey.

"Danger," continued the inebriated schoolmaster. "What do boys know about danger? The ship's all ri'; I'm all ri'; but the winds blow. It pleases them and doesn't hurt us. I shall go and turn in. Call me when the bell strikes for dinner."

And he rolled away to his bunk with an unsteady gait.

"There's not much help to be expected from him," said Jack. "We are in the hands of Providence, and as we have sighted land, we may hope. As for you Hunston and you Maple, you tried to murder Harvey and myself."

"We——" began Hunston.

"Be silent!" cried Jack, authoritatively. "I am captain here. By leaving us in the ship when all the others were going, you were guilty of intent to murder; and when the time comes, you shall see that I can repay my debts with interest."

"I am very sorry," said Maple. "It was Hunston who did it."

"You crammer," replied Hunston, "you suggested it to me. I should have been off in the first boat with Sinclair, if it had not been for you; and to show you, Harkaway, that I wish to make amends, tell me what to do and I'll do it."

"You can do nothing," answered Jack; "at the pumps your strength would not be of much use. My opinion is that the ship has taken in as much water as she will. The captain abandoned her too soon, but it's all of a piece with his antecedents. All I want you and Maple to do is to clear out; get out of my sight, for I hate to look at you; only mind one thing, don't play any more tricks, for if you do, by Heaven, I'll shoot you!"

The boys slunk out of the cabin, and Jack was alone with Harvey.

"We're in for it," said the latter.

"So long as we can drift ashore, I don't care," remarked Jack, thoughtfully. "While there's life there's hope."

"So there is."

"I'm peckish. We must keep up our strength. Go to the steward's cabin, and see what you can find. They killed some fowls yesterday."

Harvey went away, and presently returned with a couple of cold roast fowls and the remains of a ham, of which they partook heartily, washing down the repast with some bottled ale.

"That's the stuff, Dick," said Jack. "I don't believe in spirits when you've got to keep your wits about you. What's the time?"

Harvey looked at the clock. It had stopped.

"I should guess it was about three," he said.

"Then at the rate we are being driven by the tide, we shall strike about midnight—an awkward time, but there's no help for it."

"About those islands—are there not always coral reefs?"

"Nearly always."

"Then we shall be some distance from the shore. Why not set Hunston and Maple to work, making a raft," suggested Harvey.

"Not half a bad idea. If we can save some of the stores, and knock up a camp, we shall be all right, though we are rather out of the course of ships, and may look forward to a long captivity if we fall into the hands of the natives," answered Jack.

"Are they cannibals?"

"Some of them are, and the Malays are terrible pirates. Still we needn't funk. It's better to be here than in the boat that went down—poor fellows. They are all gone to their account."

"Mole will be ashamed of himself when he comes to," remarked Harvey.

"So he ought, the beast," Jack answered indignantly.

Jack was one of those who are eminently fitted to take the lead in anything and everything.

It has been well said, that some are born to command; others to obey.

The only man left on board, who ought to have been of use by his matured judgement and ripe experience, was incapacitated, by indulgence in drink; of all vices the most injurious and debasing.

The position of the boys was extremely critical.

Every wave that struck the ship threatened to knock her to pieces, and without boats, what help could there be for those on board, if she foundered in deep water.

Going on deck, Jack set Hunston and Maple to work, directing their efforts, and helping them occasionally.

Before night fell, a large serviceable raft was constructed, and they waited with impatience for what would happen next.

They made out the land distinctly now.

A strong current seemed to have set

into the shore in which the ship was caught, for she moved with greater quickness, and in a straight line, instead of rolling about, first this way and then that, with every turn of the wind.

The land was low lying, and a heavy surf broke on the beach, and from the white clouds of spray that dashed into the air, about the distance of a mile and a half from the beach, they fancied there must be a ledge of rocks straight ahead of them.

"Sleep is out of the question," said Jack, "we must keep on the look-out—to be ready to launch the raft, if she goes to pieces when she strikes."

The moments passed anxiously.

Drenched with spray, and worn out for want of sleep, the boys looked ill and haggard.

In that hot region the air was warm, though not sultry, and they did not experience any of the evils which attend upon severe cold.

The current in which the ship was involved set in shorewards, and in the clear, beautiful moonlight, the boys could see her gradually nearing the line of surf.

So imminent grew the danger that Jack exclaimed—

"One of you go below and wake up Mr. Mole—bring him on deck, drunk or sober."

Harvey set out to execute this mission.

Mr. Mole had turned in "all standing," and when roughly shaken, jumped out of his bunk in a fright.

"What's the matter? Is dinner ready?" he asked.

"You'll have no dinner to-day, sir," replied Harvey, "except what you can cadge anywhere."

"Cadge," repeated Mr. Mole, "that is not a word in my dictionary. Your tendency to slang, Harvey, will bring you to a bad end. If there's no dinner, why rouse me from my sweet and refreshing slumber?"

"Because the ship is deserted, and we shall strike almost directly on the rocks."

So emphatically and earnestly did Harvey speak that Mr. Mole began slowly to comprehend the position in which they were placed.

"If they have all gone, why did they leave me?" he inquired.

"You'd best ask them. I don't know," replied Harvey.

"Who is managing the ship?"

"Jack is, as well as he can, though she is not capable of much management. We've got a raft made, and that's all we can do."

"Where are the boats?"

"One is stove in, and the other is gone off with the captain and part of the crew."

"The danger is pressing. I will come on deck and support you with my presence in this trying emergency," said Mr. Mole.

Harvey did not care much for his presence, but was glad that he was sober enough to save him the trouble of carrying him up.

When they reached the deck the scene was a grand one.

The moon was rising high in the heavens, and the wind had somewhat subsided, though the ocean was in a state of perturbation.

Every wave broke splendidly over the rocks ahead, and a cloud of spray dashed high into the air.

Suddenly Jack cried out—

"Mind yourselves, it's coming."

And, in a few seconds, the ship trembled from stem to stern.

She had struck.

Fortunately the wave which carried her on to the coral reef had placed her in a high position, and though the waves broke over her in constant succession, she did not go to pieces.

The boys sheltered themselves as well they could, and Mr. Mole, after he had been twice taken off his legs, followed their example.

"Shall we launch the raft?" asked Harvey.

"Not till this sea is over," answered Hunston. "I am an old sailor, you know, and if you take my advice, you will remain where you are. Stick to the ship as long as she will hold together."

It was impossible to go below now, as each wave dashed into the hold and filled the ship. All the boys could do was to hang on with might and main and wait for a cessation in the war of the elements.

By morning they might hope for a calmer sea.

"This is painful," said Mr. Mole, as a small quarter-cask rolled up against his legs, and he rubbed his shins.

"Hold tight, sir, or else you'll be food for fishes," cried Jack.

"It's all very well, my young friend, to say, 'Hold on,'" replied Mr. Mole, "when you have had your shins hurt and your arms are every now and then wrenched from their sockets."

"That's nothing," answered Jack; "my shins were barked long ago, and I don't know whether I have any arms or not."

"Truly a draught of brandy would revive me. Oh!"

The latter exclamation was caused by a huge wave, which struck him in the face and filled his mouth with water.

"Won't that do as well?" asked Jack, when the water had rolled off.

"It is nauceous; very much so. Brine is not exhilarating; far from it."

"Look out, sir; there's another coming!" replied Harvey, turning his back to the wave.

Mr. Mole was not so fortunate; he received it broadside on, and spluttered dreadfully.

"If this goes on I shall never get the salt out of my system," he said. "Pickled pork will be nothing to me. If you love me, Harkaway, go below and get me a drink of something."

"And be drowned in the attempt. Thank you," answered Jack, "I'd rather not. Hang on till morning, and it will be all right."

"Morning is far distant. I shall be pickled before then," groaned Mr. Mole.

However, there was no help for it, and the boys had to "hang on," as Jack phrased it, for dear life, while the waves at intervals dashed over the devoted ship.

CHAPTER XII.

THE RAFT.

IMPATIENTLY the boys waited for morning to dawn, and when it did, the scene which met their eyes presented a singular contrast to the horrors of the day before.

The sea was comparatively calm. No rain fell. A warm, glowing sun shone out in all the fierceness of tropical splendour.

It was found that the vessel, though water-logged, was placed by the violence of the storm in a hollow bason in the reef.

Her store rooms were free from water, and though their contents were somewhat damaged by the sea, there was reasonable expectation that a large quantity of provisions and stores would be available for their use.

When the storm abated and the dawn broke, Jack looked around him.

Mr. Mole had fallen asleep on the deck so had Hunston and Maple; only Jack and Harvey remained awake.

"Nice fellows to help a lame dog over a stile, aren't they?" said Jack sarcastically.

"What are we to do now?" asked Harvey.

"I'll tell you, for I've been thinking all night. The storm is over, the ship is high if not dry, and she'll live where she is till the next storm come."

"When will that be?"

"Who can say? In these beastly latitudes storms come on, of their own sweet will, at any time. The island we see before us looks as if it was deserted, All the better; there will be no niggers to eat us up."

"Don't," said Harvey, with a shudder.

"I didn't mean to funk you," continued Jack, "but you can't trust the inhabitants you find on those outlying islands in the China Sea. We must launch the raft, and take a lot of things on shore, and build a castle in which we can put our stores, because everything must be saved from the ship that is possible to carry away, and we have no time to lose. Another storm will finish the old 'Fairy.'"

"I wonder where Captain Cuttle is," remarked Harvey.

"Perhaps he's made some land."

"He'd have been glad if he had remained on board if he could see us now."

"I'm very glad he didn't," said Jack. "He is a selfish, dangerous, bad man. The way in which he left the ship showed that he cared for nobody but himself. We have got the island we see before us to ourselves."

"If there are no niggers."

"If the niggers, as you call them, don't show themselves for a few days, I'll make a castle which will enable us to defy any number of them, and we'll call it Jack's castle," answered Jack.

"May I have a nap somewhere? I'm dead beat," exclaimed Harvey, with another yawn as he rubbed his eyes with his knuckles.

"Not yet; dive into the cabin, and bring up what you can find. Something to eat and drink will put us both right—or, stop a bit. I'll come with you."

They went below together and found something to satisfy their hunger with, and lighting a fire, they made some tea, which was very refreshing.

"Now to work," said Jack.

"Right you are," replied Harvey. "I feel another man."

"You'll stick to me, Dick," cried Jack, who looked at a pistol he had in his pocket.

"Never fear," replied Harvey again.

"I'm captain now, and you are my lieutenant. I'm not going to stand any nonsense from anybody."

"Give your orders," said Harvey, laughing.

"Go and kick Mole, Hunston, and Maple in the ribs till you wake them."

"Right."

"I find the brains, and they'll have to find arms. In other words, they'll have to do the work."

"I'll lay into Mole first," said Harvey, "and then I'll let Hunston and his dirty sneak Maple have it."

He went away grinning, as if he liked the idea of the task he had taken in hand.

A vigorous kick in the side roused Mr. Mole, who sprang to his feet, and looked wildly around him.

"Where are we?" he cried; "and what is the meaning of this outrage? Harvey, you kicked me; are you aware that you actually had the hardihood to kick, in the neighbourhood of the fifth rib, your late respected senior master and the proprietor of innumerable Hyson shrubs in a China tea garden, near Canton."

"Captain's orders, sir," replied Harvey.

"The captain! I thought all but ourselves had left the ship."

Jack now made his appearance, and said—

"I have made myself the captain, Mr. Mole, and I shall act with the utmost severity to those who refuse to obey me."

Hunston and Maple had been roused by Harvey, and stood sleepily surveying the scene, which was a lovely one.

While they had been slumbering, some magician seemed to have shaken his wand, and the whole situation had been changed.

Wind had given place to a gentle breeze; huge waves were now ripplets. Black clouds gave way to a bright, sunlit sky, and inside the coral reef the water was calm as a millpond.

Mr. Mole was carried away by the situation.

"My dear boys," he exclaimed, "we have been saved by a miracle from a watery grave, yet we do not know what dangers may confront us. You are singularly fortunate in having me to direct your efforts—with my mature judgment and ripe experience, you will find me a tower of strength, and——"

"It seems to me, Mr. Mole, that you do not know what you are saying; and as this is a time for acting, and not talking, you may oblige me by helping to launch the raft," replied Jack. "Now then, Hunston, wake up. Lend a hand, Maple."

"I want some breakfast," replied Hunston.

"Happy thought!" exclaimed Mr. Mole. "The inner man begins to rumble, and thereby gives warning that there is a hollow space which wants filling up."

"It will have to want," answered Jack, "until the raft has been to the island and back; I'll stand no nonsense. My orders must be obeyed."

So determined was Jack's manner that the raft was launched, and several things which it was considered would be of the first importance, was placed upon it.

"Now then," cried Jack; "steady all, away we go."

As they were about to push off, they heard a whining noise.

"That's the captain's dog, Nero," said Harvey. "He's in the cabin. It's a wonder he wasn't drowned."

"Go and cut him loose. A good

watch-dog will be just the thing we want," replied Jack.

Nero was a fine specimen of the black curly-haired retriever, and when Harvey cut the rope which fastened him, he rushed on deck, and springing on the raft, caressed the boys, who had always been kind to him, with every demonstration of affection.

After this, the raft was not long in reaching the shore, it being propelled by a light wind and the sail which Jack hoisted.

A small inlet or creek was espied, and up this the raft was pushed with a long pole, until a landing-place was reached.

Jack sprang ashore, and sticking the pole in the earth, cried—

"I take possession of this island in the name of our gracious Sovereign. Hurrah for the Queen!"

"Hurrah! hurrah!" cried everybody except Mr. Mole, who had been overhaul

ing the "luggage," as he called what had been placed on the raft, and discovered a case of spirits, a bottle of which he was raising to his lips.

Jack saw this, and snatching the bottle from him exclaimed : "At it again, are you? Say 'Hurrah for the Queen!'"

"God save the Queen!" cried Mr. Mole, adding. "Don't be so violent, Harkaway. I am sure I'm as loyal as anybody, but after what we have gone through we must keep our spirits up."

"When you've earned your rations you shall have them, not before," replied Jack. "I shall call this Harkaway Island. Dick, light a fire, and give them something to eat and drink, while I go inland and explore a place for us to pitch our tent."

Leaving his lieutenant to follow his instructions, Jack climbed up a sandhill and commenced his exploring expedition.

CHAPTER XIII.

BUILDING JACK'S CASTLE.

If Jack had not been so anxious, his walk would have been a delightful one.

The island on which his lot had been cast was well wooded and the vegetation rank and luxuriant.

As he struck inland he came upon groves of tall trees, mixed with cocoa and betel nut palms.

It is scarcely possible to convey an idea of the rich grouping of the palms and shrubbery and festooning vines as the sun shot into the abundant foliage, long horizontal pencils of golden light.

Coffee trees grew wild, and were covered with berries nearly ripe.

The sharp hiss of a snake, as it glided away in the long grass, warned him to be careful.

Before him, in the distance, loomed a mighty mountain, rising majestically from the earth.

Its high top, hundreds of feet above the level of the sea, was hidden in the early morning by horizontal clouds, which parted while he was gazing upon them, and let down a band of bright sunlight over its dark clefts.

The unbroken sweep of its sides, from

its summit to the sea, was most majestic; but from narrow grooves that he perceived, Jack thought it was a volcano, and had been recently in a state of eruption.

He had not gone more than a quarter of a mile from the sea, along a level country, when he came to a slight hill.

Behind this was a clump of trees of a moderate height, and of a circular shape.

It immediately occurred to him that if those in the centre were cut down, and more trees planted, or stakes—which would grow in that fertile climate—stuck in between the spaces, an excellent wall for a castle would be made.

The hill hid the trees from the shore, so that smoke from a fire would be dissipated before it reached the summit of the eminence.

On the other side, or inland, a perfect forest of trees encircled a space of about thirty acres of rich land, covered with long grass and brushwood.

This land Jack saw would do to grow corn or potatoes, or, indeed, anything which he could rescue from the wreck.

So he determined to select this as his dwelling-place.

Whether the island was inhabited or not, or what animals infested it, he could not tell.

His first care was to make a house, into which he could take everything that he could rescue from the wreck.

Storms were so violent and so sudden in those regions that they might go to sleep at night and find the next morning that not a single vestige of the ill-fated "Fairy" remained.

Returning to the creek, where he had left his companions, he took them to look at the spot he had selected for a dwelling-place.

They all approved of it, and he set Hunston and Maple to work with an axe to clear the interior, leaving a circle of trees all round.

Mr. Mole dug holes, in which were placed the trees cut down, so as to fill up the gaps, and by nightfall there was a thick fence, through which nothing could pass.

A small opening was left to serve as a door, and a large sail was spread over the top to keep out the rain and dew.

While this was being done, Jack and Harvey made several trips to the ship on the raft, and brought back a variety of articles, which they piled in a heap on the land.

They made their dinner on salt beef and biscuit, washing it down with some excellent water, which welled up from a spring near the castle, as they already called their future habitation.

For more than a fortnight they worked incessantly.

Planks brought from the ship divided the interior of the castle into rooms. Each one had a bedroom, and bedding brought from the ship supplied them with something to lay upon, and the covering they had been accustomed to.

The rooms were comfortably furnished with the ship's furniture, and in one large room, which they termed the warehouse, all sorts of things were stored—guns, powder, shot, provisions, in short, all they could save from the wreck.

By tearing up the deck they made their partitions, and the doors of the cabins were easily fixed. Planks, placed slantingly against a central beam, made a capital roof, and they were able to defy the weather, while sails nailed all round the inside of the castle, kept out the wind from the chinks between the trees which made the outer wall.

The bedrooms ran round the castle, and the sitting-room was in the centre, being divided from the other room, or the warehouse, by long planks placed in the earth.

They had several casks of oil, and lamps in which to burn it, as well as candles, biscuits, potted meats, salt beef, and other things saved from the ship—provisions to last them for at least six months.

They knew not what animals and birds the island could supply them with, as they had been too busy in building their castle to look about them.

At length it was finished, and very proud Jack was of it.

Hidden from the sea and protected from the wind in front by the hill we have mentioned, it was equally protected in the rear by the forest of trees.

The dog, Nero, was chained up close to the entrance, so that no one could approach without his giving notice.

When the ship had been ransacked of nearly everything that was worth having, another storm arose and shattered the wreck to pieces.

Jack, however, did not care for this. It was no longer a misfortune.

His companions had worked with a will, and recognised his leadership, being well satisfied with the result of his clever devices.

They had an excellent house to live in, with ample stores to last them for some months, and though on a desert island in a remote part of the uncivilised world, they had many of the comforts and luxuries of civilisation to console them in their enforced exile.

When the castle was finished, and they could cease from their labours, when the floor was planked over and the wind kept out by sails, which hung like tapestry on the walls, Jack determined to give a banquet, which he did in good style.

After dinner wine was put on the table, and he rose to make a speech.

"Gentlemen," said he, "I have to thank you for your laudable exertions on behalf of our little commonwealth. We have now a house to live in, which is by no means contemptible. Our stores of provisions will last us for six months or thereabouts. Now, our next care will be to explore the island, and to dig up and plant the land which lies about our castle. We have a sack of corn, some barley, and potatoes.

"How long we shall be destined to live upon this island, or what our adventures may be, none of us can venture to say, but this I will assert, we have a great deal to be thankful for; and I trust that we shall live in harmony and be good friends. I know one thing, and that is, I mean to keep order in our little settlement, and, without being a tyrant, I will be obeyed. Mr. Mole knows that nothing can be done without discipline."

"Hear, hear!" from Mr. Mole.

Jack sat down, and Harvey got up, saying—

"I beg to propose the health of Jack Harkaway, our monarch. Jack the First the king of Harkaway Island!"

The toast was drunk with apparent enthusiasm for however much Hunston and Maple may have disliked him in their hearts, they did not think fit to give their opinion free vent at that time.

It was agreed that the next day they would explore the island.

Each of them was supplied with a gun and powder and shot, so as to be ready for any emergency.

CHAPTER XIV.

MR. MOLE COMES TO GRIEF.

MR. MOLE did not in any way attempt to thwart Jack, for he was afraid of him. Jack kept the key of the warehouse, and distributed the stores impartially; but when Mr. Mole and Hunston and Maple got together, they gave expression to their discontent.

"It's true," said Mr. Mole, "that we have a good house and that everything goes on well; but we have worked hard to get things together. Why should Harkaway keep the command? My age and my position entitles me to be the commander."

"Of course," replied Hunston. "If Harkaway's vanity didn't blind him, he would see that in a minute."

"I vote," said Maple, "that we take his gun some night, and make him our servant."

"Don't you know," replied Hunston, "that he and Harvey never sleep at the same time?—either he is on guard or Harvey; it's like fellows keeping watch on board ship."

"Perhaps," said Mr. Mole, "our time will come; we must not do anything in a hurry. If we were to make an attempt and fail, our position would be particularly unpleasant."

"I'm not going to be his slave longer than I can help," remarked Hunston.

They had been digging up the ground and planting potatoes for some hours, under a hot sun, which did not improve their temper. As Jack kept the key of the warehouse, they could get nothing to eat or drink without his permission, and were entirely in his power.

Jack and Harvey had gone out with their guns to explore the neighbourhood and bring home some fresh meat if any could be found.

Some thick clouds that had been gathering began to pour down a perfect flood of rain.

The drops were so large, and fell with such momentum, that it seemed like standing under a heavy shower-bath.

Lightning gleamed as it only does in tropical lands, and the thunder roared as if a park of artillery was at work.

The little party took refuge in the castle, and were presently joined by Jack and Harvey, who had shot several parrots and a small antelope; these were prepared for dinner, and with cocoa nuts and mangoes, made an excellent repast.

"The island," said Jack, "appears to be much bigger than I had any idea of. It is long and rather narrow. I think if we ascended the mountain, we could see about a couple of miles inland. We should get a good view with a glass."

"Let's go this afternoon," exclaimed Hunston. "I'm tired of planting 'taters."

"Very well. Maple shall stop at home and guard the castle and look out for tigers, for Harvey declares he saw one in a bit of jungle," replied Jack.

"That's pleasant," answered Hunston. "Did you see any niggers?"

"Not the slightest, and I should fancy that the island is uninhabited."

"I propose," remarked Mr. Mole, "that I should build a little hut on the top of the hill, near our house, erect a flagstaff, and spend a portion of each day on the look-out with a telescope; because I have no wish to pass the remainder of my valuable existence on this island, and if I should attract the attention of a passing ship, we should all be taken off."

"I have no objection to that," replied Jack.

The idea was considered so good, that they postponed their exploring expedition, and that very day set to work and erected Mr. Mole's observatory.

An excellent view of the ocean was secured from the hill, and the Union Jack waved gaily in the breeze from the summit of the flagstaff.

"I hope it won't attract the attention of the Malay pirates, if ever they get into these regions," remarked Hunston.

Mr. Mole was charmed with his device, and passed hours in the box looking through a telescope, which he had placed on a stand.

Everything soon got into good working order. Mr. Mole was the signalman, and his duty consisted in keeping a look-out. Harvey and Jack looked after the castle, and went out shooting. Maple was the servant and did all the drudgery; while Hunston had the management of the farm, and sowed the crops.

As we have said, there was a good deal of lurking discontent at Jack's high-handed manner, but as yet it had not shown itself in any marked degree.

Choosing a very fine day, an exploring expedition was formed to ascend the mountain, which had all the appearance of an extinct volcano.

Jack, Harvey, Hunston, and Mr. Mole formed the party, Maple remaining behind to wash the plates and dishes saved from the wreck, and cook the dinner.

Several hours were occupied in ascending the sides of the mountain, but a splendid view was attained when the summit was reached.

The land extended as far as the eye could reach, and seemed rather to be part of some large continent, than the little island they had imagined it to be.

A hollow cone, resembling the mouth of a huge well, enabled Mr. Mole to speak with certainty about the origin of the mountain.

Standing upon the edge of the extinct crater, and pointing with a bamboo to the black and yawning gulf, he exclaimed—

"My dear boys, we should never neglect an opportunity of imparting useful knowledge. This is a volcanic-mountain. It may have been silent for centuries, and it may break out again in five minutes."

The boys started back a little at this declaration.

"Yes," continued Mr. Mole, waving his arm grandly, "who can tell? Amidst the crash of empires and the fall of worlds, what is the silence of one volcanic mountain? In these dark and murky depths was once a fountain of smoke and flame. The shaft may descend miles into the bosom of the earth. Woe to the unlucky wretch who tumbled down it!"

Suddenly there was a slight noise, as if the lava crust on which the speaker was standing, was giving way.

Mr. Mole had vanished.

Two hands were seen for a moment clutching at the treacherous surface, there was a dismal yell, and the late senior master of Pomona House academy for young gentlemen had, with as little fuss as possible under the circumstances, glided down the crater.

"Good-bye," cried Harvey.

"Why, he's gone!" exclaimed Hunston. "He might have said he was going."

"It's nothing to laugh at," remarked Jack. "I don't suppose we shall see him again till the next eruption."

"How about the tea-garden?"

"Hunston," said Jack, in a tone of mild remonstrance, "you're an unfeeling beast. Here we are, on a desert island, like orphan children, and yet you laugh."

"Who could help laughing? It's so comical," replied Hunston.

"If you're not serious I'll chuck you after him," said Jack, making a threatening gesture.

Hunston retreated to a safe distance.

"Can't we do something for him?" asked Harvey.

"'Fraid not," replied Jack. "It's dangerous to go near. Poor old Mole!"

It seemed as if Mr. Mole had disappeared for ever from the scene, as the

"TAKE POSSESSION OF THIS ISLAND, HURRAH CRIED JACK."

depth of the hole down which he had fallen might be very great.

His only chance was to alight on some inequality in the sides. It was useless to try to help him, and the boys sorrowfully wended their way homewards, never expecting to see him again.

The loss of one of their number saddened them.

CHAPTER XV.

THE BURNING MOUNTAIN.

THE accident which had happened to Mr. Mole was of so sudden a nature that the boys could not actually believe for a time that one of their party had been snatched from them by a mysterious and awful death.

It seemed but a moment ago that he was talking to them, and explaining the nature of the extinct volcano that had engulfed him.

He had probably sunk deep down into the bowels of the earth, losing his life in the thick vapours which hovered about the shaft, if he was not dashed to pieces in his descent.

Even Hunston grew grave when the serious side of the matter overcame the laughable one.

"I didn't mean anything," he said; "I'm as sorry for Mole as you are, though he wasn't much good, and he'd never given me any cause to like him."

"Never say anything bad of the dead. Let him rest. We don't know whose turn it may be next," said Jack.

"You're right there," remarked Hunston. "In these countries you may put your foot on what seems to be a stick, and get bitten by a snake, or a tiger may have a go in at you for looking at him too closely, or the niggers may take a liking to your head. Hullo! hold up."

They had reached the level ground again, and this exclamation was occasioned by a sudden movement of the earth, causing the boys to stumble.

The next minute there began a low heavy rumbling, deep down in the earth.

It was not a roar, but such a rattling or quick succession of reports as is made when a number of heavily-laden coaches are driven rapidly down a steep street paved with round cobble stones.

The following minute it seemed as if some invisible giant had seized the boys and thrown them forward, and then pulled them back with the greatest violence.

"Lie down! lie down!" shouted Jack. "It is an earthquake, and a stinger, too."

"You needn't say 'lie down' when a fellow can't keep his legs," replied Hunston who was one of those boys who will have their say, even when death and danger are staring them in the face.

For a brief space the boys lay perfectly still, rather expecting that the earth might open and swallow them up.

The first shock, however, was not followed by another.

Jack computed that the time which elapsed between hearing the rumbling noise and the feeling of the shock was about five seconds.

It was the time of year when the monsoon prevailed, and the wind blows refreshingly day and night.

But after this earthquake there was not the slightest perceptible motion of the air.

The tree toads stopped their steady piping, and the insects all ceased their shrill music.

"I say," cried Hunston, looking up.

"What?" asked Jack, shivering.

"Old Mole's been waking them up down below, hasn't he? Perhaps they've been waiting for him down there, and think it the cheese to give him a chyaike on his arrival."

"How can you joke at such a time as this?" asked Jack.

"Doesn't it look like it?" replied Hunston, in an argumentative tone. "Here is old Mole gone and fallen down the crater of a volcano. Nobody asked him to. He did it all of his own free will, and directly afterwards there's this shindy—it's cause and effect."

No one answered him. Jack and Harvey were too much upset at this perturbation of nature to care for chaffing.

Everything was so absolutely quiet that it seemed as if all nature was waiting in dread anticipation of some coming catastrophe.

Such an unnatural stillness was certainly more painful than the howling of the most violent tempest, or the roar of the heaviest thunder.

The utter helplessness which one feels at such a time, when even the solid earth groans and trembles beneath one's feet, makes the solitude most keenly painful.

It was half-an-hour—and that half-hour seemed an age—before the wind began to blow, or before at last the animals and insects resumed their cries and humming.

Jack had often wished to see an earthquake, but after he had witnessed one there was something in the very sound of the word which made him shudder.

The boys, finding the earthquake was over, went back to their castle, and ate the dinner which Maple had provided for them.

Although they did not care for Mr. Mole, they could not help feeling his loss; and Jack brought some wine out of the warehouse after dinner to cheer them up a little.

It seemed to grow dark sooner than usual that evening.

Maple, who had gone outside for some purpose, rushed in again, saying—

"The mountain's on fire!"

"What does he mean?" asked Jack.

"I thought the earthquake meant more than we saw at first," answered Hunston. "If the mountain's on fire, as Maple says, then there must be an eruption. Old Mole can't let us alone."

"I wish you'd let him alone. You've no respect for anyone, dead or alive," exclaimed Jack, angrily.

"I haven't much for you," growled Hunston.

Jack and Harvey ran outside the castle and perceived that the mountain was actually in a state of eruption.

Volcanic influences were at work.

Three distinct columns of flame had burst forth, all of them within the verge of the crater, and their tops united in the air in a troubled, confused manner.

At intervals showers of stones about the size of walnuts were thrown into the air, and these were followed by clouds of ashes.

Jack and Harvey gazed at the terrible sight with awe.

Red lines, like fiery serpents, were to be seen on the side of the mountain, showing the course taken by the burning lava.

"Look out for Mole," said Hunston, who had followed them into the open air. "He'll come out like a fossil presently."

Jack did not feel pleased at this constant levity of Hunston's, and hitting out at him, he sent him into Maple's arms, saying—

"If you have no decency left in you, I must teach you that I have. Get out."

Hunston retired with Maple, and his hatred of Jack increased at the blow he had received.

"Tell you what, Map, old boy," he said between his teeth, "I shan't stand this much longer. I'd rather cut the camp, and go and do my best with a gun in some other part of the island. It's been King Harkaway long enough. I'll make it King Hunston or die for it."

"You know I'll stick to you like bricks," answered Maple.

"We'll wait till we see what this jolly old mountain means to do, and then leave everything to me," said Hunston. "This state of things isn't good enough for me by a long way. I can't get a glass of grog unless his majesty Jack the First is in a good temper and chances to produce a bottle from the warehouse."

The mountain continued to burn and throw up stones and lava and ashes until the middle of the next day.

Then the eruption subsided as rapidly as it had begun.

It was dreadful to think that Mr. Mole's grave had been the crater of a volcano, and that his was a winding-sheet of molten lava.

CHAPTER XVI.

HUNSTON PROCLAIMS HIMSELF KING OF THE ISLAND.

ALL danger of the lava or the ashes covering the castle was at an end for the present.

Some weeks passed, and everything went on at the little settlement as well as the boys could wish.

Such was the fertility of the island that the land they had dug up and planted began to show a favourable return, and a promise of excellent crops.

Jack did not expect to live there all his life, but he knew that his stores would not last for ever, and if they did not make the most of their opportunities they would have to undergo great privation, if they did not die of starvation.

A good look-out was kept at the signal station which the unfortunate Mr. Mole had caused to be erected.

It seemed that the island on which their lot was cast was not in the track of ships—for not a sail was to be seen.

One day, however, Harvey, who was engaged in sweeping the sea with his glass, reported a sail, and every effort was made to arrest the attention of those on board.

A huge fire was lighted, and guns were fired without avail.

The ship passed on its way, and was soon lost to sight.

"No go, Dick," said Jack with a sigh, as the vessel's outline sank below the edge of the horizon.

"Better luck next time," said Harvey.

"I hope so. Turn it up for to-day, and come and talk to me. We'll send Maple up here, and give Hunston something to do."

Jack had put his gun down by the side of the shed. A dark figure passed quickly by him, and seized it.

"Will you give Hunston something to do?" he exclaimed. "Perhaps it will be the other way."

Jack looked up and saw Hunston. At the same time Maple had seized Harvey's gun, and the two friends were helpless.

"What do you mean?" asked Jack, clenching his fists.

"Just this. We've had enough of your reign," answered Hunston. "I'm going to be king, and if you don't obey me, why, I'll put a bullet through your head. The tables are turned now. Harvey will stop here and keep a look out, while you go and hoe the potatoes. When Maple and I have had our dinner, you may come and eat up the scraps."

"How do you feel now, Jack?" asked Maple, with an odious grin.

Jack gave him a kick on the shin which made him howl.

"That just served you right—who told you to speak?" remarked Hunston. "I'm king, I tell you, and I can say all I want to. Give me the key of the warehouse, Harkaway."

Jack saw Hunston place the rifle against his shoulder, and knew him well enough to be sure that he would fire if he was thwarted, so he tossed the key towards him.

"That's right," said Hunston, triumphantly; "that's how things ought to be. Go and hoe those 'taters, and keep the parrots out of the corn; and you, Harvey, look out, or I'll let you both know the reason why."

He walked off to the castle with Maple, and the two friends were together.

"What an ass you were to leave your gun where Hunston could see it and collar it," exclaimed Harvey.

"I didn't know he meant treachery," answered Jack, looking very crestfallen.

"What shall you do?"

"Go and do what he told me," said Jack. "He's got the run of the spirits now, and he'll be drunk in an hour or two, and then——"

"What will you do?" asked Harvey.

"Wait and see. He'll never more be officer of mine. I'll start him. He shall see how living on cocoa-nuts and mangoes in the woods agrees with him. Perhaps he'll make a good dinner for a wild beast. I don't care. I wish he'd tumbled down the hole in the mountain instead of old Mole. Hunston always was a bad lot, but Mole had something good about him, if he was an occasional ass.

At sunset Maple came out to Jack, who had been hard at work, and said insolently—"You may come and have your dinner now."

"May I?" said Jack, flinging a dead snake at him, which he had killed with his spade.

"Will it bite?' asked Maple, starting back, and dropping his gun.

Jack sprang forward and seized the weapon.

"If he won't, this will," cried Jack. "Down on your knees and beg my pardon."

Maple hesitated, and Jack fired one barrel over his head, which had the effect of causing Maple to sink down with his hands clasped.

"That's it; I knew you'd do it. Where's Hunston?" continued Jack.

"In the castle," replied Maple.

"What's he doing?"

"Drinking."

"Is he tight?"

"Not quite; but getting on that way," answered Maple. "He says he's the king now, and he's going to hang Harvey to-morrow."

"Is he?" said Jack, between his teeth. "I'll let him know. Get up that tree, and stop there till I come back and tell you to get down. If you dare to move, I'll shoot you like a parrot."

Maple was up the tree like a flash of lightning, and Jack went to the castle.

"Is that you, Maple?" asked Hunston as the door opened.

"Yes," said Jack, altering his voice.

"Come and give me a hand up. I think there's been another earthquake or something. I've tumbled off my chair, and the beastly place goes round with me like winking."

Jack darted forward and had Hunston by the throat before he could seize his gun and attempt to defend himself.

"Hullo! What's this? Let me go, Harkaway," cried Hunston, becoming sober.

"Not yet, my boy; you must come with me. I'll show you how I deal with rebels."

Jack dragged him into the open air, and half carried him, half pushed him to the place where he had left Maple.

"Now, Maple, come down. I want you," he said.

"What is it, Jack?" replied Maple, in a civil voice, as he made his appearance.

"Take a spade, and dig a hole five feet deep and about two wide. Look sharp, unless you want a tanning."

Hunston let his eyes close, and pretented to be asleep, while the work was going on. In about an hour the hole was dug, and Maple perspiring from every pore, left off.

Jack dragged his enemy to the hole, and put him in feet foremost, and let him sink till his head was on a level with the soil.

"Shovel in," he exclaimed.

"I say, Jack," cried Hunston, coming to himself, and growing alarmed. "Don't be a savage—remember that there are wild beasts and snakes, and birds of a carrion kind here. What do you mean to do?"

"It's a nice bed for a king. Shovel away, Maple," answered Jack.

The earth was quickly thrown in, and pressed down by Jack's feet, until Hunston was buried in the soil, unable to move hand or foot, and only his head appeared above the surface.

"Give me that spade," said Jack.

Maple did so.

"You will stop here all night," continued Jack, "that is to say, if you care for your friend, and you can keep off the snakes and wild things that he seems so much afraid off. I will see what is to be done with him to-morrow morning.

In vain Hunston appealed to Jack to let him go—he turned a deaf ear to his entreaties, and went to seek Harvey, to whom he related what he had done.

"Serve the begger right," said Harvey.

"He said he meant to hang you to-morrow," continued Jack with a grin.

"Did he?" exclaimed Harvey. "Perhaps he'll think better of it."

They went to the castle, and amused themselves by playing at chess, having saved a board and men from the wreck.

Maple sat down near Hunston, and was quite unable to render him any assistance. He had neither spade nor pickaxe, and could not remove the earth.

"You've betrayed me," said Hunston, who was quite clear and sober now, under the influence of the danger that threatened him. "Why don't you get me out of this?"

"I can't," replied Maple, sullenly. "It's bad enough to have to sit here all night and watch you."

"Don't leave me—for Heaven's sake don't leave me alone!" cried Hunston, in a voice of deadly terror. "Harkaway only means to punish me—he don't want to kill him. Look in that thicket. I can see the eyes of a tiger gleaming."

"A tiger?" repeated Maple.

"Yes! Look—look!" repeated the terror-stricken youth.

"Oh! If there are tigers about, I shall step it," said Maple, coolly. "I don't care about being eaten up by the wild beasts. Good night."

Hunston's voice failed him, and he could say no more. His tongue clove to the roof of his mouth, and he thought his last hour had come.

Maple walked quickly away, showing his former friend how much reliance there was to be placed upon his partnership, for Maple was one of those who always go from the losing to the winning side.

King Hunston was in a pitiable plight.

CHAPTER XVII.

THE SAVAGES.

MAPLE went to the castle, and knocking at the door, was admitted.

"What do you want?" asked Harvey.

"Tell Harkaway, please," replied Maple, "I saw tigers about, and want to come in."

"Have you left Hunston to his fate?" asked Jack, coming forward.

"Yes. I couldn't do him any good."

"You dirty little cur. Shall I poleaxe him?"

"He deserves it, but I don't think I would, because we want a servant," replied Harvey.

"All right," said Jack. "Go inside. Dick, come with me. I only want to frighten Hunston, and should be sorry if any harm came to him."

Maple went inside, and Jack, followed by Harvey, walked by the soft moonlight to the place where Hunston was buried up to his neck in the ground.

When Hunston saw them he exclaimed—

"Thank God you have come. You were always a generous fellow, Harkaway. Knock me on the head, but don't leave me here to die in the night."

"I'll dig you up," replied Jack, who had brought a spade with him.

In a few minutes the earth was sufficiently loosened to admit of the captive being dragged out, and he was placed upon his legs, which for a time trembled so that he could scarcely stand upright.

"Now, what are you going to do?" asked Jack.

"I hate you, and I'll never make terms with you," replied Hunston. "I've roughed it in various parts of the world, and I daresay I can do so again. I'll work my way down the island, and if I can't turn anything up I'll come back to you and be your servant."

"You'd best make friends, and say you won't kick over the traces again," replied Jack, good-naturedly.

"I shan't," Hunston said, sullenly. "I want to get away from you, and start on my own hook. You can give me a pistol and a few charges of powder and shot if you like."

"Thank you. I'll trust you as far as I can see you and no farther," Jack said. "You can stop if you like, or you can go. Take your choice."

Hunston put his hands in the pockets of his pea-jacket, and holding down his head, walked away, being soon lost to sight amongst the trees that fringed the outskirts of the little farm.

"He'll come back. It's only temper," said Jack.

"What else can he do?" answered Harvey. "He's got no arms. Perhaps he might make a bow and arrow, but he'll be glad enough to come back in time."

"If he doesn't, it's not our fault. Perhaps things will go on smoother now, Dick. We never had a row when we were alone."

"And Maple is just fit for our servant," said Harvey.

"Of course he is—make him work."

"It will serve him right. He backed up Hunston in his revolt, and pretended to be such a friend of his, and when the fortune of war went against him, he was the first to leave him."

"He always was a sneak. Didn't he show just the same spirit at Crawcour's?" replied Jack.

Talking in this way they returned to the castle, and finished their game at chess. Jack slept while Harvey watched, and, when Jack woke up, Harvey took his place.

Their little band was diminishing gradually. First Mr. Mole had been cut off, and now Hunston had left them.

A couple of days passed, and they saw nothing of him.

Jack grew uneasy.

"I don't think I ought to leave that fellow Hunston to wander about wild in the woods," he said to Harvey.

"He's lurking about somewhere, and means to drop down upon us when we least expect it," replied the latter.

"I don't think so."

"What will you do? Let him take his chance?"

"No," replied Jack, " I shan't do that. Will you stay here with Maple? I'll take my gun and go out and look for him. I don't like the idea of leaving even Hunston to take his chance in the woods."

"You're more generous than I should be."

"Now, Dick," said Jack, "you know you've got a good heart, and it won't do for you to try to make yourself out a beast."

Jack would have his way, and shouldering his gun, he sallied forth to look for Hunston, forgetting in his generosity how badly he had treated him.

He walked for some hours, and traversed several miles of ground.

The sun was setting when he halted, weary and thirsty.

Throwing some stones up at a tree, he knocked down some ripe cocoa nuts, and quenched his thirst. Suddenly he heard a noise.

Looking before him he saw, to his consternation, a band of savages.

He was only hidden from them by a small fringe of brushwood.

They were dancing round and round in a ring, in the middle of which was a human being tied to a stake.

Crawling on his hands and knees to the edge of the brush, Jack took a closer view.

The savages were about twelve in number, and the man in their midst was Hunston.

"It seems to me," muttered Jack, "that my presentiments did not deceive me, and I have come just in time."

His first idea was to fire, but that would have been folly, considering the number of the natives.

Yet Hunston must be rescued.

How to render him material aid was the question.

Lying still on his stomach, Jack ruminated.

It was clear that the natives were performing some savage rite, and that Hunston, who had unluckily fallen into their power, was the object of it.

"I'm king of this island any way," said Jack to himself, "and I'll let them know they're not going to have it all their own way—not much."

Twelve to one, however, was great odds. For once in his life Jack was at a loss.

CHAPTER XVIII.

JACK TO THE RESCUE.

THE savages whom Jack now saw for the first time were very singular-looking beings.

In height and general appearance they closely resembled the Malays.

The colour of the skin and hair was dark, the latter short and crisp, confined on their heads by a red handkerchief, obtained from the natives on the extreme eastern coast.

Their clothing was simply a strip of the inner bark of a tree, beaten with stones until it had become white and opaque, and looking much like rough white paper.

This garment was three or four inches wide, and about three feet long.

It passed round the waist, and covered the loins in such a way that one end hung down in front as far as the knee.

On the arm, above the elbow, some wore a large ring made, apparently from the stalk of a sea plant.

Each of the warriors was armed with a cleaver, which he raised high in the right hand.

Some had shields, three or four feet long, but only four or five inches wide, and others again held long spears.

Their dance was merely a series of short leaps backwards, and forwards, with an occasional whirl round, as if trying to defend themselves from an imaginary attack in the rear.

They sang a wild song, as fast and as loud as they could.

At length the dancing warriors became more excited, and flourished their cleavers, and leaped to and fro with all their might until it looked as if their eyes were on fire.

They worked themselves up into a state of temporary madness, and it was easy to believe that while in this condition, they would no more hesitate to cleave off a human head than they would to cut down a bamboo.

These creatures belonged to the tribe of the far-famed head hunters, a race of which every traveller in the Eastern Archipelago has heard and trembled at their barbarous customs.

It is a custom with them, which has become a law, that every young man must, at least, cut off one human head before he can marry.

Heads, therefore, are in great demand.

Hunston was evidently a windfall for them, and they were rejoicing accordingly.

New heads must be obtained to celebrate such events as a birth, or a funeral, as well as a marriage.

One man, taller than the rest, had a neckless made of human teeth.

Small holes had been drilled in several score of teeth, which were strung on wire, long enough to pass three times round the neck of the hero who wore it.

Jack rightly supposed this to be the chief of the ferocious band.

On the piece of paper-like bark which hangs down in front, and which we have just described, the wearer makes a mark when he cuts off a head.

This mark was in the shape of a circle;

and some had as many as ten or twelve of these circles, while others only had one or two.

When the dance was over, they all sat down and indulged freely in an intoxicating liquor, made from the juice of the flowering part of a palm.

Then they began to dance again, and the chief tossed into their midst a human head, apparently not long severed from its trunk, for it was all smeared with clotted blood.

This they proceeded to kick wildly about as if it had been a football.

A sickening sensation, akin to fear, crept over Jack, as he lay hid, watching the awful carnival of those fiends.

"Very jolly sort of neighbours to have," muttered Jack. "I wonder what they are going to do with old Hunston? He don't look happy."

Nor did he.

As he was bound to the stake, Hunston's face had assumed an expression of utter and hopeless terror, and at times he closed his eyes as if he could not bear the hideous sight before him, and wished to shut it out.

It was clear that when Hunston gave way to his temper, and left his party, he had wandered about the island until he fell in with the natives, and was captured.

Perhaps he intended to return, and try and surprise Jack and Harvey again, and make them his slaves.

He was bad enough for anything.

However Jack was far too generous to allow his companion to perish.

He could not find it in his heart to leave him in the hands of the barbarians, whom he saw dancing around him, and celebrating a feast of blood.

When he was at Mr. Crawcour's academy, he had produced a singular effect upon everybody by his talent in ventriloquism.

It occurred to him now that if Mr. Crawcour and his masters could be startled by the exercise of this singular art, the savages were much more likely to be impressed by it.

No sooner had he imbibed the idea, than he determined to put it into execution.

It was true that he was armed with a double-barrelled breech-loading rifle, but he did not like to take life unnecessarily and without due provocation.

Besides the killing of one or two

natives would only make the others more savage.

Blood for blood is a principle of the savages' creed.

Suddenly throwing his voice into the air, he exclaimed—

"Hunston, old man, how do you find yourself?"

The effect of this speech was magical.

The savages stopped their war dance, and looked up anxiously and inquiringly.

Neglected lay the head they had been kicking about.

But it was upon Hunston that the effect of the observation was most marked.

He recognised Jack's voice, and he knew he was a ventriloquist.

Just as the wretch reprieved on the scaffold may go from despair to hope, so did Hunston's face give up it blackness and assume a happier look.

"Keep up your pecker," continued Jack "I'm not far off."

Hunston made no answer, but looked at the chief in a peculiar way.

Jack saw this significant look.

"He means something," he thought. "I must be careful.

For a time he remained silent.

When the natives had recovered from their astonishment, the chief, whose name was Banda Navia, called by his followers the Tuan Biza, or great chief, approached the captive.

Now Jack saw why Hunston had put on such a singular expression.

The Tuan Biza had, by meeting traders on the coast of Coram, whither he had been taken when young, picked up a knowledge of English, and Hunston was afraid Jack might say too much.

The suspicion of the Tuan Biza would be at once aroused if he heard any familiar phrases.

It was Jack's object to make him think that the great spirit was speaking.

All the savage tribes on these islands believe in a great spirit, and in witchcraft.

It was their well-known superstition that Jack hoped to play upon.

Speaking to Hunston, the chief said—

"Was that a spirit we heard?"

"Yes," answered Hunston, "It was my guardian angel."

"What did it say?"

"Listen. It will speak again."

Jack heard this conversation, and immediately exclaimed—

"Kill him not. If you do you will incur my vengeance."

"It says you are to spare my life," cried Hunston overpowered with joy.

The Tuan Biza translated this to the warriors, who seemed much concerned.

One of them, named Buro, who was famed for his cruel and wicked disposition stood forward and spoke.

"He is our captive," he said, pointing to Hunston, "and by our laws we are allowed to kill him, What is the spirit which forbids us doing so? One of our young men, Keyali, is about to be married and wants a head. It is not well that the captive should be spared."

Keyali, who had regarded Hunston as his special property, gave a grunt of approval.

"You hear what the spirit speaking from the clouds above our head has declared," replied the Tuan Biza.

Jack spoke again, and this time his voice was so near the chief as to make him start.

"If he is hurt," he exclaimed, "dread the fiery mountain, which shall cover you with stones and ashes. It does not please me that he shall die, as he is under my protection,"

"Why, then, O, spirit, did you let him fall into our hands?" asked the chief.

"Because, O, Tuan Biza," replied Jack, giving the chief his title, "he had displeased me. It is the custom of some of your tribe to tattoo their skins, and I doubt not that you will find one of your number who understands the art. Let the captive, then, be pricked all over in curious devices, and marked with the juice of a nut."

The Tuan Biza turned to his friends, and related the order of the spirit, which seemed to please them immensely.

Hunston, however, did not relish the order at all.

"I say, Jack," he said, "don't for goodness sake, tell them that. They'll do it. I shall be as ugly as a Red Indian."

"Serve you right," answered Jack, coolly. "You and I have had a score to pay off this ever so long."

"I'll tell them where the castle is, and make them come and fight you," continued Hunston.

"They'll get pepper if they do," Jack said; "and if you threaten me, I'll tell them I've changed my mind, and that interesting youth, Keyali, or whatever his name is, who is going to be married, and wants a head, according to custom, shall have yours."

"Jack, dear Jack," cried Hunston, "don't let them tattoo me. Fancy what I shall look like if I ever get back to England."

The Tuan Biza thought Hunston was saying his prayers, and beseeching the spirit to intercede for him.

"What you call your spirit? Is it Jack?" he asked,

"Yes," replied Hunston.

The chief informed the savages that the spirit who watched over the white man was called Jack, and they imbibed a great respect for the name at once.

"Tattoo him at once," said Jack.

The chief being thoroughly awed by the voice, ordered Hunston's clothes to be removed; and a sharp fish bone was procured with which to puncture holes in the skin.

Into these the dark juice of a nut was to be squeezed, which would penetrate under the skin, and make the marks lasting.

"Will the spirit like him to be marked with birds and fishes?" asked the Tuan Biza.

"Birds, fishes and serpents," answered Jack, "with a parrot on each cheek and a small crocodile on the nose."

"I say, Jack," cried Hunston, again, "this won't do. I'd rather die. Fancy going about the Strand or Regent Street with a parrot on each cheek, and a small crocodile on the nose. Don't; I'll pay you out if you do."

"You've done all the malicious and beastly things to me you could do," replied Jack, "and I'm not afraid of you. Those who offend a greater power than themselves must pay the penalty. O,

Tuan Biza you have found favour in our sight. Proceed at once with the—a— what do you call it?—tattooment."

The chief, Banda Navia, and Buru understood the art of tattooing, for they had travelled about the Archipelago, in prahus, or large boats, trading with nutmegs and spices which grew in abundance on trees in the group of islands on which the "Fairy" was wrecked.

They had seen sailors do it, as well as remote tribes, and Banda Navia was not a bad artist.

Hunston was stripped naked to the waist.

The fish bone was wielded by the chief, and its point proved as sharp as that of a needle, as if it had been rubbed on a stone.

Buru was prepared with the juice to make the stain when rubbed into the pricked skin.

The warriors began to sing and dance again, and determined to have some fun over this ceremony, if they could not have any over that of cutting off his head.

"Jack, Jack," cried Hunston, as the fish bone began to describe circles over his face.

Jack remained obstinately silent.

"I'll say you're not a spirit, and it's all humbug," continued Hunston.

"Go it, my tulip," answered Jack, "they'll only cut off your head. It makes no odds to me particularly, but you're so jolly ugly as you are, I thought I'd have you beautified, and make you look pretty, that's all, my hearty."

Jack said this in his own voice, and from the thicket where he was concealed.

In a moment he saw his mistake.

The chief, who was a shrewd fellow, began to move in that direction.

There was a danger of the trick being found out.

CHAPTER XIX.

HUNSTON IS TATTOOED.

FORTUNATELY Jack could see all that was going on.

His presence of mind did not desert him.

When the chief had reached the edge of the cleared space in which the savage rites were being celebrated, and was gaining Jack's hiding-place, the latter imitated the hiss of a snake.

This was done to perfection.

It seemed just under the foot of the Tuan Biza.

He started back with an expression of horror, and Jack shifted his position.

A large tree was close by, and he hid behind its trunk.

The Tuan Biza changed his mind, and did not search any farther.

The natives proceeded with the process of tattooing, and as Hunston was tied to a stake, he was unable to offer any opposition.

After tattooing his face and nose, his back, chest, and sides were operated upon.

A stinging sensation like that produced by the bites of mosquitos, assailed the victim of this cruel joke.

But it must be recollected that Hunston had done many things to make Jack his enemy.

He and Maple had actually tried to leave him and Harvey to drown in the sinking ship.

There is a limit to generosity, and, though Jack could be a good friend, he could be a good hater.

When the tattooment was completed, the chief, looking upwards, said—

"O, spirit, is it well?"

Hunston was writhing in agony.

He actually foamed at the mouth, not altogether through physical pain, but because he thought of the singular figure he should present ever afterwards.

There is no process which will effect tattooing. When the marks are once made with the point of anything sharp, and the dye, *if it is a lasting one*, rubbed in, they last a man's lifetime.

"You have done well, O, Tuan Biza," replied Jack, still speaking from the air near the stake. "Keep the captive till the sun sets, and then release him."

The chief bowed his head, for he was superstitious enough to think that when the snake hissed, it was a serpent sent by the spirit to sting him for listening to what Hunston had said.

At any other time Hunston would not have betrayed his companions.

Indeed he had been threatened with death by the savages, before Jack came up, because he would not tell how he came upon the island or how many companions he had.

This must be stated in his favour.

Now he was so maddened and furious at being tattooed that he felt no pity for any of his comrades.

"Let me go," he said, "and I'll tell you something worth knowing. I have companions on this island. We were wrecked here about a couple of months ago."

The Tuan Biza pricked up his ears, thinking he was going to hear something agreeable.

"How many?" he asked.

Hunston was about to reply when Jack, seeing the danger that threatened him, imitated his voice and made him say—

"Fifty-five."

The chief looked grave.

"There were four with me, but now there are only three," exclaimed Hunston.

"Just now you said fifty-five. Why do you say one thing one minute and then alter your number?" asked the Tuan Biza.

"It wasn't me; it's Jack," answered Hunston, driven wild with pain and annoyance.

The chief shook his head.

It was his opinion that Hunston was going mad.

Buru, the savage-minded native of whom we have spoken, approached with his cleaver and threatened the captive.

"IN VAIN HUNSTON APPEALED TO JACK TO LET HIM GO."

Speaking in his own language, he said that he and his companions were not satisfied with the conduct of the chief.

The captive had said that he and and his companions wanted heads.

The Tuan Biza replied that the spirit had forbidden him to touch Hunston.

Buru made a derisive gesture, and danced round contemptuously, cutting what we should call a caper.

He snapped his fingers in the air, and again threatened Hunston with the cleaver.

" Ugh !" he exclaimed, " what can the spirit do ? Keyali, our young man, must have his head."

Keyali stepped forward, much elated at the turn affairs were taking.

" Beware !" thundered Jack. " Fire and smoke will come down from Heaven and consume you. Release the captive at sunset. Dare to touch a hair of his head and you will die."

Buru had been drinking rather too freely of the intoxicating liquor we have alluded to.

He snapped his fingers again, and led Keyali towards Hunston.

The other savages hung back.

Jack saw it was necessary to act.

Bringing his double-barrelled gun to a level with his shoulder, he prepared to fire.

It was not his object to kill either Buru or Keyali, as he wanted to make an example and strike terror into them.

So he aimed at Buru's leg, because he was the foremost in opposition, and the most ferocious-looking.

" Strike !" said Buru to Keyali.

At that moment Jack pulled the trigger.

Buru fell to the ground weltering in his blood.

Keyali ran away into the bush, and did not stop until he had gone some miles.

Then he sat down on the ground, and began to examine himself to see if he was hit.

The warriors were thunderstruck for a brief time, after which they chattered like a lot of monkeys.

Some examined Buru and bound up his wound, while others, headed by the Tuan Biza ran into the thicket from whence the smoke came.

But Jack was too quick for them.

Directly after firing, he had run away,

and hidden himself again at some distance.

They could find nothing, and their dismay was immense.

It was their firm belief that fire had come out of Heaven, as the spirit said it should.

From that instant Hunston's life was sacred in their eyes.

Even Buru would not have thought of harming him.

The wound inflicted upon the latter was situated in the thigh, and though painful, not dangerous, or necessarily fatal.

Feeling that he had saved Hunston's life, Jack hurried home to the castle, where he knew that Harvey must be waiting for him with the utmost impatience.

He had established a certain power over the natives; but he feared that since Hunston had told them there were other white people on the island, they would never rest until they had found them out.

Whether the savages lived at the extreme end of the island, or had come to this particular one to celebrate some custom, he could not tell.

It was enough for him just then to have come up in the nick of time, and prevented Hunston from having his head cut off by Keyali.

The mention of head-cutting was conclusive in Jack's mind that the natives he had seen were the dreaded and far-famed head-hunters.

Tired and hungry, he reached the castle.

Harvey was on the look-out, rifle in hand.

" Hullo, Jack," he said; " I thought you never were coming back. Seen anything ?"

" Yes," replied Jack.

" What ?"

" Niggers."

" No ! Have you really ?" said Harvey, much excited. " Have they got Hunston ?"

"There's no mistake about that, they've got him hard and fast. It serves him right for playing tricks with us and being treacherous. If he hadn't given way to his temper, he'd have been all right."

" Will they eat him ?"

" I don't think they are cannibals; they didn't look like it," answered Jack, " though they are ugly enough for anything. In my opinion they are a tribe or off-shoot of the Dyak head-hunters of Borneo, and nothing like nice neighbours."

"Didn't you try to save him?" asked Harvey.

"I did save him. As it happened I came up just at the time they were going to perform upon him, about a dozen of them. Such savage-looking beasts!"

"Why didn't you bring him with you?"

"You'll see him before long," said Jack, laughing, "and I'll bet you a sovereign, which, by-the-bye, I could not pay if I lost, as we haven't got any money amongst us, that you won't know him."

"Why not?" replied Harvey.

"His own mother wouldn't know him. Ha! ha! ha!"

"What are you laughing at?"

"Never mind," said Jack, "I've paid Master Hunston out for all he has done to me. You will know all about it soon enough. Give me some grub. I'm dead beat."

"I don't know what you'll have to eat?" replied Harvey; "the ants have got into the biscuits, and there is nothing but the kegs of salt beef I have not opened."

"I'll tell you how to dodge the ants," answered Jack.

"How?"

"Put a saucer full of water under each leg of a table, and they can't get up. Look out! There's a parrot. Odds I pot him."

As he spoke Jack fired at a gaudy-plumaged bird, and brought it down.

"Put him in some hot water," he continued, "the feathers will come off, then clean him and cut him open. He'll do fine on the gridiron; or, look here, where's Maple? Make him do it."

"All right. Maple's civil enough. He's been on his knees, as one may say, ever since Hunston cut it?" replied Harvey.

"Here, you, Maple," cried Jack, "you're to be head cook and bottle washer; take this parrot, and get him ready for my dinner! If you are not slippery over it, I pity you."

Maple set to work with alacrity, and in a quarter of an hour Jack had a very good broil, for it must be recollected that they had saved from the wreck all the cooking utensils and things for use that they wanted.

What Harvey had said about the ants was quite true.

They were pests.

The little insects got into everything that was not protected.

If a bird was shot and laid down for an hour there would not be much of it left, and they ran up everything in swarms.

While Jack was having his dinner, Maple approached him and said—

"Is it true that Hunston has been caught by the savages?"

"Yes; and so will you if you don't watch it," answered Jack, with his mouth half full of broiled parrot.

"You won't give me to them, will you?"

"That depends upon how you behave yourself."

"I'll never do anything to offend you again," said Maple, with tears in his eyes, "and I'm glad now they've got Hunston, because he set me on against you all along. If they eat him, it will only serve him right."

"Get out," exclaimed Jack in a tone of great disgust. "I hate you more now than I did before. You are a worse sneak than I thought you were."

"Why, Jack?" asked Maple.

"Don't call me 'Jack,'" replied he. "You and Hunston have been friends ever since you have known one another. You're as bad as he, and it's cowardly of you to let him down. Get up."

"Oh! if you've taken a spite against me, I can't help it," replied Maple, surlily.

Jack threw a biscuit at him, and he made his escape into the open air, looking more like a cowardly sneak than he usually did, and that is saying a great deal.

When Jack had satisfied his hunger, he called Harvey.

"You must keep a good look-out to-night," he exclaimed.

"Why more to-night than any other?" asked Harvey.

"I'll tell you why, Dick," answered Jack. "Those head-hunting niggers have an idea that there are white people on the island, and they will search for them. That's for sartin, as the African observed, when he was told he'd be hanged for eating his grandmother."

Harvey laughed.

"It wouldn't be pleasant to wake up in the morning, and find our heads gone," Jack went on.

"If our heads were off, we shouldn't wake any more," Harvey said.

"Yes, we should, we should wake in another land," answered Jack, smiling. "Don't interrupt me. I'm tired, and you must watch till twelve; then call me. Let Maple sleep. We can't depend on the little varmint. If Hunston comes in, wake me at once, only don't take him for Tippoo Saib in his war paint."

"I wish you'd tell me what has happened to Hunston," exclaimed Harvey.

"I won't spoil the fun. All I say is this. Hunston will be let go at sunset. I've worked the oracle so far, and I shan't say any more at present," replied Jack.

"I daresay it will keep," rejoined Harvey, in a tone of annoyance. "But about the natives? My only wonder is the beggars haven't found us out before. We've got quite a little farm about here."

"Yes; but we're in a sheltered nook, and they wouldn't spot us now, if they didn't follow Hunston."

"You think they'll do that?"

"I don't think; I know it. Niggers all over the world are the dodgiest beasts out. So keep your swivel eye open."

"Never fear," replied Harvey. "I'm wide awake. They won't catch this weazel with both eyes shut."

Jack was satisfied with his answer, and though the sun had not yet set, lay down to rest.

The fatigue in the hot noontide he had gone through was enough to make an ordinary mortal sleepy.

And sleep he did, like a top that hums, for he snored loud enough to scare the mosquitoes away, as Harvey observed with a laugh to Maple.

CHAPTER XX.

TREACHERY IN THE CAMP.

MAPLE was thoroughly cowed in the absence of Hunston, and obeyed every command which was given him by Harvey without a word.

His evil, malevolent nature could only plot—he had not the courage to carry out his wicked designs.

Coming up to Harvey about sunset while the latter, gun in hand, was keeping guard during Jack's sleep, as he sat down on the trunk of a fallen tree outside the castle, he said—

"Do you want me any more?"

"Yes," replied Harvey.

"What for?"

"That's nothing to you."

"But I should like to know. I've been weeding the corn all day, and I'm as tired as—as—help me to a simile."

"I shan't," answered Harvey. "If you can't find similes, go without them, or, if you must have one, say 'as sleepy as an ass,' which is what you are."

"You're always on to me," said Maple, with a subdued growl. "I suppose you think you can do as you like with me because you've got me on a desert island, and Hunston's sloped."

"It isn't deserted. Jack's seen savages."

"Has he? How many, and what are they like?" asked Maple, in surprise.

"You'll know in time. Hunston will be here soon."

"Will he? That's good news. He won't have me slave-driven. But what am I to do now?" Maple said, his face brightening at the news of Hunston's return.

"Skin a deer."

"Where is it?" Maple inquired, looking round.

"You'll see directly. I'm on the watch. The deer have been at the corn. They come about this time, and I mean to have a shot at one of the gentlemen," replied Harvey.

It was a lovely evening.

There was a constant changing of beautiful colours in the clouds that rested on the high mountain peaks in the south, while the day was fading into twilight, and the twilight in its turn subsiding into a fine, starlight night.

A little way off they could hear the sandpipers come and trip to and fro on the beach when the tide was full.

Many long-winged night-hawks swooped back and forth, feasting on multitudes of insects that came out as evening approached.

The deer of which Harvey spoke were most destructive.

They were accustomed to come into the prairie-lands in great droves, and frequently an area of a quarter of an acre was so completely rooted up by them that it looked as if it had been ploughed.

This was annoying, as the corn the boys had planted was making good progress under the fertilising influence of the climate.

Presently there was the sound of hoofs clattering on the hard ground.

Harvey fired, and brought down a fine deer.

He had learnt how to shoot, and having a quick eye, was as good a shot as Jack.

"Well shot," cried Maple. "You potted him splendidly. It was stunning."

"It'll be more stunning when you've skinned him and cut him up. Take a sharp knife, and I'll make a cat gallows to hang the flesh on," replied Harvey.

Accordingly, he cut down a couple of saplings, and placed them in the ground.

Over these he tied a horizontal bar.

Then he made a hole in the ground at the foot of each upright pole, and puddled the bottom with clay to make them hold water.

By this means he prevented the white ants climbing up the poles.

They would have eaten all the meat before morning if he had not adopted the plan of surrounding the sticks with water.

When the strips of fresh meat were hanging on the cross-bar, he lighted a fire underneath, and smoked them, placing a couple of steaks on the flames for his and Mapel's supper.

"Not bad tackle this," observed Maple, as he cut into his steak. "Venison's fine when you've had nothing but salt junk and biscuit for a week."

While the boys were eating their supper there was a sound of footsteps.

Harvey sprang to his feet and shouldered his rifle.

"Fire! fire! It's a nigger," said Mapel.

The intruder held up his hand, and said—

"Don't you know me?"

"I"ll be hanged if I do," replied Maple; "and yet it is—no, it can't be—yes, it is Hunston."

Hunston it was.

But how altered!

His face was haggard, and his eyes blood-shot.

Naked to the waist, as when the Indians let him go, in obedience to what they considered the command of a spirit, he appeared in all the grotesque horror of his recent tattooing.

His back presented a perfect nest of snakes, and a huge python coiled on his shoulders.

Parrots and other birds were represented on his chest and arms, while his stomach gave one a very good idea of a tiger crouching for his spring, and underneath all was a belt of fishes,

On each cheek was a parrot and on his nose a small crocodile.

He was smarting with the pain of the tattooing, and his skin presented an angry and inflamed appearance.

A more diabolical-looking object could not have startled his companions.

Mapel began to laugh.

He could not have helped it.

"Why, Hunston, old man," exclaimed Harvey, joining in the merriment his condition excited, "what have they been doing to you. Is it paint?"

"I wish to goodness it was," answered Hunston, in a hollow voice, "then it would wash off but now I'm marked for life."

"I must say you look pretty, You're quite a work of art. I never saw such a picture. You ought to be stuffed and sent to the British museum."

"I'll stuff you if you chaff me," answered Hunston. "Give me some of your grub. I'm very nearly starved."

"How did you get away?" asked Maple, putting a slice of dear meat on the fire.

"It was Jack's ventriloquism that did it," replied Hunston with a groan.

"He funked the critters awfully, and there was one buffer, the Tuan Biza, or chief, who quite thought he was a spirit, but I wish he'd left me to die, I do. What good am I, pricked about like this? I'll have my revenge, though, see if I don't!"

Maple had been trying to smother his laughter, but he could not do so any longer.

"Ha, ha, ha! ho, ho, ho!" he broke out, ducking his head, and laughing till his sides shook.

"What are you grinning at, ugly?" cried Hunston, seizing him by the ear. "I'll give you something to howl at."

"Oh, don't Hunston!" exclaimed Maple. "I couldn't help it. You look so comical."

Hunston dragged him to the fire, and bending him down by his superior strength put his head in the flames.

In a minute almost all his hair was singed off, and he would have been seriously burnt if Harvey had not pulled him away.

"Now you look comical, and I'll make you more so if you don't watch it," replied Hunston, savagely.

Maple did look funny without his hair and retired to a distance, rubbing his scorched head and crying.

When Hunston had satisfied his hunger he was a little better tempered, and Harvey gave him a little bottle of wine which had been saved from the wreck.

"Stop that bellowing," he exclaimed, to Maple, who was still roaring.

"You can go to roost as soon as you like," said Harvey.

"How can I sleep with a singed head? It stings so," answered Maple.

"Go and get some grease, and rub it well in, and put on a sailor's cap," suggested Harvey.

"Your thatch will grow again," remarked Hunston, "while my beauty will never come back. My figure-head is ornamented for life, but I'll be one with Master Jack Harkaway."

Harvey did not like the persistent way in which he spoke of his cherished vengeance.

"Don't rile Jack too much?" he said, " or he may wipe you out altogether."

"Two can play at that game," returned Hunston; "and you'd better keep out of it. I've no row with you at present."

"Your bad or good opinion doesn't matter much to me," answered Harvey carelessly.

"Doesn't it? We shall see. I'm desperate now, and if you quarrel with me, you'll find it no bottle, as the sailors say; so shut up before there's any harm done!" Hunston exclaimed threateningly.

"Why can't you live on friendly terms with us?" asked Harvey. "I am sure we ought to be more friendly than ever in our lonely position, with all sorts of dangers staring us in the face."

"You'll have enough of them soon," said Hunston, significantly; "and you should have more sense than to suppose that I can ever be jolly with any of you after this."

He pointed to his face.

"Jack did not do it."

"He told the savages to do it, which comes to the same thing."

"At the same time he saved your life, which you did not deserve."

"What's the use of my life to me?" asked Hunston. "I can never return to a civilized country with a face like this. I tell you he has just made me desperate, that's all."

"Did you not try to drown Jack, and I, and poor Mr. Mole when the 'Fairy' was abandoned?"

Hunston was silent.

"If you want to argue, you shall have enough of it," continued Harvey. "I suppose Jack thought you were only good enough to live among savages. It's what your bad disposition has brought you to."

"You'd look foolish if I brought the savages down on you," remarked Hunston.

"What good would that do you?" asked Harvey. "We are your friends, are we not? At least we are as friendly as you will let us be. The fact is, you were always a bad fellow, and I don't blame Jack for what he's done. But there may be hope for you yet."

"What hope?" cried Hunston.

"All the tattooing I have seen on board ship has been done with Indian ink, which won't come out."

"Well?"

"Suppose the dye of the berry the savages used is not lasting."

Hunston's face grew positively radiant at this suggestion.

"God grant what you suggest may be true. It sounds too good, however. A week or two will show. It's kind of you, Harvey, to try to comfort me. I thought you all hated me."

"Jack doesn't hate you in his heart. He's not the sort of fellow to hate anyone; only remember your last attempt to take the command here and make us your slaves. You can't be trusted—you are so treacherous and evily disposed."

"Jack had best look out."

"I wonder you don't feel grateful to him for saving you," Harvey said. "I'm not exactly a pious sort of a fellow, as you know, though I try to steer clear of anything wrong, and——"

"Ah, yes, I daresay!" sneered Hunston. "You're one of those saints who carry a Bible in their pockets."

"I have got a Bible, I am thankful to say in my pocket. It was my mother's last gift, and I find a good deal of comfort in it now and then, though I am sorry that I don't read it so much as I ought."

"You have got one."

"Yes, and I'm not ashamed of it," replied Harvey, resolutely. "But what I was going to say is this——"

"I shall slip my cable and sleep in the woods if you are going to preach."

"Only a word or two. Don't you think you are better here with us, than if you had been killed, and sent as you are to be judged? One ought to pay a little attention to these things."

"Oh, don't bother me!" answered Hunston, uneasily. "I want to be quiet and think."

Harvey said no more.

As he watched Hunston doze, after his dinner, he fancied his face assumed a villainous expression.

Bad thoughts were evidently lurking in his mind.

Of course the tattooing disfigured him, and made him look repulsive and even ferocious, though there was a comical side to that also.

"I must warn Jack," muttered Harvey. "There is something in the beggar's look which I don't like. If he does not mean mischief, I can't read faces."

Full of thought, he paced up and down, keeping a good look-out, and breathing with more ease, now a cool current of air, such as the evening brings, took the place of the garish light of day and its sultry atmosphere.

CHAPTER XXI.

JUST IN TIME.

HUNSTON, who was thoroughly exhausted, fell asleep.

The wind, in heavy gusts, sighed through the dense foliage over his head, while in the distance rose the deep, pulsating roar of the ocean surf.

Inland was a deep ravine, and from its furthermost recesses rolled out the reverberating, moaning cries of monkeys, who all the night long kept up a piteous calling, each answering his fellows in the same mournful tones.

Hunston's dreams were not pleasant.

A storm was coming on, to avoid which Harvey entered the castle, still on the look-out.

At midnight a troubled dream disturbed the rest of Hunston.

An indefinite horror thrilled along his veins as he fancied for a moment that he was whirling round and round a deep yawning maelstrom.

Then a change occurred, but scarcely one for the better.

He fancied he was fixed in the midst of a water-spout, and in his struggles to escape, awoke to find that a great stream of water was pouring down upon him from the leaves of a palm under which he was sleeping.

A heavy shower had come on.

Getting up, he went to the house the boys had built, and was about to enter, when he was stopped by Harvey.

"You can't come inside," said the latter.

"Why not? Do you want me to catch rheumatism out in the wet?" answered Hunston.

"I'll ask Harkaway. It's time to call him, but the fact is, after the threats you used, I am afraid of you."

"I shan't hurt you," said Hunston, with a laugh. "It would be easy enough, if I felt inclined. What's to prevent me from cutting your throat like a rabbit?"

Harvey shuddered.

Hunston spoke in such a cold blooded way, that he feared him more than ever; but, touching his gun, he exclaimed—

"Only this, my boy. This will stop you."

"Let me in to-night, and I'll cut the shop to-morrow," Hunston said, pleadingly. "I shall be better off with the savages."

Harvey woke Jack, saying—

"It's your turn to watch now. I am pretty well done up."

"Has Hunston come back?" asked Jack springing up.

"Yes; he's at the door. It's pelting with rain. Shall he come in?"

"Oh, yes, let the poor beast in."

"Be on the look-out. He's in a nice state of mind, I can tell you."

"Is he? Well it isn't to be wondered at. What does he look like?" asked Jack, with a grin.

"Beautiful. He's a sort of cross between a zebra and a chimpanzee with the measles."

Hunston stepped forward.

He had heard this remark, and he exclaimed—

"What are you? I should call you a cross between a laughing jackass and a baboon, with a dash of Tom Fool in you."

"Look here! stash that sort of thing," cried Jack· "I'm cock here, You must not cheek, Harvey."

"Why can't he let me alone?"

"It's his playful nature. He is not savage like you."

"Enough to make me savage. Look at my face," growled Hunston.

"I will in the morning, when there's more light; at present our lamp is rather dim. But you ought to feel flattered at the delicate attention the natives have paid you."

"Why?"

"Because, when you get back to England, if you ever do, you need not be hard up," answered Jack. "All you've got to do is to hire yourself out to some cove with a caravan, and he can take you round the country and show you, at a penny a head, as the 'wild man of the Unknown Islands, by nature painted as you see him, born with a parrot on each cheek, and a small crocodile on the nose. Walk up ladies and gentlemen, walk up; only a penny. Positively only a brown to see this wonderful natural phenomenon.' Then will come a touch of the big drum, and the coppers will roll in like steam. Tie a sheepskin round your waist, and you'll draw. Your fortune's as good as made."

"Go on," said Hunston. "It pleases you, and it doesn't hurt me."

"Or you might be advertised as the marvellous man monkey, ornamental if not useful."

"I shan't answer you. I'm going to pitch in the corner. My unfortunate nut aches fit to split," Hunston observed.

"'Behold him ladies and gentlemen, but at the same time beware,'" Jack went on, "'for he takes the most lovely maidens into the topmost branches of the highest trees, regardless of their piteous cries, and the agonized entreaties of their frenzied relatives.'"

"Shut up, you fool!" cried Hunston, who could not keep his temper.

"I'm only doing the showman," Jack answered.

"You might let a fellow get a few winks of sleep after all he has gone through."

"All right. Dick be quiet. The pictorial ape sleeps.

Hunston pretended to snore, but he did not go to sleep.

He was watching his opportunity, which came sooner than he expected.

Harvey threw himself down, and also made him believe that he was worn out and wanted rest,

But he distrusted Hunston and determined to watch him.

Only the humming of the night birds and insects, with the occasional hiss of a snake, and the wild and horrid noise made by some wild beast in the jungle, broke the silence of the night.

The rain had cleared up as suddenly as it had come on.

Jack took a peep outside, standing half in, and half out of the doorway.

The rain that had fallen rose again in thick heavy vapour from the hot ground.

Knowing that this very often gave rise to fevers, Jack did not venture out.

Hunston had not taken his snake-like eyes off him.

Seeing his back turned, he rose on his hands and knees.

Opening his clasp knife, he placed it between his teeth, and crawled stealthily towards his victim.

In an instant Harvey was after him.

Just as he started up in the dim mist of that tropical night to plunge his knife into the back of Harkaway, who was totally unsuspicious of his intention, Harvey was upon him.

Throwing his arms round his neck, he put on a hug that nearly strangled him.

He fell on his back on the floor of the

hut, and Harvey placed his knee on his chest.

"Would you?" he said.

"What's the shine, Dick?" asked Jack, turning round.

"Can't you see?"

"I can't make out exactly."

It would have been all up the Baltic with you in a brace of shakes if I hadn't guessed what his game was and watched him. He'd got a knife to stab you with."

"Had he, by jingo?" replied Jack, who now began to realise the narrow escape he had had.

Hunston glanced sullenly and defiantly at them.

CHAPTER XXII.

AN UGLY FIX.

PRESENTLY Jack spoke.

"I'll tell you what it is, old man," he exclaimed, "if you play tricks with me, it's either your life or mine, and as king of this island, I shall have to. try you by court-martial, and let the daylight into you with an ounce of lead."

"I didn't mean anything," answered Hunston, cowering before him.

"What had you a knife for?"

"You see, I was dreaming, and walked in my sleep."

"It won't wash," said Jack.

"What I've gone through upset my mind. I thought I was going to attack one of the natives, and make my escape."

"It isn't good enough," continued Jack.

"Don't you believe me?"

"Not by a long way. You're a bad lot, Mr. Hunston, and you'll have to make tracks."

"What?"

"Walk your chalks!"

"You won't send me away! How can I live unarmed, in the open?" pleaded Hunston.

"You stepped it of your own accord a little while ago, and now you'll hook it to please me."

"That was temper. I meant to come back, only the natives copped me," replied Hunston. "Come, Jack, make it up. I swear I didn't mean any harm. You were always more generous to me than I deserved. Don't kick me out like a dog. There are wild beasts on the islands, and I saw snakes. These are not nice companions, let alone the head hunting natives."

"It's your own fault."

"Don't be hard on me," continued Hunston.

"I'll leave it till the morning, and then we'll decide what's to be done with you," replied Jack. "It's beastly to think there is treachery in the camp. I don't like it."

"I know what that means," said Hunston, gloomily. "You'll let me be quiet till the morning, and then you'll shunt me. If I go by myself on this island I must croak, you know that."

"No, I don't. Forage for yourself."

"You don't seem to see exactly what you are doing," Hunston said. "But I'll tell you if Harvey will let me go."

"Let him get up, Dick," said Jack.

Hunston rose and shook himself, like a Newfoundland dog on getting out of the water.

"Go ahead," continued Jack. "I'm so far up to you, that you don't perform on me. I'm wide awake enough."

"If you send me away, you drive me into the hands of the natives. They won't kill me now, because they consider me under the protection of a spirit, and they will be glad enough to have me, when I tell them who the spirit is, and what a nice, little, well-stored crib he's got here."

"You're villain enough for anything," exclaimed Jack.

"If I'm driven to it."

"Were you driven to trying to annoy me at school, or to drown me on board ship, or to make yourself master here, or to go in for stabbing me to-night?" said Jack, looking pointedly at him.

"Let the past drop. I'm talking about what you're driving me to now," answered Hunston.

"You double-distilled ass," exclaimed Jack, impatiently. "Do you think I can't see through you?"

"I don't want to be master," Hunston

continued. "But I don't see why a fellow with my experience, who has made more than one voyage, should be put on the shelf, because you choose to make a favourite of Harvey."

"Dick and I are old chums. Dick is a gentleman, which is what you never were, and never will be."

"His father's only a clerk, a half-and-half City banking Clerk, and my father has got his own property," Hunston said.

"I'm talking about the man himself, and not about fathers," replied Jack. "I say Dick's an old pal of mine, and he has always gone straight, which you have not, and that's why I made him my lieutenant."

"Won't you trust me?"

"I can't. If you were to go down on your knees, and take all the oaths you ever knew, I shouldn't feel any more comfortable with you in the place, than I should with a young cobra copella between my ship's blankets."

Hunston looked foolish.

"You asked me for it, and now you've got it," Jack went on.

"Then you'd rather have me as an enemy," said Hunston.

"What are you now?"

"Willing to be your friend."

To Hunston's offer of friendship Jack simply replied—

"Bosh! over the left."

"All right, my hearty. It don't make much difference to me," cried Hunston. "If I can't have your friendship, I'll have——"

"What?" asked Jack, as he hesitated.

"*Your head*," replied Hunston.

Jack and Harvey regarded him with amazement.

Was he going to make another attack upon them?

What did he mean? Jack scarcely knew how to deal with Hunston.

He was in a sort of fix.

Hunston was not slow in taking advantage of the impression that he had made upon Jack.

"I suppose you know," he went on, "that the natives you saw to-day are head-hunters?"

"Yes. I gathered as much as that," answered Jack.

"Very well, then we can sail fair," continued Hunston, who stooped down to repossess himself of his knife. "Am I to go?"

"How can I keep you here, when you are always trying to prod me with knives, and won't knock under?"

"I never did, and never will. The man isn't born who shall call me master."

"But don't you know," exclaimed Jack, "that even the savages have a chief? There must be some head to keep things in working order. What is it you want?"

"My idea is that of a republic. One man's as good as another. Let us live like brothers, and share and share alike."

"Yes," Harvey said, derisively, "a nice brother you'd make. If you had the key of the spirit chest, you'd be as tight as a drum in an hour."

"A good job, too," replied Hunston. "But don't you put your say in. I'm talking to your master."

"Who's that?"

"Harkaway; didn't he say he was king? Very well. If he is, of course he's your master as well as mine, though that's not what I'm driving at. I'm to go, that's flat. I don't care much, for I shall go to the natives and make terms with them. They will plan an attack on you here, and I shall show them the way, so you know what you've got to expect."

"That's a nice return for all our kindness," observed Jack.

"Kindness," repeated Hunston, scornfully.

"I don't see that we have treated you badly."

"Oh, don't you! I'm sorry for you then."

"You have tried more than once to take away my life, and I suppose you know that is murder," exclaimed Jack, severely. "If you were at home you would be tried and hanged for it."

"Hanged for killing a thing like you!"

"Never mind what I am. You need not be so cocky. I could shoot you now and be justified in doing so," Jack said, colouring.

"Why?"

"Simply because you have basely and treacherously tried to take away a life you cannot give back again. You're like a dog that bites the hand that feeds it."

"Well, I'm off. My name's Walker, and I can see the sooner I slope out of this caboose the better. It won't take me long to find better diggings. Will you give me a gun and some powder and shot?" said Hunston.

"Not likely," answered Jack, "you don't take me for such a flat, do you? I may be green, I know I am green in some things, but I'm not so jolly thundering green as all that."

"I only want to shoot something."

"Somebody you mean, and that somebody is myself. No thank you. When I'm tired of my life, I'll make you a present of our best double-barrelled, but not before."

"I meant I wanted to kill something to live upon," said Hunston, looking confused.

"Over the left," remarked Harvey.

"Join your friends the niggers. You're worth your grub to them; they'll board and lodge you," replied Jack.

"I may not find them at once."

"Why not?"

"They don't live here," replied Hunston, becoming confidential. "This is a desert island, with no inhabitants except ourselves. They came over in proas or long boats."

"How do you know that?" queried Jack, who was much interested in this announcement.

"I heard the Tuan Biza talking, and asked him a lot of questions. They call this Pulo Kapul or Ship Island, because it is a dangerous coast, and ships have been wrecked here before."

"What did they come here for?"

"For a spree, I suppose. There was some ceremony on, and it was a sort of excursion," answered Hunston.

"I don't understand the habits of the beggars," exclaimed Jack. "But are you sure you are not humbugging us?"

"No, I'm not really. I tell you the truth. The natives you saw come from some distance. They had, as far as I can ascertain, boarded an English merchant vessel, for they are awful pirates, and they had killed all the passengers and crew except a young girl, whom they led captive to their town or village."

"An English girl?" asked Jack, his face flushing indignantly.

"Yes."

"Well, cut along, Hunston," Jack said; "you can't stop here until you get better ideas, I won't say into your head, but into your heart; that's where you are wrong, old boy."

"Good-bye," muttered Hunston, as Harvey left the doorway to make room for him to pass.

"I'll tell you one thing," Jack went on, "if you come back ready and willing to make one of us, I shall always be glad to forget what's happened. I can't say more than that, can I?"

Hunston was silent.

"Can I, Dick?" repeated Jack.

"I'm sure you can't," replied Harvey.

"Oh, yes," sneered Hunston, "you want to be a couple of jolly good-natured fellows, don't you? That sort of lingo is only meant to glorify yourselves, and make me look small."

"I won't waste any further words with you," Jack said, in a tone of annoyance. "Clear out."

He stood on one side, and Hunston quitted the castle in the grey dawn of the early morning, and was soon lost to sight in the distance.

"A good riddance," remarked Jack.

"Yes, he's useless; and I suppose I can take my forty winks now," replied Harvey.

Jack replied in the affirmative, and walked up and down outside the castle, gun in hand, so as to be ready in the event of a surprise.

He thought over his present position, and thoughts of home came into his mind.

Would he ever see his home again?

Surrounded on all sides by peril, it was extremely doubtful, but he kept a good heart and did not despair.

Thinking of what Hunston had told him about the wreck of an English ship on a neighbouring island, and the capture of a young lady by the natives, caused his thoughts to turn to Emily.

It was pleasant to think that she was happy with her friends.

To know that the natives had only visited his island was consoling, because they were not so likely to attack him.

What would Hunston do?

He had, in his bullying, blustering way, threatened to make friends with the natives if he fell in with them again.

Very likely he might be able to effect an union with them.

And flushed with the hope of plunder as well as human heads, they would not be a force to be despised.

Yet he could not blame himself for letting Hunston go away.

While in the castle, he was always plotting against Jack and seeking his life.

"HARVEY PLACED HIS KNEE ON HUNSTON'S CHEST."

He was his enemy anyhow.

All Jack could do was to be always on the watch.

He resolved that he would go out the next day and once more explore the island, so as to see if the savages were still upon it.

In his belt he placed pistols and knives, and over his shoulder he carried his breech-loading gun.

When Harvey heard his intention, he begged to be allowed to accompany him.

This he could not agree to, as it would not have been safe to leave the castle in the charge of Maple.

So Jack started alone.

Having set off before the heat of the day came on, Jack, in about three hours, had done his ten miles.

He passed several lakes, fringed with ferns; hot, sulphurous fumes exhaled from them.

On one was a flock of wild birds, which he longed to have a shot at, but did not deem it prudent, as he might give an indication of his presence to enemies.

Occasionally he came across springs and pools of steaming, boiling water, showing the volcanic nature of the ground for miles near the burning mountain.

A range of hills rose up before him, and from these descended a variety of streams which formed themselves into a river.

This gradually increased in size and volume till it reached the sea.

It was magnificently wooded on both sides, and, as Jack stood on the bank and gazed up and down, he thought what a lovely place it would be to come and fish in.

Vines, shrubs, and large trees, were mingled together, while guardy-plumaged birds disported themselves in the dense foliage.

Even a photograph could scarcely convey a correct and adequate idea of the magnifience of the scenery.

Being hot and tired, Jack made up his mind to have a bath.

For a moment he forget that there might be dangerous reptiles in the river.

The water looked so cool and tempting that he could not resist it.

Laying down his gun, pistols and knives, he took off his clothes, and selecting a good place on the bank to jump off from, plunged in with a header.

He came up with the sparkling water bubbling over his head.

"This is jolly," he exclaimed, "I wish old Harvey was here. How he would enjoy it."

And he struck out to cross the river, the stream of which was not very strong.

He had not gone more than a dozen yards before he heard a shouting behind him.

Turning round he saw three men.

A glance seemed to show him that they were savages.

They gesticulated and held up their hands in which were spears, as if to arrest his attention.

Luckily he had taken the precaution to hide his weapons and clothes under a carraway tree, the long, needle-like leaves of which effectually protected and concealed them.

It seemed as if the natives were telling him to come back.

"Thank you," muttered Jack to himself, "I'd rather not. I've no doubt you're very nice when one knows you, but I've no desire to have the pleasure of your acquaintance, we'll postpone the honour."

His intention was to swim to the opposite bank and make his escape.

He could return for his gun and clothes when they were gone.

Anything was better than falling into their hands.

The noise made by the natives redoubled.

"What a row the varmints are kicking up," Jack said, wondering what they meant.

He was very soon to find out.

Suddenly he saw something in the water ahead of him.

Something ugly and scaly, like the head of a monster in a pantomime.

A thing with dull eyes, but big jaw, which he knew in an instant belonged to a crocodile.

It was between him and the shore.

Behind him were the natives.

It was death to retreat, and it looked very much like death to advance or stay where he was.

Jack's blood turned cold, and he felt as if the water, which he had hitherto thought temperate, had become icy.

"I'm a gone coon," he said to himself; "either the crocodile or the niggers must have me, and its odds on the croc."

It was certainly an awkward meeting, and showed the danger of bathing in a river in the tropics.

What was he to do.

Jack had not the remotest idea.

He stared at the crocodile, and the repulsive brute glared back again at him.

CHAPTER XXIII.

THE FEAST OF THE CANNIBALS.

"Yes," continued Jack to himself, "I'll back the fish. It's long odds on the scaly monster of the deep."

But in spite of his apparent levity, he was very much alarmed.

His position seemed a hopeless one.

He was afraid to move much, and kept treading water and floating gently down the stream.

If he moved, he had an idea that the crocodile would at once make a dive at him.

All at once he heard something whizz past his ear.

"A short stick floated on the water near him, and he fancied that the natives were shooting arrows at him, and trying to kill him.

"That's coming it too strong," he muttered. "It's getting, hot now and no mistakes."

Another and another of these short stick fell close to him, and Jack grasped one, remarking that it was sharpened at both ends, and seemed to be cut from a very hard sort of wood.

This action of his may have roused the crocodile, who was of average size, for the monster moved towards Jack.

His huge jaws opened, and the formidable teeth he possessed became visible.

"God help me," cried Jack, as the beast rushed at him. "It's all over now. Good-bye to everybody and everything. I should have liked a better grave than that beast's stomach."

The instinct of self-preservation was very strong within him.

Scarcely knowing why he did so, he put out his hand.

In it was the short stick shot at him by the natives.

This he thrust into the crocodile's mouth quite suddenly.

His jaws tried to close, to bite off the boy's appetising arm, but they shut on the sharp edges of the hard stick.

Unable to open or shut his mouth, the creature lashed the water into foam.

The natives had been very quiet for a time.

Now they set up a shout.

This led Jack to believe that they had purposely sent him the sharpened sticks, and not with the intention of injuring him.

Whether their intention was friendly or not he could not tell.

Perhaps they wanted to eat him themselves, and did not like the idea, of a crocodile having such a tit-bit all to itself.

"They may be friendly, and they may be t'other. Very much t'other, I should suspect," thought Jack. "However, I shan't give them the chance of chawing up this child."

Anxious to get out of the water as soon as possible, he swam with quick stroke to the opposite bank to that on which the natives were standing.

The crocodile followed him, though it was as inoffensive as a lamb now.

Once on the shore, Jack sank on his knees and thanked Heaven.

Then he took up a stone and threw it at the crocodile, upon which it made no impression,

"The brute's like a hog in armour," remarked Jack.

He ran for some distance, but finding the heat of the sun inconvenient, he climbed up a tree and hid himself among the thick leaves.

Here he remained until the sun's power decreased.

He was so delighted at his escape from the dangers that had menaced him, that he did not care much for such little evils as being scorched by the sun, or parched with thirst.

When he could conveniently do so, he intended to seek a place near the river's source, where he could ford the stream.

Nothing would have induced him to swim across the water again.

To be face to face, when bathing, with a crocodile, is quite enough once in a lifetime.

He learnt afterwards that it was not at all an unusual thing for the natives to thrust sharp-pointed sticks into the monster's jaws, and so render him incapable of closing them.

That some natives still lingered on the island he had no doubt.

On dry land, and armed, he did not fear them.

It appeared, from what he learnt subsequently, that when they saw him in the water, they took him to be one of their own party.

Their shooting the sticks with their bows towards him was no proof of their friendliness to him.

Perhaps they were not a little surprised when they saw him get out of the water, with his white skin shining in the sun.

In time Jack descended from the tree, and made his way, as well as he could with his naked feet, along the river bank.

He found a ford, about two miles further up, crossed, and went towards the spot where he had left his clothes.

To his joy, he discovered them just as he had left them.

It did not take him long to dress, and with his gun and pistols, he felt himself a man once more.

It was time to get back, so he started on the homeward journey, not having done much that day.

That the island was larger than he had imagined he had found out, as well as that it had a water-shed from a range of hills of some importance.

In addition to this, the natives had not yet gone away.

There was a source of danger in this fact, for if Hunston was as good as his word, and made friends with these savages, he might at any moment lead them against his former companions,

While thinking of the dangers ahead, Jack stopped abruptly.

A wild sound fell upon his ears, which he knew from his experience of the day before, was the festival chant of the nation

Approaching very cautiously, he saw that he had arrived at the spot where the savages had been singing joy songs over the capture of Hunston.

Had they got him again?

A glance sufficed to show him that the victim tied to the bamboo stake was not Hunston, nor did he see any trace of that young gentleman.

Fascinated by the expectation of some horrible spectacle, Jack halted, being well concealed, and looked on.

"Here's the show gratis for nothing, and I don't see why I shouldn't peep at it," was Jack's remark.

A sharpened prop was placed under the prisoner's chin, so that he could not move his head.

One look at the wretched man's face proved conclusively that he had given up all hope of life.

It was possible to read nothing there but blank, hopeless despair.

Presently the barbaric chant ended.

The Tuan Biza stepped forward with a large, sharp knife in his hand.

As the chief, it was his privilege to cut out of the living victim any piece he liked best.

The parts of the human body which are esteemed the greatest delicacies by these cannibals are first, the palms of the hands, and then the eyes.

When the chief has gratified his choice the others are entitled in turn to advance and cut out bits.

The savage feast proceeded quickly, and the victim's shrieks and moans were pitiful to hear.*

Jack ground his teeth with rage, but on looking to his rifle, found that he had lost the percussion cap off the nipple, and had not another with him. Besides the man might have been a criminal for what he knew.

It was evident that those men did not eat human flesh for lack of animal food.

Abundance of game was to be met with, as Jack knew.

They indulged their appetites in this beastly manner, because they liked it.

It was a very long time before Jack got the sight of the hacked and bleeding form from his eyes.

Sick at heart, and faint, he glided away from the spot, and struck out for home.

When he reached the castle, he related his adventures to Harvey, who listened with increasing horror at each fresh detail

---

* For confirmation of this revolting custom, refer to Bickmore's and Pfeiffer's travels among the Battas of the East Indian Archipelago.

Maple was equally impressed.

"I'm glad you got away from the crocodile," said Maple. "But it would have been worse to fall in with the natives. Do you think they would eat us?"

"Yes, like a shot," answered Jack. "But I don't mean to give them the chance."

"Will they attack us?" said Harvey, "that is the question."

"Yes, a hundred to one on it," answered Jack. "Hunston will make his peace with, and become one of them, solely by promising them the plunder of our castle, and the enjoyment of our bodies. I don't expect him to-night, though we shall not be safe from one hour to the other."

"Let me watch, Jack," exclaimed Maple, "and give me a gun. I'm sure I can shoot."

"I can't trust you," replied Jack.

"Not when our lives are in danger? I should not, for my own sake, let the natives capture us."

"Yes, you might if Hunston got hold of you, and promised you your own life. That's what it is to have a bad character," Jack continued. "You might in this crisis help us a great deal, but we know what you are; so, while Harvey and I do the watching and fighting, you must be the indoor servant, Sally the housemaid, and Polly the cook, rolled into one; so set about your business at once, and let me have some dried venison and something to drink."

Maple slunk away, ashamed of himself, and annoyed at not being allowed to act the part of a man.

It was his own fault, however, and he had only himself to thank for it.

"You're dull, Jack," observed Harvey, pouring him out a glass of wine.

"My nerves are a little shaken," answered Jack, drinking the wine at a draught.

"No wonder."

"And I've got an idea that stirring events are going to happen."

"I wish a ship would come and take us away," said Harvey, with a sigh, as he thought of home.

"So do I, but I don't know that I should go in her," replied Jack.

"Why not?" asked Harvey, in surprise.

"You heard what Hunston said about a ship being wrecked on another island?"

"Yes."

"And an English girl being saved?" continued Jack.

"And taken into the interior as a captive or slave, or something," said Harvey.

"That was it," replied Jack, adding, "well, I want to save that girl, and bring her away with me; and I shouldn't consider myself a man, or be happy all my life, if I had the chance of going away, and did not make something more than an effort to rescue that English girl."

"By Jove! you're right, Jack. I always said you were a fine fellow," cried Harvey, his face speaking the admiration he felt.

Involuntarily the boy's hands met in a cordial grasp.

It was a silent compact between them to save their fair and unfortunate countrywoman at all hazards.

CHAPTER XXIV.

KEPT IN SUSPENSE

A FEW days passed without bringing any cause of alarm to the castaways.

Jack did not decrease in vigilance.

He and Harvey kept a good look-out, distrusting Maple, who was treated as their drudge, for they knew his deceitful nature, and feared lest he might in some way be in communication with Hunston.

The captain's dog, Nero, of which we have spoken, was tied up outside the castle, so that he might give notice of the approach of any foe.

He would not bark at any of the boys, and not knowing what Hunston's real character was, he rather liked him in return for meat and biscuits he had given him, but the slightest tread of a strange footstep would make his loud bark resound through the woods.

"I wish I knew the worst," Jack remarked to his friend. "If Hunston is going to lead the natives to attack us, he might do it and get the thing over."

"Perhaps he's not so bad as we think him, and will change his mind," answered Harvey.

"Not he," said Jack, with a shake of the head. "I know him of old. He only cares for himself. He would like to be king of the savages and have all our stores and firearms, but he hasn't got them yet."

"That reminds me of an idea I had," said Harvey.

"Out with it then; don't be afraid of it."

"If we were attacked it would be from the clearing we've made, as the enemy could act more compactly together. My idea is to load, say twenty guns, and fix them nearly all together so that we could tie a string to the triggers, pull it and fire a volley, which would kill the lot."

"All right," said Jack. "I loaded about thirty guns yesterday, and put them in a corner, so that I could take up one after another and let fly at the niggers on the principle of one down, t'other come on."

This idea of Harvey's was adopted, and a formidable battery erected in a few hours.

The boys felt more comfortable when they had taken every precaution against a surprise that prudence suggested.

"Some of these guns are oldish. I hope they won't 'bust' up," remarked Jack, with a smile.

"If you think that," answered Harvey, regarding the battery fondly, "let's make Maple pull the string. If he was blown into little bits and smithereens, he wouldn't be much loss."

"I should like to take a stroll and see what is going on," Jack said, anxiously.

"You mustn't venture a yard from the castle, Jack," cried Harvey. "I won't have it. Our only chance is in the bundle of sticks dodge. We must hang together. How do you know that we are not being watched now from some bush, and that your departure on a stroll would be the signal for a rush in and a surprise of the place. It makes my hair curl to think of it."

"All right. I won't leave you," Jack replied, "though this continued suspense is not at all to my liking. Perhaps the natives have left the island, their game of jinks being over, and Hunston can't find them."

"No," said Harvey, thoughtfully. "He's found them. If he hadn't, he'd have been back. How could he live without arms to kill birds and things? He's met with them, and is getting something up for us."

"He'll meet with a hot reception. Our guns will astonish the weak nerves of his new friends."

"That's what he's afraid of. He wants to catch us napping."

"Don't he wish he may get it?" answered Jack, adding, "I say, Dick, have you noticed those fine birds that look like pheasants—the beggars that eat our corn up! Look at them now; they're wiring in like steam. Here, Maple, you little humbug, why don't you go and bird-flap? It's all you're fit for."

"They won't go away," replied Maple, who was hoeing the weeds out of some potatoes that had just begun to sprout.

"You've only got to show your ugly mug and they'll have fits," replied Jack. "Whistle, howl, do something. Give them a 'lul-li-e-ty' like that we used to wake old Crawcour up with, and drive Mole mad on the winter evenings at Lillie Bridge."

"I wish I was back there again," said Maple, almost tearfully.

"You ungrateful little viper," exclaimed Jack sarcastically. "Do you mean to say that you don't appreciate the honour of being head cook and bottle washer to King Harkaway and Duke Harvey, his prime minister, home secretary, and all the rest of it."

"Duke Humbug," muttered Maple.

"What's that you say?" asked Harvey. "I'll give you something, my fine fellow. Come here and do homage. Come on."

"Do what?" said Maple, laying down his hoe and advancing.

"Do homage. Kneel on both knees, and put my feet on your head in token of submission. You won't? Lend me that stick, an' it please your most gracious majesty. I must welt this disobedient subject."

Jack handed him a stick he carried in his hand, and laughed heartily.

"Lamm in to him," he said.

"Oh, don't hit me, Harvey," roared Maple. "I'm sore all over from the last hiding you gave me. I'll do homage or any other rot you like."

Accordingly Harvey refrained, and Maple, kneeling down, put his head under the prime minister's feet, and was afterwards allowed to resume his work.

"That will teach you not to be cheeky," observed Harvey. "We don't allow any Radicals here."

Maple gave him a spiteful look, and went to the cornfields to drive away the gaudy-plumaged birds that were making such sad havoc with the corn.

They rose in a body as he approached but when he went away they soon came down again.

Jack tried to get a shot at them, and found them too wary, for they would not let him get near them.

In appearance they resembled phesants and seemed as if they would be excellent eating.

"I never saw such wary brutes," Jack observed. "It's a nuisance, too, because if we could kill a few, we could see what they would be like in the pot, and we should also be able to make some scarecrows to keep the rest away. I can't get near them."

"I'll tell you a dodge," remarked Harvey. "Although I'm a Londoner and the gov's a clerk in the City, I've been a good deal at my uncle's farm in Gloucestershire, and I'll tell you how he gets his game."

"Shoots it, I suppose?"

"No; he doesn't shoot it either; so you're out there. The landlord wouldn't let him start a feather with a gun," answered Harvey, with a knowing wink."

"How is it done, then?" asked Jack.

"I'll show you. You know those fowls we saved from the wreck?"

"Yes; they're in the coop now. A cock and three hens. I had an egg for my breakfast this morning. What of them?"

"Go and bring the cock, will you? He's a regular old Turk to fight, and I'll show you some fun."

Jack went to the hen coop and brought out the cock, which was a thoroughbred game fowl.

During his absence, Harvey had broken off two blades from his penknife, which he had in his pocket.

Taking the bird from Jack, he fixed the blades on to the creature's legs.

"Those don't make bad spurs, do they?" he asked.

"Not at all," answered Jack.

"Follow me, then, and you shall see a match between the English barndoor fowl and the East Indian nondescript."

They approached the cornfield, and the handsome birds flew away, perching as usual some distance off on high trees.

Harvey put down the cock, which began to crow loudly, and the boys hid behind the trunk of a tree.

The birds came cautiously back to their food, and one of the males, not liking the appearance of a stranger on the scene, flew down and gave him battle.

The birds flew at one another, and the issue was not long doubtful.

The English bird struck his enemy, and the blade of the penknife cut into his head, causing him to fall down with a death flutter.

"Dead as mutton," whispered Harvey, gleefully.

"What a lark!" said Jack, in the same tone.

"Hold your noise," cried Harvey. "There's another coming to have a pitch in.

He was right.

Another of the beautiful birds came to fight the intruder, and with an angry screech, which the cock met with a crow of defiance, the battle began, and ended quickly with the same result.

In a short time, half-a-dozen fine cock-birds were lying on their sides.

Harvey thought that enough, and took the victorious game-fowl back to the coop, having previously removed his formidable spurs, and then he rewarded him for his prowess with a handful of corn.

"What do you think of that?" asked Harvey, rejoining Jack, who was examining the spoil.

"Stunning. Your uncle was a genius, Dick," replied Harkaway.

"That's how we used to get the squire's birds, as the keepers never heard a gun fired, they never twigged the caper. But I'll show you something else. My aunt was very fond of partridges, and we used to give them her. First of all we spotted a covey, and when this was done, we were bound to have them."

"How?"

"Give me about an hour, and I'll show you. I've got to make my preparation," answered Harvey.

"Cut along, then," said Jack, adding—
"Maple."

"Yes, Jack," answered Maple.

"Don't 'yes, Jack' me," exclaimed Harkaway, with an affectation of anger. "I'm king. Speak to me with proper and becoming respect."

"Very well, my lord," said Maple.

"That won't do. It's not grand enough."

"What does your majesty require? Will that do?"

"It's better. Take a brace of those birds; pluck them, and stick them before a fire. I want to see how they eat."

Maple sat down and began his task with a groan.

He hated plucking and cleaning birds.

But grumbling was no use, and he had to do it.

CHAPTER XXV.

HUNSTON'S RECEPTION BY THE NATIVES.

To use his own expression, Hunston was rather "down in the mouth" as he threaded his way through the luxuriant vegetation of the tropics. The day had broken with its usual splendour, and though not insensible to the beauties of nature, he had no inclination just then to give rein to his admiration.

His mind was full of dark black thoughts.

"I hate Harkaway," he muttered; "I always did dislike him, and now I detest him more than ever. We never cottoned at school, and it's clear we can't pull together."

He forgot that Jack's hostility was entirely provoked by his own bad conduct.

He had never kept faith with his companions, and he had not hesitated to act in the most murderous manner towards them.

Was it any wonder that Jack was obliged to use harsh and strong measures?

But the wicked are always slow to blame themselves.

Their evil thoughts lead them to think unkindly of the virtuous and good.

As he went along he passed groves of nutmeg trees growing wild.

This useful tree is in such abundance that the land is full of it without its being planted by anyone.

All the islands in the Archipelago produce it more or less.

When June and September come, the nutmeg, which produces the mace outside the shell, is ready for gathering, and when the natives are inclined for trade, it brings a rich harvest.

Feeling thirsty, Hunston threw a heavy stone at a cocoa-nut palm, and brought down a rich cluster of the ripe fruit.

Cutting them open with his knife, he put his mouth to them and sucked out the rich juice.

Then he stooped down and cut a pine-apple.

The Malays and Javanese call it *nanas*, and are very fond of it.

"Fancy a fellow cutting pine-apples and sucking cocoa-nut," said Hunston. "Those who go to sea have a chance of meeting with strange things. Some chaps like it. I don't. I'd rather be smoking my pipe and dipping my beak into a foaming pewter of malt in some quiet pub, going out of the Strand or Tower Hill, than running wild in this beastly hole."

He had not gone much further before he saw a tall dark form in front of him.

"Scissors!" he ejaculated.

He had come face to face with a native whom he had not much difficulty in recognising as the Tuan Biza.

The recognition was mutual.

"Ha!" exclaimed the chief. "Has the great spirit sent you to us again?"

A cruel smile played round the corners of his ugly black mouth.

"Fiddlesticks," said Hunston. "I've nothing to do with spirits, although I shouldn't mind four of pale brandy, cold, with a lump of ice in it. This land of yours is so jolly hot."

"Why do you seek our camp then?" continued the Tuan Biza, who did not know whether to regard Hunston as a friend or enemy.

"To put you up to a good thing. Do

you know enough English to understand that?"

The chief nodded his head in token of assent.

"I want to be your friend," continued Hunston. "Let us enter into an explanation. When you caught me a few days back, I had had a row with my companion."

"Ah!" said the Tuan Biza, with a significant look. "Those who with you were wreck."

"Just so."

"How many?"

The chief counted on his fingers one, two, three, four.

Then Hunston stopped him.

"There were four," he said. "But one is dead. That is to say, we were five in all. One being dead, and I being here, the number is reduced to three. Do you understand?"

"Yes," replied the Tuan Biza.

"Very well. They have arms, guns, pistols, and powder. Do you know what those are?"

"No," replied the chief. "I learn English when I work in the hold of a ship; but I never see what you speak of. I go to the coast, but not know much."

"I'll enlighten your ignorance then," said Hunston. "You remember Buru being hurt, as you thought, by the spirit? Well, it was a shot fired from a gun held by one of my late companions."

The chief intimated that he had heard of such wonderful things, though he had never handled them, and he thought he had seen them, but he had never taken any particular notice of or interest in them.

In fact, the Tuan Biza knew very little about the habits, customs and weapons of civilised countries.

He had obtained his knowledge of English from some traders to whom he sold spice, and who employed him to load the cargo; but that was long ago.

With great difficulty Hunston made him understand that guns could kill anything at a certain distance, and that his three companions had a good store of them, together with powder and shot.

He added that they lived in a house they had built, not far from where they were then standing, and that they had saved a variety of valuable things from the wreck of their ship.

The Tuan Biza was a sharp man in his way, and he comprehended Hunston's meaning so far as to say—

"You want to be one of us, a head-hunter?"

"Yes. I should like to have Jack's head and Harvey's," replied Hunston, savagely.

"Who Jack? Who Harvey?" asked the chief.

"The people in the castle—Jack's castle."

"And the other, the three one?"

He meant the "third" one.

"Oh, he's a pal o' mine; a friend, I mean, and I'll entice him out. I don't want his head."

"And you will show us how to get the lightning guns and the stores?"

"Of course I will. You and I with your men can do it," answered Hunston. "But tell me, why are you stopping here?"

"Buru is badly hurt," replied the Tuan Biza. "I thought the spirit struck him by lightning, but I now see that it was the fire gun. We came here to have a feast, according to our customs. We not live here. Our island many miles, fifteen, twenty, thirty from here. When Buru well, we go back in two boat."

"Oh, that's it? Will you take me with you, and make me your king?"

"First give us the fire-gun and the ship's things. Do this for us, and we will make you king," answered the Tuan Biza cautiously.

"That's an agreement. I'll lead you against Jack's castle."

"When?"

"Oh, there's no hurry. We'd better wait a few days, as they expect an attack now, and if we are quiet, they will not be so watchful. You see we have no guns, and they have an advantage over us."

"Come with me," said the chief. "I will make you friendly with my young men. You are tattooed, and they will not hurt you, because they think you are under the protection of the great spirit."

"You won't let Keyali have my head? Keyali wants a head, you know," remarked Hunston.

"I am Tuan Biza," answered the chief, drawing himself up grandly.

"All right. I only want to be on the safe side. No tricks upon travellers. Don't you try any games on with me. It won't wash."

This speech was not very comprehensible to the Tuan Biza, but he seemed to catch the sense of it, and, taking Hunston by the hand, led him some little distance to the camp.

The warriors were surprised to see Hunston.

His appearance, owing to his recent tattooing, was rather savage and ferocious, but they might not have received him favourably, unless the chief had told them that he was their great friend, and was going to get them heads and many good things belonging to the white men.

When the Tuan Biza's companions understood the benefit that Hunston was going to confer upon them, and realised that their chief had made a compact with him, they crowded round Hunston, and gave him signs of friendship.

This was enough for Hunston.

When he felt that his life was safe, he became arrogant once more.

"Give me some of that spirit stuff you make out of the palm," he exclaimed.

They brought him what he required in the half of a cocoa-nut.

Then he threw himself down on some leaves under a tree, and prepared to go to sleep.

"Keep your friends away from me, will you?" he continued to the chief. "I may be a worthy object of curiosity, but I want to be quiet for a spell, and your nigger friends don't smell nice when the wind blows this way."

The Tuan Biza ordered the open space around Hunston to be kept clear.

He collected his companions in another spot, and told them all that Hunston was going to do for them.

At the prospect of heads and plunder into the bargain, they all grew jolly.

The palm spirit passed freely from one to another.

War songs were sung, and they talked of nothing else than the coming murder of the whites, against whom their new associate Hunston was to lead them.

Hunston and the savages had made friends.

The alliance boded no good to Jack and his companions in the castle.

But some people's consciences are elastic.

At all events Hunston slept calmly, and did not seem to be troubled with bad dreams.

CHAPTER XXVI.

A MASSAGE FROM THE SEA.

In about an hour Harvey came out of the castle with a basin full of peas.

"What have you got there?" inquired Jack.

"Peas—soaked in oil of vitriol," replied Harvey, "you'll see the birds pick them up and roll about quite groggy, when we can go and wring their necks. The peas will burn a hole in their crops, and fall out of themselves, so that the game won't be injured at all."

"You and your uncle were up to a few rummy dodges," remarked Jack. "I should call him a scientific poacher."

"He was all that. It was a lark to hear the squire's keeper come and say, 'I can't make out, Mr. Harvey, where the birds go to. Covey after covey vanishes. There must be some desperate poachers about somewhere,'" replied Harvey, laughing as he thought of it.

Walking to the edge of the clearing, Harvey scattered the peas about, and retired to watch the result.

The timid birds did not come down from the trees until the coast was clear.

When the flock found out the peas, which had been partially boiled in hot water, and then soaked in vitriol, they snapped them up savagely.

The effect was soon visible.

They were unable to fly, and staggered about in eccentric circles.

Jack and Harvey rushed up and seized them easily, wringing their necks, and bagging several dozen, which thinned the flock considerably.

The finest they reserved for eating—the others they tied to stakes driven in the ground, and used as scarecrows to frighten the others away.

"We might have tried that dodge on

with old Mole's pigeons at Crawcour's," remarked Jack.

Maple now appeared with Jack's dinner. The birds were done to a turn, and found to be excellent eating.

"I don't know what this fowl is called, but it eats better than parrot," Jack remarked, "and your plan of killing these things will save our powder and shot, of which we haven't got too much. Try a wing."

"Don't mind if I do," answered Harvey.

It was the custom of Maple to go to the signal station that Mr. Mole had built, for an hour every day, to sweep the sea with a glass in the chance of seeing a passing sail.

Approaching Jack, he exclaimed—

"Shall I go to the look-out now?"

"Have you done your work?" replied Jack.

"Yes."

"Cut along, then, and don't go to sleep as you did the other day. If I come up and find you winking even, I'll take it out of you," Jack said.

Maple put a telescope under his arm, and went to the beach.

Harvey and Jack liked the birds so much that they cooked another brace.

It was a lovely day, and after looking through the glass, and seeing nothing in the shape of a ship, Maple thought he would like a bath.

"The sea looks jolly tempting," he muttered. "I'll chance a wallopping. Jack's gorging those birds, and he's a beggar to eat when he gets anything he likes. I'll have a dip, if I die for it,"

Quickly throwing off his clothes, he walked along the hot sands, which almost burned his naked feet, until he came to a rock-bound pool, clear as crystal.

The retiring tide had left it full of water, and its depth was about three feet, while its circumference might have been a couple of dozen yards.

Beautiful shells and sprigs of coral glistened at the bottom, which, like the beach, was lined with soft, golden sand.

Plunging in, Maple splashed about like a young and sportive porpoise.

"This is something like," he exclaimed, as he beat the water back in childish sport. "The sun has just made the water deliciously warm. This is Jack and Harvey's bathing-place. They'll warm me if they catch me."

Suddenly his eye caught something round and black lying on the top of the water, half hidden by a patch of seaweed in which it had got entangled.

"What's that?" he cried. "It looks like a bottle."

It was a bottle.

Wading up to it, he grasped an ordinary black bottle, which, once upon a time, might have contained port or sherry.

It seemed very light.

A cork was stuffed firmly into the neck, and as it rode on the surface of the water, it could have had nothing but air inside it.

"Only a bottle somebody has shied overboard for a lark," he muttered, being about to throw it away.

He however, was struck by a brilliant idea.

"I'll make a cockshy of it," he said to himself.

Selecting a prominent piece of rock at the edge of the basin in which he was bathing, he placed the bottle on it.

Then he picked up half a dozen round middle-sized pebbles.

The first one he threw at the bottle missed it, but the second caught it plump in the middle, and it fell down cracked in twenty pieces.

"Well, shied, sir; good shot, indeed, sir!" he exclaimed, exulting over his own prowess, just as if he was applauding the delivery of the ball from "Long on" in a cricket field.

Just at that moment Jack came up and thought Maple had gone mad, but the latter soon stopped the noise he was making when he heard the king's voice.

"What's all this hullaballoo about?" cried Jack; "and what do you mean by leaving the signal station when you're on duty?"

"I wanted to bathe," replied Maple.

"I believe you will be all the sweeter for washing, and on that ground I won't say anything more about it," Jack exclaimed, with a smile. "But what was that I heard break? It sounded like glass."

"So it was. I found a bottle and made a cockshy of it. There is what remains of it."

Jack approached the broken bottle and the wind gently wafted a slip of paper towards him.

JACK HARKAWAY.

"THE INSTINCT OF SELF-PRESERVATION WAS STRONG WITHIN JACK."

He bent down and seized it between his fingers

"I say?" he cried; "it's lucky I came up."

"Why?" asked Maple.

"Because it's a message from the sea."

"What's that?"

"Don't you know that very often when a ship is sinking, people will write something on a bit of paper, and putting it in a bottle, cork it down and chuck it into the sea, in the expectation of its being washed ashore or picked up by some one?"

"And is that a message?" asked Maple, coming out of the water and basking in the sun to dry himself before he put on his clothes.

Jack was too much absorbed in the perusal of the messsage to pay him any further attention.

"What is it, Jack? You might tell a fellow," continued Maple, who really felt curious.

"Find out," answered Jack.

Holding the paper in his hand, he hastened back to the castle to find Harvey.

The latter was lying under a tree in front of the castle, to protect himself from the heat, which, being the middle of the day, was very great.

As near as possible the sun was in its meridian.

"What's the shindy, Jack?" asked Harvey, noticing that he was agitated.

"Come inside and I'll tell you," replied Jack.

"Just like my luck," muttered Harvey, "I no sooner settle myself down for a snooze than somebody rouses me. I'm like the old woman in the story, who said she was doomed to be flustrated."

He entered the castle after Jack, singing—

"I feel—I feel—I feel—
I feel like a morning star;
I feel—I feel— I feel——"

"I wish you'd make some allowance for my feelings, Dick, and not be howling that rubbish in my ear," interrupted Jack.

"What's come to your royal highness?" asked Harvey.

"A message from the sea."

"The deuce there has! That's interesting. Let's have it," Harvey exclaimed, adding—

"The most devoted and obedient subject of your august majesty impatiently awaits your pleasure. Speak, oh king, and don't make any bones about it."

"I'll break your bones, Dick, if you chaff," answered Jack good-humouredly.

"Start with Maple or send him into the woods to catch a nigger, if your majesty is in a savage humour," replied Harvey.

"Do you want to hear the message?"

"Yes. What did I leave my nest under the palm tree for? I'd rigged up a punkah—a beautiful one.

"It is an old door, hung on a branch, I have tied a piece of string to it, and can move it up and down, which makes a splendid draught just over one's head.

"I shouldn't have left, it I can assure you, unless I thought urgent affairs of state required my presence in the council chamber. Fire away."

Jack straightened the paper, and prepared to read.

CHAPTER XXVII.

WIDE AWAKE.

THIS was the message from the sea :—

"Having come to the conclusion that I might improve my circumstances by emigration, I embarked with my wife and child in the 'Eastern Monarch, but on gaining the Indian Ocean, we encountered bad weather, which ultimately made us a wreck.

"At the time I write, the boats are being lowered, and we are going to seek safety where we may find it.

"This is to let my friends in England know how dreadful our situation is. God help us!"

Jack paused, and looked up.

"Well, what is there in that?" inquired Harvey.

"The signature is 'J Scratchley, late

of Highgate, London,'" answered Jack.

"What then?"

"Haven't I told you that I was brought up by a Mr. Scratchley?"

"Ah, I see."

"And Emily, his dear little daughter, is the only girl I ever loved in my life."

"Excuse my forgetfulness," said Harvey. "I remember it now. Of course you were spooney on Emily, and you think that she has been wrecked with her father in the 'Eastern Monarch.' It's as plain as a pikestaff now. But don't fret. She's somewhere about. No doubt she's saved."

"I don't know," replied Jack, with a shake of the head.

"Oh, yes; she is. It's better than if she'd 'gone to Brigham Young, a Mormonite to be.'"

"I'll tell you what I fancy," continued Jack. "I fancy Emily is that girl that Hunston's savages spoke about. It's my firm impression that she is on one of those islands."

"Shouldn't wonder," answered Harvey, after thinking a moment. "It's very likely; and if it is Emily, won't it be jolly to save her?"

"She must be getting a big girl now. Who'd have thought old Scratchley would have emigrated?"

"Who'd have thought of Mole going to China."

"True," said Jack. "It's a curious world; so full of changes. We never know one year where we shall be next."

"Was this letter corked up in a bottle?"

"Yes."

"What's the date?"

"It isn't dated. I suppose Scratchley was too much flurried to think of dates; and if it were it wouldn't help us, for I don't really know the day of the week or the month of the year. I can only guess at them."

"What's the odds, so long as you're happy?" said Harvey.

"I'm not happy," answered Jack. "I don't mind being here so much because I've got you, and it's always jolly to have a friend. Robinson Crusoe is all very well on paper, but in reality it becomes tiresome when it goes on too long. I must rescue Emily."

"She's getting a big girl by this time," observed Harvey.

"Yes; and I'm a big boy. Within the last few weeks I feel as if I had become a man, Dick."

"So do I. Being in one's own house makes one feel manly."

"What's that?" cried Jack, suddenly.

"What?"

"Hush!" Jack continued, putting his finger to his lips; adding, as he lowered his voice to a whisper—"There is some one in the bushes to the left. Keep a good look-out. I'll go and fox him."

In a moment Jack had glided away. Before Harvey had recovered from his astonishment, he had disappeared.

Five minutes had elapsed. It was an age to Harvey. Then Jack returned.

"That's worth something," he exclaimed. "I've found out what's going on. Wasn't there a cove in ancient history who had a hundred eyes?"

"Argus. Mythological sort of buffer," replied Harvey.

"That's the man. Well, one ought to be like him to keep one's head on one's shoulders. What do you think? You'll never guess."

"I shan't try. Put me out of my misery at once," answered Harvey.

"I saw Maple talking to Hunston."

"No!"

"I did though, and no flies," replied Jack.

"You should say mosquitoes. Mosquitoes are the customers one meets with here," remarked Harvey.

"It's all the same. A 'muskeeter' is only a big, overgrown, stinging sort of fly. But listen to me. Maple has been talking to Hunston, and has agreed to betray us."

"Did you hear that?"

"Yes; I was just in time. If I'd had my gun, I do think I should have felt justified in peppering Mr. Hunston."

"The brute!" said Harvey.

"There is to be a night attack," continued Jack.

"When?"

"To-night. Maple is to ask us to be on guard, and to kill the dog. Then the niggers, led by Hunston, are to come up and tomahawk us."

"A very neat arrangement."

"Isn't it? Fortunately we are wide awake, and they've got to spell 'able' before they do it."

"It doesn't matter so much now we know what their little game is," said

Harvey. "Because we can choke them off if they don't surprise us."

"I don't mean that enterprising young nigger Keyali, I told you of, to have my head," replied Jack.

"And he shan't have mine. Not much. I guess we shall be too many for them."

"Rather. Just a few," answered Jack. "Still it is as well to know what we've got to expect."

"We ought to have started Maple when we kicked Hunston out."

"So we ought. They always did hang together."

"What a reptile he is," Harvey observed.

"Reptile. He's worse than that. I'd rather make a friend of a boa constrictor than of him," replied Jack, indignantly.

"What shall we do with him? Drown him like a kitten, or kill him with a back hander like a rabbit?"

"Neither one nor the other. When we are attacked he is to go over to the enemy with as many loaded guns as he can carry. He knows where the loaded guns are. We will change the position, and put some empty ones there."

"That's not bad, but he ought to be done something to," said Harvey.

"Wait till the battle begins. The savages will think their guns, stolen by Maple, are loaded, and they will advance pluckily. You'll see Maple and Hunston among them, and if I get a cool shot at either of them, I shall think I'm justified in pulling the trigger.

"I should think you would too," said Harvey.

"We shall kill the whole boiling of them, and a good job it will be. It's very hard we can't be left alone. We're not interfering with any one. However, they'll get it hot this journey, or I'm very much mistaken."

Presently Maple came up, looking rather sheepish.

"Hullo, Maple, what's the row?" asked Harvey.

"I'm all right," replied Maple, "bar the heat. This country takes it out of a fellow, and makes him want to sleep half his time."

"Oh! I thought you'd seen somebody?"

"I haven't seen anybody, and don't want to."

"Don't stand there jawing. Go and do something," exclaimed Harvey.

"What do you suppose we keep you for?"

Maple slunk away, and pretended to busy himself in some way.

"It'll soon be over," he said to himself. "They don't know as much as I do."

And he chuckled quietly.

In the afternoon Jack placed some empty guns where the loaded ones had been, and transferred the latter to another spot.

He and Harvey did not appear to have any idea of what was going on, and treated Maple just as they had done before.

This threw the latter off his guard.

Jack was on guard, but he lay down, and Maple thought he was asleep.

Taking advantage of his apparent slumber, he removed the guns and put them under a tree in the clearing.

All this was observed by Jack.

It was about twelve o'clock when Maple disappeared altogether.

Jack rose and touched Harvey on the shoulder.

"Now for it," he exclaimed.

"Are they here?" asked Harvey, who, in accordance with their arrangements, had been having a nap.

"I don't think they are far off. Wake up. Maple's stepped it."

"Are the guns gone?"

"Yes."

"I'm ready," said Harvey. "Give us your hand, Jack. Think of me if I'm picked off."

"God bless you, Dick. If you die, I shall lose the only friend I ever had," answered Jack, whose eyes were moist with tears.

"I can say the same. But I say, this won't do. You're blubbering, and so am I. Suppose you turn the cock on in another direction. Let's have a drop of something."

Jack produced a bottle of brandy, and they both took a sip.

Nero began to growl.

"The dog's growling," exclaimed Harvey.

"Then they're coming. Look out. The loaded guns are in that corner. I have made two loopholes, one on each side of the door. You take one. I'll take the other."

"Right you are," replied Harvey, who was freshened up by the brandy.

"Cover your man before you fire.

There are a dozen of them, besides Hunston and Maple.

"They've got nothing but spears," exclaimed Harvey. "They're not worth their salt as fighting men against us."

All at once the dog gave a moan.

Jack peeped out, and saw him lying on his side.

It was evident that he had been killed by an arrow.

Setting his teeth together, Jack said—

"Stand close, Dick. They've killed the dog. There is just light enough to enable us to see the dark-skinned brutes. It's their lives or ours."

"So it is," replied Harvey. I don't like the idea of shooting any one, but it's their look out, and not ours. We don't attack them."

As he spoke, a troup of dusky savages emerged from the trees that skirted the clearing, and approached the castle.

The natives, with Hunston, walked behind Maple, who was some yards in front.

Jack sank on the ground, and simulated sleep again.

"Jack—Jack, old man," said Maple.

There was no answer.

"I say, Jack," continued Maple.

Still no answer.

Maple retired.

"It's all right. They're both asleep, and I've stolen the guns," Jack heard him say.

Then Hunston spoke to the Tuan Biza, and the natives, in obedience to a sign, again advanced.

"Now, Dick, let 'em have it. Remember, it's us or them. Aim low," whispered Jack.

In an instant a couple of reports were heard.

These were followed by another and another in quick succession.

Loud cries arose on every side.

All was darkness and confusion.

The defenders of the castle continued to fire as rapidly as they were able.

It must be acknowledged that Hunston displayed great courage.

His voice could be heard incessantly urging on the savages whom he had led against his former friends, and when he found that the guns Maple had supplied them with would not go off, his rage knew no bounds.

The defenders of the castle kept up a steady fire. Such weapons as the natives possessed were of no use against the walls of the castle.

Seeing his companions falling around him, the Tuan Biza gave the orders to advance in a body, and storm the castle.

This was what Jack was waiting for.

With his own hands he pulled the string connected with the battery of fire-arms.

"There was the report of a volley of musketry, loud cries followed the discharge, and then there was a solemn stillness, which intimated that the attacking party had either all perished, or had thought it advisable to beat a retreat.

Jack was completely victorious.

He did not, however, cease his vigilance —for it was impossible to tell what plans the savages might have made.

They might have had reinforcements, or be meditating an attack in another quarter.

So two weary hours passed, and then the much longed-for daylight came.

Neither Jack nor Harvey had made more than a passing remark occasionally.

Now they joined one another, and cautiously ventured outside.

Their victory had been more complete than even they had anticipated.

Eleven dead bodies lay upon the ground.

First of all they passed the dog, which had been killed at an early part of the engagement, and Jack said—

"Poor Nero!"

Ten of the bodies were those of fine, handsome, full-grown natives.

The eleventh was a white.

Passing in front of the corpse, Jack said sorrowfully—

"He has brought it upon himself. In the confusion and the darkness I cannot say whether you or I caused his death, Dick."

It was Maple.

The boy was lying on his back, and a tranquil expression sat upon his features, as if death had been instantaneous, which perhaps it was, there being a wound in the region of the heart, through which the bullet probably passed.

"Poor little beggar," remarked Harvey. "I'm sorry he's gone. It makes one feel lonely, though I can't say I really liked him. He never did anything to deserve pity at our hands."

" Still," said Jack, " it's one more gone. We were five when we were cast on this island. Mole was the first to go, then Hunston left us, and now Maple's dead."

" He'd have killed us, Jack, if he had won the fight."

" So he would, but I would rather Hunston had been killed. Maple was led by him."

" Not always. Maple had a wicked mind, though as he's gone, I won't say anything against him. If you will look at the matter in the light I do, you will come to think that it's a good thing we are left to ourselves. It strikes me we shall get on better."

" You and I, Dick, could jog along anywhere; we were made to run together in double harness."

" There don't fret any more about Maple," replied Harvey. " He was killed in fair fight, and deserved his fate; for a more treacherous trick than to steal our guns was never thought of."

" He and Hunston arranged it; by the way, I suppose Hunston has got off clear with the Tuan Biza. I don't see the chief among the slain."

" We have killed nearly all of them—that's a comfort," Harvey remarked.

" After what has happened, Hunston will never come back to us," Jack said. " He'll go over to the Tuan Biza's island and perhaps organise a fresh expedition against us."

" I can't understand two English fellows like Hunston and Maple fighting against their own friends," Harvey said. " It licks me altogether."

" I've been thinking about it," replied Jack; " and it seems to me that when a man gives way to his wicked thoughts and passions, ever so little, he opens the door to temptation, and he goes on doing low and dirty things till it becomes a habit with him, and he doesn't know when to stop."

" There's a good deal of truth in that; a fellow becomes a villain by degrees, not all at once."

" Examine the history of a thief," continued Jack, " and you will find that he has been bad in other things, before he brought himself to steal. People are not born bad. Its giving way to temper, idleness, and one's passion, and being self-willed, that does it; but I don't want to preach a sermon. Maple's dead, and we must bury him decently, as well as those others."

" Better dig a trench for the natives," Harvey suggested.

" Very well," answered Jack, " and give Maple a grave to himself. Fancy, Dick, our having killed all those. It seems very dreadful, doesn't it?"

" Killing's no murder in self-defence. We didn,t begin the row. Take a spade and make a start. I'll wire in on this side and meet you half-way."

They selected a sequestered spot, some little distance from the castle, and in about four hours had dug a trench sufficiently deep to bury the natives in.

Reverently they placed the bodies in the hole and covered them up with the soil, for they knew that all, whether Christian or savage, go, after death, to meet their Creator.

Their next care was to bury Maple, which they did in a green spot, on which the sunshine played, and around which the birds sang and sported.

Neither Jack nor Harvey said anything, but they both cried heartily as they laid the little fellow's body in the grave.

They were not ashamed of their tears.

Nor had they any reason to be so.

We like a boy, or a man either for that matter, to be able to shed a tear when there is ocasion for it.

It shows that he's got a heart and not a bit of stone in his bosom.

When the last sod had been beaten down, Jack fell on his knees and said something in a low voice.

Harvey did not hear every word, but he knew it was a prayer.

When Jack had done, Dick slowly said—

" Amen."

All the rest of that day Jack was busy carving a little cross, which he placed at the head of the grave.

As they went away after performing their last office of respect for the memory of the dead, Jack's eyes were moistened again.

He seized Harvey's hand, and wringing it, exclaimed—

" I can't help it, Dick. I know I'm an old fool; but I thought I should make a decent man of him some day if I could only get him away from Hunston's influence."

" When sow's ears make silk purses, then," began Harvey.

"I know all that," interrupted Jack. "Perhaps you're right. Let's talk about something else. Come for a stroll; were safe enough now. The savages have had enough to last them some time and they won't bother us again, I'll bet."

"I don't like to leave the castle," replied Harvey.

"There's no danger. I think we have killed the lot with the exception of the Tuan Biza and Hunston.

"The very two I should have liked to see fall."

"Yes. They are the ones who are likely to give us future trouble," replied Jack.

As they went along they remarked that the volcanic mountain was in a state of agitation.

On the south-west side, about one fourth of the distance from its summit, was a deep, wide gulf.

Out of this arose thick opaque clouds of white gas, which in the still clear air, was seen rolling grandly upwards in one gigantic, expanding column to the sky.

On its top were thin, veil-like clouds, which occasionally gathered and then slowly floated away, dissolving into the pure ether.

These cloud masses were chiefly composed of steam and sulphurous acid gas.

As they poured out they indicated what an active laboratory nature had deep within the bowels of this old volcano.

"Look out, Jack?" cried Harvey all at once.

In a moment Jack had raised his gun to his shoulder.

"What is it?" he exclaimed.

"I don't know exactly, but unless I am going to fancy things, I could swear I saw a nigger in the bush."

As he spoke a native emerged from the concealment of the jungle.

He advanced on his hands and knees in token of submission, and finding that no harm was done him, he stood upright in a submissive attitude.

Of middle height, the fellow had a good-humoured, ingenious countenance, though he appeared to have suffered recently from hunger.

His only clothing was the strip of the inner bark of a tree, beaten with stones, until it looked very much like rough white paper, and which we have described before as being peculiar to these islands.

It passed round the waist, and covered the loins in such a way, that one end hung down as far as the knee.

He was unarmed, and Jack refrained from firing at him, as he did not seem as if he had the slightest intention of harming them.

"Take care," said Harvey, as he saw Jack lower his gun; "perhaps there are more behind, and it's only a dodge."

"I don't think so. You keep guard, while I make signs and try to find out what his game is."

CHAPTER XXVIII.

MONDAY.

THE native went through a performance which, as Jack said, would have puzzled a deaf and dumb man.

It was clear that the signs he made were intended to convey to the boys that he claimed their protection, and would be their servant.

The native climbed up a tree, and bringing down fruit, placed it at Jack's feet, kneeling before the boys; and taking Harvey's hand, he struck himself on the head with it, meaning he would not resent a blow.

Then he pointed to the sea with every expression of horror, as if his enemies were in boats.

"It's quite a pantomime," remarked Harvey.

"My idea," answered Jack, "is, that this fellow is one of the victims brought over here by the natives who attacked us. I saw them kill one, you know. Perhaps this one escaped, and so disappointed them in their expectation of his head."

"Shouldn't wonder," replied Harvey.

"Now Maple's gone we shall want some one to drudge about. Suppose we enlist this Mr. What-d'ye-call-him."

"Old Bob Crusoe had his man, and he called him Friday. I vote we christen Thingamagig there Monday. I like Mondays. We used to get our pocket-money at Crawcour's on a Monday. And he sang—

> "He had a man Friday
> To keep his house tidy;
> Fortunate Robinson Crusoe!

Or we might say—

> "It happened on one day,
> We came across Monday;

*   *   *   *   *

Finish the verse for me, Jack. I was never good at poetry."

"I couldn't finish it, if you paid me for it," replied Jack. "But I'll bet a pound of snuff, that this will turn out an honest fellow."

While they were talking, the native appeared very anxious, as if they thought they meant to kill him.

Jack, however, took him by the hand, and shook it, giving him to understand by a variety of signs that they would do him no harm.

They led him back to the castle and fed him on such food as they had ready to hand, which he seemed to like very much.

Jack showed him how to do various things, and he evinced an aptitude and willingness that made him a valuable acquaintance.

Monday saved the boys a great deal of trouble, and the poor creature was as faithful as a dog, and as grateful as possible for their kindness.

He began to learn English, and acquired a great proficiency in a short time, being singularly quick.

If he once heard a word and was given its meaning, he never forgot it, and would repeat it over and over again to himself to impress it on his memory.

Monday was not more than two-and-twenty, strong and healthy, and not bad-looking, for one of his people.

It was to Jack that he attached himself more than Harvey, though he liked both and obeyed orders from each.

Still he was more Jack's man than Harvey's, if any distinction could be fairly drawn.

Both the boys used to take the greatest interest in teaching him their own language, to which task they devoted several hours each day.

Of course, when he knew English, he would be of more use to them, and a better companion.

Fully three months passed.

Their corn and their potatoes came up and were gathered into the warehouse in the castle, before the rainy season began.

Nothing had been seen or heard of Hunston.

Whether he was alive or dead they did not know.

But Jack had made a tour of the island which took him three days, and he saw no signs anywhere of other occupants than themselves.

The grass was growing green and waving over Maple's grave.

Both Hunston and Maple were in a measure forgotten.

At length Monday began to talk.

His English was broken and imperfect, as is generally the case with those who are commencing to learn a language, for it takes time to make one's self proficient in the moods, tenses, ect., of a strange tongue.

However he spoke well enough to enable Jack to understand him.

This is in effect what he said—

About twenty-four miles off, or six hours' sail, there were two islands not more than one hour's sail from each other.

One was called Ship Island, which was the one Hunston had heard of from the Tuan Biza.

The other was named Limbi.

From this one Monday came. In his own country his name was Metabella, but he was quite reconciled to the name given him, and even seemed rather flattered at it.

The inhabitants of the two islands were pretty nearly equal in point of numbers, and they were all head-hunters.

They continually made war upon one another.

The victorious party always ate its captives, and generally in fine weather made a voyage to another neighbouring island, and had a sort of a picnic.

"Lively amusement," remarked Jack to Harvey, as Monday was proceeding with his recital.

"Nice neighbours," answered Harvey.

Once, Monday said, a Hukam Tua, or missionary, as far as Jack could make him out, came to Limbi in a ship.

The day after his arrival the natives killed and ate him.

"Did you have a bit?" asked Harvey.

"Yes," replied Monday; "me have bit. Hukam Tua good, fat, much nice, Monday eat him up quick!"

"You cannibal beast, I shall never like you again," cried Harvey, turning away in disgust and loathing, which the horrid confession was quite calculated to produce in the breast of a European.

Monday saw the expression of his face.

"No eat mans now," he said hastily. "Monday know better, and never more eat up mans. No; never—no."

The poor fellow kept on saying this until Harvey told him he forgave him, because in those days he did not know any better.

"Are you sure you won't wake up some night and make a meal of me?" asked Harvey.

Monday said there was no chance of that. The teaching he had received and the affection he had for his masters, would prevent him from doing anything of that sort.

Some little time after this conversation Jack thought of a question which he wished to put to Monday.

From what Hunston had told him of the remarks of the Tuan Biza, and from the letter in the bottle that Maple had picked up, he fancied his dear old friend Emily was a captive in the hands of the savages.

The latter was signed by Mr. Scratchley of Highgate, and it wasn't likely there would be two people of that name.

Nor was it surprising that a scheming, unscrupulous man like Scratchley should make up his mind to emigrate.

Thousands of people do the same thing every year.

"If then, Mr. Scratchley, his wife and child didn't remain on board the "Eastern Monarch," when she was deserted in a sinking condition, it was fair to suppose that they escaped in the boats.

Still there was a stretch of the imagination on Jack's part in supposing that the girl in captivity, of whom the chief had told Hunston, was Emily.

Nevertheless, Jack had got hold of the idea; and when, as he said, "he got a thing fixed in his nut, it wasn't easy to get it out again."

So he took Monday on one side and said—

"Did you hear in your country of an English girl being shut up?"

He did not say in captivity, or use any long words, because he thought they would be beyond Monday's comprehension.

For this reason he always used as plain language as he could pitch upon.

"Not my country," answered Monday; "on Ship Island, a girl; that's why call Ship Island."

"Oh, indeed," said Jack; "then on Ship Island they have got a girl from an English vessel?"

"Yes," answered Monday, nodding his head up and down.

"How do you know this?"

"Oh, I hear from one my people who go there to make war. We beat them last time, though they take me and one more, and carry over here to eat."

"Which are the best warriors, your people or the other islanders?"

"Sometimes one, sometimes another. It's not always one," answered Monday.

"I should like to go to your natives and help them to make war, and save this English girl," continued Jack.

Monday's countenance brightened.

"Come, come," he cried. "You shoot your powder shot, you kill all, and we never have no more war."

As he spoke, he danced round and round in a sort of ecstasy.

"But I thought your people liked war," said Jack.

"Me teach them better. If no one make no more war on them, then my people no more war," said Monday.

"Do you think we could build a boat and go over to your country?"

"Oh, yes; me build boat."

Jack knew that the natives could build boats.

They have no iron, and therefore, the whole boat is made of wood; but it is not the less sea-worthy on that account.

The central part is low, and the bow and stern curve up high.

These boats generally resembled those used in the South Sea.

"Give Monday axe," exclaimed the faithful fellow. "He soon make boat, but"—and his face assumed a sorrowful expression—"no send Monday away. Save Monday's life. Kill Monday if you part him."

By which he meant to say that he should die if Jack sent him away.

"I won't part with you," answered Jack, "so long as you do as I tell you.

But I want to go to your island and make friends with your chief."

"Why make friends?"

"Will they not thank me for being kind to you?"

"Oh, yes! Much thank. You be great chief."

"Very well. I will lead them against their enemies, and we will rescue the English girl," said Jack.

It was annoying to him to think that Emily, if it was she, should be amongst the natives with whom he supposed Hunston had gone to live.

Sending Monday about his business he sought Harvey, who was having what he called "a jolly," that is, he was lying on his back under a tree, and sipping a drink he had made through a straw, while he read a book.

"Dick," cried Jack, "we're going to build a boat."

"Bully for you!" answered Harvey.

"And we're going over to Monday's savages, and intend trying to make them fight Hunston, and rescue the English girl."

"Good again. I'm on."

"It's worrying me to think that Emily may be in the power of Hunston and the Tuan Biza."

"Gall and wormwood, as the novels say," remarked Harvey.

"What do you say to it?" continued Jack.

"I like the idea much," replied Harvey. "To tell the truth, this sort of life is all very well for a month or two, but it gets very wearing after a bit. I'd do anything for a dust up."

"All right. Help us to make the boat."

"Like a shot. Is Monday a naval architect?"

"He says so," replied Jack.

"His accomplishments come out one by one. First of all he knows how to cook and eat a human being, next he learns English, then he builds boats. Monday's developing. It's a good dodge, in a wild and unknown island, to have a tame nigger."

Jack smiled.

That afternoon they commenced building the boat, in which they were to make the adventurous voyage which had for its object the rescue of the girl Jack supposed to be Emily.

Whether he was right or not we shall soon see.

CHAPTER XXIX.

BUILDING THE BOAT.

THE arrival of Monday proved very valuable to the boys.

He grew much attached to them.

They could both sleep at night, for the young savage soon learnt to load and fire a gun, and kept watch while his masters slept.

His progress in learning English was very quick and showed him to be sharp and clever.

The project of building a boat proceeded satisfactorily.

Monday had helped to make boats on his own island of Limpi.

Selecting a spot near the sea he set to work.

The trees in the tropics grow for centuries, and then fall down from decay, literally dying from old age.

A constant source of danger in these regions arises from these falling trees, which topple down without any warning.

Choosing a mighty tree which had just fallen, Monday began to hollow out the trunk.

It was a work that took some time.

Monday called this species of boat a "leper-leper," though in the far west it would be spoken of as a "dug-out."

When the tree was sufficiently hollowed pieces of plank were placed on the sides to raise them to the proper height.

Both sides are sharp and curve upwards.

About four feet from the bow a pole is laid across, and another the same distance from the stern.

These project outward from the sides of the boat, and to them is fastened a bamboo, the whole forming what is known as an outrigger.

This is necessary, because the canoes are narrow and crank.

Monday declared that with a small triangular sail and a paddle he could manage a leper-leper in the fiercest storm.

Jack's inventive genius supplied a rudder, of the use of which Monday seemed profoundly ignorant.

It was rare fun for the boys when at work, singing, laughing, and talking.

They kept up their spirits in spite of the danger that surrounded them and their lonely position.

Imagine them on the skirts of the thick woods, where troops of large black monkeys kept up a perpetual hooting or trumpeting.

Their cries resembled a score of amateurs practising on trombones.

Sometimes the din they made was quite deafening, and Jack could not hear himself speak.

Then he fired his gun amongst them, and they scampered off, their chattering ceasing for a time.

But they would return, as if they took a curious interest in what was going on, and rather liked boat building than otherwise.

Both Jack and Harvey were rather sorry at the idea of leaving the island.

Their corn and potatoes were got in, and the castle had become quite a dear spot to them.

"It's no use grumbling," remarked Jack. "We must go some time or other, and if we don't like Monday's friends, we can come back here again."

"I know what is driving you on, Jack," exclaimed Harvey.

"What?"

"A wish to rescue Emily, if it should, indeed, be your little friend who is in the hands of the savages."

"I don't mind owning it," answered Jack. "Fancy Emily in the power of the head-hunters, and the indignities she may be daily and hourly subjected to.

"Hunston is with the savages, and he would protect her."

"Would he?" said Jack, angrily. "That's all you know about Master Hunston. He is much more likely to add to her worries."

"Why?"

"Because Emmy is a pretty girl, and Hunston's got an eye for a handsome face."

"Well," replied Harvey, "I am game to go anywhere with you, and if there's any fighting to be done, old boy, I shan't shirk my share of it, as you know."

"Give us your fist, old fellow; you're a trump," said Jack.

The boys shook hands, and no more was said about Emily just then, for Jack's eyes filled with tears, and Harvey saw that he felt deeply about the matter.

Jack had an additional reason for wishing to leave the island.

He never knew at what moment Hunston and the Tuan Biza might sweep down upon them with an overwhelming force.

That the chief would wish to revenge the death of his comrades who had perished in the attack upon the castle, there was no doubt.

A second assault might be more successful.

What were three people against perhaps a hundred.

In the island of Limbi, with Monday's friends, they would be safe.

There was just as much chance of a ship's passing by Limbi and taking them off, as there was of one approaching Harkaway Island.

So it was resolved to abandon the castle, for a time at least.

According to Monday's account, Limbi was only about twenty English miles off.

Not a very formidable voyage after all.

They had scoured Harkaway Island from one end to the other, by making a circuit round it, and they had satisfied themselves that Hunston and the Tuan Biza had quitted it.

The island on which the Tuan Biza and his followers lived was visible from Limbi, and had the name of Pisang.

Limbi and Pisang were always at war.

In the last battle between the rival tribes, the Limbians had been surprised, and Monday was captured.

But Monday said, "We much fight, and more win than the Pisangs. Next time, we take plenty Pisangs and cut off heads."

"You won't cut off heads and eat your enemies any more, will you?" asked Jack, looking crossly at him.

Not me. Monday no cut and eat," replied the poor fellow. "My people not know what you told me about the Bible, and that it wrong to eat man flesh. Mon-

"'WHAT IS IT, JACK? YOU MIGHT TELL A FELLOW,' SAID MAPLE."

day tell them all and then they must change, alter."

"We'll wake up the Pisangs or whatever they call themselves," observed Harvey.

"Yes," replied Jack, "we shall have to go on the war path, for Emily's sake."

"We'll lick 'em into 'eternal smash," replied Harvey, loudly. "I should like to see the half-dozen niggers that can stand against one pure-born Britisher."

Jack laughed.

"You may laugh," continued Harvey. "But there is something about an Englishman that scares a nigger and a Frenchman. I suppose it's our roast beef."

"Not much of that here," Jack said.

"That's the worst of this outlandish hole," Harvey replied, "you can't get your proper grub. If ever we are licked, I shall put it down to that."

"So I would, Dick."

"It's a theory of mine that a man ought to have his proper grub," Harvey said sagely. "Do we ever have puddings? Have we seen a cow, dead or alive since we landed?"

"I've seen a calf," remarked Jack.

"Jack, who's your friend?" demanded Harvey.

"You are, I hope."

"Then don't run the risk of losing him through idle chaff. You called me a calf. Veal's all very well in its way, but to call me a calf, and before Monday too. It's lowering the dignity of your lieutenant."

"I apologise, Dick. It shan't occur again," Jack said, anxious to soothe his friend's wounded vanity.

"I accept the apology, but it wasn't kind," Harvey answered, becoming good-humoured again. "Let's see, as the blind man said, what were we talking about?"

"Grub."

"So we were. Now I'll tell you what I should like to have a turn at, that's tripe and onions. Oh, my! fancy a go in at tripe, Jack!"

"I can't fancy anything half so beastly in this hot climate," replied Jack; "and I am surprised at your vulgar tastes. Mark that poll parrot. There he goes—flying over our heads. Mark! mark!"

"He's settled. I see him."

"So do I," answered Jack, as he fired.

"Monday will stew the bird with a clove of garlic. That will beat all the tripe in Whitechapel," said Jack.

"Never mind," said Harvey with a grave shake of the head. "Parrots are not bad, but I'll stick out for stewed eels and tripe."

"What next will you want?" asked Jack, adding—"I wish you'd be more like the sailor's parrot."

"What did he do?"

"He didn't talk much, but he was a beggar to think."

"Thank you," said Harvey, biting his lip. "Sorry I spoke; but I'm much obliged to your majesty, and I'll not forget you."

The boat was nearly finished.

All that remained to be done was to step the mast, and rig a sail, the rudder being already shipped.

Monday was digging a channel in the sand to float her.

In appearance the boat was not exactly handsome, but she was very long and deep.

It was Jack's intention to load her with all sorts of stores almost up to the gunwale, as he knew that guns, powder, and bullets, would be of the greatest use to him and the savages with whom, through Monday's influence, he hoped to make friends.

Provisions did not matter so much, as the natives were known to be good hunters; but a case or two of spirits would not be unacceptable, he thought, to the chief and his principal advisers.

Jack turned away from Harvey, and watched Monday as he was digging.

Each spadeful he cast up glittered strangely in the sun.

Peering more curiously into the sandy mixture, he stooped down, and took up some in his hand.

Then he blew away the lighter particles, and there remained some golden dust, among which were a few large rugged lumps about the size of a small pea.

"What have you got there, Jack?" inquired Harvey.

"Gold," replied Jack, quietly.

"Nonsense."

"If I haven't, I'm a Dutchman," Jack exclaimed.

Harvey approached nearer, and looked wonderingly at the auriferous particles.

"Well," he ejaculated, "that's the greatest lick out. Fancy finding gold here."

"Why not?" said Jack. "We're in the land of romance, my boy, and if I found a diamond as big as a pigeon's egg, I shouldn't be surprised; though, to tell you the truth, I never thought there was gold here, but I have heard the sailors say that the natives of these islands trade in gold dust."

"I say Monday," cried Harvey.

"What now, Mast' Harvey?" asked the black.

"Have you ever seen this stuff before?"

He showed him some of the glittering ore which he took from Jack's hand.

Monday looked at it carefully before he replied.

CHAPTER XXX.

THE VALLEY OF DEATH.

"OH, yes," answered Monday, after a moment's examination. "It's gold. We find much like this, and sell. We make things for the nose and ears."

"Rings?"

"Yes, rings. Plenty stuff like that. We think nothing," said Monday, in a tone of indifference.

"They wouldn't say that in Europe," remarked Jack.

"Not exactly," answered Harvey. "It wants washing and sifting; but it's my opinion one might make a very tidy little fortune out of this island."

It is a fact that gold is found in the western and southern parts of Borneo, as well as in Luzon and the Philippines, and in the peninsula of Celebes.

The gold is bought and sold in the form of dust, as the natives do not understand the art of coining.

"We have no time to spare to collect it," said Jack, looking wistfully at the beautiful golden grains in his hand.

"It's all very well for you to talk like that, Jack," exclaimed Harvey.

"Why?"

"You are rich, and your guv's got lots of tin, while mine is poor, and it's a scramble at home often enough among the kids for the potato skins."

"You can gather some if you like."

"I do like, and if your majesty will graciously condescend to finish the boat and give me a day or two's holiday, I'll just roam about this island, and see if I can't turn up a nugget."

"You won't do that. Gold is only deposited in the shape of dust in these islands," Jack replied.

"All right. I'll have a go in and chance it. I want to make a pile, and when I've got a belt full, I'll cry a-go, as they say at cribbage."

"Cut along at once, then, Dick. I'll see to the boat, and dodge that up all serene, for I want to be off at once."

"At once?" asked Harvey, who saw that Jack's manner was urgent.

"Oh, I don't suppose a day or two will make much difference, but I'm anxious. It's some time now since Hunston hooked it off with the Tuan Biza, and he'll be back again without letting the grass grow under his feet."

"He can't hurt us. I wouldn't give a rap off a common for him and his niggers," said Harvey.

After the way in which the blackskins were beaten off in the last attack, Harvey had got into this manner of deriding them.

"You hold them too cheap," exclaimed Jack. "But it doesn't matter. If you must go gold seeking, go, though you'd get more by raking this dust up."

Harvey would have his own way, however, and, armed with a pistol, in case of accidents, he started on his journey.

He fancied that if they could find deposits of gold on the sands, they would certainly discover lumps inland.

Jack had given him his opinion upon the subject, and, muttering to himself— "I suppose he'll be back when he's tired of it," went on with his work.

By evening the boat was ready for launching, and, knocking away some supports, Jack and Monday, with a good English hurrah, let her slide into the dock they had dug for her.

This dock communicated with the sea, and all they had to do, when they wanted to start, was to push her along till they got clear.

Monday said that he knew a break in the coral reef, which surrounded the island through which they could sail.

The next thing to do was to get in the cargo; but, as it was growing late, Jack deferred this till the morrow.

"Where Mast' Harvey?" asked Monday, as he shouldered some tools to take back to the castle.

"Oh! he's up at the castle I should think," answered Jack. "Perhaps he thought we should have returned before this."

"S'pose him got much big gold lump!" cried Monday, with a smile.

"You heard my opinion, Monday. What is your experience?"

"All dust—no much good—no lump. Poor Mast' Harvey! How him grin wrong side of him face!" replied Monday laughing.

They entered the castle, and Jack was surprised, and not a little alarmed, to see nothing of Harvey, who certainly ought to have returned before this.

Jack's first thought was that the savages had landed again, this time under the command of Hunston. If so, Harvey would fall an easy prey to them, as he was wandering about the island.

"You stop here, Monday," he said, shouldering his rifle, "and I will take a stroll."

"What for you go?" asked Monday.

"I can't make out what has come to Harvey. I must look for him. I don't take kindly to sitting at home when a friend may want my services."

"Me go with you?" asked Monday.

"No! Stop at home, and keep a sharp look out. Shoot at the first darkskin you see!"

Monday was already too well trained to dispute his master's will.

Jack set out alone.

Not knowing in what direction he was likely to find Harvey, he wandered about in much perturbation of spirit.

"I'd rather have my right hand cut off," he muttered, "than any harm should happen to Dick!"

And he was sincere in what he said.

The purest and most romantic friendship existed between the two boys, which had been strengthened by their solitary exile.

He might have walked for half-a-dozen miles in the interior of the island, when he came to a barren plain, which he had never remarked before.

The volcano mountain towered high into the clouds behind him.

Not a shrub or a blade of grass was to be seen on this desolate plain.

Sulphurous gases appeared in the moonlight to arise from fissures and holes in the earth.

The ground was of a pale grey or yellowish colour.

Avoiding the steaming gases, Jack walked a little way along the valley.

On all sides of him he saw a number of dead animals of various kinds.

Deer, tigers, birds, and even snakes spread their ghastly skeletons upon the ground.

All these had lost their lives in the fatal place. It was a veritable Valley of the Shadow of Death.

Sulphuric acid gas broke out under his feet, and he retreated, half suffocated by the noxious vapour.

This it was which had caused such certain destruction to all the animals he saw lying around him, who had wandered thither.

The soft parts of many of the dead victims, as the skin, muscles, hair, or feathers, were entire, but the bones had partially crumbled.

No fabled upas tree could have worked more or swifter desolation.

The smell of the gas which assailed Jack's nostrils was just like the smoke of a common lucifer match when first struck.

It may be readily imagined how dangerous and poisonous it was.

This vapour was generated under the mountain, and when the volcano was not in action, it escaped through the earth as we have described.

Just as Jack was hastily turning round to retrace his steps, a dim object on his right caught his eye.

It had the form of a man, and was stretched out on the ground.

"Can that be Dick?" was the exclamation that involuntarily escaped him.

Making a circuit to avoid a dense volume of gas which came up from a hole, he approached the singular object.

A glance sufficed to show him that it was Harvey.

He was lying on his back, and though breathing, seemed to be perfectly stupefied and insensible.

It was no time for deliberation or hesitating.

Jack himself felt dizzy, and was sure that if he remained long in that dreadful valley he would sink down like his friend, probably to rise no more.

Tightly clenched in Harvey's hand was the end of a large lump of gold.

The glitter of this piece of precious metal had probably attracted him.

Gas might have broken out near him and caused him to fall down half suffocated, for the deadly vapour springs out at all times from all sorts of fissures, and does not steadily emanate from any particular one.

Jack put the gold in his pocket.

It was, from its appearance and weight, worth some hundreds of pounds, and quite a rarity in that region.

At all events he considered it a windfall for Harvey, which would prove most acceptable to him if he should ever return to civilised life again.

It would be hard indeed to lose it after having risked so much to obtain it.

When he had secured the lump of gold, Jack seized Harvey in his arms, and with a desperate exercise of strength, carried him away from the valley.

Several times he stopped and staggered like a drunken man, for the pestilential gas assailed him, and very nearly subdued his energy.

At length the end of the open and blighted space was reached.

Reeling a few yards further, Jack let his friend sink to the ground on the grass, which even here was sparse and stunted.

The blight of the Valley of Death had tainted it.

Now Jack could understand how animals coming into this dreadful space sank down to die.

Now he could imagine birds flying over it compelled to flutter to the earth in deadly agony.

Now he could conceive a horrid serpent, which had crawled to the fatal precinct to enjoy the promised heat, inhaling the poison rising from the earth, and twisting about in useless convolutions.

He always carried a little flask of brandy in his pocket in case of an emergency like the present arising, and he poured a few drops down Harvey's throat.

It stimulated the action of the heart, which was beating slowly.

Presently he opened his eyes, and stared wildly round him.

"Is it you, Jack?" he gasped.

"Yes, Dick. It's all right. Do you feel better?" replied Jack.

"I'm getting better; but I've had a dream. I thought someone was choking me with the smoke of matches. How was it?"

"You went after some gold, didn't you?" said Jack, trying to help his memory.

"That's it. I was going home, as it was getting dark, and I had found nothing, when I saw something glittering in the imperfect light, on a dry-looking plain."

"It was lucky I came up when I did. You could not have lived long there."

"It wasn't more than half-an-hour ago. I remember picking up the gold. Such a whopping big lump! and then this beastly smoke I tell you about came up. I tried to run, but couldn't; and then I went to sleep, dreaming this horrid dream."

"That is the valley of poison. It is full of deadly gases, and nothing can live long upon it."

"I have heard of such places near the base of volcanoes. But how can I thank you, Jack, for rescuing me?"

"Perhaps you'll have a chance some day of doing as much for me."

"Won't I, that's all! Give us another pull out of the flask, and I shall be as right as a trivet," replied Harvey, who was rapidly regaining his strength.

"I couldn't rest," continued Jack, handing him the brandy, "when I found you did not come home. That there was something wrong, I felt positive."

"You thought the niggers had got me."

"I did."

"By the way," exclaimed Harvey. "where's the bullion? Was it bullion, or was that part of the dream?"

"No, here it is. I collard that at the time I rescued you, and a very tidy-sized lump it is.

Harvey clutched it eagerly.

"This is worth running a little risk for. It must be worth a lot," he said, gazing at it with admiration.

"It may lay the foundation of your fortune if ever we get back again to England."

"Tell you what, Jack," said Harvey. "I'll give it to you. After what you've done for me, I ought to think more of my life being saved than what good money will do for me. Take it, old fellow, and my love with it."

Jack was much affected by this proof of his friend's generosity of heart, and liberality.

"Keep it, Dick," he replied, "though I thank you all the same. As you reminded me this morning, I have plenty. My father's well enough off."

"Won't you have it?"

"No. It's all your own, Dick."

Harvey reluctantly put the gold in his pocket, and, leaning on Jack's arm, they returned to the castle, where the faithful Monday was anxiously awaiting their coming.

From the account Harvey gave of his adventure as they went along, Jack gathered that he had not long been insensible in the valley.

The jet of gas which had assailed him, had darted suddenly out of the earth, and as quickly died away again.

If it had continued, life must have been speedily extinguished.

Those fumes are for ever rising and vanishing all over the fatal spot, and sweeping hither and thither in white, dense clouds.

It was a narrow escape, and one for which the companions were both deeply grateful.

That night Harvey did not forget to say his prayers, which he uttered with rather more than his usual earnestness.

A little danger is sometimes a wholesome stimulus to our devotion, and to the proper regulation of our thoughts.

It checks our pride, and makes us remember what helpless creatures we really are.

The next day was occupied in taking stores to the boat.

She was carefully laden, and moored near the signal station, so, that all the crew had to do was to jump in, and push off.

The wind being rather high, the boys deferred their departure for a few days.

This delay gave rise to a peril which, though not unexpected, came upon them with all the severity of a surprise.

—+◦◦◦◦◦+—

CHAPTER XXXI.

BURNING OF THE CASTLE.

As we have stated, all was in readiness for the voyage to Limbi.

Jack was only waiting for the wind to lull a little, as he did not deem it prudent to embark in half a gale with a roughly-made and heavily-laden boat.

The stores which they had placed on board were chiefly guns, powder, and shot.

Both Harvey and Jack were sorry to leave the castle, where they had spent some pleasant months; though Maple's death, and Hunston's desertion, with Mr. Mole's sad end, had damped their enjoyment.

Trouble, however, makes people selfish.

They thought a good deal of themselves, and saw the necessity of making some move, unless they wanted to spend their remaining days on the island.

This was not an agreeable prospect to high-spirited boys, who wished to take their places in the world once more, and rise amongst their fellows.

Monday was delighted at the chance of seeing his friends and relations again.

"My father prince. Much great chief," he said.

"Is he the king of Limbi?" asked Jack.

"Yes; him king. Tuan Biza. Great chief, we call him."

"Will he make us welcome?"

"You save Matabella's life. That me —Monday," replied the black. "He much thank for saving Matabella—him only son."

"What's your governor's name, Monday?" inquired Jack.

"Lanindyer, him call."

"That's a nice crackjaw name. I suppose you'll be king some day?"

"No. Make Master Jack king. Monday be him servant, as he is now."

"Oh, so you want me to be your king. All right," replied Jack; "I'll astonish the natives."

"Lead them against Pisang with shot-gun, and make Limbi one big, great peoples, with plenty heads," said Monday.

"I won't have any head-hunting. Drop that idea," Jack said.

Monday looked contrite, and said that he had forgotten for the moment that head-hunting was wrong.

"You no fight. No war where you come from in big canoe?" queried Monday.

"Well, yes, we fight when we're attacked," replied Jack.

"So we do. No 'tack, no fight. Live quiet at Limbi, if Pisang not come take head."

Jack did not care to continue the conversation, because he knew, from what he had read of the history of his own and other countries, that the European nations had waged wars as dreadful as any fought by the savages of the Eastern Archipelago.

"Monday," he cried, "get the guns ready. I am going to have one more ramble over the island before we leave it—perhaps for ever."

"Happy have we been, and happy may we be," remarked Harvey. " I like this jolly old place."

"So do I; but it does not do to stagnate and stand still. We must push on Dick," said Jack.

"So we must, and I wonder where we shall push to at last."

Harvey was in a tearful mood at the prospect of leaving the island, but Jack shouldered the rifle Monday brought him.

"Are you coming?" he said to Harvey.

"Of course I am. You don't think I'm going to shirk behind when there is sport going on," replied the latter. "Give me a gun, you, Monday."

"Yes," replied Monday, handing him one.

"What did I tell you to call me?" asked Harvey, severely.

"Sare. I forget, sare."

"No; it wasn't ' sare,' either. It was sir. So don't you forget another time or——"

He lifted his foot threateningly.

Monday grinned, and showed his white, gleaming teeth,

"No kickee, sare. No kickee poor Monday," he cried.

"Well, I won't this time; but I will have proper respect paid to one who was until lately an officer in the British mercantile marine. That licks you, old sharpshine, doesn't it?"

"Yes, Mast' Harvey, that one lick for me," replied Monday, who only yet imperfectly understood the slang terms of his young masters.

"That's what you may call a lick for the mind, and it's better than a lick on the head," said Harvey, laughing.

Jack now led the way into the interior of the island, but they did not see anything to shoot at.

After walking some distance, they felt tired, and lay down under a spreading palm tree, while Monday knocked down some clusters of the rich, ripe cocoanuts.

They were filled with a deliciously cool water, which was peculiarly grateful to them during the noontide heat.

"We shall get a shot or two when the sun goes down," remarked Jack.

"Everything has gone to sleep now, and I'm going to follow everything's example," replied Harvey.

"You always were a lazy beggar, Dick."

"Why shouldn't I be? I hate taking trouble, and if this climate wouldn't make a fellow lazy, I should like to know what would."

"Monday," exclaimed Jack, " where's the powder flask?"

"Is it him powdare? Monday been and forgot him," answered the black.

"Oh, have you? then you'll have to tramp back to the castle and get it."

"Well, I'm blowed," exclaimed Harvey " you're a nice young man for a small tea party, up Islington way, I don't think."

"Let him alone; walking to the castle and back will be a sufficient punishment for him without bullying," cried Jack.

Monday did not wait to be told twice; he set off at a jog trot to the castle to repair his forgetfulness.

"How the fellow runs," remarked Harvey, " I couldn't cut out the pace like that if anyone paid me for it."

Without appearing to put himself to any great exertion, Monday could run a mile in about seven or eight minutes.

Half an hour elapsed, during which time the boys remained in the shade.

Then Monday was seen coming back with the wings of the wind.

"He's running full tilt," said Jack. "It's wonderful. I believe he's going quicker now than when he started.

Monday came up, but with his hands empty; he had no powder with him though he had been sent expressly for it.

His manner was agitated, and his breast heaved with exertion.

For some moments he was unable to speak.

"Something's up," observed Harvey.

"Yes, he's had a scare," answered Jack, "and he's forced the running to such an extent that he is pumped out—can't find wind enough to speak with."

"Shall I stir him up?"

"If you like."

Harvey gave him a dig in the ribs and a slap on his back.

"Wake up, you imp of blackness," he exclaimed. "Have you seen your own face in a pool of water, or discovered that there is a strong family likeness between your nose and a parrot's beak? Speak, you sable duffer, and put us out of our misery at once!"

"Oh, Mast' Jack! oh, Mast' Harvey!" was all he could reply.

"Oh, oh!" repeated Harvey. "If you go on like that we shall take you for a West-end swell who has got into debt and 'Oh's' everybody."

"Be quiet, Dick. There's something serious about this," said Jack. "Keep a look out; he may be pursued, or perhaps he's wounded."

Harvey grew grave as this view of the case was presented to him.

It was not at all unlikely that he had seen some of his old enemies, with Hunston at their head.

He waited eagerly for the black to speak, which he did as soon as he could command his voice.

"Oh, sare!" he exclaimed, addressing himself to Jack, "Oh, such a sight! Ten, twenty, hundred Pisang on island! The Tuan Biza and white man with the strange face, both near the castle."

"He means Hunston," said Harvey.

"No doubt," answered Jack, turning pale, and setting his teeth together, which was a way he had when anything put him out. "Go on, Monday."

"They take much thing out of castle and pile in heap. Many Pisang drink much strong wine, spirit. They sing; they dance."

"Getting drunk, eh?" remarked Harvey. "They've not lost any time over it."

"White man with the fancy face——" continued Monday.

"Fancy face!" repeated Harvey, laughing. "That's not bad. Monday makes shots at his English, but he's hit the mark this time. Hunston's mug is of a fancy character. You might say of it, 'He was all my fancy painted him.'"

"Let Monday speak!" cried Jack, in a rage at his companion's thoughtless interruptions. "We can't afford to lose valuable time with your confounded interruptions."

"All right, I'll subside. Monday, proceed," answered Harvey, who never disputed Jack's will.

"White man with the face," continued Monday. "Him take stick from a fire, which some Pisangs make, and throw it into the castle. Soon it all one, much large blaze."

"They've burnt the castle, Dick!" said Jack.

"Blow them!" was all Harvey could say.

"White man take more fire and throw it in the corn," Monday went on. "Soon it all one big smoke, fire. White man do everything. All Pisangs look to him as if he great chief. Oh! how all burn. The Pisangs—they dance, they laugh and drink, and the white man, he much grin like me when I cut off my first head."

It was clear, from Monday's confused account, that Hunston had suddenly landed on the island, with an overwhelming force of savages.

These were buoyed up by the hope of plunder, and burning, no doubt, to have revenge for the death of friends and relatives who had fallen by Jack's rifles in the late attack.

How Hunston felt towards him, Jack knew well enough.

Hunston was sufficiently vindictive to wish that Jack had half a dozen lives, that he might take them cruelly, one after the other.

The enemy was on the island.

They were dancing even then round the burning castle.

The corn, upon which the boys had intended to subsist when the ship's provisions were exhausted, was in flames.

All the havoc and mischief of which savages are capable was accomplished in a few brief hours.

No wonder that a sigh escaped Jack at the distressing news brought him by Monday.

CHAPTER XXXII.

A GHOST FROM THE GRAVE.

"This is bad news," said Harvey, dolefully.

"Not so bad as it might have been had we been caught napping," replied Jack.

"Fancy our dear old castle being burnt. But after all it does not matter so much, as we were going to cut our stick and leave it. Hunston does not know that we have our boat ready."

"His plan is to destroy everything we have belonging to us and condemn us to starvation. He would like to see us wandering about with no powder and shot to kill our food or protect us from the wild beasts, and no roof to shelter us— that's his game.

"And a villanous plot it is too."

"So long as our boat is not discovered, it is all right. If they find that, Heaven help us!" said Jack.

"What's that?" cried Harvey.

All listened intently.

A loud noise, coming from the direction of the castle, was heard.

It resembled a clap of distant thunder.

"I think I can explain that," said Jack, with a smile.

"How?" asked Harvey.

"You remember what I called the magazine?"

"The hole in the warehouse, in which you put the kegs of powder?"

"Exactly. After stowing away as much as I could in the boat, there still remained a considerable quantity."

"I see," cried Harvey. "The flames have caught it, and there has been an explosion. What a jolly lark! I hope some of the noble savages have copped it hot."

"So do I, and Hunston into the bargain. You may depend it has done some damage. But now to get off the island. We must make the attempt, wind or no wind."

"I shan't bother myself to sweat about till the sun goes down," Harvey said with a yawn.

"Be firm, Dick; no foolishness," cried Jack, in a tone of encouragement. "Every hour we stay here is fraught with peril, and though our enemies are savages, we can't afford to despise them, more especially as they are led by Hunston."

"I wish Hunston was afflicted with all the plagues of Egypt. What a nuisance the brute is, bothering us like this."

Turning to Monday, Jack continued—

"What do you say?"

The black had been listening to their conversation attentively.

"Me say, go now. No wait for night. When him dark, um boat not go easy through the reef," replied Monday.

"Your opinion and mine are alike," answered Jack. "We will get down to the coast, going as cautiously as we can and if we meet with the Pisangs, as Monday calls them, we must either show them a clean pair of heels or make the best fight we can."

"I don't like the idea of running away from niggers," replied Harvey.

"Neither do I, but there is no help for it," answered Jack.

"Let us go in Indian file. I'll take the lead. Monday shall be in the middle, and you bring up the rear, Dick.

They started in this order, and walked at a quick pace, in spite of the sun's heat to the sea shore.

Each kept his eyes on the alert, in case of a surprise, and to avoid the castle and the savages they made a considerable circuit.

They reached the boat, which was lying in the water, concealed under some rocks, near the place where the boys had first landed and Jack had taken possession of the island in the name of the Queen.

He wished now that he had placed the little vessel in another spot, as she was too near Hunston and his savages to make her builders feel comfortable. As they passed within half a mile of the castle, a thick smoke apprised them of the truth of Monday's story.

Desolation, wrought by fire, reigned in the once happy spot, where the boys might have dwelt peacefully had it not been for Hunston's wicked passions.

Creeping cautiously through the forest, they reached the skirts, and a long tract of rank grass, fringed towards the sea with sand, stretched down to the shore.

Hitherto they had not had much cause for apprehension, as the trees in the woods had sheltered them.

But now the case was altered.

If the savages had spread themselves over that part of the island, as there was every reason to believe, they might observe the fugitives as they crossed the open space.

"Halt," said Jack, in a low tone.

Harvey joined him, and Monday stood still, scouring the plain with his quick eyes.

The explosion, for such it was, had done considerable damage.

Hunston had never been allowed to go into the warehouse, and therefore did not know where the powder was kept.

He had, when the castle was taken possession of, searched everywhere for it.

His hunt had been unsuccessful.

A case of spirits was found, and a cask of wine.

As is usual in such cases, the marauders had all helped themselves to some intoxicating liquors.

Not being accustomed to such strong drinks, the Pisangs became uproarious.

They danced, and sang, and went roaring and bellowing about.

Their leaders were unable to control them.

They yelled for heads, and demanded to be led against Jack and Harvey.

Of Monday's existence they knew nothing.

Hunston's annoyance at not finding the powder was very great.

It is true he had captured a large stand of arms, but the guns were useless without powder.

Suddenly the explosion took place.

The savages were dancing round the burning castle, unsuspicious of danger.

Several were killed when the magazine was blown up.

Hunston was thrown on his back, and much hurt.

His face was getting well, for, to his great joy, he found the dye used by the natives in tattooing him was not lasting.

The marks were gradually dying out.

Every day they grew fainter.

There was a prospect of his recovering his usual appearance in a few months.

The explosion, however, blackened his face and singed his hair, making him look hideous.

Roaring with rage, he rose to his feet, dizzy, and looking unutterably hideous and ferocious.

While Jack was on the look out he saw some one crossing the sandy plain between himself and the sea.

"Dick," he exclaimed, "who is that? —his face is white!"

"Blessed if I know. It isn't Hunston; but, as you say, it is a white man," answered Harvey.

"Cover me well with your rifle," continued Jack; "and you, Monday, do the same. Fire if you see me in any danger. I am going to reconnoitre."

He stepped into the open.

"Who goes there?" he exclaimed.

A well-known voice replied—

"A friend."

Jack advanced boldly.

The next moment he was face to face with the intruder.

The latter was tall and gaunt, his hair hung down his neck in tangled locks, his clothes, which were of European cut, were tattered and torn, and his broad-brimmed straw hat had more than one rent in it.

"Why, bless me! it is—and yet it can't be! Is it Mr. Mole?" cried Jack.

"My dear boy!" replied the voice of Mr. Mole. "It is indeed I. No wonder you do not recognise me."

"But I thought you fell down the mountain and perished in the eruption," said Jack, beside himself with amazement.

"I did fall down, but only a little way. Providence was good to me. I climbed up again, but in seeking to rejoin you I lost my way, and fell into the hands of the savages."

"It's a wonder they did not have your head."

"I am indebted to Hunston for my life. The savages intended me for a grand sacrifice, but Hunston, who seems to have acquired great influence with the savages, caused them to spare me," replied Mr. Mole.

"And since then?"

"Since then they have made me their slave. I have been a hewer of wood and a drawer of water. Truly my lot was hard."

"Where did they keep you?"

"They took me in a boat to the island of Pisang," said Mr. Mole. "But though absent in the body, in spirit I have been with you."

"Well this is the most out-and-out extraordinary thing I ever heard of!" cried Jack. "Dash my buttons! I can scarcely believe it. We have been mourning you as dead."

"How are Harvey and Maple?" asked Mr. Mole.

"Dick's all right, and is hiding in the wood. Maple is dead. But am I to regard you as a friend or an enemy?" replied Jack, with a look of distrust.

"As a friend. It is true that your castle is burnt, and that the island swarms with your enemies the Pisangs; you will be hunted, even to the death, I fear, yet will I not desert you. Isaac Mole's heart is in the right place."

"Things are not quite so dicky as you imagine," Jack said, with a smile.

"Did you know the castle was burnt and that the Pisangs had landed in force?"

"I did."

"You are on your guard?"

"Rather," replied Jack. "I have too much regard for my head to let Hunston steal a march upon me. By the way, how is he?"

"Getting better. It was a cruel joke you played him, and his phiz looked so comical when he came to Pisang that I laughed in derision, whereupon he kicked me—me Isaac Mole—upon my seat of honour."

"Just like him."

"How did Maple die?"

"You heard of the attack on the castle, which failed?"

"Yes."

"Maple betrayed us, and joined the enemy; but his treachery cost him his life."

"He was always of a shifty disposition. I will not let fall a tear to his memory," said Mr. Mole, "nor would I to that of Hunston, should vengeance overtake him, for he hath used me sorely and his kicks rankle in my mind."

"Look here, Mr. Mole," said Jack. "This is a critical time, but you have always acted like a gentleman, and I esteem you for it."

"Thank you, Harkaway."

"There is my hand on it."

"I grasp it as that of an honest man," said Mr. Mole, as they shook hands.

"I can't tell whether you mean to betray us or not. If you try it on, I shall feel no compunction in shooting you like a dog. I am, however, disposed to trust you. You think our position desperate, yet you have offered to join us?"

"Verily I will cast in my lot with you. Hunston is an arrogant upstart. There was over much liquor found in the castle but to me he denied a drop, when I would fain have solaced myself with a gill of brandy, and he allowed his friends the savages to wallow in Martell's best and Kinahan's LL whisky, like the swine they are."

"I've got whisky, and I've got powder and shot," said Jack, "so come on."

"Believe me or not," continued Mr. Mole, "it was my intention in seeking you—for I did set forth to seek you—to warn you of your danger, and I thanked Heaven when I found you were not at home at the castle."

"It is lucky, perhaps," answered Jack.

"Hunston has promised your head and that of Harvey to the Pisangs, and you are to be killed, with great pomp and display."

"When captured," repeated Jack. "It is as well to catch your hare before you think of cooking it. But come on. It is not safe to stand here."

"Lead, Harkaway. I will follow you, for you were always a brave boy. Your country shall be my country, as the Scripture hath it, for truly my spirit is much vexed with over serving," answered Mr. Mole.

Jack, looking cautiously around him to prevent a surprise, led the way back to the wood, where he had left Harvey and the black.

"THE SAVAGE KNELT BEFORE THE TWO BOYS."

CHAPTER XXXIII.

MR. MOLE'S VALOUR.

THE singular meeting between Jack and Mr. Mole was like an incident in a romance.

His story, however, was intelligible enough.

He had struck upon a ledge in the uneven shaft of the crater of the mountain.

By dint of great energy and perseverance he succeeded in reaching the top once more.

His companions had gone away, giving him up for lost.

Losing his way in trying to retrace his steps to the castle, he had been captured by the Tuan Biza and his band.

The savages would have eventually killed him, had not Hunston interposed in his behalf.

For two days before he was captured, Mr. Mole had wandered about, lost, subsisting on such fruits as he could find.

Jack had always had a liking for his old master, and he was much pleased to meet with him again.

Harvey was as much surprised to see Mr. Mole as Jack had been.

"Is it a ghost?" he exclaimed. "Can I believe my eyes? Have you come back from the grave, sir?"

"No, my dear Harvey, I have been simply a servitor to a degraded race of negroes—I, the proprietor of a tea-garden in China have been beaten by them, and made to toil in the fields, while Hunston has amused himself by brutally kicking me," replied Mr. Mole.

He then briefly related his adventures, to which Harvey listened breathlessly.

"What made them bring you here to join in the attack on us?" asked Jack, who could talk more at his ease while concealed in the dense foliage of the wood.

"I was to be a decoy. I am even now sent out into the woods to find you, and throw you off your guard."

"And you accepted such a post?" cried Jack, eyeing him suspiciously.

Harvey grasped his rifle tighter.

"I did, though in my heart I secretly determined to warn you of your danger. It is not supposed that you knew of the landing and what has followed it," answered Mr. Mole.

"Did you see the explosion?"

"I did not. I came up at the sound, and found Hunston, who is much blackened by the powder, cursing like the Pagan he is at the disaster. He has guns in plenty, but no powder."

"Ha! ha!" laughed Jack, "I thought his lordship would be nicely done in that direction."

"Six Pisangs are killed by the explosion and five more wounded. The Tuan Biza raves like a maniac, and his amiable fellows call loudly for heads. What, my dear boys, shall you do, to avoid the cruel death that menaces you?"

"Step it," replied Jack.

"Whither?"

"Across the wild sea."

"You cannot swim the distance," said Mr. Mole, doubtingly.

"I don't mean to try, but our name is Walker before another hour is over. We meant to hook it to-day, and all our preparations are made."

"Indeed! may I inquire the nature of your conveyance and your destination."

"We have a boat, and we're going to Limbi that's the name of the crib, isn't it, Monday?" said Jack.

"Him Limbi, safe enuf," answered the black, who had been hidden behind a tree.

"Dear me," exclaimed Mr. Mole, "is that a friendly black? He gave me quite a turn. I thought he was a Pisang. They all have a family likeness."

"He is Monday."

"And why Monday?"

"Because we found him on a Saturday," said Jack, laughing.

"That is an absurd reason. I am, however, content to know that he is not an Amalekite, that is to say a Pisang. But I will also make a joke. When you get to Lim*bi*, mind you don't find yourselves in lim*bo*."

"Not bad for Mole, eh, Dick?" remarked Jack, with a smile.

"He's improving," answered Harvey.

"You may make as many bad puns as you like, sir," exclaimed Jack; "we're too glad to have you amongst us again to find fault with anything you do or say."

"Harkaway, you're a good boy," replied Mr. Mole, much touched with his kindness; "you have placed me under several obligations to you at various times, and I shall esteem it a favour if you can give me to drink a small portion of your spirituous liquor."

"Here's my flask, lay hold, and don't pitch into it too hard," answered Jack.

Mr. Mole snatched it eagerly, and a quick gurgling sound was soon audible.

"The patriarch was right when he said that wine, whereby he meant fermented liquid generally, as well as distillations, gladdens the heart of man," remarked Mr. Mole.

Again he raised the bottle to his lips.

A second time was the gurgling audible.

"Dash my wig," exclaimed Jack; "you'd drink the sea dry, sir, if it was filled with gin and water."

"No water, Harkaway. I abominate adulteration, and will take my stand on pure spirit."

"You won't stand at all, if you don't watch it. Give me my flask. Well, I'll be hanged if it isn't empty," exclaimed Jack, regarding the bottle.

"Now," said Mr. Mole valiantly, "I have courage. Show me the villain Hunston, and give me a sword that I may hew him in pieces."

"Here's a pistol, sir," replied Harvey, handing him a revolver, "mind you shoot straight."

"I am incapable of a crooked action. I hope you believe that I am thoroughly incapable of a crooked action. 'True as steel' is my motto, and I have resolved to defend you poor helpless boys against the savages who are thirsting for your blood," Mr. Mole rejoined.

Harvey laughed.

The late senior master at Pomona House rolled his eyes in a peculiar manner, and staggered a little bit on one side.

"How infinitely superior is the brandy of the Christian," he observed, "to the palm spirit of the savages, in which I indulged deeply this morning on the sly.

But my heart is good; lead me against the Pisangs. I burn to avenge my slavery, and to strike a blow for the liberty of my friends."

"I wish you'd talk less and do more," exclaimed Jack. "Look alive, sir, and just put a stopper on your tongue till we're afloat, then you may jaw for a month if you choose."

Thus rebuked Mr. Mole was silent.

Jack gave his orders, and soon the little party were engaged in crossing the open space, to gain the boat, which was concealed under the rock about half a mile off.

A path led down from the rocks to the sea-shore, and when the commencement of this was reached, Jack, who led, and was some yards in advance, looked below.

In an instant he held up his hand.

This was a signal.

Harvey halted and did the same.

Mr. Mole and Monday, who followed, imitated his example.

Each looked to his weapon.

"Monday," observed Mr. Mole, "I perceive that you have attached yourself to the white people, and I trust you are prepared to acquit yourself like a man.'"

"Monday fight till no use fight no more. Then he run 'way," replied the black.

"A very sage native, upon my word," remarked Mr. Mole. "There is more wisdom in you, Monday, than I thought there was. You mean to do the very thing I had intended to do myself."

"What good one fight twenty? What use um die? No more brandy drink," Monday said, grinning.

"My worthy black creature," Mr. Mole answered, gravely, "you are facetious, but you must not make jokes at my expense, or I shall, as my friend Harkaway would put it, be under the painful necessity of tanning your hide, though nature and the hot sun of the tropics have done that pretty effectually already."

"Mast' Mole, mind um pistol," exclaimed Monday, as Harvey made a second signal to them to be on the alert.

"Do you think there will be any fighting, my sable friend?" asked Mr. Mole.

"Some Pisangs not far off. Much fight soon."

"Ah, dear me! I perceive a small rocky fissure in the sand. I will step within it. Tell me, my good blackskin, when the fighting is over."

In fact, there happened to be just in front of Mr. Mole an inequality in the ground, which he called a rocky fissure.

It was, however, nothing of the sort.

Jack had dug a hole in the sand to serve as a rifle-pit, from which he could fire at the enemy, and be concealed himself if he should be attacked.

Into this Mr. Mole crept.

He was securely hidden in the hole.

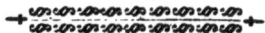

CHAPTER XXXIV.

ESCAPING FROM THE ISLAND.

MONDAY was much incensed at what he considered Mr. Mole's cowardice.

"Sare!" he exclaimed; "you sare! Come out dat. Won't you help fight? Come out dat hole, sare!"

"Not if I know it, my amiable negro," replied Mr. Mole. "You want this hole yourself, but I've been too quick for you. I shall relinquish this hole to no man breathing. Not much!"

We must now describe what had excited Jack's alarm.

The path in the rock was about five-and-twenty yards in length.

Immediately below lay the boat.

To his surprise, he beheld six Pisangs standing near her.

They had evidently not been there long, for they were talking rapidly, and making wild gestures, as if pleased with their discovery.

Two were overhauling the stores, though they did not attempt to remove anything.

If the savages took possession of the boat, Jack knew that his doom was sealed.

It was a time for action.

Retreating a few steps, he was joined by Harvey.

"What is it, old fellow?" asked the latter. "You look as if you had found sixpence and lost a shilling."

"The Pisangs have found the boat."

"Nonsense!"

"They have, though," replied Jack.

"How many of them are there down there?"

"Six. Come and look."

"Six!" repeated Harvey. "That's three to one."

"You forget Mole."

"Oh! Mole's an old woman. He don't count. And besides, he's been swigging the natives' palm spirit till he's top-heavy, and your brandy will about settle him."

"I wish we hadn't met him. He'll only be in the way. Yet we must not grumble. It will be a charity to get him away from the Tuan Biza and Hunston," said Jack.

The boys approached the edge of the cliff and looked down.

They retreated almost immediately.

One of the Pisangs was ascending the winding-path.

"He's going to tell his friends of the find they've made," said Harvey.

"That's just my idea. Stand fast, Dick, and back me up like brick. I don't like taking a man's life, but it's a case with us, if I don't stop this cove."

"We shall all be up a gum tree if he gets away. Shall I tackle him?" replied Harvey.

"No. Leave him to me."

"Shall you shoot."

Jack replied by drawing a case-knife from its sheath.

"It'll be a rough and tumble, but I shall have the best of it, as he will be taken by surprise. If you see me getting worst off shoot, Dick."

"Never fear."

Harvey laid down on his side, and Jack crawled on his hands and knees to the edge of the cliff, with the knife opened, and held between his teeth.

He did not want to shoot if he could help it, as the noise of the shot would arouse the attention of the main body of the savages.

The messenger must, however, be stopped at all hazards.

Scarcely allowing himself to breathe, Jack crouched as he waited for his enemy.

The inhabitants of Pisang Island had come over under Hunston's leadership to attack him, and were even then searching for him to cut off his head.

Could he be blamed for taking life in self-defence?

A few moments of breathless expectation.

Then a head appeared above the summit of the cliff.

This was followed by the shoulders of the native.

Stretching out his arm, Jack threw it round the man's neck.

He drew him forward with a hug like that of a bear.

"How do you find yourself, old boy?" he said, gleefully.

The Pisang turned his eyes upon him, filled with a look of deadly terror.

Jack's grasp tightened.

The native laid on his back.

Disengaging one hand, Jack, took the knife from his mouth and plunged it into his body, burying it up to the hilt.

The native made a convulsive spring.

Thinking that all was over, Jack had relaxed his grasp, which allowed the spasmodic effort of the native to jerk his body over the cliff.

He rolled down a corpse.

When his body fell at the feet of his companions they crowded round him gazing at him with wonder not unmixed with terror.

This passed away, and raising a horrible war whoop, they looked upwards for their enemies.

"I managed that badly," said Jack, "but it can't be helped. Call up Mole and Monday, Dick, and follow my fire."

Selecting the most prominent of the natives, Jack discharged his rifle.

The fellow started forward and fell dead on his face.

The Pisangs began to run.

"Fire, Dick, fire," cried Jack while he reloaded.

Harvey took a steady aim, and a native fell to the earth biting the sand in his death agony.

By this time Jack was ready to discharge his piece a second time.

A fourth native fell.

Monday came up and also fired his piece, but the two remaining Pisangs, running with incredible celerity, were out of danger.

"Now for it, Dick," exclaimed Jack, "it's no use following those two skunks. We couldn't catch them if we did."

"What shall we do?"

"Get down to the boat and make a start; the wind is still blowing stiffly from the shore, though not so roughly as it did this morning; now then, Monday, down with you; look slippery, Dick. I'll bring up the rear."

"Where's Mole?" asked Harvey.

"Mr. Mole, where are you sir!" cried Jack. "We're off, come along."

A head appeared above the sand.

"I—I felt a little faint, Harkaway," said Mr. Mole in a confused voice. "But I'm all right now."

"Come on then," exclaimed Jack.

Harvey and Monday were already half-way down the cliff, slipping along like wild cats.

Jack followed them.

They knew that their lives depended upon their speed,

The Pisangs had come over in boats, and they could follow them, and perhaps there would be a battle on the sea.

A hundred Pisangs, in perhaps ten boats, would be a formidable fleet to attack or resist.

Mr. Mole emerged from his place of concealment, and looking round him, saw nobody.

"Oh! Jack, good Jack, don't leave me," he exclaimed, "I'm taken very bad all at once; don't leave me, Jack."

There was no answer.

"Harkaway, my dear boy, this is wrong," he continued. "I am one of you. I have joined you, and yet you desert me. Why, where the deuce have they gone? Have they found a hole as well as I?"

He ran to the edge of the cliff, and looking down, saw them already in the boat.

Harvey was in the middle, setting the sail; Monday stood at the bow, with a paddle in his hand; and Jack manfully grasped the tiller.

"Whoa!" cried Mr. Mole. "I say, hold hard. I'm coming. Whoa, there! Whoa!"

In his hurry to get down the cliff, he missed his footing after he had gone a few yards.

This caused him to roll down very gracefully until he reached the bottom.

He was bruised and breathless.

Picking himself up with a naughty exclamation, he ran to the boat, and stepping into the water, crawled on board, and lay down exhausted at Jack's feet.

"Away we go. Bravo! Mole, you've done it. Off we are, Dick," cried Jack, in a loud voice.

"Right," replied Harvey, allowing the little sail to belly to the breeze.

"We've got the start of the wretches. Hurrah! Steady, Dick, steady," added Jack, as the heavily-laden craft heeled over a little.

"Steady she is," answered Harvey, slackening the sail.

"She'll weather it, sir. Bravo!" continued Jack.

"We've got our ballast on board," remarked Harvey, pointing to Mr. Mole.

The late senior master heard the observation.

"Ballast, Harvey, is not a fitting noun substantive to apply to me," he said.

"Got your wind again, sir, have you?"

"I thank Heaven for all its mercies, and that is one of them."

"You came down that hill with a fine run. It was a proper come down, sir," Harvey said, with a laugh.

"You may jeer, my young friend, but should the savages overtake you, I trust that my influence with them may be sufficient to save your lives. Ballast, indeed! A nice term to apply to one in my position. Ballast! Well, it isn't worth talking about; but I never was called ballast before—no, not even by the Pisangs," said Mr. Mole, in high dudgeon.

"I didn't mean any offence, sir."

"When none is meant, none is taken. I accept your apology, Harvey, and will you be good enough to ask your friend Harkaway for some stimulating beverage? I bore myself bravely during the scrimmage, and I have reason to believe that one, at least, of the savages fell before my unerring aim."

"Not now, Mr. Mole," replied Jack, smiling in spite of his preoccupation; "wait a bit, please, till we get clear of the reef."

"As you please, Harkaway. Can I make myself of any further use?" said Mr. Mole, with a sigh of resignation.

"Lie still where you are, that's all you can do."

"I should like Mr. Crawcour and all our old friends, if any of us reach England again, to know that I bore myself bravely, and did not shrink in the hour of danger."

"I'll see to that, sir. It shall be put down in my diary."

"With that promise I am content. Call upon me, Harkaway, when peril is pressing; Mole will be to the fore."

"Right you are, sir. Steady, Monday; mind the reef!" replied Jack.

The boat was laden nearly to the water's edge.

She was now nearing the passage in the reef through which Monday intended to conduct her.

He lifted his paddle first one side, then the other, as he wanted Jack to steer.

It was evident that he had been in a boat before, and knew well how to handle one.

In five minutes she would be floating fairly on the open sea.

"I wonder," said Harvey, "where the boats of the Pisangs are?"

Scarcely had he spoken when loud cries assailed his ears.

Turning round to look from whence they proceeded he saw a confused mass of men, about three hundred yards from the spot at which they had embarked.

Several boats, which he had not before noticed, were lying on the beach.

"What is it, Dick?" asked Jack, who could not turn his head round.

"Pisangs," answered Harvey, "and a jolly good heap of them too. They swarm like flies!"

"What are they doing?"

"Getting into their boats. They have unfortunately landed close to the castle, and will be after us in a twinkling."

"Never mind; we shall be through the reef in a brace of shakes, and perhaps they don't know this opening."

"What a pity they don't! they must have come through it."

"Perhaps so," said Jack, thoughtfully; "at any rate, we have one advantage over them. They have no guns, or, at least, if they have stolen ours, they have no powder; so we shall beat them that way."

"Keep um boat straight, Mast' Jack," replied Monday.

The opening in the reef was reached.

As it was a very narrow channel and the wind was high, the utmost caution was necessary to steer clear.

Monday used his paddle in the water with great dexterity.

The surf ran up in a dangerous manner, but Jack did not allow the boat at any time to get broadside on, and so she did not ship a sea.

She rode gallantly upon the waves, and showed herself thoroughly seaworthy under good management.

Jack kept her well before the wind and she met the surf with her bows, steaming the tide beautifully.

"Well done, Mast' Jack," cried Monday, "that your sort, all ri' soon."

In the meantime the cries of the Pisangs redoubled.

They were rapidly taking to their boats.

The chase threatened to be a hot one.

Hunston's blackened figure was discernible in their midst, and from his frantic motions he appeared to be dreadfully annoyed at the escape of his former friends.

"There's Hunston," said Harvey, "I'd swear to his ugly mug in a thousand."

"If there's any mischief brewing he's sure to be in it," replied Jack.

"Don't he look wild that's all," continued Harvey.

"Perhaps he'll be wilder, when he sees us scudding before the wind, and finds that we've slipped our cable just in time to put him in the hole. Steady, Monday, that's it, my man; another moment, and we shall be clear," Jack exclaimed, in his usual tone of command.

They were half through the dangerous passage.

The enemy were in pursuit of them and a short time would decide their fate.

Several boats, manned by the enraged Pisangs, started in pursuit of Jack and his companions.

Their fury knew no bounds when they saw their prey escaping.

The explosion which had killed and disabled several of their number, had first of all put them out of temper.

Loss of the powder they had expected to capture, and without which their guns were of no use, made them worse.

The death of the larger part of the party who had discovered the boat did not tend to increase their good humour.

And the escape from the island of those whom they had regarded as their sure victims, put the finishing touch to their rage.

Hunston and Keyali were in the first two boats that went after the fugitives.

The Tuan Biza, and others, followed quickly.

Hunston had promised Keyali Jack's head, and as Keyali could not marry until he got a head belonging to somebody, he was very anxious to have it.

He had made sure of catching Jack on the island, and in his anger at being disappointed, he danced about in the boat at the risk of upsetting it.

Hunston had to remonstrate with him and make him sit down.

His loud cries and exclamations were heard by Jack and Harvey, who had learnt a good deal of the native language from Monday.

This was a natural consequence of teaching Monday English.

Mr. Mole also understood the language spoken by the Pisangs and Limbians, owing to his having been a captive amongst the former.

The same tongue was common to both the tribes.

"I'll have your head!" shouted Jack, in derision, as his boat shot through the narrow opening in the reef.

He had heard Keyali's ravings, and meant to chaff him and Hunston.

But he spoke in the native language, so that he might comprehend by both, as Hunston was by this time thoroughly well able to converse in the dialect.

"Take care we don't have yours," replied Hunston, shouting in the same loud tone.

"No fear, old boy," replied Jack.

"I don't know that," said Hunston.

"Take a fool's advice," continued Jack, "and don't come too near us. We've got guns and you haven't."

"What of that? We've got bows and arrows and spears, and our arrows can fly as straight as your shots."

"Perhaps, but they can't carry as far, and we shan't let you get within shot of us."

Hunston was silent.

He saw the force of the argument.

"Give me his head; you promised me his head, and Tecona, my beloved, will not be my wife till I get a head. I must, I will have his head!" Keyali continued to shout.

"Keep that great calf quiet, can't you?" cried Jack.

"He wants his rights," replied Hunston

"Then he'll have to want."

Harvey was hard at work setting the sails, and he had surprised Jack by rigging up a flying jib, which gave them an advantage over their pursuers, who only had a mainsail.

"Bravo, Dick!" exclaimed Jack, as the breeze caught her and she sped onward like a thing of life.

Monday stood at the bows till the boat was clear of the rocks.

Then he sat down and looked contentedly at their pursuers.

"They plenty of them, Mast' Jack," he said, with a long face.

"We shall be a match for them, Monday," replied Jack.

"Hope so, sare; no want lose head. I hear Keyali cry for you. He do same for me once; but I 'scape and you save me. Keyali have mine 'fore yours," said the goodhearted fellow.

"I'll take precious good care he don't have either," returned Jack, dryly. "If he does, I'll forgive him. Which way shall I steer, Monday?"

Monday made a gesture which indicated west by north.

And following the direction of his arm, Jack put the boat about.

"Wire in, Jack, and get your name up. That's your sort," said Harvey.

"You shut up, and mind that flying jib of yours," replied Jack, laughing.

"You look fine, standing there, and coaching the canoe. Hunston's also standing up, but he isn't a patch upon you," continued Harvey.

"Stow it, Dick," answered Jack. "I don't want any buttering, and it isn't a time for humbug."

In fact it was not a time for chaffing.

But the boys kept their spirits up wonderfully well, and were delighted at getting away from the enemy.

They were showing them what sailors call a "clean pair of heels."

Mr. Mole was with them too.

They had every reason to believe him loyal and true.

If so, he was an addition to their strength.

The boat ran splendidly before the freshening breeze.

The gale had lulled, but began to get up again, though Jack did not anticipate much more of it.

Wind in those latitudes often sink as rapidly as it rises.

"There will be a fine sunset," remarked Monday.

"So I think," replied Jack, "and worse luck for us."

Everyone looked, as he spoke at the pursuing boats.

It was true that they were distancing them, and that every moment left them farther behind.

But in the event of a sudden calm, they could strike their sails and use their oars.

Jack had no oars.

He had not thought of being chased on the ocean, and for that reason did not make any.

Harvey attended to the sails with great skill, and obtained praise from Jack, who said—

"Bravo, Dick! A better fellow than you never loosened a topsail."

"We only want a flag to make us perfect," replied Harvey.

"Run up Mr. Mole's tile. It won't look bad, and I see its owner has gone to sleep."

"Right you are," said Harvey.

He took Mr. Mole's hat, and, without much exertion, secured it at the head of their small mast.

"We can't call it the British standard waving at the topmast," he observed. "But it will show them that we have got Mole on board, and they will know there is one more of us to fight."

"Hurrah for the blue sea!" said Jack, as they shot ahead, and the cries of their enemies grew fainter behind them.

At this exclamation, Mr. Mole was aroused, and looked languidly around him.

"Harvey," he said, "I will thank you for my hat. You imagined me asleep, but I was only revolving mighty ideas in my mind, and I saw you make free with my Panama straw."

Harvey pointed upwards.

"The wind's caught it, sir, and it's stuck up aloft," he replied.

"Now, that's a curious thing," remarked Mr. Mole. "Stop your ship, Harkaway, and get down my hat."

"Strike our flag? Not if I know it. That's the banner of independence, and meant as a defiance to the Pisangs," responded Jack.

"Oh, if it's meant as a defiance to the Pisangs, all right," replied Mr. Mole, wrapping a handkerchief of the bandana species round his head.

"Mast' Jack," said Monday, "give um Monday a drink of rum."

"Certainly," answered Jack, taking out a bottle, and handing it him. "You've had some not work, and you deserve it."

The bottle was given to Monday, who took a pull, and seemed much relieved.

Mr. Mole eyed it wistfully, and said in a low voice—

"My faithful savage, hand me that bottle. I will replace it in a secure position."

Monday gave it him, and he pretended to stow it away, but, when no one was looking, he solaced himself with a secret draught, which did not tend to improve his usefulness to the party.

In fact, he soon fell into such a deep sleep, that he did not wake, although important events were passing around him.

As Jack had anticipated, the wind fell towards evening.

Their pursuers were out of sight, but they could not be far off.

The boat made slow progress, and such advance as she did make grew less every five minutes.

In the tropics, when the sun sets, it is high time for everyone to hurry home.

There is no fading twilight.

Darkness presses closely on the footsteps of retreating day, and at once it is night.

In addition to the coming darkness a thick mist began to rise.

This might serve to conceal the runaways from the prying eyes of their pursuers.

In the absence of wind it was necessary to remain quiet till morning.

There was no current that would run the boat back to the rocks.

She might drift a little with the motion of the waves, but that was all.

Furling the sails, a watch was set.

Harvey and Monday lay down in the bottom of the boat and sought that sleep of which they were in need.

Jack sat on one of the thwarts and kept his ears open, for his eyes were not of much use in the thick mist and darkness.

Hours passed and nothing was heard but the rolling of the waves.

The boat was some miles from the shore, and Jack could not distinguish the breaking of the surf upon the rocks.

A speck of light appeared in the east. Day was about to break.

Jack who was nearly worn out, touched Harvey on the shoulder.

The latter sprang up.

"What is it?" he exclaimed, "are the Pisangs upon us?"

"No. I can see no signs of them, but I want to have a pitch, and as I've been on duty for so many hours, I thought you might take a turn."

"Of course," replied Harvey, "why didn't you wake me before?"

"It's time enough. I wonder how long the calm is going to last?" said Jack; "we must look out, as I expect the beggars will be upon us as soon as the mist rises."

He was about to lie down in the boat, when his practised ears detected the sound of oars in the distance.

"Hark!" he said, "do you hear that, Dick?"

"Oars," replied Harvey; "they are cruising about for us, knowing that we are stuck somewhere in this infernal mist."

"If it's only one boat, I don't mind," Jack continued, "or we might tackle two, but if the whole fleet are together, it's a case of Jack's up the orchard with us!"

"I should think they have been separated in the night, and that the one we hear is a solitary vessel which will be as much astonished at seeing us, as we are at meeting her," observed Harvey.

"I'd give something if the wind would blow, if it was only a capful, it would show what's behind, and we'd soon let them know what stuff our craft is made of."

The sound of the oars, which fell into, and were recovered regularly from the water, grew more distinct.

"Stand close, but don't fire till I give the order," exclaimed Jack.

Harvey nodded, and his companion woke Monday and Mr. Mole, whispering to them not to speak above their breath, as the enemy were not far off.

Monday grasped his rifle tighter, and looked to his pistols. Mr. Mole handled a revolver, which was his only weapon, with a carelessness that suggested danger to those around him, rather than to the enemy.

His contempt for the latter may perhaps be accounted for, from the fact that they were up to this time invisible.

"Don't let a shot be fired till I give the signal," Jack again said. "Let them run alongside of us, nearly, so that we can make sure of our men."

"Four of us," remarked Monday under his breath, "um Pisang boat generally carry six to row, and one to steer."

"That's seven. It's odds against us, but we have powder and shot, and they have none, so that makes us equal."

"Mr. Mole must get um head," said Monday, "and then him marry black princess at Limbi."

"Thank you, my worthy friend," replied Mr. Mole in a tone of disgust. "I don't care about dusky beauties."

"With us, a great chief can have three wife. Mr. Mole great chief. He cut off Pisang head, and then he have three wife," continued Monday with a grin.

"The Lord deliver me from such a fate!" said Mr. Mole, inwardly shuddering at the prospect.

Monday was about to speak again, when Jack said, "Hush!"

The dim outline of the proa hove in sight.

All held their breath, and nerved themselves for the coming encounter.

The battle would be short, sharp, and decisive.

CHAPTER XXXVI.

A FIGHT UNDER THE SEA.

PRESENTLY a shout from the occupants of the boat showed Jack that he was perceived.

It was useless to remain on the defensive any longer.

"Let them have it. Pour in a volley," he exclaimed. "Aim low, and hurrah for old England!"

There was no white man in the boat, but Jack recognised as the one who was steering, Keyali, who had evinced such a longing for a white man's head.

Keyali was evidently in command.

He had no idea that he was so near those of whom he was in pursuit, and would have put back out of harm's way, had it not been too late.

The Pisangs ceased rowing, and seized their spears. With such force had the boat been propelled, that its momentum threatened to carry it alongside of the boys.

As soon as Jack had given the word there was a report of firearms.

At the same moment, the wind began to lift.

A faint breeze was springing up.

Four of the Pisangs fell under the well-directed shots.

The remaining three sprang from their boat into Jack's, and a hand-to-hand fight ensued.

Keyali, with an eye like a hawk, singled out Jack, whom he caught round the neck and waist, with such a determined grip that he could not use his firearms.

Harvey was wounded in the thigh by a spear, and lay at the bottom of the boat helpless.

Monday tackled one Pisang, and Mr. Mole, in self-defence, grappled with another.

Jack and Keyali rocked to and fro in a deadly embrace.

Suddenly they lost their balance, and fell into the sea.

Down, down, they sank, as if they were so much lead.

Jack feared they would both be drowned, as it was impossible to live long under water.

Mr. Mole saw them disappear and was so alarmed that he forgot to go on fighting, and the Pisang with whom he had been battling was about to stab him with a murderous-looking knife, when Harvey crawled up.

He seized the savage's leg, and made his teeth meet in the flesh.

This caused him such pain, that he dropped his knife, and fell on his knees, howling loudly.

Mr. Mole had begun to say his prayers, thinking it was all over with him.

He regained his courage, however, and fired a pistol close to his ear.

The Pisang fell forward with a groan.

Taking up the knife, Mr. Mole prodded him with it in various parts of the body.

"That will do, sir. He's dead as mutton," said Harvey.

"I like to make sure," replied Mr. Mole, inflicting more savage thrusts with the knife.

At the same time, Monday settled accounts with his antagonist; and, cutting off his head, held up the bleeding trophy in triumph.

"You all right, Mist' Mole? You much hurt, Mast' Harvey?" exclaimed Monday, adding, with a look of bewilderment, "Oh, de debbel! Where Mast' Jack? Him gone!"

"Gone!" said Harvey. "Isn't Harkaway here?"

"I saw him fall overboard not long ago," replied Mr. Mole, "locked in the arms of one Keyali, whom I know to be a very truculent ruffian."

Monday and Harvey looked blankly at one another.

In the meantime, Jack had continued to descend into the bosom of the deep.

He managed to keep his senses about him.

Keyali would not let go, but suddenly Jack felt one arm relax, which allowed him to make use of his right hand.

He remembered that he had a sheath knife in his belt.

If he could draw this he might deal his adversary a blow which would save his life.

Apparently the same idea occurred to Keyali, for he began to feel for his knife.

Luckily for Jack it had fallen out in the struggle, being only slenderly secured with a string round his waist.

It did not take more than a second to assure Keyali of this fact.

He now struggled to regain his hold of Jack, and endeavoured to move one hand to his throat, so as to strangle him.

Being the stronger of the two, the Pisang might have succeeded in this effort, had he not given Jack an opportunity when he first loosened his grasp to feel for his knife.

This was a fortunate chance for Harkaway.

Had it not been for this he would probably have soon floated, a blackened and swollen corpse, before the eyes of his friends.

As soon as he had drawn the knife, he stabbed Keyali repeatedly about the legs.

The water was soon crimsoned with blood.

Keyali tightened his grip, and Jack, whose strength began to fail him, and whose head grew dizzy with the pressure of the water, made frantic efforts to reach a vital part of the Pisang's body.

This fight under the sea was terrible.

They had been beneath the waves nearly three-quarters of a minute.

Short as the time in reality was, it seemed a lifetime to Jack.

Maddened with pain, Keyali succeeded in grasping his opponent's throat.

The stifling sensation that had attacked Jack increased.

A mist swam before his eyes.

Making one last effort, he plunged his knife up to the hilt in the Pisang's body.

Gradually his hold relaxed.

The arms fell down, and the man was dead.

Raising his feet, Jack struck the lifeless body, sending it down into the sea.

At the same time he began to ascend.

It was time.

A very short period more, and he would have gone to the bottom, locked in that death-grip.

Suddenly he appeared above the surface, close to the boat.

Monday stretched out his arms, and dragged him on board, breathless, panting, and exhausted.

It was some time before he could speak.

When he was able to use his voice, he gave an account of the fight beneath the waves.

"Thank goodness I am none the worse for it," he added. "But I hope never again to have such a tussle. Here, you Kafoozlum—what's your name, Monday—give me some brandy to wash the salt water out of my mouth."

Monday did as he was requested, and Jack began to revive sensibly.

"I need not ask how you got on," he continued, "for I see you have disposed of your enemies. Are you hurt, Dick?"

Harvey was tying a bandage round his leg, and he replied—

"I've got an ugly thrust in the leg from a spear, but it's not much."

"Throw the carrion overboard," Jack said, pointing to the two dead Pisangs.

Monday proceeded to do so.

"I think you will all bear witness to my bravery," observed Mr. Mole.

"HARVEY WAS LYING ON HIS BACK, PERFECTLY INSENSIBLE WHEN JACK ARRIVED."

dispatched that wretched creature whom Monday is about to consign to the deep. I, Isaac Mole, dispatched him with my own hand.

"If I hadn't bit him in the leg with my teeth," said Harvey, "you would have gone to the mole country, sir."

"No jokes, Harvey; you may have distracted the poor fellow's attention, but I had him well in hand throughout, and was never for one moment afraid of him. Harkaway, pass the bottle in a friendly spirit, and let us drink to our noble selves."

Jack granted his request, and Mr. Mole took a deep draught.

"Drink deep, the poet says," remarked Mr. Mole. "And truly he was right, for this spirit comforteth the inner man and keepeth out the rawness of the fog, which I perceive, is disappearing.

In fact, as he spoke, the sail which had been lying idly by the mast began to flap to and fro.

"Hurrah," cried Jack, "the wind is coming."

"I'm sorry I can't lend a hand," said Harvey."

"You be still," replied Jack, who put some boating jackets under Harvey to make his position more comfortable.

"You want rest as much as I, for you were on the watch all night."

"Never mind me. I can't sleep when there is anything to do, but I make up for it afterwards. If the wind lasts, and Monday is right in his steering, we shall make Limbi in four or five hours.

Jack set the sails, and the little craft, as the wind caught her, ran before it in splendid style.

The sails bellied to the breeze, and Monday took the helm.

"Harkaway," said Mr. Mole, "take the rest, of which you stand so much in need and leave the management of the boat to this trusty savage and myself."

"Very well," said Jack, who thought he might safely do so, as there was nothing of consequence to attend to.

Accordingly he threw himself down, wet as he was, knowing that the hot sun would soon dry him, and fell fast asleep.

Mr. Mole applied his lips frequently to the bottle, much to Monday's delight.

"Mist' Mole got um best friend," he observed, as Mole hugged the bottle tightly.

"If that observation is intended to apply to this case bottle," replied Mr. Mole, "all I can say is that you are a very rude and impertinent negro."

"No offence, sare; beg um pardon," said Monday. "Me 'fraid of you sare, you fight so well."

This compliment mollified the object of it.

"You are right," he said; "by my bravery I have saved you all from a dreadful fate. I hewed mine adversary in pieces; but you must not repeat your remarks. In this climate the European requires stimulants to protect himself from the trying effects of the weather. What I take is taken with reluctance, and strictly as medicine."

"Monday not mind a drop of same sort of medsun."

"Not a drop. It is not good for you who are young and strong, and accustomed to the climate."

"Very well, Mist' Mole know best. Monday get him three wife."

"If you suggest such a thing again," cried Mr. Mole, in a rage, "I'll—I'll wring your neck like—like a sparrow's."

"No wring um poor Monday neck. Monday do what him like in Limbi. His name Matabella, and his father, Lanindyer. Great chief. King of Island. All obey Monday. If Monday say Mole great chief, him cut off all Pisangs heads, the woman all love him and he be 'bliged to have one, two, three wife."

"Is your father really the Tuan Biza of Limbi?" asked Mr. Mole.

Monday nodded his head vehemently.

"It's quite right," exclaimed Harvey, who could not sleep through pain, and had been an amused listener to this conversation.

"Is he not joking? I have found him of a facetious tendency."

"No. Monday's a howling swell in his own diggings, ain't you, Mon?" said Harvey.

"Matabella, him show Mist' Mole," answered the black, drawing himself up proudly as he stood in the stern, rudder-lines in hand.

"Take the bottle and help yourself, my young and intelligent friend," exclaimed Mr. Mole.

Monday did so with a grin.

"I hope nothing I have said has given you offence," continued Mr. Mole. "I had no idea you were a prince in your own country. But for Heaven's sake, say no more about the wives."

The conversation dropped, and the boat went on her course, the wind continuing to rise, as if impatient at having been still during the night.

No more boats belonging to the Pisang fleet were visible.

The sun rose high in the heavens, and the heavily-ladened craft which carried the boys and their fortunes slowly ploughed her way along the deep.

Harvey and Mr. Mole covered themselves with a tarpaulin, and sought forgetfulness in slumber.

Monday was alone in command of the boat.

He could not steer and see to the sails as well, and when the force of the wind increased, and the sea rose, he thought it advisable to wake Jack.

Nearly five hours had passed since the dispersion of the Pisangs.

Jack had had time to recruit his wasted energies.

The boat made one or two dangerous lurches over, and Monday was afraid she might capsize. Jack started up with alacrity.

"What is it?" he asked.

Monday explained to him, and pointing to a dark ridge visible on the verge of the horizon, added—

"That Limbi."

"Oh, is that Limbi?" asked Jack. "You know your way about in these waters. How shall we land?"

"No land in the surf—not in this boat," answered Monday. "They send out boat when see us, and then we land in our fashion.

"Very well. I leave it all to you," replied Jack, well pleased at the prospect of reaching their journey's end without further danger.

The land was not more than five or six miles distant.

Their voyage would soon be over.

━┽•∘⊶૭⅋₂∾•┾━

CHAPTER   XXXVII

RECEPTION   AT   LIMBI.

THE first sight of Limbi was not a re-assuring one.

A straight open beach descended abruptly beneath the sea, so that the high swell never once broke before finding itself suddenly stopped in its rapid course.

The water rose up in one huge wall that rolled forward and fell on the steep shore with a roar like thunder.

Every few moments the water would rebound from the sand until it rose twice and a half as high as the natives standing near it, for several of the islanders had collected at the novel sight of a vessel standing in for their shore.

"My dear Harkaway," said Mr. Mole, who was roused from his sleep by the breaking of the surf, "you surely do not intend to run the risk of landing on such a coast?"

"Monday says he will make it all right," replied Jack.

"We near 'nuff now," exclaimed Monday, "please take in sail, Mast' Jack."

Jack did so, and the boat ceased her onward career, merely drifting a little with the tide.

Monday put his hands to his mouth, and gave utterance to a peculiarly shrill and piercing cry, which he repeated three times.

"That to let them know me come, sare," he observed.

The noise awoke Harvey, who looking round him in astonishment, said—

"What's that beastly row?"

"It's only Monday," answered Jack.

"I thought it was um Pisangs, as he calls them. I never heard such a din in my life. It was like a baked 'tater boy on a cold night in winter, singing out, 'all 'ot, all 'ot!'"

"That our war cry," explained Monday; "all my people know my voice; they say 'That Matabella,' and my father come out to me in a proa and take us all on shore."

"Your father! Is he on the beach?"

"Yes. Monday see him. Look, look; he telling them it me, and they shake head. Now he order boat, because they all think me dead—killed, eat up by

Pisang. See! father, how um run, Mast' Jack; how um skip, Mast' Harvey, how um talk, sare."

The black grew quite excited at the prospect of meeting with his father.

In fact, Jack saw that the few natives whom he had at first distinguished on the beach had grown into a crowd, which numbered upwards of two hundred.

An elderly man moved in their midst, and to him they paid the strictest attention, as if he were entitled to command.

His manner was that of a prince or chief, and it was clear that Monday's peculiar cry had produced a singular effect upon the inhabitants of the island.

For a few minutes it was not evident what the Limbians were about.

They ran to and fro carrying pieces of wood, and all seemed confusion.

"What are the beggars trying to do?" asked Harvey.

"Blest if I know," replied Jack. "They are like bees in a hive, when they're going to swarm."

The natives did not keep them long in suspense.

They soon made a rude skid or wide ladder with large poles on the sides and small green ones with the bark torn off for the rounds.

This was laid down on the beach while the wave was forming, and a heavy boat, with a sort of awning in the middle to keep off the spray, was pushed on to it as the wave broke and a broad sheet of surge partially buoyed her up.

As this wave receded she was successfully launched.

The boat, guided by native hands, reached Jack's boat, and an affectionate greeting passed between Monday and his friends.

His father, the Tuan Biza of Limbi, was a man of commanding stature, but his self-possession was great.

He had given up his son as lost.

When a prisoner falls into the hands of his enemies, he rarely, if ever, escapes.

To see Matabella again, was to Lanindyer a resurrection of his son.

Monday threw himself on his neck and kissed him affectionately, but the old man displayed no emotion.

It was evident, though, that he was affected, for teardrops trembled in his eyes.

When Monday recovered himself, he pointed to Jack, Harvey, and Mr. Mole and told them in the native language who they were, and what they had done for him.

In teaching Monday English, Jack and Harvey had, of necessity, learnt his language.

So that the conversation between the father and son was intelligible to them.

Mr. Mole also knew the native dialect, which was common to all the tribes about these islands, for he had picked it up during his captivity.

Turning to Jack, the aged chief said—

"Saviour of my child, you are welcome to Limbi, and you shall live like a prince among our people."

"Thank you," replied Jack. "It is my pride to be the friend of so great a chief as Lanindyer, who is alike renowned in war and peace."

The Tuan Biza now set his men to work and all the stores were moved out of Jack's boat into the proa, and in the latter they all embarked, leaving their own craft to ride at anchor in charge of a native.

Harvey was lifted carefully from one boat to the other, being unable to walk, as his wound was painful in the extreme, and his leg much swollen.

When all was ready, they ran into the shore over the heavy rollers.

Other natives appeared on the shore with a huge coil of rattan an inch or more in diameter.

Two or three of them seized an end, ran down and plunged into a huge wave as coolly and unhesitatingly as a diver would leap from the side of a boat into a quiet bay.

The end of the cord was fastened to the front part of the boat.

The other was carried up a long way on the beach, and the natives ranged themselves in two rows, each grasping it with one hand ready to haul in when the signal was given. A number of heavy seas now rolled in and broke, but the natives on board kept the boat from being swept forward or backward.

A smaller swell now came on.

Every native gave a wild yell, and those on shore hauled in the rattan with all their might.

Away darted the boat on the crest of a wave with the swiftness of an arrow.

Soon the boat was in the midst of the surf.

The next instant it was on the skid,

and away it glided with the speed of a locomotive.

Before Jack could realize the fact, they were high and dry upon the bank before the next wave came in.

In this way was their landing in Limbi effected.

Monday had not exaggerated his influence with the natives of Limbi.

There were about a thousand in number, living in a town called Tompano, which was built on a hill.

This made it healthy, and afforded some security from attack.

Monday's father had ruled over the inhabitants for some years, as his father had done before him.

He was, in fact, descended from a long line of princes.

The people who lived in the neighbouring island of Pisang were the hereditary enemies of the Limbians.

War was almost always going on between them, and with varying success.

The town in which the Pisangs lived was called Palembarg.

A few years ago the Limbians had invaded Pisang, and being victorious, burnt Palembarg to the ground.

This made the Pisangs very angry and vindictive.

They had vowed vengeance ever since, and threatened an invasion of Limbi.

Jack's supply of powder, shot, and guns was exhibited to the Limbians, and their use explained to them.

They hailed Jack and his friends at once as great chiefs.

A house was given them to live in near the king's palace.

They were delighted at the restoration of Matabella, or Monday, who was much beloved.

These simple people, savage though they were in their habits, were not wanting in gratitude.

Jack got all their fighting men together, and instructed them in the use of firearms.

But he was very sparing with the powder and shot, because when his supply was gone, he could get no more.

He knew of what advantage it would be to him and his friends in the event of an invasion of Limbi.

That Hunston would carry on the war he did not doubt.

If, indeed, the Pisangs should be afraid to invade Limbi, he determined to land an army on their island.

For some time everything went on quietly.

The Pisangs did not show themselves.

Monday would not leave Jack.

He might have lived in his father's palace, but his attachment to the boys was so great that he lived in their house, and was Jack's body guard.

He never allowed him to stir out unless he accompanied him.

"You save my life, and you teach me do what right," he said. "I spend my life with you. It is your life, and Monday still your servant."

"My friend, you mean, Monday," replied Jack.

"You do as you like with me, Mast' Jack," continued the grateful fellow. "You ask me die for you, I do it, because I then give back the life you save."

Both Jack and Harvey were much attached to Monday, and liked to have him near them.

Harvey's leg got well in about six weeks, and he could walk again.

They had plenty of servants, and did not allow Monday to do any menial work, though he was always ready to lend a hand when necessary.

As the Pisangs did not show themselves, Jack planned an invasion of their country on a large scale.

A fleet was provided, and the army, which numbered four hundred men, was drilled every day.

The inhabitants of Pisang and Limbi were about equal in number.

Making an allowance for the women and children, the aged and the infirm, they could put four hundred, or a few more, in the field.

CHAPTER XXXVIII.

MONDAY'S NEWS.

THE white men were an object of attraction to the ladies of Limbi.

Every chief was entitled to have three wives.

It was reported that the strangers had killed their enemies, and, therefore, were, by the laws of the land, able to marry

Jack and Harvey were too young to indulge in any idea of the sort.

If they had not been, they would not have fallen in love with the Limbian women, who were far from being attractive.

Besides which, Jack was in love with Emily, and his principal reason for wishing the Limbians to attack the Pisangs, was to find if she really was on their island, and if so, rescue her.

Jack found his new friends very idle.

They would fight, hunt, and fish, but nothing more.

The women were made to do the principal part of the work on the island.

All were very fond of dancing.

The principal dance was called the minari.

It consisted of men and women arranging themselves in two rows.

They slowly twisted their bodies to the right and left, at the same time moving the extended arms and open hands in circles in opposite directions.

The only motions of the naked feet were to change the weight of the body from the heel to the toe, and reverse it.

Monday had two cousins, Alfura and Ambonia.

They expressed a wish to marry the white men, as a mode of showing their gratitude for their having saved Monday's life.

The king summoned a council to discuss the idea.

Monday heard of it.

Alfura and Ambonia were his near relations, and he hastened to tell his masters the news.

Jack and Harvey were together, talking about Emily.

Mr. Mole had gone out for a walk, to think alone about his tea gardens in China.

"Mast' Jack," exclaimed Monday, coming into the house, "what you think?"

"I don't know," replied Jack. "Have the Pisangs come after us?"

"No; not them, but the Tuan Biza and all the chiefs met in council to-day."

"What about?"

"Alfura and Ambonia—you know them. They are my father's brother's daughters."

"That's a roundabout way of describing them; but no matter. Go ahead," remarked Harvey.

"They have said they want to marry a white man, and the chiefs are to decide whether they shall or not."

"Scissors!" exclaimed Jack. "Suppose the white man don't see it?"

"Then he must leave the island," replied Monday. "If one of the Tuan Biza's family want to marry and chose a man, and he not have her, then he go."

"Oh, that's it, is it? I wish I'd got a return ticket," Jack remarked.

"If the chiefs say yes, they send for you, and it is our custom to place sometimes seven, eight, nine women together."

"Yes."

"Then you go and pick out one, two, three, if you like; but of course you take those who have asked for you."

"I see; you pick out the ones who have honoured you by their preference," replied Jack.

"That is a dodge to spare their blushes if they have any," observed Harvey.

"Yes," said Monday, quickly, "You not supposed to know they ask for you,"

"But I don't want to marry," exclaimed Jack.

"Nor I," said Harvey.

"You should have kept us out of this, Monday. It's not kind of you," Jack continued.

Monday grinned.

"What do you stand grinning there for like the ugly baboon you are?" said Jack in a rage.

"'Scuse me, Mast' Jack. I not grin at you," replied Monday.

"Then you're indulging at my expense," said Harvey. "Where's my crutch? I'll lamn into you Master Monday, if you were twenty king's sons."

"No lamn in, sare," Monday cried in alarm. "You say you too young to marry. You wait a year and let Mr. Mole marry Alfura and Ambonia; that my idea—that why I grin, sare."

Jack smiled, and Harvey put down the crutch with which he had walked while his leg was bad.

"That's a rattling good idea, too," said Jack. "It will be a rare spree to see Mole with—how many did you say Monday?"

"Two at first."

"Oh, yes, two to start with, Alfura and Ambonia. Two beauties they are, too—aren't they, Dick?"

"Stunners," replied Harvey. "Alfura's got a nose like a squashed pumpkin, and her ears stick out like a cow's, while her mouth would enable her to eat mince pies whole."

"And Ambonia's fat and pudgy, with a temper like a wild hyæna. I saw her chivey a cove down the street the other day, and wallop him awfully," said Jack.

"What for?"

"Because he bagged something out of her father's garden. She did give it him and no mistake."

"Monday's a genius," said Harvey.

"If they send for me to the council," continued Jack, "I shall treat them to a little ventriloquism, and say that the great spirit does not wish us to marry for a year, as we are too young."

"And that Mole is to have Alfura and Ambonia, or be cast adrift in a boat without oars, sails, rudder, or grub," put in Harvey.

"Exactly."

"That's the ticket," Harvey went on. "You'll fog them beautifully with your ventriloquism."

"Monday," exclaimed Jack.

"Yes, Mast' Jack," replied the black with his usual respectful manner.

"Don't you let on to anyone about my gift'

"About you talkee in the air?"

"That's it."

"Monday never say nothing."

"Then you say something. "Never say nothing' isn't grammar, Monday. You ought to go to Crawcour's if ever you reach England with us," observed Harvey.

Monday shook his head.

This speech was beyond him.

But he protested that he never mentioned anything that the boys told him to keep secret.

He had heard Jack ventriloquise once or twice, and the mystery had been explained to him.

Jack and Harvey felt perfectly happy when they saw a way out of the new difficulty which now presented itself.

It was nothing unusual in the archipelago for girls of thirteen to marry boys of sixteen.

The natives arrive at maturity so much earlier in warm climates than we do in our colder latitudes.

To plead that they were too young would have been a poor excuse.

"Mole shall be the victim," said Jack.

"How many wives shall he have?" asked Harvey.

"Monday says he can't have more than three by the law of the land. I'd give him a dozen if I could work it."

"Let him have Alfura and Ambonia to begin with. Mole hates women, I think. He was never very civil to them, and if he doesn't care about marrying English beauties, he'll faint at the idea of two full-blown niggers," observed Harvey.

"As brave a fo'castle man as ever broke biscuit would steer clear of them."

"And naturally a loblolly-boy like Mole will fight shy."

"He's in a narrow channel, and he'd better take soundings," said Jack; "for, if I'm not mistaken, here's a messenger coming up the street to tell me to come to the council."

"That right, sare," replied Monday. "Him de message, sure enuff."

"Then it's all 'u p' with Mole; for, to get myself out, I must get him into the mess."

It was as Monday had predicted.

Alfura and Ambonia, ladies of high rank, had in accordance with the custom of the country, expressed themselves willing to bestow their hands and hearts upon the adventurous stranger.

This proposal, owing to their high position, had to be considered by the chiefs in council.

They had come to the determination that the ladies' wish should be granted.

In the event of non-compliance with the desires of the fair ones, expulsion from the island would be the result.

The council consisted of twenty-five members, who sat on mats in a sort of barn.

Room was made for Jack.

The Tuan Biza himself informed Jack that he might have his choice of his relatives, or take them both for his wives if he liked.

Jack coughed, and replied that he was, indeed a fortunate man to be so highly honoured.

He shouldn't mind one of the ladies.

With one, however, he would be content, and his friend, Harvey, might have the other.

A murmur of applause arose.

Then Jack, throwing his voice into the centre of the apartment, near the ceiling, changed the tone, which became serious, if not awful.

"Forbear," he said. "I, the spirit of the white men, speak."

A general consternation seized the chiefs in council.

They looked at one another terror-stricken, for, as we have said, they were all very superstitious, and believed in witchcraft.

"Jack and Harvey are your guests," he continued. "They are about to lead you against your enemies, the Pisangs, over whom you shall be victorious.

"Their customs are not your customs, and they must not marry until one year has passed, for they are too young to have wives."

A murmur of approbation, mingled with astonishment, ran through the council.

"But," continued Jack, "I, the spirit of the white men, do not wish the ladies Alfura and Ambonia to remain single."

As Jack spoke in the native dialect, his words were perfectly intelligible.

"Who, then, O spirit!" asked the king, "is worthy to have their matchless charms?"

"Who but the Tuan Biza of the whi[te] men—who but the great chief Mole, wh[o] has qualified himself for marriage b[y] cutting off a head?"

"Good, good," broke from the a[s]sembly. "The spirit of the white me[n] speaks the words of wisdom. It is ve[ry] good."

"Let the Tuan Biza Mole be unite[d] to both ladies at once," Jack went on.

"It shall be done, O spirit!" said th[e] council, as with one voice, and bowin[g] their heads.

Jack pretended to be disappointed [at] this interruption, and said that he ha[d] taken a fancy to Alfura.

"We have other beauties," replied th[e] king, "and you shall marry when th[e] year has run, O friend of my soul!"

"I was afraid the spirit would inte[r]fere," continued Jack.

"Does he often do so?"

"Always, when we do anything again[st] the laws of our priests."

"And is it unlawful to marry before [a] certain age?" asked the king.

"Of course it is; that's at the botto[m] of the mischief," answered Jack.

"Rest easy, O son of my adoption[,]" replied the king. "You shall do [a] wrong through us."

Rising, the chief said a few words [to] his friends, and they dispatched a messen[n]ger to fetch Mr. Mole.

"Shall I go, O Tuan Biza, and a[c]quaint my countryman with his go[od] fortune?" asked Jack.

The proposal was accepted, and Ja[ck] went in search of Mole.

He left the chiefs in council, holdi[ng] Jack in higher veneration than ever.

They had not the slightest idea th[at] they had been imposed upon.

To their simple minds the great spi[rit] of the whites had spoken.

His dictates must be obeyed.

Though Jack and Harvey were for [a] time lost as husbands to their princess[es,] they had Mole to fall back upon.

For him there was no escape.

Little did he suspect what news was [in] store for him, as he wended his way ba[ck] to the town of Tompano.

CHAPTER XXXIX.

MR. MOLE'S DESPAIR.

WHEN Jack returned to Harvey, who was waiting for him with impatience, he began to laugh heartily.

"I've done it, Dick," he said, when his merriment was over. "We're under the protection of the spirit. Has Mole turned up?"

"Not yet. It's feeding-time, though, and Mole is generally pretty punctual at knife-and-fork-time. How did you do it?"

"I told the council that you and I were highly honoured, and would marry the ladies. There was applause at this. Then I changed my voice, and you should have seen the beggars stare."

"Of course the spirit forbade the banns, and suggested Mole as the bridegroom. Which is he to have?"

"Both of them."

"Both?" repeated Harvey. "My eye, Jack! it will give him fits. He's always going on about women, and saying he shall die as he has lived—a bachelor."

"Will he? We shall see him with a couple of young papooses on his knee. I wonder what colour they'll be."

"Chocolate and cream—half and half."

"Piebald, perhaps. What a lark!" said Jack.

"It's all a spree," remarked Harvey.

At this juncture Mr. Mole entered, looking hot and tired.

He had been botanising, and carried in his hand some rare specimens of the flora of the island.

"Something more for my collection," he remarked. "I shall have quite a cabinet of curiosities soon."

"I think you will, sir," replied Jack.

"What do you mean? Your observations have a doubtful tendency in them sometimes, Harkaway."

"No doubt about this last start, sir."

"What on earth are you talking of?"

"The council is waiting for you," replied Jack, "and you are destined to a high honour."

"Ah! I suppose they want to make me prime minister or chancellor of the exchequer; very good! I will give these savages a constitution, and bring in an education-bill. We must have a school here."

"It isn't that, sir, though that may come afterwards."

"What is it, then?"

"You're to be married, sir."

Mr. Mole gave a high bound.

Harvey sang—

"For I'm mar-ry-ed to a mer-may-ed,
    At the bottom of the deep, blue sea."

"You are joking, Harkaway. Do not indulge in merriment at my expense. Explain this to me. No foolishness?" exclaimed Mr. Mole.

"It's quite true, sir. Two ladies have chosen you, and by the law of the land you must marry them, or——"

"Or what?"

"Leave the island in an empty boat—no provisions, no cars, no anything."

"Why, that's certain death!" replied Mole, with a groan, adding—

"Who are the—ahem? the females?"

"Miss Alfura and Ambonia, relatives of the royal family."

"What, those she-dragons? I know them," exclaimed Mr. Mole. "Alfura's forty if she's a day, and has lost all her front teeth. Ambonia's got a temper of the old gentleman himself, and squints awfully."

"Consider the honour, sir."

"Honour be——but no, I will not give way. I will command myself. I shall proceed to the council chamber, and remonstrate with those savages."

Jack laughed.

"What is fun to you is death to me, and if I find that you have got this up for me, I'll—I'll——"

Mr. Mole could not find words dreadful enough for what he would do.

"Go on, sir," said Jack. "Who's afraid."

"I didn't mean anything," Mole replied. "Come, Harkaway, stand my friend in this matter, and get me out of the mess."

"Can't be done."

"Why not?"

"If you don't at once marry those ladies, you'll be put in the boat."

"I don't know which is the worst prospect," Mr. Mole said. "Confound the natives! Confound everything."

He began to tear his hair, and danced about like a madman.

When he stopped with a handful of hair in each hand, Jack said—

"That's lively, sir. Can't you favour us again?"

"He's as good as a dancing dervish," cried Harvey.

"Jack, dear Jack," said Mr. Mole, "you always were my friend, and a generous fellow; tell me you're only chaffing."

"I'm not indeed."

"Then I'm a lost man. Two wives! Oh, Lord! oh, Lord!"

"In a month's time you'll be entitled to take a third."

"A third!" cried the wretched Mole. "Tell me, Harkaway—tell me, if you love me, if there are any lunatic asylums in this beastly country?"

"Not that I know of."

"If not, I shall wander about the island a raving maniac. Oh, Isaac Mole, why were you ever born? Wretched man, what have you done to deserve such a fate?"

Monday, who had been down to the council-room again, now came back.

"The council has broke up," he said. "They all gone to bring Alfura and Ambonia here."

"Here! Are the furies coming here?" asked Mr. Mole.

"They not long first."

"But they can't take me until the ceremony is performed."

"We no ceremony. They say they have you, and the council decide. Then it all over. No ceremony, sare. They come take you home."

"Now? Do you mean this instant."

"In one, two short minute," replied Monday.

Mr. Mole began to dance again.

"This how it done Mist' Mole," continued Monday. "They bring p'raps ten women. All stand in a row. You look at them. One by one they come to you and you shake your head to all but Alfura and Ambonia, to whom you kneel. That all the ceremony."

"Never! I'll die first," replied Mr. Mole.

"They put you in boat else," said Monday, grinning.

"Dick, give him some whisky," said Jack.

Harvey poured some brandy into half a cocoanut shell, and Mole quaffed it eagerly.

"You're a gone coon, sir. Better make the best of it," he observed.

Mr. Mole shook his fist in Monday's face, saying—

"You confounded black lump of ugliness, you have done this for me! But I'll have your life!"

Harvey forced him into a seat.

"Let me get at him! I'll do him an injury! I'll have his——'

"Life," he was about to say, when Harvey gravely put in "head," which made Jack burst out laughing.

"Harvey," said Mr. Mole, in a faint tone, "you are low and vulgar. You are raised but little above these poor, benighted savages in the social scale."

"I wouldn't bullyrag them if I were you," replied Harvey. "Remember you are going to marry a couple of the poor benighteds."

"Come, sir, don't give way. I'm sure Alfura's got beautiful, shiny skin," said Jack.

"And Ambonia's hair is curly and oily," exclaimed Harvey.

"Better not say much," remarked Monday. "They beat you, sare; they scratch, they kick."

"Well, it's only for life, that's one comfort; and I shan't live long under the infliction," answered Mr. Mole, with a moan.

As he spoke, a loud noise was heard in the street.

The procession was approaching.

First came the band, which consisted of a score of men carrying gongs.

The gongs increased regularly in size from one of five or six inches to one of a foot or fifteen inches in diameter.

Each had a round knob or boss in the middle, which was struck with a small stick.

When made to reverberate in this manner, their music was very agreeable.

It resembled closely that made by small bells.

This instrument was called the bonang.

After the bonangs came the chiefs of the town.

Behind these were the nine virgins, Ambonia and Alfura being in the centre.

The rear was brought up by a guard of soldiers, and behind these again came the rabble of the town of Tompano, who, like crowds all over the world, had collected to witness what they could of the unusual ceremony.

CHAPTER XL.

TAKING HIM HOME.

WHEN Harvey heard the bonangs, he exclaimed—

"Chingarings and chopsticks! hongs and gongs! That's your sort! Go it, ye cripples! Have some more whisky, sir!"

Mr. Mole began to recover his composure a little.

"I think I will even follow your advice," he answered, "if only to nerve myself for the dreadful ordeal. I want a little something."

"Nothing like a drop of whisky for a nerver," replied Jack.

"That's right, Mist' Mole. Show um pluck, sar," chimed in Monday.

"Very well, my black friend," replied Mr. Mole. "I owe you one—yes, sir, I owe you one—and we'll square accounts some day.

"Keep up your pecker. Let them see what stuff you're made of. Don't funk, sir."

"I hope an Englishman never shows the white feather, Harkaway. Nor will I. No, not even under the most trying circumstances."

"Good again," cried Harvey, who was in an ecstasy of delight at the anticipated fun.

"I will bear myself bravely, like one advancing to the sacrifice. I have before my eyes the gladiators of ancient Rome."

"Who were they, sir!"

"Have you so soon forgotten the lessons of your early youth, Harkaway? I cry shame upon you."

"Set of coves who fought in the arena," observed Harvey.

"You are right," continued Mr. Mole. "But I object to the word 'coves.' However, let it pass. They had their 'Ave Cæsar,' or 'Hail Cæsar!' and they added '*Morituri te salutamus*,' which, being translated, means 'Being about to die, we salute you.' My fate is worse than death; but I will be brave."

"I have remarked, sir," said Harvey "that these Limbi ladies have a peculiar scent or odour of their own."

"Smell—odour. Don't be delicate, Harvey. Call it a smell, which is highly suggestive of polecats."

"All right, sir; anything to please you."

"However agreeable it may be to native noses, my English nasal organ revolts at it. They are rank, Harvey, very rank; and all the perfumes in Rimmel's shop would not convince me to the contrary."

"You'll like it, sir, when you're used to it," exclaimed Jack.

Mr. Mole darted a ferocious look at him.

The noise of the bonangs increased, and the hoarse shouts of the multitude grew nearer.

Again the wretched man applied himself to the whisky bottle.

"Go it, sir; nip away," exclaimed Harvey, singing—

"Whisky killed my poor dad;
Whisky drove my mother mad.
    Whisky, whisky,
Whisky for my Johnny!"

Fortified with a sort of Dutch courage, Mr. Mole awaited the coming of the procession, with the resignation of a lamb going to the slaughter.

"How do you find yourself now, sir?" asked Jack.

"Agonized, my young friend."

"Pity the sorrows of poor old Mole," said Harvey.

Mr. Mole was about to reply when the band halted outside, and ceasing playing, allowed the members of the deputation to enter.

First came the chiefs of the council chamber, and those were closely followed by the nine virgins.

"JACK DREW HIM FORWARD WITH A HUG LIKE THAT OF A BEAR."

The soldiers kept guard at the door.

Ranging themselves in a row, the young ladies cast down their eyes and prepared themselves for the ceremony.

The king, addressing Monday, exclaimed—

"Matabella, does the Tuan Biza of the white men know what is required of him by our customs?"

"He does, O king, live for ever," answered Monday.

"Is he aware of the high honour the alliance will confer upon him?"

"He is; and feels deeply gratified, O king; may thy victories increase," replied Monday.

"Let the rites commence."

"At once, O king. May you always be victorious in war," said Monday.

He then filled a calabash with whisky, of which spirit the Limbians had learnt to be very fond, and handed it round to the company.

All partook of it but the women.

"Now, then, sir," said Jack to Mr. Mole, "go in and win. All eyes are upon you."

"Faint heart never won fair lady," exclaimed Harvey. "Keep up the honour of old England."

The nine virgins stood apart, and Mr. Mole staggered rather than walked towards them.

Deep groans broke from him.

The perspiration stood in beads upon his forehead.

At a signal from Monday, the band again struck up a quick, jig-like sort of tune.

The nine virgins looked up.

First one left the rank, and walking past Mr. Mole, he shook his head at her, and she took up a position at the other end of the row.

The second did the same with a like result.

The third was Alfura.

As soon as Mr. Mole saw Alfura, he sank gracefully on one knee before her.

This was the signal of acceptance.

She took a place on his left side.

A loud shout of applause from the assembled spectators rent the air, which was taken up by the mob outside.

Number four now passed Mr. Mole, and was rejected.

The fifth shared a similar fate.

So did six, seven, and eight.

Ambonia was the ninth and before her Mr. Mole bowed as before.

Again the shouts arose as she placed herself on his right side.

Each wife seized an arm, and held him in a tight grip, as if afraid that he was going to run away from them.

The calabash was refilled, and the health of the bridegroom drunk heartily.

"Long live the Tuan Biza of the whites!" exclaimed the king, "and may his children people the land."

The chiefs now filed out of the room, and the seven virgins, surrounding Mr. Mole and his wives, followed them.

He was dragged from the apartment, and the procession, led by the band, proceeded down the principal street of Tompano, at the end of which was the house of Alfura and Ambonia.

Mole cast an appealing glance at Jack who was looking out of a window.

"Never say die, sir," cried Jack.

"They'll comb your hair for you, sir," exclaimed Harvey.

A curse not loud but deep burst from the unhappy man, who was soon lost to sight by a bend in the street.

The ceremony was over.

Mr. Mole was a married man, very much married indeed, and his wives were taking him home to the nuptial board.

It was not until two days had passed that the boys beheld their old friend and instructor.

On the morning of the third day, Mr. Mole paid them a visit.

He looked wistfully around him as he entered, and seemed afraid of being followed.

"Hullo, sir!" exclaimed Jack. "How goes it with you?"

"Badly, my dear boy, very badly," replied Mr. Mole."

"How's that? We call you the Great Pasha, the Grand Turk."

"Brigham Young is nearer the mark," said Harvey. "Mole's a Mormonite."

"Bring 'em young, you should say," returned Mr. Mole. "Tempers grow with age, and Ambonia's a perfect fiend. It's too late in life now to correct either of them."

"What's happened, sir? We thought you'd have looked us up before now?"

"So I should have done, but I've been locked in, bolted in, barred, and had the liberty of the subject painfully infringed."

"Bottled up, eh, sir? That's nothing extraordinary in married life, is it?" replied Jack.

"I don't know. It's all new to me."

"You ought to be an authority in these matters. Perhaps it's a custom of the country."

"When you're in Turkey, you must do as the Turkeys do," remarked Harvey.

"Oh, the life I've led!" continued Mr. Mole, with a sigh. "Alfura's not so bad but Ambonia is an incarnate fiend. She has boxed my ears, and has threatened me with a bamboo cane."

"So you have come out on the loose, sir?"

"I escaped through the window, and, thinking you would comfort me with some spirituous liquor, I have sought you,"

"It's very wrong to encourage a married man in staying away from his home; but for the sake of old times, you shall have what you like," said Jack, gravely.

"Spoken like yourself, Harkaway. Whisky, if you please, and plenty of it."

Monday supplied his wants, coming in as Harvey clapped his hands, as a signal for him to appear.

He could not help laughing at Mr. Mole, but a sign from Jack caused him to withdraw.

"It's very hard to be jeered and gibed at by a miserable savage like that," observed Mole, "and I think you ought not to encourage him, Harkaway."

"What did he do, sir?" asked Jack.

"Never mind, he is gone; and the memory of his offence shall go with him."

"Have you put your marriage in the paper, sir?" asked Harvey, innocently.

"How could I do so when there are no journals in the island, and the natives are unable to read?"

"Oh, I forgot that."

"I think, sir," Jack remarked, "you might have been content with one wife at a time. It is bad form to have two."

"You know as well as I, Harkaway, that I had no voice in the matter."

"You must have liked the girls in your heart, sir."

"Harkaway," said Mr. Mole, very gravely, "did you ever see a snake?"

"I'm sorry to say I have seen a good many since I have been in this part of the world," replied Jack.

"Did you ever take a fancy to one?"

"I've admired them at a distance, but I can't say I ever thought of cuddling one up in my arms."

"Then don't ask me if I like the Limbi women. Let us talk of something else. I am degraded in my own eyes. Harvey, you keep that bottle too much on your own side. I am afraid you have taken to drinking lately."

"I, sir!" cried Harvey. "No, sir. A sailor always likes his allowance. I don't go beyond it."

Mr. Mole helped himself, and his temper improved.

CHAPTER XLI.

STARTLING NEWS.

"HAVE you heard the news, sir?" asked Jack, after a pause.

"News," repeated Mr. Mole. "I was not aware that in this wretched country they had anything of the sort."

"You ought to take an interest in anything that is moving, because you have a stake in the country."

"If it will gratify you, Harkaway, I will say that I have a feeling of intense interest in anything that may befall this unhappy land," continued Mr. Mole, adding, "Harvey, oblige me by letting the bottle alone. I am quite capable of taking care of it."

"Right, sir," replied Harvey.

"There's going to be a war," continued Jack.

"Going to be. There always is a war isn't there? The beasts are always fighting."

"He's thinking of his wives," said Harvey.

"Harvey," exclaimed Mr. Mole, in a

tone of rebuke, "it is unkind of you to remind me of my misery—let the bottle alone, if you please."

Repeated application to the bottle of whisky made Mr. Mole's eyes swim in his head.

"A war," he said to himself. "What do I care for a dozen wars?"

"We are to start to invade Pisang this day week, sir, and you shall have an independent command," said Jack.

"An independent humbug," answered Mr. Mole.

"What, sir?"

"Humbug, I said," repeated Mr. Mole, who, in spite of his growing inebriety, grew alarmed at the prospect of war. "I said humbug, and I'll stick to it. What have I got to do with war?"

"We are going to fight Hunston."

"Fight him and welcome. Kill him if you like. It is fitting and proper for you to do so. You and Harvey are young. I am—ahem!—I am a married man, settled down, you know, Harkaway, and it would not be right to take me away from my wife."

"Wives, sir."

"I stand corrected," continued Mr. Mole, with a bland smile. "Go, by all means, Harkaway, and fight those despicable Pisangs. I will stop at home and organise the militia, or whatever the reserve forces my be."

"Won't you come with us?"

"No. My place is here in Tompano. I am a family man, Harkaway. No fighting for me, unless it is for hearths and home; then Isaac Mole will be to the fore, and woe to the foe."

"That's a rhyme, sir. You should wish——" said Harvey.

"I do wish. I wish most devoutedly that—that there will be an earthquake which will swallow up Ambonia," replied Mole.

"Then you don't mind Alfura?"

"She's ugly, but she's not vicious," said Mr. Mole. "I can put up with Alfura; that is to say, for a time."

"Until you can get to your tea-garden in China, sir?" hazarded Jack.

"Precisely, my dear boy."

"You can sing, sir, 'Happy could I be with either, were, t'other dear charmer away," said Harvey.

"With your usual impulsiveness, you have jumped to a wrong conclusion, Harvey," answered Mr. Mole. "I could

not be happy with either, and my only time of peace is when they are fighting amongst themselves."

"Fighting!"

"Yes, like bull-logs. When they are not throwing stones and vegetable refuse at me, they are engaged in the mild amusement of tearing each other's cheeks, which is a pleasing pastime for a husband to stand and look on at."

"Sorry for you, sir. Knock 'em down and jump on 'em," said Harvey.

"You are a brute," replied Mr. Mole. "A little while ago you exhorted me to keep up the honour of my country, and behave like an Englishman."

"Dick, shut up," said Jack.

"No," Mr. Mole went on, "I will not reduce myself to the level of a Whitechapel costermonger. I will not even floor them. What though Alfura punches me on the nose, and Ambonia hurls a dead cat in my eye."

"That's nothing, sir," exclaimed Jack.

"Nothing? Isn't it? Did you ever have a dead cat settle on your left eye?" cried Mr. Mole, sharply.

"No, sir, and don't want to. But let me tell you the news. It's rather startling."

"What is it, Harkaway?" said Mr. Mole, handling the bottle with an unsteady hand.

"Excuse me a minute, and then I'll tell you," replied Jack, as Harvey came over and whispered to him. "Make Mole tight, and carry him home to his wives."

Jack nodded, and went on—

"Help yourself, sir. Don't be afraid of it. There's more where that came from."

"I wish you'd come to your news," said Mr. Mole, snappishly.

"We are going to invade Pisang at once. Harvey and I take the lead. Our fleet is ready; our soldiers number four hundred, and it's either to be victory or Westminster Abbey."

"You told me that before, and I persist in my resolve to patrol the town. I will be governor of Tompano," answered Mr. Mole.

"I thought you imagined I was joking, sir, and did not believe what I said," Jack rejoined.

Mr. Mole got up, and staggered towards the door.

"Is your floor straight?" he asked.

"Lie down and try sir."

Mr. Mole sat down with an imbecile chuckle, and said—

"Tell Ambonia I'm very jolly. Say we're jol' good f'lows, ev'ry one. I don't care, Ambonia. I'll let 'bonia know if she givesh me any of her nonshensh."

"Here's your health, sir, and death to Hunston and the Pisangs. You'll drink that toast, won't you?" said Harvey.

He tendered him a glass, which Mole tossed off.

It was the finishing stroke, for he rolled backwards, laughing heartily, as if it was a good joke."

"He's a settled member," exclaimed Harvey.

"Collar his legs, Dick; I'll take his nut, and we'll cart him off home."

"I pity him when Ambonia gets her fingers nicely twisted in his hair," replied Harvey.

They took him up, and were not long in conveying him into the presence of his wives.

The ladies had wondered what had become of their husband, and had been indulging in a little quarrel on their own account.

Various articles of domestic use lay about the room in some confusion.

There were all the signs of a free fight.

When Mr. Mole was deposited on the floor, the wives guessed what had brought him into that state.

Each abused him in the choicest and most flowery terms which their language allowed them to employ.

The boys turned round and went away leaving them at it, lest they might fall in for their share.

"Ambonia's a caution," said Harvey. "Didn't she slip in a good un?"

Jack made no answer.

"You might have the civility to answer me when I speak to you," continued Harvey.

"Excuse me, Dick. I was thinking of something else. Shall we find the king in, do you think, if we call at the palace?" replied Jack.

"Sure to, I should fancy."

"Step up with me, will you? We must arrange all the details of our invasion, and see how the guns are to be given out."

"Every man in Limbi wants a gun, and two-thirds of them would only shoot their nearest neighbours or pot themselves."

"I think I shall give two guns to every five-and-twenty men, and select the best shots."

Harvey agreed with him, and talking of military matters they strolled along.

Suddenly an old woman fantastically dressed, stepped in front of the boys.

"Who's this?" said Jack.

"Hush!" said Harvey. "Don't anger her."

"Why not?"

"It's Nuratella," said Harvey, under his breath.

"Who is she?" returned Jack, as much in the dark as ever.

"Nuratella is a sort of sorceress, witch, prophetess—what you like. All I know is that the people here think a lot of her," replied Harvey.

Nuratella raised her arms, as if commanding silence.

She did not understand the English they were speaking, but she saw from their faces that they knew who she was, and that her appearance had produced some impression upon them.

CHAPTER XLII.

NURATELLA, THE WITCH.'

WE have already hinted that all the inhabitants of the numerous islands in the East Indian Archipelago were strong believers in witchcraft.

Nuratella was regarded as a prophetess of the highest order.

She professed to have the power of divining future events, and had been known to still the wind when raging at its highest fury.

Perhaps her knowledge of the weather was superior to that of those around her, and she did not attempt the hazardous task of commanding the storm until she saw some indication of a cessation of the tempest.

At all events she imposed upon the ignorant beings amongst whom her lot was cast.

Her influence over them was remarkable.

Strange, weird, thrilling stories were told about her.

It was said that in her youth she had met with, and dared to love, an illustrious chief of the Pisangs.

For this offence she was condemned to death by her own countrymen.

It was treason of the worst sort for a woman of Limbi to look favourably upon a Pisang warrior.

On a man, in fact, whose hands were red with the blood of her kindred.

She was led forth to die.

At the moment when the executioner had uplifted the fatal sword, a volume of light shot out from the sky.

The lightning, for such it was, struck the executioner, and killed him on the spot.

This was considered as an interposition of Providence on her behalf.

She had called down fire from heaven.

The lurid flame was supposed to be of her own conjuring, and she was liberated in all haste.

Ever afterwards she lived a secluded and wild life, but her influence as a witch was established.

All feared her, if none loved her.

shrewdest among the Limbians that she was still in correspondence with the Pisangs.

That she could not forget her early love.

Sometimes the Pisangs obtained information of the movements of the people of Limbi in a mysterious manner.

Nuratella was known to set sail in a frail canoe, and be absent for several days.

Who so likely as she to visit Pisang, and inform the chiefs there of the plans of their enemies?

She was allowed to attend the councils of her own people, and her advice was much valued.

Yet no one liked to denounce her, nor, had they done so, was there any proof of her guilt.

The boys had often heard of her strange and mysterious power.

They did not believe in her magical gifts, but they did not at the same time think it advisable to slight or offend her.

Far better would it have been for Jack if he had never listened to her.

"Well, mother, what do you want?" exclaimed Jack, addressing Nuratella in her own language.

"Follow me, and you shall quickly learn," she replied.

"Shall I come?" asked Harvey.

"Perhaps I had better ask the old girl," said Jack.

He put the question to Nuratella.

"No," she answered, decisively. "It is you I want. Let your friend return to his home."

"She says no," said Jack, addressing Harvey.

"So I heard. I suppose the old cat means you no harm," replied Harvey. "They don't speak too well of her, though they all funk her."

"She won't hurt me. What does it matter if she is a witch, and rides on broomsticks? I don't think she'd find me a light weight if I ride behind."

"All right; you know best. Good-

Harvey shook his head as if he did not half like his friend to go away with Nuratella.

But Jack was not to be interfered with when he had made up his mind.

There were few things that frightened him, and as he said to himself, he was not going to be afraid of an old woman.

Nuratella led the way into the country, and walked for about a mile, keeping ahead of Jack, to whom she did not address a word.

Occasionally she turned her head to see if he was following her.

The road, was simply a rough path, a few large stones having been removed.

The ragged coral rock everywhere projected so completely through the thin soil that it was a wonder to Jack how his conductor could travel barefoot with such apparent ease.

They soon came to a circular hut, enclosed by a low stone wall.

It was the most wretched abode for a human being that could possibly be imagined.

The walls, instead of being made of boards or flattened bamboos, as in the town of Tompano, were composed of small sticks, about three feet high, driven into the ground.

These supported a conical roof, thatched with palm leaves.

An ugly-looking pig, with long bristles on his back, was raking about this detestable hovel.

Near the hut was a burial place.

A low wall enclosed a small angular plot that was filled with earth.

This contained one or more graves, each of which had for its foot and head stones small, square, pyramidal blocks of wood, with the apex fixed in the ground.

A pack of wolf-like dogs saluted Jack with a fierce yelping and barking as he approached the miserable dwelling.

A word from Nuratella calmed them.

Sitting down upon a rude block of stone outside her dwelling, she motioned Jack to stand before her, which he did.

Perhaps if she had been talking to any of her countrymen, she would have had recourse to some mystic rites.

She rightly judged, however, that on one of Jack's education and sense such conduct would not make much impression.

Nevertheless there was something weird if not awful about the hag.

"They say she was good-looking once," thought Jack; "if so, it must have been a precious long while ago, and no mistake."

"Young man from the great kingdom over the sea, where the lightning owns the power of your wise men, and machines carry you faster than the bird can fly, listen to the words of Nuratella, the scorceress of Limbi," she exclaimed.

The speech showed that she had enjoyed some intercourse with white men, and had gained an insight into their civilisation.

But when, where, or how it was difficult to say.

"At your service, mother," answered Jack. "Ease her! stop her! go ahead!" he added in English, as he was unable to put the latter into what he called "understandable" Limbian.

"You are going to place yourself at the head of my people and invade Pisang," she continued.

"It didn't require a witch to tell me that, when all the island knows it," Jack answered.

"And the Pisangs, too. They are prepared for your coming."

"Are they?" Jack replied. "Have you been kind enough to give them information?"

Nuratella raised her arm threateningly.

"What have I to do with the enemies of my country?" she exclaimed. "To me it is given to pierce the future and to know what has happened in the past, as well as what is taking place in the present."

"Do you mean to sit there calmly, old girl," said Jack, "and tell me that you can prophesy?"

"Put me to the test," she answered. "Ask me anything you like, and as I reply to you, so will I be judged."

Jack thought a moment.

"I'll ask her about Emily," he thought.

Nuratella regarded him with her wild-looking eyes, which seemed to possess the fire of insanity, tempered at times by gleams of reason.

"Can you tell me if there is a white captive in Pisang?" he said.

"There are two," she replied.

"Two! Men or women?"

"One a man, the other a fair-haired girl, barely seventeen."

"Perhaps you've been there and seen them," cried Jack, who guessed at once that she referred to Mr. Scratchley and his daughter Emily.

Again Nuratella threatened him with her upraised arm.

"Boy," she said, "to whom do you speak? Many leagues divide Limbi from Pisang."

"But you've got a boat of your own."

"I tell you that I know them not. The Pisangs and I never meet."

"Well," said Jack, impatiently; "cut along. What have you brought me here for?"

There was a certain bluntness about Jack which would not be checked by any amount of murmuring.

Nuratella had thought to impress, but she found that she had signally failed.

"You love this fair-haired girl," she exclaimed.

"You're not far out there," replied Jack.

"And she loves you."

"That's stale news," replied Jack imperturabably, "though how you got to know it is a puzzler."

"You must meet again. Emily—that is your darling's name— is in peril," continued Nuratella.

"Of what nature?"

"The persecution of a wicked and bad man."

"Hunston."

The name escaped Jack involuntarily.

"That is he,' continued Nuratella. "Hunston wishes to make Emily his wife. She, mindful of you, will not consent."

"Of course not."

"But Hunston is the chief adviser of the Pisangs," Nuratella proceeded. "He is their great chief. What he orders, they do."

"I feared this," said Jack, almost tearfully. "I have been wrong to delay so long. We should have attacked the Pisang brutes long ago, but I'll give them a lesson."

His tone was bitter, and his manner almost ferocious.

"Will you not try to save your Emily?" asked the witch, watching his growing anger with a smile.

"What's the use of asking such a stupid question?" he replied sharply.

"Would you like to see her?"

"When?" he cried.

"At once. This very night. My power will suffice to bring her here."

"Here? On this island?"

"Yes, here; at this very spot. I will ask the spirits with whom I deal to transport her hither."

"Spirits be blowed!" Jack said in English. Adding immediately afterwards, "I don't care how you do it, so long as you get Emily."

"It shall be done. I swear it to you. I, Nuratella, say that you shall meet the girl with the flaxen hair here, when the darkness falls upon the earth."

"I will reward you for it," said Jack.

"No reward does Nuratella want. You will lead their victorious army against the Pisangs, and Limbi will enjoy the blessings of peace."

"I'll do my best for it," Jack answered.

"Come hither at sundown, and you shall clasp your Emily in your arms."

"If you can do this, I shall say you are a very clever old women, and our fortune-tellers are not a patch upon you, but——"

He hesitated.

She interrogated him with her eyes.

"If you trifle with me," he continued, regarding her with a savage look, "I will shoot you with as little compunction as I would knock that bird off his perch.

As he spoke, he raised his gun and fired at a bright-plumaged bird in a thicket.

The creature fell dead almost at his feet.

Nuratella saw that she had made an impression upon her listener by the mention of Emily's name.

She followed up her advantage.

"If I, by my arts, contrive that you shall see Emily," she continued, "you must promise me one thing."

"What is it?" asked Jack.

"Do not mention the circumstance to anyone."

"I generally tell my friend Harvey everything," he exclaimed hesitatingly.

"This time you must not do so."

"I should like him to come with me."

"No, no!" said the witch imperiously. "You will break the charm, if you do not come unattended."

"What's the odds?" Jack replied.

"You must trust me. Are you afraid of a poor old woman?" said Nuratella, with a scornful smile.

"I'm afraid of nothing and nobody, if it comes to that. You shall have your way. I'll come alone."

"And you will keep your purpose a secret?"

"I will."

"Can I depend on you?" she asked

"I am not in the habit of breaking my word," replied Jack. "If I say a thing, I mean it; so good-bye, mother, for the present. I shall be here at dark,"

"For your own sake and that of Emily, mind you do not fail," she answered, impressively.

Jack turned on his heel, and walked back to the town of Tompano.

His mind was filled with comflicting emotions.

At one moment he was delighted with the expectation of meeting Emily, whom he had believed to be on one of the islands ever since he read the message from the sea; and the next he feared treachery.

Though what shape this danger would take he could not say.

"It was a great fact to have ascertained that Emily had really been wrecked, and that he was near her.

His heart warmed towards the little playfellow of his youth.

With the romantic passion of a young man he loved her dearly.

His blood boiled when he thought that she was in the power of Hunston and his associates.

To liberate her he would sacrifice everything.

CHAPTER XLIII.

MRS. MOLE NUMBER TWO.

JACK was very thoughtful when he reached his house in Tompano.

His native servant told him that Harvey had gone to Mr. Mole's habitation.

Having nothing better to do, he strolled down in that direction.

When he neared the house, he heard the sound of crockery being smashed.

An earthenware pan flew through the window near his head.

"That's a close shave," he muttered. "I suppose Ambonia's showing her nasty temper."

Harvey met him at the door.

"Look out Jack," he said; "Mrs. Mole Number Two is going it in fine style."

"What's the row?" asked Jack.

"Ambonia slipped into Alfura, who has gone to an aunt's somewhere near here, and now Mole's catching it hot."

Jack stepped inside.

Every article of furniture in the room was upset, and Mr. Mole was standing in a corner, in vain striving to stem the storm.

A bucket of water had been thrown over him, which had brought him to his senses, and the effect of the spirit he had drunk was going off.

Ambonia, looking like a fury, held a handful of her husband's hair in her hand, and occasionally amused herself by throwing about in various directions anything she could lay her hands on.

"My dear sir," said Jack, "what is the meaning of this scene! Is Mrs. Mole mad?"

"You may well ask that question, Harkaway," replied Mr. Mole. "I was a little overcome when you brought me home. Alfura took my part, and she has been obliged to fly the house. Mrs. Mole *secundus*, as we used to say at school, is behaving very strangely, but now there is not much more left to break, she will probably calm down soon."

Ambonia was doing a war dance, and she chattered all the time like a monkey in her native language.

Presently the leg of a chair caught Jack on the side of the head.

"Draw it mild," he observed, rubbing the injured part.

"Don't stand it, Harkaway. "Resent it," cried Mr. Mole. "I wouldn't if I were you."

"It's for you, sir," replied Jack, "to keep order in your own household."

"I can't do it. It's beyond me."

"Shall I put her in the water butt?" asked Jack.

"We haven't got one. That article of civilization is *minus* in this establishment——"

Mr. Mole would have said more, but a bunch of ripe cocoa nuts hit him on the nose, and he held the injured organ with both hands while he capered about with the pain.

"That's a flop—if you like," said Harvey grinning.

"Never laugh at a fellow-creature in distress, Harvey," exclaimed Mr. Mole. "I wish you had my nose. Oh! my nose, my poor ill-used nose!"

Ambonia advanced with a long light bamboo, and hit her angry spouse on the head with it.

"One for his nob," remarked Harvey.

Jack advanced, thinking Mr. Mole would be seriously injured, and caught Ambonia in his arms.

He drew here to the window and gave her a kiss.

"Now, my little beauty," said Jack, holding her tightly, "what are you going to do?"

"I shall do nothing. I am calm now," Ambonia replied. "If he would only treat me with kindness, I should not behave like that. He likes Alfura best, and—and——"

"And you're jealous, eh?"

She nodded her head while she lay passively in Jack's arms.

"Will you promise me not to kick up any more row?" asked Jack.

"It is over now," she sighed.

"Bravo!" cried Harvey. "The way to manage a woman all the world over is to be kind to her."

Mr. Mole emerged from his corner.

He looked very grave.

"Harkaway," he exclaimed, "what are you doing with my wife?"

"Doing, sir?"

"Yes; you have her in your arms."

"You may take her, sir. I am not ambitious of the honour," replied Jack.

Mr. Mole ventured to embrace his spouse, but she no sooner felt him touch her than she began to scream and kick.

He laid her down on the floor, and the screaming and kicking continued.

She was in a fit of violent hysterics.

"Oh, Lord! what shall I do?" cried Mr. Mole.

He stood with his hands upraised, the picture of despair.

Ambonia went on with her hysterical symptoms.

"Holler, boys!" said Harvey; "here's another guy!"

"A pair of 'em," remarked Jack, dryly.

"Ambonia's in high strikes," continued Harvey, "and Mr. Mole's——

"Silence, Harvey," interrupted Mr. Mole. "When you speak of my wife, mention her as Mrs. Mole. To me only is she Ambonia."

"All right, sir. Sit down, and take it easy for a spell," replied Harvey. "She'll be a good ten minutes before she comes round, and she'll have worn herself out then and want to go to bed."

"It's a mercy," said Mr. Mole, "for which I am devoutly thankful. Make fast the window, Harvey. I will fasten the door, and we'll adjourn to another apartment. Be sure you fasten the window. I should not like Mrs. Mole to be interrupted.

"No fear, sir; only isn't it rather heartless, not to say brutal, to leave her like this?"

"Harvey," replied Mr. Mole, "I have no hesitation in saying that you're a humbug."

"Say it again, sir," answered Harvey. "We're old friends, and I shan't punch your head."

They left Ambonia in her hysterical fit, and locked the room up.

On a table in another apartment were some very fine shell fish, resembling enormously large oysters.

They had just been brought up from the sea-shore, and laid open in their shells for Ambonia's refreshment.

"Ah! oysters! Big ones, though," remarked Mr. Mole. "Try one, Harkaway."

Jack looked at the shell fish and took one up.

It was about fifty times the size of one English oyster, and he did not know how to get it into his mouth.

"How am I to do it, sir?" he asked.

"Bolt it," suggested Harvey.

Jack made an effort, and the oyster disappeared.

He gasped for breath, and Harvey patted him on the back with a large board.

"How do you feel?"

"Very thankful it's down; and even now I can't help thinking I've swallowed a small baby," answered Jack.

Harvey laughed, and Jack continued, "Ta, ta, sir; I must toddle."

"Don't leave me, Harkaway. Why go so soon?" said Mr. Mole.

"Urgent private affairs, sir."

"You have rendered me a service. You have soothed the savage breast, Harkaway, and it is the only gleam of sunshine I have yet had in my married life."

"Sorry I can't stay, sir," answered Jack. "You must knock under."

"There she is again," cried Harvey.

As he spoke a furious yelling was heard, and a desperate kicking at the door of the room in which Ambonia was shut.

"I'll leave you to it, sir," exclaimed Jack, with a laugh.

In vain Mr. Mole tried to stop him.

Taking Harvey's arm, he left the house, and the happy couple within it.

CHAPTER XLIV.

JACK WON'T TAKE ADVICE.

As Jack and Harvey proceeded towards their own house in Tompano, the latter could not fail to perceive that his friend was full of thought and care.

"Has anything happened?" he asked.

"No," replied Jack, rather more sharply than Harvey liked. "What should happen?"

"You need not snap me up like that. I only asked kindly, but I forgot for the moment that you went away with that old witch hag, and I daresay that has upset your royal highness."

"Suppose it has, what then?"

"You are more of an ass than I took you to be. She is a rank impostor, and is said to be friendly to the Pisangs. Has she advised you not to undertake the invasion, warning you that you would be beaten."

Jack made no answer.

"Oh! if you have lost your tongue, and don't like to speak, please yourself," said Harvey. "I'll talk to Monday."

"Don't be annoyed, Dick," exclaimed Jack, at last. "I can't tell you what passed between Nuratella and myself."

"Why not?"

"Because I promised I wouldn't."

"That is a pity. Two heads are better than one," said Harvey; "and I might have been able to advise you. Not that I want to know anything out of idle curiosity."

"No; you never did, Dick," said Jack with a smile.

"That's what I call a nasty snack," replied Harvey.

"Well, you know you were a nice cup of tea at Crawcour's, Dick; and if you could get to the far end of anything, you always did."

"You mean to say that I was a regular old washerwoman. That's not kind, Jack; and I did not expect it from you. If we are to be really friends, there ought to be perfect confidence between us."

"So there should be; and so there shall be. Only wait for to-night," rejoined Jack. "I'll tell you all then."

He shook Harvey cordially by the hand, and the latter's wounded dignity got better.

"I don't think you meant to worry me," he said. "Still I wish you would take my advice."

"What is it?"

"Don't listen to anything that old hag says."

"Too late. I have made her a distinct promise," replied Jack.

"Are you going to meet her again?"

"Don't ask me any questions, Dick, there's a good fellow, because I can't answer them."

"Very well. I'll dry up," was Harvey's response.

When they reached the house, they found Monday, whose eager face denoted that he had important news to communicate.

"Oh! Mast' Jack," he exclaimed, "there have been um fight; um sea fight."

"Where?" asked Jack.

"Off the island. Two boats Pisangs meet one boat Limbians. They fight quite close here."

"Which licked?" questioned Harvey.

"Um Pisang lick, 'cos they more number; though we kill one, two, three, four."

He counted on his fingers as he spoke.

"Killed four, eh? And the others got off. What did they want cruising round our coast?" said Jack.

"There's mischief brewing," remarked Harvey.

"JACK GAVE THE WORD AND THERE WAS A REPORT OF FIREARMS."

"We'll double the guards round the city to-night," said Jack. "It won't do to be surprised."

"I don't like those fellows being so near us. It doesn't look healthy," observed Harvey.

"Nor I. It isn't rosy, and it is like their cheek to risk it."

"They kill three our men; others come back with news," Monday went on.

"Did they see Hunston with them?" asked Jack.

Monday nodded his head violently, as he always did when excited.

"Yes, they say white man chief—Tuan Biza white face with them," he answered.

Jack walked up and down the room impatiently.

"I don't half like it," he exclaimed, as if talking to himself. "There is something in all this."

After a time, feeling fatigued with the heat, he threw himself down upon a rude bed, telling Harvey that he should be obliged if he would rouse him at sunset.

He was soon asleep.

In a couple of hours the sun sank to rest, and Harvey touched him on the shoulder.

He jumped up, uttering the name "Emily."

"You're dreaming," said Harvey.

"I believe I was," replied Jack, rubbing his eyes. "I thought Emily was by my side."

"Are you going out?" asked Harvey, as he saw him put on his cap.

"Yes; I shan't be long. Don't funk about me."

"I can't help it. You're going to see that witch Nuratella. It's no use denying it."

"You're welcome to your own opinion, Dick," replied Jack.

"Well," answered Harvey, "God bless you, Jack. I wish you would take my advice, that's all, or——"

"What?"

"You might let me come with you, if there is any danger."

"But there isn't."

"I'm not so sure of that. Nuratella has been suspected before now of playing her own people false. The Pisangs have been seen off the island this very day. Hunston was with them; and, hang it all, if there is any danger, you might let me share it with you."

"You've got a good heart, Dick, and I am very grateful to you. However, don't fret on my account. I shall be all right," replied Jack.

Squeezing his friend's hand, he rushed out of the house, leaving Harvey gazing with pity after him.

He took the direction of the witch's dwelling, and was soon out of sight.

CHAPTER XLV.

THE MEETING.

NURATELLA was anxiously awaiting his appearance.

"Still sitting on the rugged stone, she did not seem to have changed her position since he left her.

"Well, mother," exclaimed Jack, "here I am, like Regulus returning to Carthage—though, as that is a little beyond your comprehension, I will say that I resemble the bad penny which is sure to turn up, whether it's wanted or no."

"Are you alone?" she inquired.

"Yes."

"You have no one within call?"

"Not a soul."

"Good!" exclaimed the old woman, over whose forbidden countenance stole an expression of satisfaction.

The shades of night had fallen with the rapidity peculiar to the tropics after sunset.

It was difficult to discern objects at a few yards distance.

Nuratella clapped her hands.

Once, twice, three times.

At the third signal a fairylike form stepped out of a thicket of trees to Jack's right, and though the light, airy European garments were torn and travel-stained, he knew that a countrywoman of his own was near.

How his heart throbbed at that moment.

"Emily," he ejaculated.

The form halted when close to him, and then as if obedient to an irresistible impulse, she threw herself into his arms.

"Oh, Jack," she exclaimed, "under what circumstances do we meet again?"

"They're not very lively, certainly," he said. "But I am so delighted at seeing you that hardships vanish, and I seem to be treading on enchanted ground."

"I have so much to tell you," she continued, "though I am afraid I ought not to waste precious time."

"Tell me, at least, how you came here."

"It was decided by the Pisang council that I should be given up to the Limbians, where a man named Hunston informed me that I should meet you."

"That is unlike Hunston, He's not usually so generous," said Jack, musingly.

"And it is unlike the treatment I have received all along from the Pisangs. My father is dying, I fear, from their ill-usuage."

"Mr. Scratchley?"

"Yes; and my poor mother went down in the wreck."

"Have you any reason to think there is a plot hatching against us?" asked Jack.

"Indeed, I fear so," returned Emily; "for we came over to Limbi, as they call this island, in two boats, full of armed men."

"And you encountered a hostile boat, which you drove off."

"We did."

"How were you conducted hither?" asked Jack.

"By Hunston, and one they called Tuan Biza, They brought me here, and left me with this old woman, who told me to remain in the thicket till she clapped her hands."

"What became of your guides?"

"They said good-bye, and left me. I cannot understand their generosity; it seems too good to be true. But had we not better fly at once?" said Emily.

"At once. We will talk at our ease. Take my arm, dear Emily. We shall soon be in Tompano. It is not far off. I know every inch of the way; and once amongst friends, we can enjoy our newly-found happiness."

Emily placed a trembling hand on Jack's arm, and without taking any further notice of Nuratella, who, by the way, had disappeared, they turned to make their escape.

Suddenly dark forms appeared behind them.

A voice exclaimed, "Not so fast my fine fellow. You and I have a score to settle."

Jack's heart leaped in his bosom.

"Betrayed, by Heaven!" he cried.

He faced the foe, but ere he had time to draw weapon in his defence, a heavy blow on the dead felled him to the ground where he fell insensible.

Emily uttered shriek upon shriek.

Her misery was complete when she saw Jack borne off by the Pisangs through the darkness.

It was for her sweet sake that he had ventured into this ambuscade.

The Pisangs, with serpentine cunning, had made her a decoy.

"Stop that noise!" exclaimed the harsh voice of Hunston, as he seized her brutally by the arm.

"Oh, do not kill him," she replied.

"Not yet. I'll make him feel his position and suffer a little first. Come along; you've done your work, and we must get back to Pisang."

Again Emily uttered piercing shrieks

"Hold that row, miss," exclaimed Hunston again, "or I shall have to hit you on the head as I did King Harkaway. Be quiet, for your own sake; you will neither do yourself nor your friend any good."

Emily remained silent, and was hurried along a narrow path which led to the coast.

"Did you think," continued Hunston, "that I was such a very innocent baby as to give you up to the only man I hate like poison?"

"I did not know what amount of villany you were capable of," she answered.

"You'll know in time. You'll find it all out when you're my wife."

"Heaven defend me from such a fate. I would die sooner!" she cried, horror-stricken.

"You'll have to do one or the other. Death or marriage. Take your choice when the time comes."

Emily shuddered.

"It was not a bad dodge of mine to

get Harkaway into our power," he went on with a loud laugh.

"It was mean and cowardly to use me as a means of entrapping him."

"All's fair in love and war. I knew he'd nibble at the hook if you were the bait at the end of it."

"What will be his fate?" she ventured to ask·

"Death? A cruel, horrible and lingering death, unless——"

"Unless?" she repeated under her breath, as her companion broke off abruptly.

"Unless you consent to be mine."

His fierce grey eyes seemed to pierce her soul in the darkness.

"Then he must die, and I will perish with him," she murmured.

As the words left her lips a feeling of faintness came over her, and she would have fallen had not Hunston caught her.

She lay like a log in his arms.

He carried her insensible form for the remainder of the distance.

The Pisangs were waiting for him.

Springing into the boat which was nearest to him, he gave the word and the sails were set.

One boat contained Harkaway, the other his beloved Emily.

They were both in the power of Hunton, from whose tender mercies they had as much gentleness to expect as the dove receives from the cruel hawk.

It was an infamous stratagem.

But at the same time it was a clever and important capture.

CHAPTER XLVI.

HARVEY GETS UNEASY.

THE hours glided by and nothing was seen of Jack.

Harvey began to grow uneasy, as did Monday.

"Something happen to Mast' Jack. What um be?" asked the black.

"I more than half suspect that treachery has been at work," replied Harvey.

"Where him go?"

"I am nearly sure that he went to see Nuratella."

"She bad woman, sare," said Monday. "We all much 'fraid Nuratella, because she um witch-prophetess."

"Wasn't she a friend of the Pisangs once?"

"Yes, one very great friend Tuan Biza, and now she go to their island in um boat."

"Do you know where she hangs out—where she lives, I mean?" asked Harvey.

"Yes, Monday him know."

"All right. Let's lie down till daybreak, and we'll go and look after him. Poor Jack! I shall never forgive myself if anything has befallen him. I ought to have followed with half a dozen rifles, whether he liked it or no."

In spite of Harvey's impatience, nothing could be done in the dark.

He slept little, and he was up as soon as the first rays of light streamed in through the mat-covered windows.

"Now, Mon, look alive!" he said.

"Alive him is, sare," replied Monday, yawning.

They ate a piece of rough bread and drank some water, then they were ready for the start.

It did not take them long to reach the witch's dwelling.

She was nowhere about, and they supposed had not yet arisen.

"What's this?" cried Harvey, casting his eyes on the ground.

The object that attracted his attention was a piece of paper, such as might be torn from the pocket-book of a European.

On it was something written in pencil.

"English, by Jove!" he said; "and in a lady's handwriting too."

He did not hesitate to read its contents, which ran thus:—

"I, Emily Scratchley, having fallen into the hands of the Pisangs, have been liberated by them to-day, and left in concealment in this thicket, until an old woman shall give me a signal that my old friend, Jack Harkaway, who I hear is on this island, comes to take me to the chief town of Limbi.

"Feeling doubtful about the good faith of the Pisangs, whom I have since my captivity found cruel and treacherous, I fear some villany is intended, and write these hurried lines in the hope that some friend may find them, in the event of any foul play taking place."

Harvey set his teeth tightly together.

"I see it all now, Monday," said he.

"What him all 'bout, sare ?" asked the black.

"Nuratella has helped the Pisangs to take Jack a prisoner."

"Mast' Jack taken ! That bad news. But we go after him and lib'rate him, or we kill and burn all Pisangs."

" Of course we will, but they may kill him before we get there."

"Look here, sare ! Mast' Harvey, come here, quick ! See 'um blood on the ground !" cried Monday, excited at the red-looking spots he saw.

Harvey came to his side, and regarded them mournfully.

"It's as clear as daylight," he observed. "Jack's been taken by surprise, and they've tapped his claret for him. Well, it can't be helped."

"Matabella go to King Lanindyer, and he make Nuratella say all she know," said Monday. "No one like her. All glad her die."

"I'd roast her over a slow fire. Does she live in that kennel?"

He pointed to the hovel as he spoke.

"That where she lives."

"Have her out, Monday. We'll take her back with us to the town, lest she gives us the slip, and goes to join her precious friends the Pisangs."

Monday hung back.

He could not forget the superstitions of his youth, and the prejudices of his nation.

"What are you afraid of ?" asked Harvey, contemptuously.

" She put some charm on me. Nuratella very great witch. She make and un-make storms. She hold the lightening in her hand," replied Monday trembling.

"Go on, you great cake !" said Harvey. "I'll dig her out, witch or no witch, or I'll burn her den about her ears."

Putting his shoulder against one side of the hut, Harvey gave it a shove, which made it rock like a poplar in a storm.

"Come out, you old cat !" he said in the native language.

There was no answer.

Not being in a humour to be trifled with, Harvey gave the hovel another shove, and down it went in a heap.

Presently the form of Nuratella appeared from a thicket a few yards off, the same in which Emily had been concealed, and from whence she had watched the destruction of her house with rising wrath.

"Why do you come to my dwelling and scatter ruin around ?" she asked.

"I am quite ready to answer for what I have done to the Tuan Biza of this island and his chiefs assembled in council," replied Harvey.

"Do you not fear my power?" asked Nuratella, still more threateningly.

"No more than that," said Harvey, snapping his fingers.

" I could make the earth open and swallow you up. I could call down the lightning from the sky, and summon wild beasts from the forest, together with venomous serpents, to destroy your life."

"Go ahead, then. Let the music strike up and the show begin," exclaimed Harvey.

Nuratella glared at him with the savageness of a tiger.

"The fact is you are an imposter," continued Harvey. "I repeat that I am ready to answer for what I have done and mean to do, though I don't think you will get off so easily."

"Go, rash boy," she exclaimed. "I have no quarrel with you."

"Oh, it's like that, is it !" Harvey said, derisively. "You find that you can't frighten me, so you slacken sail. Now it's my turn. I don't boast of what I can do; you'll see in time. So come along with me."

He seized her by the arm, and attempted to draw her along.

But she threw herself on the ground, and refused to stir.

Like most sailors, Harvey generally had some cord in his pocket.

This he produced, and quickly tied her hands and legs together.

Then he ordered Monday to lift up her head, while he took her feet.

In this way they carried her to Tompano, in spite of her cries, struggles, and protestations."

They proceeded at once to the king's palace, where the king and his chiefs were assembled in council.

A large crowd followed them, hearing that Nuratella was a prisoner, and that the white chief had mysteriously disappeared.

Harvey demanded an audience, which was granted him.

Leaving the witch in a passage guarded by Monday, he entered the great hall.

All eyes were instantly turned upon him, for alarming rumours had already reached the council.

CHAPTER XLVII.

THE WITCH'S DOOM.

BOTH Harvey and Jack possessed great influence over the savages of Limbi.

Cruel and vindictive as they were to their enemies, they nevertheless possessed the invaluable properties of gratitude.

The boys had saved and treated kindly Matabella, the heir apparent, the son of their Tuan Biza, the Prince of Wales of Limbi.

This was in itself sufficient to make them popular.

In addition to this, they had given them powder and shot; they were going to lead them against their old, old enemies, the Pisangs.

We can fancy the English in the days of their hatred to France, when war was waging, hailing an ally in a similar manner.

Besides this, the boys were not at all haughty in their manner.

They did not show or boast of their superiority in cultivation, and the arts of civilization.

On the contrary.

They made friends with the simple islanders, and endeared themselves to one and all.

Mr. Mole, who no one knew exactly why, was accounted a great chief, had married two princesses.

It was gravely debated whether or not he should have a third wife.

The Limbians thought they could not have afforded him a greater honour.

Mr. Mole thought otherwise.

He had certain domestic reasons of his own for thinking so.

But he had not yet found out the secret of governing a wife.

The Limbians did not hesitate to lay a bamboo cane across the shoulders of their refractory spouses.

Mr. Mole had yet to make that important discovery.

Unlike the chiefs of the Red Indians, about whom we have read so much, the inhabitants of the great Indian Archipelago were fond of talking.

They did not confine themselves to the utterance of grunts, and the guttural "yah yah!" with which we have been nauseated.

They were genial, and, what is more, they possessed a good deal of sound common sense.

Harvey told his tale as clearly and shortly as he could.

He had to struggle with and keep down his very natural indignation at the outrage to which his friend Jack had been subjected through a Limbian woman.

He translated the letter that Emily had written, alluded to the meeting with Nuratella, and ended by declaring his conviction that she was the authoress of the mischief.

After some consultation the chiefs were of the same opinion.

The religious men or priests who were members of the council had long been patrons of Nuratella.

It was their barbarous custom once a year to sacrifice a human being to the evil spirits.

The time was at hand.

They were searching for a victim.

The custom was, after the harvest of corn and fruits, to carry a certain quantity of sugar cane, rice, fowls, eggs, pigs, dogs, and a living being to the south-east point of the island.

The wretched creature selected for these rites was left on the shore, bound hand and foot, for the crocodiles to devour.

After the consultation of the council, Nuratella was ordered to be brought in.

She was unbound and surrounded with a strong guard, which rendered her escape impossible.

Some of the chiefs feared her fabled power, but the majority did not evince any emotion.

When the case was stated to her she made no reply.

Harvey stood up, and said "The silence of Nuratella is proof of her guilt. I demand her life shall be taken, as in all probability my poor friend by this time has ceased to exist."

"Confess," exclaimed the king Lanindyer.

"Of what use would it be for me to make any confession, when you are all hungering for my blood like a pack of wild beasts," she replied.

"Do you deny the charge which has been brought against you?" asked another chief.

"I do," she replied.

"Let her be put to the torture," said the king.

"No," cried Harvey. "Let her suffer the penalty of her crime, but torture would be barbarous."

"I have said it," answered the king, calmly. "Let the officers do their duty."

Nuratella was dragged into another apartment, and her cries were soon heard at intervals.

She was beaten with bamboos.

Fire was placed under her feet.

Red-hot stones were applied to various parts of her body, and a band of twisted reeds was tied so tightly round her forehead that her eyes threatened to burst from their sockets.

At length her fortitude, great though it was, gave way.

She confessed her intrigue with the Pisangs.

She admitted that she had beguiled Jack to her house on purpose to betray him, and she declared that she alone was to blame in the matter.

When this was made known, the indignant council clamoured loudly for her instant death. The cry was taken up by the populace out of doors.

Protected by the soldiers, she was led, accompanied by almost all the inhabitants of Tompano, to the seashore.

Near this fatal spot was the mouth of a small river, where the crocodiles were wont to assemble in large numbers.

She was securely bound, and laid upon the beach.

When the procession started, Harvey ran to Mr. Mole's house, and found him looking out at the doorway, while Alfura and Ambonia, who had made friends again, were anxiously looking at the crowd.

Mr. Mole had succeeded in restoring peace, for a time, to his distracted household, and he listened to the alarming rumours with impatience.

He hailed Harvey's arrival with delight.

"I say, sir," cried Harvey, "come along!"

"Come where? What is all this? Why fret the angry crowd, as I think my friend Horace has it?" replied Mr. Mole.

"Haven't you heard the news?"

"Not I."

"At least if I can't save Harkaway, I will avenge his death!" exclaimed Harvey.

"Dear me. Is Harkaway in danger? Don't say that? With all his faults he was a fine fellow. Don't tell me, Harvey, that he is——"

A tear sprang to Mr. Mole's eye.

He could not pronounce the word "dead."

"Come with me, sir," said Harvey, "and I will tell you all about it as we go along."

Harvey quickly told Mr. Mole the distressing news.

"The wretch!" exclaimed the latter, when he heard of Nuratella's treachery. "she deserves to die, but I wish they wouldn't do the thing in this cruel way. I think I shall interfere and stop it."

"Stop your grandmother!" replied Harvey.

"But an execution ought to be properly conducted."

Mr. Mole walked along thoughtfully.

They were in the rear of the crowd, but the shouts of the people were distinctly audible.

The doom of the witch had been decreed. Execution was to follow soon upon judgment.

CHAPTER XLVIII.

THE PREY OF THE CROCODILES.

PRESENTLY Mr. Mole said—

"Hunston is with these Pisangs is he not?"

"Yes, and directs all their councils," replied Harvey.

"I thought so. Well surely Harkaway's life will be safe in his hands."

"Will it?—over the left," answered Harvey.

"Do you mean to tell me that he will not spare an old friend?"

"You know all about the tattooing, and how we had to kick him out after he tried to murder us, and how he made an an attack on the castle?"

"Yes, I have heard of those things."

"Is it likely, then, that he'll show Jack any mercy?" answered Harvey. "I believe Hunston has become as ferocious a brute as any one of the Pisangs he is amongst."

"Do you, indeed?" said Mr. Mole.

"I do, and I think he would not hesitate to eat Jack if the others did."

"That's going a little too far, Harvey," said Mr. Mole with a half-smile.

"By mixing with savages may not a man get savage himself?"

"I hope we are not so."

"I mean a vicious man," replied Harvey.

"Let us hope that Harkaway is in no danger, and that he will soon be restored to us."

"I wish I could think so. I fear however, we shall only find his head in the house of some chief. At all events I shall hurry on the expedition for the invasion of Pisang."

"Do so, by all means," rejoined Mr. Mole; "and now I recollect that a short time ago, I elected to remain here as governor of the island in the absence of the fighting men."

"That was your wish, sir."

"It is so no longer," continued Mr. Mole. "When one of my companions, one of my dearest friends, I may say, is in danger in a foreign country; a boy whose mind was educated under my own personal surpervision, I can not remain idle."

"Bravo, sir! You're a trump!" cried Harvey.

"Harvey, do you know my motto?"

"No, sir. What is it?"

"It is," replied Mr. Mole, "'death before dishonour.' I may not be a fighting man, but I will hurl spear and draw trigger for Harkeway."

"Good again, sir! You're made of the right stuff!"

"And I shall get away from my wives," continued Mr. Mole, as if speaking to himself.

"Oh! that's it, sir!" said Harvey laughing.

"What did I say?" asked Mr. Mole in some confusion.

"Nothing, sir," replied Harvey. "Here we are."

Mr. Mole looked up, and beheld a vast concourse of people on the seashore.

They pushed their way through the crowd, the soldiers making room for the Tuan Biza of the white men.

A ring of armed men kept the throng back from a certain point.

Nuratella was already lying bound on the sand, the hot tropical sun streaming down mercilessly on her upturned face.

Her youth had been a guilty love.

Her life had been an imposition and a cheat.

He death was to be an atonement.

The people were at such a distance from the shore, that they could only see the dim outlines of the wretched victim.

The chiefs were assembled in a group somewhat nearer.

To these Harvey and Mr. Mole attached themselves.

As the tide rose, the bodies of the crocodiles could be seen rolling sluggishly up and down.

Presently they would scent their victim.

Then her end would draw near.

Not far off was the river of which we have spoken, and which drew the rainfall down from the hills.

As the water began to circle in ripplets round Nuratella, the excitement of the onlookers was intense.

Scarcely a word was spoken by the vast assembly.

Occasionally the priests uttered a low, monotonous chant.

At length two crocodiles saw the body and advanced towards it.

There was a snap of the huge jaws, and a dreadful shriek.

This was repeated.

Nuratella's cries redoubled as first an arm and then a leg was torn away.

Other crocodiles, attracted by the smell of blood, approached.

Soon the cries ceased.

The witch was still, and though the cruel fangs of the monsters tore her flesh, she felt them not.

Nuratella was dead.

Turning to Harvey, the king said—

" Are you satisfied ?"

Harvey had turned his head away from the sickening sight.

"Yes," he muttered, feebly.

A gong was loudly beaten as a signal that justice had been done.

Loud shouts rent the air, and the crowd, who had just before thrilled to the marrow of their bones, experienced a sense of relief.

"Let us get out of this," said Mr. Mole.

He and Harvey retreated along the shore, and tried to forget what they had seen by listening to the ripple of the waves as they broke on the beach.

"At least she deserved it," remarked Harvey.

"No doubt; but it was horrible for all that. I thought I should have fainted when that first crocodile took off her leg with as much ease as a surgeon at an hospital would amputate a limb."

"I've no pity for her," said Harvey. "I've only got to think of Jack, and I shouldn't care if she had got to die over again."

"Remember, Harvey, what you said about people living amongst savages and becoming like them," said Mr. Mole, warningly.

"But isn't it enough to make a fellow wild ?" began Harvey impatiently.

"No, it is not enough," interrupted Mr. Mole. "We are told to forgive our enemies seventy times seven."

"Then you'd better forgive Mrs. Ambonia Mole the next time she goes into her tantrums and tears your hair."

Mr. Mole was silent.

"That's a closer," thought Harvey.

As they neared the city they were met by Monday, who had come out to look for them.

" Well, Monday, old man," exclaimed Harvey, "what's your opinion of things in general ?"

" Not up to much, sare. Me miss Mast' Jack. Me grieve much. Monday very bad."

" So am I, and that's the truth."

" The king has decide to start to-night with all men for Pisang. That good news," continued Monday.

"Has he, though ? Then your governor's a brick, Monday," cried Harvey joyfully.

"Yes," said Mr. Mole; "that is indeed cheerful intelligence, and I will solace myself with a drink of that rum I see sticking out of your pocket, my worthy but somewhat dusky friend."

Monday had a flask in his pocket, for he had thrown an old jacket of Harvey's over his shoulders, the sun being very hot, and Monday not being disinclined to clothing when he could get it.

"Me not know, sare," he replied; "it Mast' Harvey's old jacket, Monday take him."

Mr. Mole received the flask, drank once, and then took another dip, and sighed deeply, while he put the flask in his own pocket.

"Circulate the liquor, sir !" exclaimed Harvey.

"Ah, pardon me ! It was a fit of abstraction," replied Mr. Mole, being detected in his base attempt to appropriate it all to himself.

The spirit was afterwards handed to Monday, and they all felt exhilarated by it.

" I begin to think," said Harvey, " that Jack won't be a croaker just yet. I'll bet a new hat !"

" Which you want badly, Harvey, that I must say," interposed Mr. Mole.

" Ditto, the same to you, sir," said Harvey laughing; "not to make any unkind remarks about your continuations."

" What's the matter with my trousers ?

I hope nothing has gone amiss with them," exclaimed Mr. Mole, in alarm.

"There is only a hole as big as a besom, sir, in the rear."

"Dear me, what an unfortunate thing! Do my coat tails cover it?"

"When the wind doesn't blow. As you're a householder since your marriage, sir, it doesn't matter, because you've got your 'rent' ready!" exclaimed Harvey.

"Ah! well. I suppose we shall have to resort to the garments of our first ancestors, which we have authority for believing were chiefly fig leaves," replied Mr. Mole with a sigh.

"You interrupted my observation, sir," continued Harvey, "which was, that I'd make a bet Jack fogged the niggers somehow. He's clever."

"I hope sincerely he may. However, we will haste to the rescue. Monday!"

"Yes, Mist' Mole; what up now, sare?"

"See to my pistols, will you? And first take care that my rifle is not overloaded; I have a great horror of a gun that bursts."

"All right, sare! Monday, him see to that."

"You may leave it all to Mon," exclaimed Harvey. "He'll put you straight, and send you out to the fight like a warrior of old, up to the knocker."

"I wish we had armour in these days. It would be a great protection," Mr. Mole observed wistfully.

"A bold spirit is the only armour a brave man requires," replied Harvey.

"By the way, did your spear-wound hurt much?"

"Didn't it?" said Harvey. "I should think it did, just."

"What was it like?"

"Like? Oh! like having all your muscles pulled out one by one by machinery, and then having them put in again."

"Ah! war is a dreadful thing; nevertheless, I will rescue our somewhat rash and foolhardy friend, Harkaway. You shall receive an example from me, Richard."

"Thank you, sir," replied Harvey dryly.

When they reached the town they were sent for to the council.

The chiefs had decided upon an immediate attack.

After some discussion, it was found that the men could not be got ready, embarked, and disembarked on the island of Pisang for a few days.

There was much to be prepared, and it was not advisable to risk defeat by indulging in too much haste.

Even Harvey, impatient to be up and doing, and to strike a blow for his friend, was obliged to admit that.

Mr. Mole accompanied Harvey to his house, and a fresh bottle was produced, for, though the store of liquor was running short, Harvey carefully concealed and took care of what they had left.

In a short time Mr. Mole got what Harvey called "jolly," with his frequent attentions to the bottle, and was only prevented from singing a song by being reminded that Harkaway was in danger.

At length Harvey rose, and said—

"I won't say your room is better than your company, sir, but I must make myself scarce."

"Why break up our little party?" asked Mr. Mole.

"I don't like keeping a married man out, that's one reason; and another is, I have to drill an awkward squad of our soldiers before sunset."

"Ah, duty before all things. I will not detain you, Harvey."

"And, as I don't want my castle stormed, I think you'd better be stepping it, sir, or you'll have the rival beauties after you."

"Mist' Mole should use um stick," observed Monday.

"What's that, my valiant black?" asked Mr. Mole.

Monday brandished a stout bamboo, and replied—

"All Limbi men beat their wives. You beat Ambonia, sare, and then you see."

"Is it so? A good suggestion. I'll follow your advice, Monday, and apply the rod."

Mr. Mole took the stick which Monday offered him, and went away.

"I say, Monday, are you up to your larks with Mole?" asked Harvey, when he was gone.

"Yes. Monday have um lark with him," was the reply.

"Do the Limbians beat their wives?"

"No; only sometimes. Ambonia never beat in her life. Won't Mist' Mole catch it?" said Monday grinning.

"Hot and strong, I expect," replied

Harvey who could not help laughing at the prospect which awaited the proprietor of a tea garden in China.

When Mr. Mole reached his house, he found his wives sullenly awaiting him.

Alfura said nothing.

But Ambonia asked him where he had been, and why he stopped away from them.

Mole was just sufficiently tipsy to be valiant, and he replied—

"To see the execution, my dear. Fine thing an execution! Crocodiles fine; Nuratella fine."

"We went also, but we have been back some time," answered Ambonia. "You have been somewhere else."

"Only stayed to crack a bottle with a friend. English custom my dear."

"And what is that stick for?"

"For you, my pet," replied Mr. Mole.

Ambonia made a dash at him, and attempted to seize the stick.

Mr. Mole brought it down sharply over her naked and unprotected shoulders.

"Must be firm," he muttered. "Monday told me to be firm. I *will* be firm."

"With a wild kind of howl, Ambonia sprang upon him, and grasping the stick broke it in two pieces.

"Playful creature!" exclaimed Mr. Mole, with an imbecile smile.

Ambonia seemed to be determined to let him know whether she was in play or not, for she began to beat him unmercifully with the biggest end of the bamboo which remained in her hand.

Mr. Mole fell on his knees before her, unable to withstand the torrent of blows.

"Ambonia," he said, "be merciful as you are strong; that stick hurts!"

"You have hit a princess of Limbi," she replied.

"It shall not occur again."

Thwack, thwack, descended the stick on his head and back.

"Behold me Ambonia on my knees," he said. "I repeat, behold me, for it is a sad sight! I am a great chief who has cut off heads in battle."

Ambonia danced before him in derision.

"And moreover," he added, "I am going to the wars with the Pisangs. You may never see me again."

This declaration altered the complexion of affairs.

Alfura's tender heart melted, and she endeavoured to calm Ambonia.

The Limbian women had a great respect for warriors.

When they were satisfied that their husband was going to fight, they lifted him up, put him on a seat, and sat round him.

"Ambonia will sing the white chief the deeds of her ancestors," she exclaimed.

"Yes, do; that's sensible! By all means let us hear the song," said Mr. Mole, glad to escape so easily.

While Mrs. Mole No. 2 sang to him in a tone of voice, not altogether unpleasing, her husband pillowed his head in Alfura's lap and soon slept the sleep of the just.

CHAPTER XLIX.

MONDAY'S NEW CLOTHES.

THOUGH Harvey was gratified at the just punishment which Nuratella had received at the hands of the Tuan Biza, he was ill at ease.

In vain he tried to sleep.

The night was warm and sultry, but towards morning a heavy storm of rain, accompanied by thunder and lightning, occurred.

This lasted about an hour with all the violence peculiar to such tempests in the tropics.

After this, the wind rose and blew in fitful gusts.

Harvey thought he heard the sound of big guns being fired.

From the direction of the sound, he imagined that they came from the sea.

They were discharged at intervals of a minute.

Nothing is more exciting than to hear a ship in distress fire the minute gun at sea.

As soon as day broke, he went into

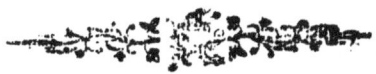

"YOU CONFOUNDED BLACK LUMP OF UGLINESS!" SAID MR. MOLE.

an adjouring apartment and roused Monday.

The black was soon on his feet.

"What um up to, Mast' Harvey?" exclaimed Monday, as Harvey gave him a poke in the ribs to wake him.

"I want you to go down to the shore," replied Harvey.

"What for? Mast' Jack come back?"

"I wish to goodness, he had; no such luck. But I fancy some ship has been driven on the rocks. Guns have been firing."

"P'r'aps you dreaming, sare," said Monday.

"No; I haven't been dreaming either, so you're out there," replied Harvey, who had been like a wasp ever since Jack disappeared. "If I didn't go to sleep, I couldn't dream, could I?"

This argument was convincing.

"Monday be off like um shot," cried the black.

"Don't be long! If I am right," said Harvey, "we will take a boat and go to the wreck, before your countrymen can know anything about it. Some lives may be saved."

Fortunately Monday did not require much dressing, and was ready to start in less than no time.

An hour passed, during which Harvey paced the room impatiently.

He reproached himself with being inactive while Jack was in danger.

The Limbians were too slow in their movements to please him.

It appeared that, before they started for the invasion of Pisang, the priests had to go through certain forms and ceremonies, to bless the expedition.

During this delay, Jack might be killed by his enemies.

"I shouldn't care," thought Harvey, "if I could die with him."

It was a relief to his oppressed mind when Monday came back.

The black danced up and down in an extraordinary manner.

"Stop that hanky panky," said Harvey. "What are you cutting all these capers for, just for all the world like a bear on hot bricks?"

"Him one big ship, sare," said Monday; "not far from land, and him stuck on um rock."

"Is there a boat anywhere near?"

"One boat, the one we come from our island in, not far off."

"That will do. Just stay your dancing performance, and come with me. When a ship is wrecked, and people may be dead or dying, it is no time for larking," said Harvey.

"Monday, him dance, because him think him get things."

"If you touch so much as a ship's biscuit without my permission, I'll skin you. Now then, lead the way; trot," replied Harvey.

Monday said no more, and they were quickly on the way to the shore.

The firing was over now, and the fate of the crew most likely decided.

With the utmost impatience Harvey hurried on, and getting into the boat, set the sail, steering directly for the wreck of a merchantman, which seemed to be fast lodged in between the rocks about half a mile or more from the beach.

As he cast his eyes back, he saw two dead bodies stretched out upon the sand, looking ghastly white in the reddening sun.

"I'm afraid we're too late, Monday. They're all dead as mutton, I expect," remarked Harvey.

"What's mutton, sare?" asked Monday.

"Sheep."

"If um sheep, why call him mutton?" asked Monday, puzzled.

"I can't explain now! I've something else to think of. You've no sheep in your forsaken country, but if you ever come to England with us, you'll know all about it."

Monday was silent for a while.

Then he said—

"Great, much wonderful place England, Mast' Harvey?"

"Rather! You'll say so, when you get there. But would you really like to come with us, if we get a passing ship to take us off?"

"Yes, Monday him come."

"And leave all your friends here?"

"Monday come back some time, and lay him bones in Limbi. Not like die out of his own country," he replied, thoughtfully.

They now reached the wreck, which was a China clipper of moderate tonnage.

The storm had done her fearful damage, and from her appearance she seemed to have been drifting water-logged for some days, so that she must have encountered more than one tempest, and have made bad weather before she was driven out of her track to Limbi.

Making the painter fast, Harvey sprang on board, followed by Monday.

Three corpses lay on the deck, and not a single living soul was to be seen above or below.

Perhaps the majority of the crew had taken to the boats before she struck and had been carried away in an opposite direction, for there were some obstinate currents in the seas.

When Harvey satisfied himself that the crew were beyond his help, he went below and found that the cargo was chiefly tea and silk.

She was the "Johnny Sands" of London, and he could only deplore the fate of the brave fellows who had manned her."

"We may as well load our boat," said Harvey, "with such things as we want. Tea and coffee are luxuries we haven't had for a long time; powder and shot, if we can find any, will be useful, and a case of spirits will not be a bad present for Mole. Lend a hand, Monday, and let's overhaul the wreck."

Monday willingly complied, and in about an hour a couple of chests of tea, a case of spirits, some wine, a bag of coffee, a keg of powder and some shot, and various other little articles, none the worse for water, were handed on deck.

Harvey packed the boat as full as it would hold, and made free with some seamen's chests containing clothes, as his own were becoming rather ragged.

When all was ready for a start, he looked round for Monday, who was nowhere to be seen.

"Where's the beggar got to?" he muttered.

Going to the companion-ladder, he shouted—"Monday!"

"Coming, sare," replied Monday. "Give him um moment."

"I'll give you a hiding, if you keep me waiting," replied Harvey. "What are you doing below there? If I catch you swigging——"

"Monday no swig, sare," replied a voice from the depths of the ship. "Him only rig himself up!"

"Do what?" said Harvey, in surprise.

"Him all right, Mast' Harvey; him right boot not fit. Never mind; one will do. Blow him right boot!"

"What on earth is he talking about?" thought Harvey.

Presently Monday made his appearance, and Harvey could not help laughing at the singular spectacle he presented.

He had seen his young master overhauling the seamen's chests, and the idea occurred to him that he ought to do the same thing.

"Mast' Harvey him dress; why not Monday? Him dress also," said Monday to himself.

He tried to put on a pair of white trousers, but tore them in the attempt, and got his left foot into a top boot, which he found in the captain's cabin.

The right one was wet, and wouldn't go on, so he managed to put one with side-springs on.

Upon his head he put a white hat with a black band round it, and this was perched a little on one side.

A white shirt was thrown over his shoulders, and tied round his neck by the sleeves.

Finding a paper collar, he had stuck that on with a pin, and tied a black ribbon round it.

"Monday, old man, this won't do," said Harvey, as soon as he could check his laughter at his ridiculous appearance; "you are a regular swell."

"Sare!" exclaimed the black, drawing himself up.

"You're going it," replied Harvey.

"Monday go to England. When him go him dress. Why not Monday dress now?"

"I don't see any particular reason. You're all the cheese; 'quite up to the knocker,' as we say."

At this compliment Monday grinned, as if he was intensely gratified.

"Monday him what you call um swell," he said, regarding his only boot with complacency.

"I should think you were a swell," replied Harvey. "Niggers can do it."

"Why you call me nigger, Mast' Harvey?"

"Because you are not white, and you're rather more greasy than you might be, only that's your misfortune and not your fault. You'd do well to sit over the wheel of an engine; it wouldn't want much train oil."

"Have him dress right?" asked Monnay, not understanding Harvey's chaff.

"Slap up!"

"Monday, him feel rather funny."

At this Harvey burst out laughing again.

"You're all right," he said, "don't flurry your fat. You might as well have started two boots while you were about it."

"Him cuss boot not go on," said Monday, in a tone of vexation.

"Don't swear Monday. Where did you learn that?"

"Mist' Mole, him swar when Ambonia go on at him. He say, 'cuss the women.'"

"Does he? That's very wrong of him," replied Harvey; "and don't you follow a bad example. Jump into the boat; never mind the other boot. You'll do. You're up to the nines, and would make a sensation in Hyde Park."

"Monday, good Englishmans."

"Stunning. I never saw a better," answered Harvey, wishing to gratify his harmless vanity.

"That all right," said Monday, smiling from ear to ear.

"I'll have you presented at court some day. It would read well in the papers. His royal highness Prince Matabella Monday of Limbi, present on the happy occasion of his finding a top boot and white hat, both rather the worse for wear."

Monday did not understand all this.

"But," he said, "now, Mast' Harvey, you chaff poor Monday."

"Chaff? I'm not chaffing. Ain't you a prince? And haven't you found a top boot and a white hat?"

"Yes, that all right."

"Dry up then, and steer the boat while I look after the sail."

They embarked with their cargo, Harvey congratulating himself upon being first in the field.

Had the natives discovered the wreck first, they would soon have carried away everything that was worth having.

As Harvey looked at Monday the more absurb his appearance seemed.

"Why you laugh, Mast' Harvey?" asked Monday.

"Because I can't help myself, and shall burst if I don't," replied Dick.

"Anything wrong with Monday?"

"I've told you there isn't; you're a toff!"

"Why um laugh then? Monday think him better dress than you sare. Him got no tear in him——"

But not knowing the name for shirt, or forgetting it in his excitement, he pointed to his covering.

"Oh! Your shirt's fine," replied Harvey.

"No holes in him?"

"I know mine is more holy than righteous; never mind, Monday. I've got something in those chests, and I'll cut you out. You shan't take the shine out of me like this."

Monday laughed, and was evidently much pleased with himself.

"Him Englishmans now," he said.

"You've done the trick, Monday," answered Harvey; "they'll take you for the British cousul at least, if we get to Singapore."

They ran their boat into a sheltered nook, and left the contents within it, intending to send down for them when they reached Tompano.

At a short distance from the city they saw a female sitting under a tree.

In her hand she held a bottle of spirits, which Harvey recognised as one he had given Mr. Mole.

She had twined some flowers in her hair, which hung down her back in untidy masses.

"Look, sare!" said Monday, "that Missy Mole."

"So it is. What is she doing, I wonder?" replied Harvey.

Monday put his hand to his mouth, as if to signify that she had been drinking.

Her wild appearance seemed to bear out the truth of his suggestion.

"If she has been imitating her husband we'd better give her a wide berth," Harvey said.

Mrs. Mole Number Two, however, was too quick for them.

Jumping up, she ran with unsteady steps to Harvey and seized his arm.

"You make my husband drink," she exclaimed. "When he comes to you, he goes home and beat me."

"My dear lady," replied Harvey, "I assure you I do all I can to stop him."

"No, no!" cried Ambonia, raising her voice to a high pitch; "you send him to me with a bamboo, and then he beat me."

"I'll swear I didn't."

"To-day," she continued, "I have taken away his spirit, and I have tasted it."

"Is it good?"

Ambonia raised the bottle to her lips and took a deep draught.

"It goes like fire through the blood," she answered; "but it has not taken away my senses. You are my husband's enemy, and thus will I punish you."

As she spoke she aimed a blow at him with the bottle.

He jumped on one side, and narrowly escaped having his head broken.

"I say!" exclaimed Harvey, "stash it. Here, Monday, speak to your amiable countrywoman. This won't do at all."

Ambonia danced round Harvey, and made a snatch at his hair.

She grasped it, and tugged away at it till Harvey danced too.

"Pull her off, Monday!" he exclaimed. "Look sharp, or I shan't have a hair left."

"Monday come, sare."

Monday seized Ambonia by the waist and dragged her to the ground.

Harvey fell with her.

She loosened her grip, and turned her attention to Monday, whom she abused in fine style.

Harvey soon tied Ambonia's hands behind her.

She kicked and screamed, but was unable to help herself.

"I'll be revenged," she cried with a hysterical sob. "I'll kill him."

"What we do with her?" asked Monday.

"I'll be hanged if I know."

"I 'pose we carry her home, sare."

"She's heavy," said Harvey.

"Never mind, sare. I take her head, you take her legs; we carry her like that."

If they had not decided to do this, it is doubtful whether Ambonia would have got home.

The whisky she had been taking had got into her head, and she staggered about in a ludicrous manner.

First she ran to Monday, and tried to bite him; then she ran towards Harvey, and tried to kick him, then lost her balance, and fell gracefully on her back.

"Now's your time, Monday; lay hold!" exclaimed Harvey.

"Me got her, sare," replied Monday.

"Lay still, mum. It's all right," continued Harvey; "we don't wish to hurt you."

She was a good weight, and it was lucky they had not far to go. It was a ludicrous procession.

Ambonia screeching, struggling, and making horrible faces.

Monday fantastically dressed, and grinning like a baboon.

Harvey enjoying the fun, but rather wishing he was out of it.

At length they got her home, and gave her into the charge of Alfura.

Then they made their way to their own home, to which Mr. Mole had previously gone.

The news of the wreck had spread.

Mr. Mole had heard of the wreck, and was looking for Harvey, to know if he would go with him to the stranded vessel.

The Tuan Biza, and many chiefs, had already started.

A wreck was a great event in those islands, and everyone, from the highest to the lowest, strove to get as much plunder as he could.

Suddenly Harvey and Monday met Mr. Mole.

"Hullo, sir!" cried Harvey. "Where are you pelting off to!"

"There is a wreck, Harvey," answered Mr. Mole; "and I am going to see what good I can do for the poor creatures. Won't you come?"

"We've been there, sir."

"Been there!" said Mr. Mole, stopping and drawing his breath quickly. "Are there not some casks of spirit on board?"

"We got a few, sir. You'd better make haste, or you'll be too late for your share."

"I'll stick up for my rights. Share and share alike is English, or at least Yorkshire. I'll have my rights, or my name is not Isaac Mole; but who, in the name of wonder, is this strange-loooking animal? Is he some one saved from the wreck?"

He pointed to Monday as he spoke whom he did not recognise in his strange attire.

"That's the King of the Cannibal Islands," replied Harvey.

"Indeed!"

"Yes; he's eaten more men, considering his size and weight than any other of his nation in existence."

"What a dreadful creature!"

"Dance, you uncultivated beast!" cried Harvey. "Show the gentleman what you can do."

And he began to sing—

"Hoky poky, wanky fum,
How do you like you taters done?
The King of the Cannibal Islands."

Monday stood still and obstinately refused to move.

"Dear me!" said Mr. Mole, "he looks to my imagination, like a wandering Christy minstrel out of work. Fancy his being an anthropophagos, or man-eater, as we should say at school."

"Don't irritate him by looking at him in that way, sir; he might do you an injury," said Harvey. "He's subject to fits."

"Fits! Bless me! Keep him off. I wonder at your fondness for such savage pets, Harvey. There is that wretched Monday, now——".

Monday showed his teeth.

He advanced to Mr. Mole with an angry look, fully entering into Harvey's joke.

"Keep him off, Harvey," cried Mr. Mole in an agony of apprehension; "I don't want to hurt him."

"Prop him, sir!" said Harvey, delighted. "Don't funk him; prop him in the eye! Give him a domino! I'll see fair play!"

"Perhaps he bites!" exclaimed Mr. Mole, drawing back.

Again Monday showed his teeth in a vicious manner.

Mr. Mole got behind Harvey saying—

"Protect me, Harvey. It is hard to be stopped in this way when I am hastening to the wreck to do Christian work."

"You needn't hurry, sir; the poor fellows are beyond human aid."

"Say you so? Then their belongings are lawful spoil, and that confounded Tuan Biza will——"

"Collar the lot, eh, sir?"

"Just so, Harvey; but I entreat you to protect me from that truculent-looking savage."

Harvey glided away, and Monday approached Mr. Mole threateningly.

Mole fell on knees, and lifting up his hands, said—

"Good, kind Mr. Cannibal don't do anything desperate. I'm only a poor schoolmaster, Don't eat me!"

"He'll only take a mouthful; he's not hungry," exclaimed Harvey, who was exploding with laughter.

Mr. Mole's distress was ludicrous in the extreme.

CHAPTER L.

HARVEY'S RESOLVE.

SUDDENLY a gust of wind blew off Monday's white hat, which disconcerted him greatly.

"You've lost your tile," cried Harvey.

"Monday, him soon catch um tile," exclaimed the black, forgetting his assumed part of the King of the Cannibal Islands.

Mr. Mole's eyes were opened.

As soon as he saw Monday without his hat, he recognised him, and rising to his feet, said—

"Why, what sort of a trick is this, Harvey? Such deception is shameful. The poor creature is Monday."

"I could have told you that, sir," replied Harvey.

"Come here, you black thief," continued Mr. Mole, as Monday approached, having captured his runaway hat. "I'll thrash you within an inch of your life.

What do you mean by rigging yourself out like that, and making fun of me?"

"Monday king; him eat um up, sare," answered Monday, who, however, kept at a respectful distance.

"I'll attend to you afterwards, my jocose friend; at present I am engaged. I shall be late at the wreck."

"There is no occasion to go sir," said Harvey. "I have secured all that is worth having. She is only a merchantman, laden with tea chiefly, and if you want a cask or two of rum or Hollands, you are welcome to them."

Mr. Mole shook him cordially by the hand.

"My dear Harvey," he replied; "my greatest consolation in this my exile, is that I have a friend like you so near me. Your words go straight to my heart. Where are the casks?"

"In our boat, sir."

"Is it safe?" Will not the Limbian thieves deprive us of our lawful spoil?"

"They've got to find it first."

"Their noses are keen, and their scent sure. I wouldn't trust the descendants of Ham."

"Gammon!" replied Harvey, by way of a joke. "The Tuan Biza would notice anything his people took. First come, first served, that's the law here, and I will say this for them, if their laws are few, they respect what they have got."

"With that assurance I will rest contented. I have over-exerted myself already in the morning sun, for no sooner did I hear the news, than I hastened away—not for what I could get, Harvey, but to do good! Don't think for a moment I went for what I could get."

"Not you, sir. You'd put whisky in a bottle, and throw stones at it."

"Well, I don't know that, exactly," replied Mr. Mole; "but I would not make capital out of the misfortunes of my fellow-creatures."

"Monday," cried Harvey, "cut on to the little village, and get some fellows to bring the stores out of the boat to our house; and look sharp, or I pity you?"

"All right, Mast' Harvey," said Monday, adding, "no eat Mr. Mole this time."

"You impudent black slave, begone; or I shall lose my temper, and be tempted to play the part of Moses in Egypt," answered Mr. Mole.

"What that, sare?"

"What that, sir? Why this, sir," Mr. Mole answered, bringing a bamboo he carried in his hand with some force down upon Monday's posteriors.

Monday uttered a yell, and put his hands behind him, as if to conceal the injured part, and then he started off at a run.

"Must be firm with those fellows," Harvey," said Mr. Mole, complacently. "Give them an inch, they'll take an ell. No foolishness. You see that I have tamed that savage, who, by the way, wouldn't be half so cheeky if you didn't encourage him."

"His hide's tough enough, sir. You didn't hurt him."

"Never mind. I did not wish to inflict any brutalizing punishment. All I wanted was to assert my authority; that done, I am satisfied."

"Walk back with me, sir, will you 1 want to have a talk with you," said Harvey.

"Certainly, my boy."

Side by side they retraced their steps towards Tompano.

"You see, sir," began Harvey, "I'm what the sailors call flummoxed."

"And what may that be?"

"Knocked out of time, upset, worried, bothered. I didn't sleep a wink all last night."

"Why is that?" demanded Mr. Mole.

"Because I am so anxious on Jack's account. If I was with him, and could share his danger, I shouldn't care half so much."

"I too am deeply grieved at Harkaway's disappearance; but I make bold to hope that no harm has befallen him," replied Mr. Mole, gravely.

"He's in Hunston's power."

"Well. So much the better!"

"So much the worse you mean, sir. He'd have ten times more chance, if he had to deal with the natives only," answered Harvey.

"I know Hunston to be bad and vindictive. He has little or no feeling. See how he kicked me, Isaac Mole, the proprietor of a tea garden in China."

"And also proprietor of two wives in Limbi."

"Don't Harvey. If you love me, don't joke on that subject. It is a sore one," said Mr. Mole with a groan.

"Very well, sir; I won't," replied Harvey. "Something ought to be done to help Jack at once."

"Are we not going in force to rescue him."

"We are; but by the time we get to Pisang we may only find his dead body."

"Nonsense, Harvey; I cannot believe that Hunston would be such an abandoned wretch as to murder an old schoolfellow in cold blood."

"Wouldn't he? I know the beast better than you do," said Harvey. "That is just why I am funking."

"The Tuan Biza will be ready to sail in two days from this time."

"Not now."

"Why not now?" asked Mr. Mole.

"Because there is a lot of drink on board the wreck, and the Limbians are not above temptation. They'll be on the spree till it's all gone?"

"Do you think so?"

"I'm sure of it. Savages are awful beggars to lush, when they get the chance, and the chiefs will be as drunk as flies for a week. I can see that."

"Perhaps you are right," replied Mr. Mole, moodily.

"They respect us, and they like us," continued Harvey; "the prompt way in which they put Nuratella out of the way is a proof that they want to conciliate us; but, after all, Jack is not one of them, and it does not much matter to them whether he lives or dies."

"Your reasoning is cogent, very cogent. What then do you propose to do?"

"This. I am determined to strike a blow for Jack at once, even if I lose my own life in the attempt."

"I commend your pluck, Harvey. Shall I accompany you? Harkaway is a dear fellow, and I will cast in my ot with you, even to the death, as you say," exclaimed Mr. Mole, animated with sudden and unusual valour.

"No; that won't do!" replied Harvey.

"You won't have me?" said Mr. Mole, secretly rejoiced; "and why not? Am I not worthy to fight in a good cause?"

"I want you to stay here, sir!" answered Harvey. "You shall do your share of fighting when the time comes, but the Limbians want some one to keep them bang up to the mark."

"Ah! I perceive."

"They have been badly beaten once or twice lately by the Pisangs, and they don't like attacking them without a white leader."

"Quite so."

"It may be a month," Harvey continued, "before they would invade Pisang of their own accord."

"Very possible."

"You are accounted a great chief," Harvey went on, "and have influence amongst them. They respect you, sir."

"And do I not deserve it, Harvey? Have I not always borne myself bravely when there was any fighting to be done?" asked Mr. Mole.

"Certainly, sir. You're a second Agamemnon. You can do it when you like; and I want you to stop here and organize the forces."

"That is just within the scope of my administrative ability. You could not have given me a more congenial task."

"See that they take proper supplies, keep their powder dry, and that every five-and-twenty men have their proper officers."

"And you?"

"I shall leave Limbi, with Monday, in a couple of hours."

"How?"

"In our boat?" replied Harvey. "I can't stop here. Pisang is only a few hours' sail, and I may be of some use to dear old Jack."

"The odds are against you."

"Have they not always been against the man who has attempted a daring enterprise, sir?" asked Harvey.

"That is true. History abounds with instances of successful daring."

"Pat me on the back, sir, and tell me to go in and win," said Harvey.

"Of course I will. But here we are at your house. Let us have a glass—a parting glass, to drink success to your expedition!" exclaimed Mr. Mole.

"You are welcome to what you like, sir. As for me, I shall not touch a drop. I never drink when I have anything to do, and keep my head cool. A glass or two when you're ashore and on the spree is another thing," answered Harvey.

"As you please, my boy. My blood is colder than yours, and wants warming. I'll drink your share and my own too," said Mr. Mole.

Harvey placed a bottle before him, and said—

"Polish it off, sir; there's more where that came from. It's a pure spirit."

"So it is, Harvey, and there isn't a headache in a gallon of pure spirit," replied Mr. Mole, who soon made himself at home.

Harvey went away to look for Monday, and apprise him of the determination he had come to.

He knew that the faithful fellow would follow him to the end of the world if he asked him, and he was also sure that he could not propose any expedition to him which he would like so well as one to rescue Jack.

Monday loved Jack with all his heart.

It would have comforted Jack in his captivity, if he had known how wildly two true hearts were beating on his account.

CHAPTER LI.

AT HUNSTON'S MERCY.

FOR some time after he was knocked down, Jack did not recover his senses, and when he did, an acute pain at the back of the head informed him that he had received a severe blow.

Gradually the fresh sea air revived him, and the dizziness consequent on his hurt passed away.

The ripple of the waves against the sides of the boat, and the swarthy faces of the Pisangs, visible by the pale moonlight, sufficed to tell him that he was being carried into captivity.

He was furious at the thought of it.

Up to the present time he had been singularly successful in defeating Hunston's designs.

To be in his power and at his mercy, was a reflection akin to madness.

However, Jack liked danger.

At school he always said that the fun of being in a scrape was the getting out of it.

"As long as they don't knock me on the head entirely, I don't care," he said to himself.

Thinking that when the landing was effected, he would be taken to some prison, he determined to give them as much trouble as possible.

If he pretended to be worse than he really was, and did not appear able to walk, they would have to carry him.

It was as he expected.

When they reached the coast of Pisang, he was lifted out of the boat, and placed upon a couple of planks tied together with reeds, and carried by four men.

The town called Palembang was reached before daybreak, and Jack found himself deposited in a square-built bamboo house, thatched with palm leaves.

It was strongly built, and no doubt guarded outside.

As soon as he was left to himself, Jack took the bearings of his prison.

He tied his bandana handkerchief round his head to keep the air and the flies from his wound.

"I don't feel much the worse," he said. "Wonder what they're going to do with me."

He could see through chinks in the wall that daylight had appeared.

"We used to sing," he remarked, "'I shan't go home till morning.' It doesn't look like going home at all. Suppose we have a look round."

Getting into a corner, he climbed up the bamboos till he reached the roof of his prison, which was made of sticks, covered with palm leaves.

It did not take him more than five minutes to push a hole through these big enough to get his body through.

Then he climbed on to the roof, and, sitting down, took a survey of the city.

There were few people about, though numbers of houses stretched away in all directions.

At the door of the house if the one-storied bamboo hut was worthy of the designation, paced two sentries, armed with spears, and bows and arrows.

"It's no good trying to escape," thought Jack. "Not just yet, at least. I should be seen and there would be a hue and cry. Don't see why I shouldn't have a game though with one of those niggers."

Some pieces of rock were laid over a weak part of the thatch, to prevent the wind blowing it away.

Taking up a little bit, he threw it on the head of a drowsy-looking Pisang.

"Morning, old fellow. It's nice and airy up here," he exclaimed.

The soldier rubbed his eyes with astonishment when he saw Jack.

"Go down again," he said.

"I'm in no hurry thank you," replied Jack.

"You're a prisoner, and it's against the rules.

"Is it? Blow me, I shouldn't have thought it. What time do you breakfast in these parts?"

"You will have something when the

other guard comes; but go down. You've no business up there," said the soldier, who wondered at Jack's speaking his language so well.

"Come and fetch me!"

"I'll call the white Tuan Biza," threatened the guard.

"Call him a thundering scoundrel, and you won't be far out," answered Jack.

Giving some orders in a low tone to his fellow-soldier, the Pisang went to a house at a little distance, and presently returned with Hunston.

The latter looked very sleepy and very cross; his face, however, was not now disfigured by a single tattoo mark.

The stain was not lasting.

It had faded away.

"Come down off there!" exclaimed Hunston savagely.

"Shan't!" Jack replied coolly.

"Won't you, by George? Then I shall have to make you."

"Try it on, old son; you're welcome."

"Give me that spear," exclaimed Hunston to the soldier.

He took it, and cast it at Jack, who bobbed on one side, and very cleverly caught it in his hand as it was whizzing by over the thatch.

"That's one to me," he exclaimed. "Now, look here, if you try to knock me off my perch, I'll give you one for yourself, Mister Hunston."

The latter looked amazed at this cool effrontry.

"Don't you know you're a prisoner?" he replied.

"What of that? It may be your turn soon. By the way, I'm glad to see that ugly mug of yours has improved a little since we last had the pleasure of meeting."

Hunston stifled a curse.

"You shall have an ornamental phiz before I've done with you, and one you'll never get rid of," he said.

"How's that?" asked Jack, unconcernedly.

"Because you'll carry it down to the grave with you in a brace of shakes."

"Thank you; much obliged, I'm sure," replied Jack.

"How's your mother?"

"Come down off there," thundered Hunston.

"Not if I know it. I shall stay here until breakfast's ready, and then I'll descend. Pray give me something nice; I'm rather hungry."

Hunston foamed at the mouth with rage.

"Fine city this!" cried Jack surveying the town with a critical air. "But not a patch on Tompano. Pity we shall have to burn it about your ears."

"We?" repeated Hunston. "I don't think you'll have much to do with it."

"Don't you? Well it's only a difference of opinion, and yours isn't worth much. I say, how's the Tuan Biza?"

"He's right enough. Come down!"

"Not by any manner of means. Can't afford it. Can't be done at the price. Lovely prospect. How's Keyali?"

"You know deuced well he's wiped out. We found his body stuck through and through with knives."

"His own fault. He was a plucky fellow, but, like you, a little too headstrong," said Jack.

"Will you come down?" shouted Hunston, who was beside himself with rage.

"Not much; unless you behave like a gentleman, and take my parole."

"What's that?"

"There," said Jack, in a tone of mock compassion, "you see the necessity for learning when one's young. I always thought your education was neglected. You should have made better use of your time. *Didicisse artes*——I forget the rest, but I will ask Mole for your edification; I'll make a note of it."

He took out his pocket-book, and coolly wrote, reading as he put it down—

"Mem. Ask Mole as to quotation— something—*artes*—to coach up Hunston.

"However," he continued, putting away his book, "I'll explain parole. It means that I will give you my word of honour not to hook it if you will let me walk about the city."

"You haven't got such a thing as honour."

"Don't judge others by yourself, old boy. Never mind; it don't much matter, I'm very jolly where I am. Best part of the day, morning. Nice cool air—breeze —not much sun."

Jack played with the captured spear.

"Fool!" hissed Hunston, through his teeth. "Don't you know you're at my mercy?"

"No, I wasn't aware of the fact," replied Jack, innocently.

Hunston gave the guard some additional orders, and stalked away to his house, unable to contain himself any longer.

CHAPTER · LII.

TRUE TO HIS COLOURS.

HAVING succeeded in annoying Hunston, which was all he wanted to do, Jack crept through the hole and sat down on the floor of his prison.

Presently the guard was changed, and something to eat and drink was brought him.

"Only a loaf of bread and some water!" he muttered. "Well, that's better than nothing; and there is one comfort in it—they don't mean to eat me, or they'd fatten me up a bit first."

A few hours glided by, and he began to feel very miserable.

Suddenly the door opened, and Emily came in.

"This is a gleam of sunshine," he exclaimed. "Emily, you are as welcome as the flowers in May."

"Oh, Jack," she replied tearfully, "can you ever forgive me for getting you into this trouble?"

"It was my fault. I ought to have been more wide-awake. Why, I haven't thought about it since last night!"

"But they will kill you!" she answered.

"Will they? When?"

"To-morrow morning. It's all settled. A council has been held."

"How are they going to do it?" asked Jack, feeling curious as to the mode to be adopted in putting him out of the world.

"You are to be hanged at daybreak. I can hardly find courage to utter the dreadful words," said Emily, with a shudder.

Jack put his head on one side, and let his tongue hang out of his mouth, as a pantomimic way of describing the tragedy.

"Oh, don't joke, Jack dear," she replied. "It is too horrible; and to think that it is all my fault!"

"All through my love for you, eh, Emmy? Never mind, darling; they won't find me show the white feather," Jack exclaimed, firmly.

"I don't think there is much chance," she said.

"Is there any?" he inquired, regarding her earnestly.

"Ye—es."

"What is it?"

"Hunston says he will spare you, if I —I will marry him," replied the girl, blushing.

"Hang his impudence, Emmy," answered Jack, indignantly. "You marry a sweep like him. Don't you do it. I won't accept my life on those terms. I thought you cared for me."

"So I do, dear Jack. I love you, very, very much indeed!"

She threw herself on his breast, and wept bitterly.

"I have no one to think of but you now, since father died," she went on.

"Is Mr. Scratchley dead?"

"Yes; he died yesterday, while I was taken to Limbi; all through Hunston's violence. He struck him, and he never got over it."

"Did he? That's another chalk to Hunston," said Jack savagely.

"I didn't expect to meet you in these islands, and when I heard you were also wrecked, I thought what a pleasant meeting we should have, but how bitterly I have been deceived."

"I knew you were here, Emmy," said Jack.

"How did you find it out?" she asked, checking her tears and looking up.

He told her about the message from the sea.

"How wonderfully things happen," she exclaimed. "Poor papa got very needy after you left us, and he resolved to emigrate. Fancy our meeting here so many miles away from home!"

"I came over to Limbi principally to rescue you," continued Jack, "for I heard that a white girl was saved from the wreck and a prisoner among the Pisangs. After reading the message, you know, I guessed it was you."

"How can I thank you? But look here, Jack dear, I have brought you a

JACK'S TUTOR, PROFESSOR MOLE.

"Here's health to you, old boy!"

"MOLL'S WIVES ABUSED HIM IN THE CHOICEST TERMS OF THEIR LANGUAGE."

sharp Malay knife, which I stole from the Tuan Biza's house, where I live."

"Thank you. What shall I do with it—cut my throat and disappoint the Pisangs?" he said, concealing the weapon in his waistcoat.

She smiled sadly, for she knew he was not in earnest.

"You are still the same old Jack," she replied, "fearless in the midst of danger, and ready at all times to laugh at death."

"Why shouldn't I? Being miserable won't mend matters! Shall I sit down and cry? But tell me, how did you get leave to come and visit me?"

"I begged permission from Hunston, and he wouldn't give it me until—until——"

"Well?"

"I let him have a kiss. I didn't mean to, Jack. It was only a little one after all; don't be jealous!" she said, bashfully.

Jack set his teeth together.

"That's another chalk to Hunston. I'll have it out of him," he exclaimed.

"It felt like the touch of a snake, Jack dear," she went on.

"So I should think. The brute, to think that he had a kiss, when I haven't dared to ask for one. May I though, Emmy, may I?"

"You know you may, Jack—a dozen if you like."

And Jack did like.

He construed this into permission to help himself, and he covered her pretty face with kisses.

"There, Jack," she said, pushing him away; "that will do. Don't be stupid."

"That's a nice thing to say to a fellow, who's got to dance upon nothing to-morrow morning," he rejoined.

"Oh! there's another thing, Jack," exclaimed Emily, "I forgot to tell you. Hunston is coming here to examine you presently."

"Is he? What about?"

"The plan of the Limbian attack, which they expect soon. The number of men and fire-arms; and if you tell them, they will promise you your life, though they don't mean to keep their word any the more for that."

"I shouldn't suppose they would. They're all thieves and liars. Don't they wish they may get it. I shan't split on my party, so they wouldn't have got a word out of me, even if you hadn't told me."

"Spoken like yourself, Jack. Be true to your colour. I shouldn't like you if you weren't," replied Emily.

"I've got one comfort," continued Jack, "and that is, you will be all safe."

"How?"

"We're sure to lick them, at least Harvey is; he will fight like a Turk for me, and you will be rescued."

"Harvey, who was at school with you at Crawcour's? Is he at Limbi?"

"Rather. Alive and kicking too, and as good a friend, and as fine a fellow as ever lived," replied Jack.

"But without you—oh! Jack—without you, how could I— how can I live?" sobbed Emily, her fears overcoming her again.

"Don't worry, Emmy dear!" he replied, kissing away her tears. "The beggars haven't done it yet; they've got to do the trick."

"Can you help yourself?"

"I think so. There is plenty of time between this and to-morrow morning."

"To do what?"

"To cut my stick. If I'm not mistaken, they'll find the cage door open and the bird gone," he said.

"Have you got any plan?" she asked.

"Not yet. I've got to think it over; ideas generally come when I want them. I'm not going to stop here, to be strung up like a dog that's flat."

"You put new life into me, Jack," replied Emily, joyfully. "Oh! if you only could escape!"

"Wouldn't it be a lark?" Jack went on. "Hunston would have a fit, and he wouldn't be able to sleep, night or day, for thinking of the reckoning he'd have to pay me."

A head was put in at the door.

"Time's up," cried the voice of Hunston.

"Good bye, Emily," exclaimed Jack, pressing her hand, and giving her a wink which was intended to reassure her, and make her believe that he was quite prepared for anything that might happen.

She returned his farewell, and stepped, with as much bravery as she could summon to her aid, into the open air.

The door closed again.

But Jack was not alone.

Hunston stood leaning against a post, with his arms folded, and regarding Jack with an air of gratified malignity.

CHAPTER LIII.

KEPT IN SUSPENSE.

"I SUPPOSE you've come to crow over me," exclaimed Jack, annoyed at his visitor's sullen silence. "Go on; I can stand it."

"It won't be for long," replied Hunston. "We are going to settle old scores, Harkaway."

"If you'd any generosity, you'd forget and forgive," answered Jack.

"It is not my nature to do either one or the other. You've made me suffer, and you shall die to-morrow morning. I'd hang you to-day in sight of all the people, only I want you to think over what I'm going to tell you."

"What's that?"

"You love Emily. Don't deny it. I remember at school that she was your playfellow, and you grew up together."

"I don't mean to deny it," replied Jack.

"It wouldn't help you if you did, for I shouldn't believe you. Well, chance has thrown you both into my power. You shall die, and when you're dead, I will make Emily my wife."

Jack made no reply.

"Do you hear me. My wife!" continued Hunston. "Think of that!"

The shaft went home.

In the imperfect light which reigned in the bamboo house, Hunston could see his former companion writhe and bite his lips till he quivered with the pain.

"She shall see your body blackening in the sun, and the birds of prey picking your flesh from the bones."

"You're a cowardly bully, to come and exult over me like this," replied Jack, forgetting his assumed indifference.

"It's a part of my revenge. I knew it would come some day. I've worked and waited for it."

"I was a fool," said Jack, "not to have shot you when I had the chance."

"Perhaps you were. However, you've lost the opportunity, and you're not likely to have another," replied Hunston.

"You might think of one thing," replied Jack, "and that is, I saved you from the Pisangs when you were bound to the stake."

Hunston smiled sardonically.

"You wouldn't have done it if you could have forseen this day," he said.

"Yes, I would," answered Jack. "I would, upon my word. I could not see a former friend in distress, and not help him. But it's no use talking to you. One might as well speak to a stone of mercy."

"I don't know the word. Still I might be induced to spare your life," remarked Hunston, carelessly.

"On what terms?"

"Tell me the plan of the Limbian attack, for our spies have informed us that you mean to invade Pisang in force."

"You got that from Nuratella."

"Never mind where the intelligence came from. We can rely upon it."

Jack thought of what Emily had told him.

"Nothing would induce me to betray my friends and allies," he exclaimed.

"Nothing? Think a moment. Life is sweet."

"Not on such terms," answered Jack, resisting the voice of the tempter.

"Die, then! Die like a dog, as you deserve!" said Hunston, in a rage; "and think over all I have said to you."

"Get out!" cried Jack, "or, prisoner as I am, I'll punch your head."

Hunston stepped back.

"Touch me!" he exclaimed. "If you dare lay so much as your lfttle finger on me, I will have you seized, and your flesh torn off with jagged stones made red-hot."

"Coward!" was all Jack ventured to reply.

"I go," continued Hunston, "but you will see me at your side to-morrow morning when you are executed, and I hope my presence will add one more drop to your cup of misery."

"Thank you," replied Jack; "I am not afraid to die, and the prospect isn't half so bad as being obliged to be shut up here with such a beast as you."

Saying "to-morrow," Hunston left him alone, and Jack brightened up a bit.

"I can breath now that serpent is gone," Jack said to himself. "What a relief. He's worse than a snake to me."

The day passed and they brought him neither provisions or water.

His fate being decided upon, they did not seem to take any further notice of him, knowing that he was well guarded.

"I'll take a squint round, and see what's going on," thought Jack.

He climbed up the wall, as he had done before, and got on the roof.

In an open space before Hunston's house some men were busily at work with poles.

They were making a huge gallows.

"That's for me," said Jack.

And then he thought what a triumph it would be if he could only get away, join his friends, capture Palembang, and hang Hunston on his own gallows.

Presently he saw the Tuan Biza going by.

"Hi!" he cried. "Tuan Biza, hi!"

The chief looked up in astonishment.

"It's all right," cried Jack. "Hunston said I might take the air; but I'm very thirsty. Chuck us up a cocoa nut or something."

Apparently satisfied that Hunston had given him permission to get on the roof there was nothing wrong, the Tuan Biza gave orders that he should be supplied with what he wanted.

"They will bring you something presently," he said.

"And some grub. What do you call it in your lingo. 'Prindu;' that's it. Send me a small parrot, or a bit of pork, cold. I see you've got some likely pigs running about loose," continued Jack.

The Tuan Biza nodded, and passed on.

When Jack saw some Pisangs coming with refreshments, he descended again, and began to attack the viands with a good appetite.

"That's something like," he muttered. "I wanted food. It will set me up for the work I've got to do to-night."

His face assumed a determined expression.

Throwing himself on the ground in a corner, he closed his eyes.

But he did not sleep.

His brain was at work, and he was thinking how he could outwit his enemies.

The gallows he had seen had an ugly look, and the thought of it quickened his perceptions wonderfully.

CHAPTER LIV.

THE VOYAGE OF DISCOVERY.

HARVEY had not long to wait for his trusty followers.

He came toiling along, with about a dozen other Limbians, heavily laden with the spoil of the wreck.

They brought the packages and cases into the house, and laid them down.

"Excellent," said Mr. Mole, rubbing his hands. "You are a capital caterer, Harvey. Truly my heart rejoices within me at the sight of all these good things."

"Help yourself, sir! You can unpack them when we are gone," replied Harvey.

"I will not fail to do so."

"There is one thing I should like you to do, sir."

"You have but to name it, my young friend."

"There are several bodies of Englishmen, some washed ashore and others on the wreck."

"Yes!"

"Have them brought on shore, and see them decently buried, will you?"

"Certainly, Harvey; a most proper request. I will see the last obsequies paid to my unfortunate countrymen. Their bodies shall be brought up to-night and interred to-morrow," replied Mr. Mole.

"Now, Monday, look alive!" continued Harvey.

"What um Monday do now, sare?" asked the black.

"First of all, take off those togs."

"Take off um beautiful dress? No,

sare; not if him die for it!" replied Monday in alarm.

"But you must! You can keep them for Sunday; that hat will make a splendid Sunday-going beaver. You and I start soon."

"Start for where, Mast' Harvey?"

"To go after Jack. He is in the hands of the Pisangs, and we must see what we can do for him. If you wear those things, you won't have freedom of action on the war path!"

"Go after Mast' Jack?" cried Monday delightedly. "That 'nother thing, sare; Monday undress, and get um ready."

"I knew you would. I'd have sworn you'd go like a bird, after Jack?"

"Like one, two, three, bird, sare. Go anywhere, and do anything for you and Master Jack?" said the savage, who, under his dusky skin, had as good a heart as ever beat beneath a white one.

"Get the boat ready at once; put in any dried stuff you can lay your claws on, and bread, with some fresh water, enough, say, to last us a fortnight."

"All right, sare," replied Monday, running off.

Mr. Mole was overhauling what he called the "salvage."

"Glorious salvage, Harvey," he said, opening a case of Hollands. "The Dutchmen know what is good; this is veritable schnaps. I feel I want taking up a peg or two. We must sample this, Harvey."

"Peg away, sir. It's all your own," replied Dick.

"Very good; I will proceed to do so. Splendid fellows those Dutchmen! They manage to put a true taste of smoke into their whisky, which is what I like. I will drink to the independence of Holland."

Mr. Mole did so, and found the liquor so good that he repeated the experiment.

Harvey busied himself in making up a few packages, and was favoured with Mr. Mole's critical approval.

"Be careful," he said, "to take plenty of powder and shot. The only argument these savages understand, is, as we used to say at school, the *argumentum ad hominem*. An ounce of lead is a powerful persuader!"

"I know all that," replied Harvey. "Don't bustle me, sir."

"Reject my advice, if you like. I know I am right, and I have your welfare at heart."

"Coach up those Limbians then, sir, and come over to Pisang as soon as you can; we shall have hot work, and Jack will want friends."

"Which he shall find."

"I am going to tell the chiefs of my departure, sir, and shall be off in a twinkling. Good bye!" said Harvey.

"Good bye, and God bless you, my brave boy! I will take care of your belongings here," replied Mr. Mole.

They shook hands, and Harvey hurried off.

He had determined to try and save Jack at all hazards.

The Limbians were sorry to lose his leadership, but they promised to obey Mr. Mole, whom they regarded as a great chief.

And they also undertook to start on the expedition as soon as possible.

They had made great progress in their drill, and had proved themselves expert shots.

Joining Monday, Harvey hurried down to the house to get his packages.

"I will see you off!" cried Mr. Mole. "I do not mind walking with you now Monday has taken off his grotesque dress, but if he were disguised as he was a short time back, I should have thought I was walking in the Zoo with the chimpanzee or the ourang outang's brother."

Harvey began to hum. "The O. K. thing at Limbi is walking in the Zoo!"

"Ah!" said Mr. Mole with a sigh. "What a thing youth is. I wish I had your spirits, Harvey?"

The latter pointed to an empty bottle, and replied—

"I think you have had your share, sir!"

"I mean animal spirits, Harvey. You have mistaken my remark."

Mr. Mole rose as he spoke, and staggered a little on one side.

"Dear me," he said, "this is odd; I appear to have lost my centre of gravity!"

"Groggy on your pins, eh, sir!" replied Harvey, laughing.

"Rather so, my juvenile but still intelligent friend. There is an inclination in my right leg to go sideways. This is more than odd—it is passing strange."

"Mind the wall, sir," exclaimed Harvey, as the late senior master of Pomona House came into violent collision with the bamboos.

"Your warning came too late, Harvey; I have collided, that is to say, struck, and the effect is painful."

"Which was the hardest, sir; your cocoa-nut or the wall?"

"Much of a muchness, Harvey," replied Mr. Mole, sitting down on the floor. "I do not think I will go with you, yet I hope you will manage to effect a start without my valuable assistance. I have over fatigued myself to-day, and exhausted nature must have rest. Fare thee well!"

His head fell back, and he was soon snoring "thirteen to the dozen," as Harvey said.

Harvey and Monday, laden with packages, now made their way to the coast.

It was growing late, and darkness would soon fall.

They got into the boat, and, hoisting the sail, began to leave Limbi behind them.

"Do you think you can manage to steer all serene at night?" asked Harvey.

"Monday know him way, sare," replied the black.

"All right. I leave it to you; but don't run us into any danger."

Night fell, and Monday, looking at the stars, kept the boat's head well before the wind.

They were both armed with revolvers and knives, while rifles lay at the bottom of the boat, ready for use at a moment's notice.

It was clear that if they encountered twenty Pisangs they would not be taken at a disadvantage.

Their firearms would give them a superiority, provided they were not struck by spears or arrows.

In the use of the latter weapons all the natives of those islands were very expert.

The night passed quickly, as it does in those latitudes, and Harvey snatched a few hours' sleep.

He dreamt that he saw Jack hanging on a high gibbit, with his enemies singing war-songs around him.

Waking in a fright, he found himself bathed in a cold sweat.

On the verge of the horizon was a dark speck.

"That's land, Monday!" he exclaimed.

There was no answer.

Monday, worn out, had fallen asleep, and the boat had drifted at the mercy of the wind and waves.

It was lucky that the breeze was not a strong one, or they would have capsized

They were travelling at a rapid pace towards the land, and it was evident they had been caught in a current, which set in strongly to the shore.

Shaking the black, Harvey succeeded in rousing him.

"Where the dickens are we?" said Harvey.

"Monday go to sleep. That bad. Mast' Harvey him kick Monday, who much 'shamed," said the black, looking crest-fallen.

"Never mind; I suppose you couldn't help it. I shan't bully you, though you deserve a blowing up. Do you know what island that is ahead of us?"

Monday shook his head.

He was out of his reckoning.

"This delay is vexatious," continued Harvey. "Every moment is precious, Jack's life may hang by a thread, as they say. Why the deuce couldn't you keep your swivel eye open?"

"Monday big stupid donkey; he worse than um child."

"I suppose we'd better run in and see. If it isn't Pisang, we must start again."

"Look!" cried Monday, as they neared a dangerous reef of coral.

"At what?"

"That post, sare. That one flagstaff. This our island; what we call Ship Island, you know. We live there once; that where you save Monday from him enemies."

Harvey looked again, shading his face with his hand.

"You're right," he replied. "That's Mr. Mole's signal station. It is our island. Shall we land?"

"If got time, sare."

"It won't make above an hour or two's difference, and we can take our bearings."

"See um old castle, Mast' Harvey; that much jolly!" cried Monday, in delight.

"Yes, I should like to have a look at the old place."

"Monday him like it too. We very happy in um old castle, Mast' Harvey."

"We hadn't much to grumble at, if Hunston and his savages had let us alone. Do you think you could start afresh, now you know where you are?"

"Start from here, sare? Easy."

"And make Pisang."

"Pisang over there; many, much

miles away;" replied Monday, pointing to the north-west, after taking his bearings.

"All right, steer steadily. Run her through the reef, and we'll have a squint round," exclaimed Harvey.

They had christened the boat "The Jack Harkaway," and riding the waters like a thing of life, she bounded joyously along, as if glad to revisit the old spot that gave her birth.

CHAPTER LV.

REVISITING THE CASTLE.

THERE was little difficulty in passing the reef during daylight, and it was with mingled emotions that Harvey stepped on that shore where he and Jack had landed, the latter taking possession of the island in the name of Queen Victoria.

Walking first to the signal station, he saw that the wind had torn the flag to rags, which fluttered feebly if not sadly in the breeze.

He then proceeded to the castle.

Nothing was to be seen but its blackened remains, for the fire kindled by the Pisangs had done its work effectually.

Some of the trees were throwing out tender shoots again, but the trunks were bare and black.

Everything of utility or value had been carried off.

It was a scene of wreck and desolation.

The birds had played havoc with the corn, and other creatures had routed amongst the potatoes, until the farm was like a wilderness choked up with weeds.

The skeletons of the Pisangs who were killed by the explosion, lay on the ground whitening in the sun.

"Who would think," said Harvey, "that this was once a flourishing little settlement?"

"Him look wild enough now, sare," returned Monday.

Harvey strolled on a little further.

Before him was Maple's grave.

He remembered how tenderly they had laid the poor misguided boy in his last resting place, and a tear fell from his eye.

The little mound was overrun with rank grass and weeds.

They had planted flowers upon it, which were choked by the luxuriant growth of the tropics.

The rough wooden cross, which Jack had in the piety of his heart erected, had fallen on one side.

Stooping down, Harvey took out his knife and cut away the grass and weeds trimming it round neatly.

Then he replaced the cross, and firmly secured it.

"If ever I see his mother," he thought, "she will ask me about her boy."

He did all he could to pay respect to his memory, though that was little enough.

He was engaged in a perilous and desperate enterprise, and he did not know how soon he might be in a similar position.

Stricken down in his youth, and laid low in the cold unsympathising ground, with no kind hands to deck his grave and shed a tear to his memory.

It is in times of danger, and in the hour of solitude, that the thought of death affects us most.

Who shall say, that death does not lose half its terrors when we know that weeping friends are round us, and that sincere mourners will bear our body reverently to the grave?

Sinking on his knees, Harvey prayed shortly but fervently.

He prayed that the poor dead boy's sins might not be remembered against him.

He supplicated that he might be forgiven for his bad faith, and his desire to injure those who had endeavoured to be kind to him.

When he rose to his feet and returned to the ruins of the castle, his face was wet with tears that he could not suppress.

Monday had been watching him, and he said. "Why you cry, Mast' Harvey?"

Harvey made him no reply.

"Why you let fall tear, sare? Why you kneel down there, and put your face in your hand?" continued Monday.

"You don't understand our religion,

Monday," replied Harvey. "That is a grave!"

"Some one dead lie there, sare?"

"Yes, a friend of mine; not much younger that I am."

"How him come to die, sare?"

"Perhaps I killed him. I know not. It was either Jack or myself, but we were fighting in self-defence. It is a sad story, Monday," said Harvey. "We won't dwell upon it. Let us get back to the boat, and go on with the work we have in hand."

Monday held his head down, as if he wished to sympathise with his master's grief, and they slowly retraced their steps to the sea side.

Suddenly they heard a sound like the growling of a mastiff.

Though Harvey had been some months in the Archipelago, he did not understand noises made by animals half so well as Monday, who had been bred and born amongst them.

He was about to advance, when Monday laid his hand upon his arm.

"What the blazes is the row now?" asked Harvey, annoyed at the interruption.

Monday pointed to a clump of trees at one side of them.

"Tiger!" he answered, with an evidence of terror he could not conceal.

"Oh, Jerusalem!" replied Harvey. "I fancy I could wop my weight in wild cats, but tigers are pussies of another colour."

They both drew back.

The growling increased in intensity.

Placing his mouth near the ground, the monster's noise reverberated around, until the dreadful roar could be heard for miles.

When the king of the forest is in a passion, every living thing within hearing is stricken with terror, even the birds ceased singing.

No other sound broke the stillness of the air.

Presently the beast emerged from her cover, and Monday declared she could smell human flesh.

She was a magnificent tigress, about four years old, and Harvey could not help admiring her beautifully-marked skin, as she walked up and down under a tree, lashing her striped sides with her long tail, which she sometimes threw right over her back.

"I have seen them do that in the Zoo,' said Harvey, in a whisper, as if speaking to himself. "That's just how they go on before feeding time. She's getting excited. Softly, my pretty dear; I'm coming."

All at once she stooped the fore part of her body, put her ears back, and opened her huge cavernous mouth.

"Stand close, Monday," cried Harvey.

He levelled his rifle for he thought she was going to spring.

Monday trembled too much to allow his fire to be of any use.

With his quick eye Harvey saw this, and continued—

"Don't shoot. Hold your gun ready for me, if I don't stop her."

Monday could only nod his head, and Harvey heard his teeth chatter.

He had no time to say more.

Away she flew, making a splendid bound of many feet, eyes flashing, jaws open, paws outstretched.

Harvey took steady aim, and let her have his one barrel full in the chest.

Monday now recovered his presence of mind, and violently pulled his young master on one side.

It was lucky he did so, for the shot did not stop her.

Had he remained where he was, she would have alighted straight upon him, so well had she calculated the distance and her own power of springing.

Seizing Monday's gun, which, unlike the rifle, had two barrels, and was a breech-loader, Harvey fired twice quickly, not daring to take regular aim, and make a "pot-shot" of it from the shoulder.

He had dropped his own piece, and the infuriated creature fell upon it with a plunge, growling over it like a cat with a mouse.

She laid hold of it with her massive teeth, and twisting it as if it had been a straw, broke it in half.

Then she jumped up, staggered a few feet towards Harvey, and fell down dead.

He waited a minute or so, to see if she was really done for, and feeling satisfied that she was past further mischief, walked up to her and fired a revolver into her head.

"That will make sure," he said.

Monday also came up, and began to make faces at the dead tiger, just as if she could understand him.

He danced before her, spit at her,

kicked her in the side, and pulled her ears in childish spite.

"What's the caper now?" asked Harvey. "The beast's dead."

"Tigers, sare, kill many Limbi people," replied Monday. "That's why me frighten. Now I tell her what I think of her."

And he began to abuse her and all her family, especially her father and mother, and her children or her cubs if she had any.

"You're a neat thing in niggers, to go on like that," exclaimed Harvey, laughing.

"We believe," replied Monday, "that the tiger spirit listen to us. Ah!" he continued, "you old wretch, how many Limbis you eaten—how many Pisang? Your father is a coward, he fly away from a monkey; your mother never fight fair, and your family not worth one pig."

"Shut up," said Harvey. "You can't be such an ass as to think that the tiger can hear you. I thought you had thrown off your old superstitions. Try and be more sensible."

Monday did not speak any more, but he shook his head, as if he had his own opinion about things in general, and that in particular.

"I should like that skin," continued Harvey. "Set to work and skin the beggar, and look slippery over it."

Monday produced his knife, and soon had the creature's handsome skin off.

He rubbed it with sand to clean it, and Harvey hung it over the side of the boat to dry in the sun.

"If ever we get back safe to Limbi, I'll keep that as a trophy. *Spolia opima*, as Mole would say," remarked Harvey.

Having embarked, they set sail, and by dint of tacking against the wind made fair progress.

Monday declared that he knew his way, and that they would reach Pisang before night.

"If you go to sleep again, I'll pound you," said Harvey.

"No sleep any more, till land in Pisang, Mast' Harvey," replied Monday.

"Mind you don't, that's all!"

Harvey was dreadfully nervous about Jack.

He feared he was in great peril, for he knew Hunston's character, and his influence over the Pisangs.

Jack was an enemy to be got rid of, for various reasons.

Nuratella had told the Pisangs that an invasion was thought of, and that Jack was the heart and soul of the Limbians.

Therefore, to kill him and get him out of the way was half the battle.

"Only let me have a slap at them, and I'll give them what for," said Harvey between his teeth.

The adventure he had embarked in, however, was more hazardous than even he imagined.

It is one of the advantages of being young—or, shall we say, one of the disadvantages—that we do not stop to consider consequences.

Young people usually act upon impulse, and impulsive actions are very often successful.

Monday was right as to the duration of the voyage.

It was not longer than seven hours, and they reached an island, which he declared to be Pisang, before night fell.

Running the boat ashore, Harvey jumped out, and said—

"What's to be done now?"

Monday did not know.

"I leave all to Mast' Harvey," he said. "Where him go, Monday follow."

"There is such a thing as going into the lion's den, and I don't mean to do that," answered Harvey.

"They have one big town like us," continued Monday; "it call Palembang. Once we have small towns."

"Villages!"

"Yes; but when war come all villages burn, now we all live together. Our town call Tompano, their town Palembang."

"Then there is not much chance of finding any one in the wilds. Shall we camp in the open, and keep watch and watch, or sleep in the boat?" said Harvey.

Monday could not offer an opinion.

He was not at any time very brilliant, and was rather formed for obeying than leading.

He had come to rescue Harkaway, and would fight for him, but how to set about rescuing him he knew no more than a baby.

"I think," said Harvey, after some reflection, "that we had best camp in the woods, and work our way up to Palembang in the morning. You speak the same language as they do, you are all a species of Malay. Can't you get into the town, and find out what's going on?"

"Yes, sare; Monday do that, though they cut um throat if they catch him."

"But you musn't allow yourself to be caught; we can't spare you, Monday."

"When um go? Now?" asked the worthy fellow.

"On consideration, no," replied Harvey. "We'll wait for morning, which will come in a few hours, and then we will work our way into the interior."

Hiding the boat as well as they could, they took a good supply of arms and ammunition, and made a camp in the woods, formed of the boughs of trees which they tore down.

"You slept last night; it's my turn now. Though, in fact, we were both in fault," exclaimed Harvey.

"Monday take first watch, sare."

"All right. Keep your weather eye open, and kick me at the slightest sound."

Harvey was soon asleep.

Monday stood with his gun tightly clasped, listening for the least noise with an eagerness that the danger of their position rendered necessary.

He was sorry for his fault the night before, and wished to make amends.

They were in the enemies' country, and the least cessation in vigilance might cost them their lives.

"Monday near eaten once," he said to himself; "no catch and try eat him second time."

They were about two miles inland, and, though they did not know it, they were not more than half a dozen miles from Palembang.

During the day the preparations for hanging Jack were finished.

On the morrow he was to die.

CHAPTER LVI.

THE ESCAPE.

WE must leave Harvey and his faithful follower in their rude camp, while we return to Harkaway.

The position in which we saw him last was not a pleasant one.

But he had kept up his spirits.

From a short distance the sounds of revelry reached him, and he concluded that the Pisangs were making merry at his approaching death.

Rude songs were being sung, and the sound of musical instruments could be distinguished at intervals.

"They are making a night of it. I should like to have a look at them," he thought. "There is time yet."

Climbing up to the roof, as he had done before, he saw his guard standing in front of his prison door.

Lamps, trimmed with palm-oil, illuminated a large, barn-like building near Hunston's house.

It was from this erection that the noise proceeded.

Jack rightly supposed this to be the council-chamber, for it was very similar to the one in Limbi, where the chiefs assembled for the discussion of public business.

One of his guards he recognised as Buru, who had accompanied the Tuan Biza on his first expedition to the island.

The other he had heard addressed as Padang.

Throwing his voice in the direction of the council-chamber, he imitated Hunston, and said—

"Buru, it is our wish that you bring the white prisoner before us."

Buru was not at all astonished at this command, and at once proceeded to put it in execution.

Opening the door of the prison, he exclaimed—

"Come with me. You must appear before the council."

"All right," answered Jack. "What is going on?"

"All the chiefs in Pisang sing the song of triumph, because the white man is in their power."

"And a jolly noise they make. Will they give me anything to drink?" asked Jack.

"They have the palm spirit of Pisang, but water is the fare of the condemned," answered Buru.

The guards put themselves on each

side of Jack, and conducted him to the council.

He passed through an open door, and found himself in the presence of about fifty chiefs, who were sitting on mats, placed round the side of the spacious hall.

Hunston was at one end, and the Tuan Biza at the other.

Both of them occupied a seat slightly raised above the others, as a token of high rank and precedence.

"How is this?" asked the Tuan Biza, in surprise, as he beheld Jack.

Hunston was about to ask the same question, when Jack made him say—

"I sent for him, O chief, to make sport of him."

An old chief rose and said—

"It is cowardly to insult the fallen."

"If it is the pleasure of our white friend, why do you, O Wahar, fly in his face?" inquired the Tuan Biza.

The old chief was about to protest that he had not intended to offend their white friend, when Jack, imitating his voice, said—

"The white chief is not worthy to be one of us. Let us hang him to-morrow instead of the prisoner."

An indescribable confusion arose at this suggestion, and another chief rose.

But before he could open his mouth, Jack made him exclaim—

"The proposal is good. Let us hang him, and dance over his grave."

The uproar increased.

Making Hunston speak, Jack went on—

"The Tuan Biza and his chiefs are old women. What care I for them? I will fight them all single-handed, and give their bodies to the birds, and their wives shall lament them in vain."

"What?" cried the Tuan Biza. "Do you attack me, O, Hunstani?" for so they had altered his name. "You dare not come to me, and say that I am a woman!"

"Daren't I?" Jack caused Hunston to answer. "You are worse than the timid deer, and your soul is as a reed."

"I have slain my foes in battle," replied the Tuan Biza. "You speak bitterly, O Hunstani, but I have the power to make you eat your words!"

"I laugh at your beard," said Jack, still making Hunston speak. "You shall die and your grave shall be defiled!"

"This is too much! Give me my spear!" shouted the Tuan Biza.

Changing his tone, Jack threw his voice close to Buru, and made him say—

"The white chief will eat you, O Tuan Biza, for he says truly that your soul is as a reed."

"Oh!" replied the Tuan Biza, "you are against me also? Take that!"

He had seized his spear by this time, and dealt Buru a heavy blow over the head with it.

Now Buru was also a great chief in his own estimation, and he did not like this sort of treatment.

Spears are hard, and if well laid on are apt to hurt.

So he retaliated, and gave the Tuan Biza a blow with a sort of mallet he carried, and hit him under the ear.

This caused him to roll over and over, uttering dismal cries.

Some friends of the Tuan Biza resented this, and attacked Buru.

He was supported by Padang, his companion, and they returned the blows with interest.

Jack jumped on a rude table, and surveyed the scene with satisfaction.

Several chiefs, thinking Hunston the cause of all the mischief, made a charge at him, against which he defended himself with difficulty.

Seeing he was getting roughly handled, Jack made his way to that end of the room, and pulled him into a corner.

The fight had now become general, and the Pisangs were engaged in a hard hand-to-hand fight amongst themselves.

The jealousy existing at all times among those distinguished warriors was easily excited, and they were only too glad of a quarrel.

During a disturbance of this sort they could pay off old scores.

They had been drinking their palm spirit, and were more or less excited by the songs they had been singing.

Hunston had been disarmed in the conflict, and looked sullenly at Jack, who held before his eyes the knife which Emily had supplied him with.

"You have got this up," said Hunston, "but you cannot escape."

"That's all you know about it," replied Jack; "but don't tremble; I'm not a coward. I might kill you in a stand-up fight, but I shall not harm you now."

"What did you want to upset the

"ARE YOU ALONE?' NUBATELLA INQUIRED OF JACK."

council for? They don't understand your ventriloquism," continued Hunston, who wanted to keep Jack in conversation till the riot lessoned and the combatants came to their senses once more.

"I was getting dull in that shed place where you shut me up, awfully slow, in fact; and when I heard you fellows enjoying yourselves, and having a bit of a barney, I thought I'd join in and sing you Rule Britannia, or something lively."

"I shall never have the same influence over the Pisangs again. Look how they are fighting!"

"The Kilkenny cats are nothing to them," Jack remarked.

"Say something and stop them; "you can do it," exclaimed Hunston.

"And get taken back to be hanged. Thank you, no; I'd rather not," replied Jack, with a grin.

"I'll promise you your life."

"Will you?"

"Yes, I will, indeed."

"What is your promise worth, do you think?" answered Jack, derisively. "You'd tell a bushel of lies for a dollar, and say your prayers afterwards with a good conscience."

"You must trust me for old acquaintance sake. Stop the row, and give them a specimen of your ventriloquial powers. It will put them in a good humour."

"You're very kind," Jack said. "Perhaps they'd enjoy the entertainment very much, especially as the show wouldn't cost them anything. But I'm sorry I can't stop."

"Can't stop? What do you mean?" said Hunston, laying his hand on his arm.

"Paws off, Pompey!" cried Jack, angrily. "If you want a domino, just say which eye you would prefer to be temporarily darkened."

"But I say you can't go. You must stop. You're a prisoner," continued Hunston.

Jack's knife flashed before his eyes, and he retreated further into the corner.

Taking up a lamp which stood near, Jack looked at it.

The wick, made of a bit of dry pith, floated in the half of a cocoa nut filled with oil.

"It will do," he said.

"Do!" repeated Hunston. "Do for what?"

"You'll see, if you live long enough.

Thought you were going to hang me, did you?" replied Jack, laughing.

He held the lamp to the side of the council-chamber.

It was built entirely of bamboo, which, being as dry as tinder, was exceedingly inflammable.

"You'll set the place on fire!" exclaimed Hunston, in alarm.

"Just what occurred to me, my pippin; and as the wind is rather high, I shouldn't wonder if all Palembang was to go to blazes before morning," Jack answered.

"Help! here, he's——"began Hunston, when the point of Jack's knife penetrated the clothes he wore and pricked his breast.

"Do you want to go to kingdom come?" said Jack.

"No," muttered Hunston, sullenly.

"Then shut up. I don't want to kill you now; but necessity has no law, and if you utter a sound loud enough for a dumb man to swear by, you shall have six inches of cold steel in the neighbourhood of the fifth rib immediately, if not sooner."

The bamboo framework had by this time caught fire, and the flames began to spread with a loud crackling noise.

Those Pisangs who had been fighting were getting tired of the amusement.

The elder chiefs, who had been trying to pacify the combatants, were beginning to succeed in their efforts.

"Good bye," said Jack.

"You shan't go! I'll——'

Jack looked for a moment as if he was going to use his knife.

But he put it in his belt, and clenching his fists, let Hunston have what he called "one, two."

Hunston fell back heavily, half stunned, as he had often done before when he made acquaintance with Jack's sledge-hammer fists.

His hat fell off, and Jack took it up and put it on.

It was made of straw, and it had a conical shape.

"Rummy sort of tile," mused Jack; "but I suppose it is a badge of distinction, or something. "I'll sport it, and they may take me for him; not that I shall be flattered at the mistake, only it may help me to make tracks."

The flames had made incredible progress, in the few minutes that had elapsed since Jack set fire to the bamboo framework with the lamp.

"They'd better call out the engines and send for the fire escape," Jack said to himself, indulging in that dry humour which he could not resist even in the hour of extreme danger.

The thick smoke and the crackling of the fire alarmed every one.

In an instant the din ceased, the uproar had subsided, and the men who had been struggling together in a sort of Irish row, looked blankly at one another.

Jack passed quickly amongst the crowd.

They raised a cry of "Fire! fire!" and ran hither and thither wildly.

A panic had seized them.

Suddenly Hunston, who had picked himself up, shouted, in a commanding voice, which trembled with rage—

"Guard the door! The prisoner has done this! Let him not escape!"

Cries of "Guard the door!" "The white prisoner!" "Death to the prisoner!" arose on all sides.

"It's getting hot," said Jack to himself. "I wasted precious time with that beast Hunston."

The smoke grew thicker, and obscured the feeble light of the oil lamps, many of which had been extinguished in the scuffle.

This dimness was much in his favour.

It was at the door itself where the real peril lay.

There Buru and some others, including the Tuan Biza, whose faces presented the appearance of so many crushed tomatoes, had congregated.

"Now for it!" exclaimed Jack, as he was within a few paces of the door. "Never say die!"

CHAPTER LVII.

ACROSS THE BRIDGE

It had not been Jack's hope or intention to escape when he determined to visit the council.

The idea was suggested by his natural daring and love of fun.

He thought it would create a sensation of some sort, and give him an opportunity; which it had done.

How he would be able to avail himself of that opportunity was another thing.

So far he had succeeded beyond his expectations.

He had got up ill blood between Hunston and his savage friends.

The Tuan Biza and the other chiefs had engaged in a dreadful riot, which had resulted in more than one broken head.

Hunston had been "chaffed and punched," as Jack said, when he was reckoning up the damage afterwards.

And to crown all, the council-chamber was in flames, the chiefs in frantic terror, and only a few cool hands guarding the door in obedience to Hunston's ill-timed summons.

Such was the situation of affairs.

Up to the present time Jack had decidedly the best of it.

One of Buru's eyes was rapidly closing, and the other wasn't of much use.

But he had heard Hunston's voice, and with native cunning guessed that the prisoner had set the place on fire, hoping to escape in the inevitable hubbub that would ensue.

"If," he argued, "Hunston is at one end of the council-chamber, he can't be at the other."

He did not believe that even a white chief, clever though he might be, could be in two places at one time.

So Jack's conical hat did not impose upon him.

Imitating Hunston's voice again, Jack said, as he reached the door—

"Let me out, my good Buru. I am Hunston, the white chief."

"You are the prisoner," replied Buru. "Yield yourself to me."

Jack's only reply was to draw his knife, and plunge it up to the hilt in his body.

Buru fell without a sound.

The Pisangs saw the deed committed, and were silent for a moment through terror and amazement.

But an instant afterwards a dozen spears were levelled at him, and half as many ugly-looking clubs aimed at his head.

Cutting right and left with his knife, he backed through the crowd.

He reached the burning portion of the

apartment, which was fringed by an eager knot of spectators.

The wall was nearly burnt through, and the roof had fallen in.

Fierce cries assailed him, and if he hesitated he was lost.

Hunston made a snatch at him, hoping to hold him fast till he could get assistance.

But Jack threw him off, saying, "You didn't do it that time, old boy!" and dashed boldly into the burning space, and falling timber.

With a wild plunge he dashed through the hole in the wall, and, half blinded, half suffocated, found himself outside.

The air was cool and refreshing.

At present the alarm of fire had not spread, and the inhabitants of Palembang were sleeping in fancied security.

His hair was singed, and his hat was on fire.

This he cast from him as a useless encumbrance, and taking one look at the burning building, ran at full speed up the street.

When his enemies had recovered from their surprise, they rushed through the open door, and gave chase.

Hunston was at their head.

"After him!" he cried. "He will take to the woods. After him! He cannot escape. Brave will be the chief who takes his head, and all the women of Palembang will smile upon him."

Jack's form could be clearly seen in the moonlight.

The pursuers halted at the extremity of the town, satisfied that they knew the direction the fugitive had taken.

They held a brief conversation, which resulted in twelve chiefs, with Hunston in command, being told off to pursue the runaway.

The rest returned to the burning council-chamber, to assist in putting out the fire, which had assumed formidable dimensions.

No sooner had Jack reached the open ground than he turned round, and skirted the town to throw the Pisangs off the scent.

They would imagine that he would go straight on, and he might gain a secure shelter in the woods.

As he moderated his pace and went round the town, he could hear the cries of the affrighted populace.

Gongs were beaten in every direction.

Dense clouds of smoke and bright flashes of flame showed him that the fire, driven by the wind, had seized on other dwellings, and was making great havoc and devastation.

"It's as good as burning out a wasp's nest," he remarked.

For more than two hours he ran without halting.

It was his impression that when those who followed him found themselves at fault they would return to the burning town.

Three several parties of explorers would be formed, and dispatched in various directions.

When day broke he had reached a dense forest, and feeling tired, he climbed into a tree to enjoy a little rest.

Lashing himself with his handkerchief to a bough, he closed his eyes.

For some time he could not go to sleep, owing to the sharp hiss of the serpents and the dred cries of the wild beasts.

He thought with horror of Sinbad the Sailor when in a similar position.

Sinbad had two companions with him, and they were lower down in a tree.

On the first night a huge snake climbed up, and dragged down one of the men.

Would the snakes of this island attempt to gratify their appetites in a similar manner?

"No serpent shall land me," he said to himself. "I'll sleep with one eye open."

But at length exhausted nature had its way, and he slept soundly.

Not for long, however.

He was awake before the sun had acquired any considerable power, and unlashing himself he descended the tree.

All nature was smiling under the grateful night dew and the cheering sun's rays.

He pushed on slowly through the forest, not daring to retrace his steps.

His only hope was to subsist in the jungle as best he might until his friends from Limbi had come over and captured the island, if they could succeed in doing so.

He felt sure that Harvey was doing his utmost for him.

But he did not suspect the length to which Harvey's devotion had led him.

Nor did he even faintly imagine that he and Monday were at that very time on the island.

"Dick won't desert me," he thought

"Dick will stick to me like a leech. That's one comfort."

He was in high spirits as he slowly trudged along through the dense underwood.

To have outwitted the Pisangs, bearded Hunston amongst his friends, and set the town of Palembang on fire was no slight achievement.

Suddenly he felt a peculiar smarting and itching sensation at the ancle.

Looking down, he found his socks stained with blood.

Turning them down, he saw both ancles perfectly fringed with little insects like leeches, which had filled themselves till they were ready to burst.

Some of the bloodsuckers had even crawled down to his foot, and made an incision which allowed the blood to trickle through his shoe.

Jack had heard of these annoying and disquieting pests from Monday.

Sometimes the stinging worms would drop from the leaves of the trees upon the heads and into the necks of those who pass under them.

It was almost unendurable to think that they were lancing him and sucking out his blood.

However, he knocked them off as well as he could, and travelled onwards.

At length he came to a river which ran through a ravine, the rocky bottom of which churned its impetuous waters into foam.

Cautiously making his way by the side of the rocky channel, Jack pushed along in a listless manner.

He wished to find a cave in which he could rest, with a few palms in the vicinity to supply him with cocoa-nuts.

He had not gone far before he came to a hanging bridge, which was thrown across the ravine.

On each side was a road, if an ordinary clearing in the forest might be dignified with that name.

It was a suspension bridge of rattan; at the middle it rested on the tops of tall trees, which grew up from a small island in the torrent below.

It was constructed by stretching across these large rattans.

On these, narrow slips of board were placed and fastened at each end; other rattans starting from the ground on the bank, passed above the branches of high camphor trees that grew on the edge of the chasm in which the torrent flowed; descending from these branches in a sharp curve, they rose again steeply at the further end of the bridge.

From these rattans, were fastened other rattans below them, just as in our own suspension bridges, and thus all parts were made to aid in supporting the weight.

As it was so light, it vibrated and shook terribly when any one ventured to cross it.

Jack had been told of these bridges, of which there are several in the islands, and had been cautioned against grasping the side, lest it might swing over and cast him into the abyss.

The difficulty in crossing this bridge, which was flexible as a manilla rope, was so great because it oscillated from left to right, and its whole floor did not move in one piece, but like a series of rolling waves.

"I don't think I'll venture across that," said Jack. "But I'll go down the rocks, if I can manage it, and have a drink of water."

As he was speaking, he heard a loud shout behind him.

The next moment an arrow buried itself in a tree close to him.

He looked round, and saw a party of Pisangs, probably forming one of the divisions that had been sent out to search for him.

Now he blamed himself for his folly in not remaining hidden.

He could not have acted more foolishly than exposing himself to view, on one of the few public roads, in the island.

To retreat into the forest, was to court instant death or capture.

The road was blocked.

The sides of the ravine were just there almost perpendicular, and impossible of descent.

If he would escape, there was nothing for it but a bold attempt to cross the dangerous bridge.

Without any further hesitation, he got on the bridge, with a hurried walk, which he hoped would break up the rolling motion.

It was nearly four hundred feet long.

Having got half-way across the first span, he saw that one of the cross boards, on which he was in the act of placing his foot, had become loose, and slipped on to one side.

He drew back, for had he gone on carelessly, he must have fallen through, and been dashed to pieces on the rocks below.

Stopping instantly, he stood still, and the bridge swung to and fro, as if it was being purposely shaken.

The Pisangs continued to fire arrows at him, but the motion of the bridge interfered with the correctness of their aim.

Going on again, he reached the centre, and reconnoitred his enemies.

One Pisang, more adventurous than the rest, was following him.

"Wait a bit!" said Jack between his teeth.

He had gained confidence now, and crossed the remaining half at a quick run, hiding himself behind a tree when on land.

The Pisangs shouted to one another, and flattered themselves that their prey was not far off.

When the whole five were together, on the second half, Jack slashed away with his knife at the supports of rattan.

Three or four parted, and the remaining ones unable to support the weight, snapped with a loud sharp crack, like the report of a pistol.

The large rattans that supported the sides, and went over the high branches of the camphor trees, had parted.

Then the bridge gave a fearful lurch, and finally the whole structure fell with a crash into the boiling torrent.

Fearful cries arose from the poor wretches thus hurled into eternity, but Jack smiled grimly, for it was their lives or his, and again he had triumphed.

His exultation was premature however.

Straight in front of him, he saw five more Pisangs, who were attracted by the cries of their countrymen.

They hurried forward, but all was still.

Probably the party had divided, one half crossing the bridge, the other, which had perished, remaining behind.

They peered down the sides of the ravine, and talked hurriedly among themselves.

One, more curious than the rest, examined the rattans, and saw that they had been cut, with a knife.

He pointed this out to his companions.

Yells of fury arose, and Jack, who was gently stealing off along the road, was perceived.

Instantly a hue and cry was raised.

"Now for it!" thought Jack, as he scudded along the road. "I must step out, or make up my mind to be cooked for dinner, and eaten without salt."

He had a slight start, but it was a question whether or not he would keep it.

His pursuers made the woods echo again with their savage outcries.

Jack's training in hare-and-hounds, at Mr. Crawcour's academy for young gentlemen, stood him in good stead now.

It was a race for life.

CHAPTER LVIII.

THE RACE FOR LIFE.

As the Pisangs knew the road and the country so much better than he did, Jack was afraid to take refuge in the forest again.

He ran on at the top of his speed, not daring to turn round to look how the chase progressed, lest he should lose time.

No arrows were fired at him; no spears thrown.

Either the Pisangs had received orders to bring him back alive, or they would not stop to adjust their bows, or hurl their spears.

It scarcely could be that they had regard for his life, or an arrow would not have been shot at him when he was bent on his perilous journey across the bridge.

Good runner as he was, he had not gone more than three or four miles before he felt his strength failing him.

Jack's head grew dizzy, and his legs seemed to drag one after the other.

The wound inflicted upon him when captured had caused him to lose blood.

This would create weakness, and even vertigo, if compelled to undergo unwonted exertion.

For some hours he had not had anything to eat and drink.

He was also running under a hot sun, which made the perspiration pour from him in streams. All this told against him.

The Pisangs had nothing to impede the free exercise of their limbs.

He had.

Therefore he was at an additional disadvantage.

"I'm coopered," was Jack's mental exclamation.

He turned round and saw the pursuers had him well in hand—three in front, two behind.

They had never once lost sight of him.

On they came; bodies a little inclined forward, elbows pressed into the side, legs going like machines.

"They've got the wind of a bellows," Jack said with a groan; "I shouldn't care if I had anything to fight with."

Like the stag, hunted to the extremity of his endurance, he turned round, faced his pursuers, and stood at bay.

"I'll die with my eyes open," he exclaimed; "at least, I'll see what kills me, and how it's done. It'll be a comfort to know the *modus operandi*."

When the Pisangs saw that he did not run any further, they halted also.

The foremost made signs that they wanted to speak, and Jack said that he was listening.

"Are you armed?" asked the Pisang.

"No; you can see I'm not. I shouldn't have cut and run if I had anything to fight with," exclaimed Jack. "That was why I heaved anchor."

"O white chief," continued the Pisang, "come back with us to the ruins of our city, for Palembang is now in ashes."

"That's a blessing, only it will make the beggars more savage," said Jack.

"You must die the death that has been decided on; I can hold out no hope of mercy, but I doubt not you will die like a brave man."

"That depends upon circumstances. What is this particular pleasant death?"

"It is the punishment of the stake. Every warrior in Pisang will be entitled to cut off a piece of your flesh, about an inch square in size, till all the flesh is gone and nothing but bones remain."

"Thank you, then I shan't come," said Jack, in his usual careless manner.

The Pisang raised his bow.

"You can tell them I am much obliged for their kind invitation, but I have a previous appointment in another direction. I hope to enjoy the pleasure another time."

"The white chief cannot escape; his Pisang enemy will shoot him down and carry him wounded to the city," replied the warrior.

"Let fly," exclaimed Jack impatiently, "perhaps I can dodge you after all."

He remembered his knife, and prepared to dash forward and close with his assailants, so as to perish, as it were, sword in hand.

The Pisang did not waste any further time in talk.

He drew his bow to its utmost capacity of tension.

The arrow quivered on the string.

Suddenly there was a loud report, and the Pisang struck with a leaden messenger of death, fell heavily forward on his face.

Three other reports made themselves heard, and as many Pisangs fell; and the fifth stricken with a deadly terror, plunged into the tangled depths of the forest and was seen no more.

Jack could scarcely bring himself to believe in the evidence of his senses.

Guns in Pisang, and people to fire them; and what is more to fire them on his behalf!

The age of miracles was come back again.

"If that isn't Dick's doings," he muttered, "it must be something that rhymes with Dick, and that's Old Nick."

Just then two forms emerged from some dense brushwood.

One was Harvey, and the other Monday.

Advancing towards Jack, they shook him cordially by the hand.

Monday danced and capered about in the wildest glee.

Jack was too much affected to be able to speak for some seconds.

"Well, my cockalorum, how goes it?" exclaimed Harvey.

"Dick," replied Harkaway, "how you managed it I don't know, but you came up just in time to save my life, and I'm deeply grateful for it."

"Don't say anything about that, old fellow," answered Harvey. "I'm modestly inclined, and don't like to be praised."

"I was dead beat; a four-mile run in this climate is a pipe-opener, I can tell you, and it was six to four on the niggers."

"I knew you'd want me, and that's why I came."

"Have you landed in force?" asked Jack.

"No; Monday and I are alone.

"Have you ventured, all by yourselves, into the enemies' country for my sake?" asked Jack, deeply moved.

"Why not? You don't think we came to explore the beauties of Pisang, in the interests of high art, do you?"

"Not exactly; but it is more than I had a right to expect."

"It is not. You had a right to expect that we should do everything we could for you," returned Harvey; "and as the bloated old Limbi chief wasn't ready, we put on steam and started. If you'd sent us a telegram we should have made a move sooner."

"There is such a thing as electricity of the heart, Dick; and I think our hearts spoke to one another," said Jack Harkaway.

"Very likely I dreamt about you, and I thought you wanted me: Didn't I, Mon?" said Harvey,

"Yes, sare. You say 'Go to Mast' Jack.' He in much big danger, and so we come," replied the black.

"You arrived in the nick of time. I was sewed up—regularly licked."

"Tell us all about it. What have you done?"

"I've seen Emily, and made it all square with her," replied Jack. "I've cheeked Hunston, and got up a small Donnybrook Fair in the council-chamber. I've been the death of six Pisangs, and I've burnt Palembang to the ground."

"By George, Jack, you're a wonder! Explain all this to me," said Harvey, in astonishment.

"I will, directly. It was more a fluke, after all, than anything else; but just now I'm like a parched pea. Can you lay your hands on any civilised or uncivilised sort of grub?"

"Certainly we can. Our ship is hidden not far off, and we have a few odds and ends in her. I'm not exactly a pocket Soyer, or a sea-cook, but I can rig you up a good breakfast."

"Fire away, then. If it's boiled snake I'm on, like a hundred bricks," replied Jack.

Harvey gave Jack his arm, for he trembled violently and needed support.

They walked to the shore, where the boat was concealed, and were quickly engaged in discussing an excellent breakfast, when we consider the materials they had to work with.

A kettle was boiled, and some tea made from some of the Hyson found on board the wreck.

This was very grateful and cheering.

After he had satisfied his appetite, and gained the strength he stood so much in need of, Jack related his adventures to Harvey.

"By Jove!" replied the latter, "you had a closer shave than even I imagined."

"I saw Hunston meant it," answered Jack, "and that put me more on my mettle."

"You are all right now, thank goodness; and the best thing we can do is to jump on board, and set sail for Limbi," remarked Harvey.

"No," replied Jack shortly.

"What!" cried Harvey in astonishment; "do you want to stop here?"

"That's precisely what I mean to do."

"Are you mad?"

"I don't think so. All I want from you, Dick, is, a rifle and a few charges of powder and shot."

"But think a bit, the Pisangs will have you; it's a moral. You've burnt their city, and they'll swarm all over the place after you."

"I'll chance it. We can but die once."

Harvey reflected a moment.

"The Limbians won't be here for a day or two. You know what slow coaches they are, as well as I do," he exclaimed.

"I've got work to do here, Dick."

"What work?"

"Can't you guess?" asked Jack.

"No; hang me if I can!" replied Harvey.

"Then I will tell you. But first of all give me another half cocoanutful of that Souchong, or whatever it is."

Harvey did so, and Jack proceeded to drink the tea with calm enjoyment.

CHAPTER LIX.

THE STRATAGEM.

THE sun was now rising high in the heavens.

Jack began to get merry.

"I'll trouble you Mr. Monday," he said, "for another of those dried fish. They're not equal to bloaters, but they're not bad."

"Um dried fish, sare? Yes, sare, very fine," replied Monday.

"I didn't ask you for your opinion; the fish is quite sufficient. You can dry up," answered Jack.

Harvey was dying with impatience to know what Jack's intentions were, though the latter did not show any signs of being in a hurry to gratify his curiosity.

"Fine day," said Jack, wiping his mouth with the back of his hand, in the absence of a pocket handkerchief.

"What's the use of telling a fellow that, when it always is fine here?" answered Harvey.

"Don't ruffle your feathers, Dick! As I'm going to stop in the island, I like to study the signs of the weather."

"What are you going to stay for?"

"Can't you guess?"

"I've told you I can't once," replied Harvey. "I never was good at riddles, as a kid."

"But you're not a kid now, and you ought to have improved. Why does a miller wear a white hat?"

"To keep his head warm, I suppose."

"Exactly," replied Jack. "That shows you're not quite a Simple Simon."

Harvey looked angry, and pressing his lips together, remained silent.

"Dick, you've lost something," exclaimed Jack quickly.

"Have I? What?" asked Harvey.

"Only your tongue, that's all. You're sulking because I won't speak fast enough for you. Did they teaze the poor old boy?" cried Jack coaxingly.

"Go on; I don't mind," replied Harvey.

"Forgive me, Dick. I feel so jolly at getting away from those Pisangs that I must chaff or die," exclaimed Jack, in a good-natured voice. "You would if you were me."

"So I should, Jack. I'm not angry."

"It's so freezingly delightful—that's the phrase out here—to have licked the skunks, that I can't help exuberating."

"That's a big word," said Harvey, smiling.

"Big words suit the occasion," answered Jack; "and now I'll tell you why I want to stay here. Emily is in the hands of the Pisangs; and, what is worse, in the power of that brute Hunston, who is a Pisang double distilled."

"I see; don't say any more, Jack. I was an unfeeling wretch not to think of that before," Harvey hastened to say.

"I don't want you to stay," continued Jack. "We may be Damon and Pythias, but it would be too much to ask you to play the part of Pythias, to empty boxes."

"No, it wouldn't; and the boxes wouldn't be empty, for my heart and my conscience are big enough to fill the house."

"Close the show," exclaimed Jack. "You're a good sort; you're a trump, and you shall help me to rescue Emily."

"Or die in the attempt."

"Good again, Dick; they've got to kill us though, now we have these little pop-guns;" and Jack handled the rifle and revolver which Monday had given him, looking at them affectionately.

"Monday help too, rescue Missey Em'ly," cried Monday.

"So you shall. All hands are welcome," replied Jack.

"You should have seen Monday's get-up before we left Limbi; there was a wreck—all the crew dead, and we had the first overhaul," exclaimed Harvey.

"What did he do?" asked Jack.

"Togged himself out till he was quite nobby, didn't you, Mon?"

"Never mind," replied Monday; "me show Mast' Jack, one of these days. All very fine, make fun of poor Monday; he know what him do know."

"Don't be riled, Prince Matabella," continued Harvey; "you shall sport your things when we get back again."

Monday retired to pack up the remains of the breakfast, and from the way in which he talked to himself in his own language, he did not seem very well pleased at the ridicule Harvey cast upon his newly-acquired European clothes.

To him, his attire was simply perfect.

It whipped that of his young masters altogether, and threw Mr. Mole's rather shabby dress quite into the shade.

"You say you have seen Emily?" observed Harvey.

"Yes, I did enjoy that happiness, but not for long, and under very trying circumstances," replied Jack.

"I should have liked to see you stir up the chiefs in Palembang; what a lark it must have been!"

"It wasn't all fun. I must confess I was in a dismal funk all the time."

"What do you think of doing about Emily?" asked Harvey.

"I fancy," replied Jack, "that as the city is burned down, they will all be up a tree; that is to say, camped out anywhere, and in the confusion we might make a dash."

"Just like a man-of-war's boats cutting out an armed vessel in harbour."

"Something of that sort," answered Jack.

"When shall you try it on?"

"To-morrow. I'm so knocked out of time that I must sleep all day."

"I'll join you. Suppose we sleep under this tree, and leave Monday to watch," said Harvey.

"That's the idea," replied Jack. "Call him; I'm so beastly tired, and can't raise my voice."

"Monday," cried Harvey. "You're wanted."

"What um want him for, Mast' Harvey?" asked Monday.

"We're going to recruit exhausted nature; in other words, to sleep, and you must keep a good look out. If you don't——"

"What then, sare?"

"We'll get some chemical stuff, and turn you white."

"He! he!" laughed Monday. "You have um joke. Mast' Harvey."

"You'll find it no joke, when you're all cream and no chocolate. So keep your eyes open, and stick something under your eyelids."

Monday promised to exercise the greatest vigilance, and there was some necessity for it.

The Pisangs were evidently swarming about the island in pursuit of Jack.

A party might discover them, and if no watch was kept they would be surprised before they could use their guns.

In a very short time Jack and Harvey were fast asleep.

They had every confidence in Monday.

The latter stood near the trunk of the tree, rifle in hand, revolver in his belt, and looked searchingly by turns in every direction.

"Monday like to see um Pisang take him in," he muttered. "Monday smell um Pisang mile off."

A couple of hours passed, and the heat of the day was at its height.

Monday, like all the other natives of the islands, owned the power of the sun at this particular time.

He felt drowsy, and had the greatest difficulty in keeping himself awake.

His eyes closed, and he was aroused in a short time by a slight noise.

A large monkey of the ourang-outang species had crept up, and was hurrying off with his rifle, which he had placed against a tree.

He did not like to take Jack's or Harvey's, for they had put them under their heads, to be ready at a moment's notice.

If he touched them he should wake them.

So he followed the monkey.

It went slowly into the forest, and Monday, not caring to go into the jungle after it, drew a revolver from his belt and fired.

The monkey threw up his ungainly arms and fell upon its back.

Monday advanced to gain possession of his rifle, and was astonished to find the skin fall off.

A full-grown Pisang was revealed to his view.

It was a disguise.

As he stooped to take possession of his rifle half-a-dozen strong hands seized him.

He had fallen into a trap.

The Pisang who had assumed the disguise had paid the penalty with his life.

But he had enabled his companions to succeed in their enterprise.

Almost before he could realise the fact, Monday was strongly bound.

He cast his eyes towards Jack and Harvey, and found that a score of dusky figures were busily engaged in securing them.

They had been surprised while they slept.

"Hullo," cried Jack, as he felt himself strongly grasped. "What's this?"

"Monday—Monday!" cried Harvey.

"You may go through all the days in the week, and it won't help you," said a voice in his ear.

He looked up.

"Hunston!" he ejaculated.

"Yes, my boy. We've been one too many for you," said Hunston, with a malevolent laugh.

Monday was marched up to the spot where his young masters were safely bound.

He hung down his head and was ashamed to speak.

"This is your fault," said Harvey angrily.

"They come one dodge over Monday, Mast' Harvey. Him think it um monkey and shoot, but then it too late," replied Monday.

"It's no good howling," said Jack. "We're copped and there's an end of it."

"I'm glad to see you bear it with resignation," rejoined Hunston. "When I set out after you I did not expect to make such a haul as this."

"Didn't it burn well? It was a proper flare up. I mean Palembang," said Jack smiling.

"You'll suffer all the more for it, and we can make another gallows, big enough for the three or you," answered Hunston.

Jack laughed again.

"You'll laugh on the wrong side of your face soon," said Hunston.

"Not I," answered Jack: "I haven't got a wrong side. I leave that sort of thing to you. I can't help laughing when I see you."

"Let them laugh who win," replied Hunston savagely.

He spoke a few words to his attendants, and the Pisangs placed themselves in a triple line round the captives.

Their legs were free, though their arms were tightly bound behind their backs.

Hunston took their revolvers from them and placed them in his own belt.

The rifle he told the Pisangs to carry.

"March!" he cried.

The party moved forward, going towards the interior.

"Cheer up, Dick," said Harkaway.

"I'm all right," said Harvey. "Only I can't help thinking that Monday——"

"Don't bully the poor beggar. They had him just as they might have had you or me. It was a dodge," interrupted Jack.

"Silence, there! No talking," cried Hunston

"Who are you when you're at home?" asked Jack, with his usual impudence.

Hunston delighted to have a pistol again, flourished it in his face.

"Shut up," he said, "or I'll let you know."

"Will you?"

"Yes; and I'll pistol the first who disobeys my orders. Silence! March!"

The prisoners moved on again, and not a word was spoken.

"Don't rile him," whispered Harvey. "It is as well to bide our time."

Jack made no reply, but his pale face and compressed lips showed that evil thoughts were passing through his mind.

He regretted now that he had not killed Hunston the night before, when he had the chance.

But the chance was gone.

It was too late to think of that now.

"LAY STILL; IT'S ALL RIGHT, MUM,' SAID HARVEY."

CHAPTER LX.

GRIN AND BEAR IT.

THE captives were placed in the midst of a guard, and the procession, if such it can be called, started for the ruins of Palembang.

Jack, Harvey, and Monday were together, their arms being bound behind them.

"It's all your fault, Monday," said Jack, with just the least tinge of anger in his tone.

"How on earth he could be such an ass, I don't know," said Harvey.

"Monday one fool," said the black. "Him deserve to be eaten.

"Perhaps they'll do it," replied Harvey; "only they may prefer white meat first, worse luck!"

"I don't know how the deuce to get out of this scrape," remarked Jack. "I shouldn't care so much for myself. It's you and Monday I am in a funk about. If you could get away, Dick——"

"Leave thee, leave thee, lad;
I'll never leave thee,"

said Harvey, quoting the words of an old Scotch song.

"I know you're a brick, and you'll stand to your guns as long as anybody," said Jack. "But hang me if I can help being riled at this turn up. It oughtn't to have happened."

Hunston was not far off, and hearing voices, he came up to the captives.

"No talking there," he said. "I don't permit it."

"You can't well stop it unless you gag us," answered Jack.

"Can't I? We'll see about that. What do you suppose you are going to do?"

"Grin and bear it," said Jack, with a laugh.

"That's what you'll have to do, until you're strung up," said Hunston.

"You said that before and yet you didn't do it."

Hunston gnashed his teeth with rage.

"Perhaps I shall have better luck next time," he said. "I've got you safe enough now."

"Didn't Palembang burn finely, and didn't I set your chiefs milling like steam?"

"Don't cheek me. If you do, you'll find yourself in the wrong box, I can tell you," said Hunston, angrily.

"You can tie my arms, but you can't stop my tongue, unless you've got a gag," said Jack.

"Can't I? What does that taste like?" was Hunston's answer.

He hit Harkaway in the face with all his might, and as Jack could not use his arms to steady himself, he fell backwards.

The blood streamed from his nose, and he was a good deal hurt.

"That's plucky," he said.

"Do you want another?" asked Hunston.

"You can pitch in as long as you like to be coward enough. I can't stop you," replied Jack. "But just untie my arms, and I'll give you toko for yam, my boy!"

"Get up."

"I shan't. You knocked me down, and you may pick me up, or ask some of your niggers to do it."

"Not likely," said Hunston. "If you don't get up, I'll kick you till you do. How would you like a toe in the ribs?"

He suited the action to the word, and Jack contrived in some way to get on his feet.

"All right, Mister Tuan Biza Hunston," he said. "I'll be one with you before long."

"You won't have the chance," said Hunston.

"You can't tell that. I've spared you once or twice, but the next time—if ever it does come—it will be a case of a tombstone, with something written on it,"

"What?"

"Oh? something like this. 'Here lies Harry Hunston, the biggest black-guard who ever disgraced the name of Englishman.'"

"You dare to say this to me?" cried Hunston frantically.

"Why shouldn't I? Do you want to give me another nose-ender? Do it if you like; you are cock now, and I'm only a hen."

"Wait till you dance on nothing, and then you'll alter your tone."

"Think so?" said Jack, beginning to whistle "The Night before Larry was Stretched!"

Going up to Harvey, Hunston said—

"Walk on with me. I want to talk to you."

"All right," said Harvey.

They separated themselves from the other prisoners, and went on a little ahead.

"I've no particular ill feeling towards you," continued Hunston, in a slightly embarrassed manner, "though you were always a friend of Harkaway's."

"I'm not ashamed of it. Jack and I are like brothers," said Harvey.

"You won't be long, for Harkaway will be as dead as a door nail before this time to-morrow."

"And I?"

"Your fate depends upon yourself. I am all powerful with the Pisangs, though I do not think my influence would suffice to save Harkaway, even were I disposed to try."

"Why not?" asked Harvey.

"The chiefs are so ashamed of being humbugged by him last night, and they are enraged as well at the burning of Palembang. He set the place on fire, and there is scarcely a house left standing. All the people are camped out."

"Can't they be generous to an enemy?"

"They don't understand the word," replied Hunston, "but you I can save. They will be content with torturing and hanging Harkaway, and that black Limbian thief of a servant you've got."

"Monday?"

"I do not know what you call him."

"Oh! he's harmless enough. Show yourself a man for once, Hunston, and let us all go free. We will undertake not to molest you any more."

"Can't be done at the price, my boy. There is an old score between Harkaway and myself, which must be rubbed out this time; and I would not spare him if I could."

"If that is all you have to tell me, you might have saved me the pain of listening to it," said Harvey, in a tone of disgust.

"It is not all."

"Let me go back to Jack. I don't care about the society of a butcher."

"Who's a butcher?"

"You are; and an inhuman brute into the bargain. I will say it, if you kill me for it. You are not so good as a butcher, by a long chalk."

"Take care," exclaimed Hunston, with a savage, vindictive glance in his snake-like eye. "I repeat that I don't wish to harm you. Listen to me. I feel rather lonely among the Pisangs, having no one to talk to, except Emily."

"And her father?"

"He is dead."

"How was that?"

"She swears I did it; but I didn't want the fool to kick the bucket. He insulted me, and I had him publicly flogged with bamboos, and I suppose his constitution couldn't stand it, though I only ordered him to receive two hundred strokes."

"Why, it's barbarous!" said Harvey.

"At all events," resumed Hunston, "it knocked old Scratchley off his perch, and Emily hates me like bricks for it So you see I want a chum."

"You've got your Pisang chief," said Harvey.

"No good at all. I could cut a better chum out of a cocoa-nut than any of them would make. You be my friend, Harvey, and you shall not die."

"What!" replied Dick, with a feeling of loathing and horror; "I pal up with you?"

"Why not?"

"After what you've just told me—after your vindictive hatred to Jack—your flogging old Scratchley to death—and your determination to make the daughter marry the murderer of her father, whether she will or not?"

"You put it rather strongly," said Hunston, cowering beneath the withering look Harvey gave him.

"Not a bit too strong," answered Harvey.

"Do you consent?"

"Consent? I should think not, indeed. I'd die a thousand deaths first. You won't catch me buying my life at such a price. I'd rather chum with a burglar. The most desperate convict is a greater gentleman than you."

"Die, then!" replied Hunston savagely. "you're a bigger fool than I took you to be."

"If I had my hands loose, I'd punch your ugly head for insulting me by such an offer," cried Harvey.

"Don't provoke me too far," said Hunston; "or I'll serve you as I did Scratchley."

Harvey turned round and walked away, without giving him any answer.

Hunston was mad with rage.

Speaking in the native language, he cried—"Halt!"

Instantly the Pisangs stopped, and looked to their leader for orders.

"Two of you seize that fellow," Hunston went on; "strip him, and tie him to a palm tree. Two more of you break off a couple of long bamboos, and give him twenty cuts as hard as you can lay them on. Twenty from each of you."

In an instant Harvey was seized, and tightly bound with thick rattans.

His jacket and shirt stripped off, and his back laid bare.

"I'll teach you to cheek me, my hearty," said Hunston, smiling bitterly. "I'm king here, and you shall know it."

Harvey made no answer, feeling that it would be of no use to appeal to his tormentor.

There was nothing for it, as Jack had said but to "grin and bear it."

Nevertheless, he gnashed his teeth angrily, and waited with a sinking feeling at his heart for the first strokes of the supple bamboos.

He was not kept long in suspense.

"Whish! whish!" They came with a sound like a hiss through the yielding air, and his back felt as if some one was stripping off the skin with a sharp knife.

CHAPTER LXI.

MONDAY'S DODGE.

IF Hunston expected to have the triumph of hearing his victim howl and cry for mercy, he was disappointed.

He bore the infliction bravely.

At times low wailing moans escaped him, which were wrung from him by the severity of the pain.

But that was all; and when they cast him loose, after giving him the last cut, he trembled violently, while they dressed him again, and then rejoined Jack, who, powerless to help him, had looked on with frantic rage.

"Did I bear it well?" asked Harvey in a whisper.

"Like a trump. Never mind, Dick I hope it's only lent. We'll pay him back again before long. What was it for?"

"He offered me my life if I'd be his friend, and I told him to go to Jericho," answered Harvey.

"Did he say anything about me?"

"Yes. You're a gone coon. Your case is past praying for; but now we're both tarred with the same brush, and I suppose the cowardly brute will have it all his own way."

"Perhaps Mole and the Limbians will come soon."

"They will come," replied Harvey. "Of that I'm certain; but the mischief is, they may come too late. How my back burns!"

"I should think so. I'll ask Hunston if his fellows have got any oil," said Jack who added aloud—"Hunston;"

"What is it?" was the reply.

"May your men rub some oil on Harvey's back!"

"Not a drop."

"You are torturing him," said Jack, whose face flushed angrily.

"Just what I want to do. You don't suppose I had him flogged for nothing do you? And you'd best shut up, or I'll give you a dose of it. Tell him he'll be out of his misery to-morrow," answered Hunston with a laugh.

Jack was about to make some reply, when Harvey touched his sleeve.

"Don't," he said, "it's no use. You might as well talk to a stone wall; and I shouldn't like you to cop it as well as me."

Much against his will, Harkaway remained silent.

"You're right. We must bide our time; though I should like to have five minutes' play with my fists with him in the open. He might tie one hand behind me if he liked, and then I'd back myself to lick him."

"He's a nice pup; but we'll make him yelp before we've done with him," replied Harvey, smarting with pain.

In a short time a halt was ordered, and a guard being established, the Pisangs threw themselves down to rest.

The heat of the sun had been great, which made the march very fatiguing.

Glad to follow their example, the captives sank on the hard ground.

Presently Monday looked around him; all was still.

"You sleep Mast' Jack?" he whispered.

"No," replied Harkaway, "for my mind is so full of disagreeable thoughts that I'm not likely to be."

"Lie still. Monday use um teeth."

"What for?"

"Cut in two the rattans; then Mast' Jack make a dive for the woods, and get off," continued Monday.

"It' not a bad dodge, but I'd rather you did it for Harvey. I can take care of myself; something always turns up for me," answered Jack.

"Very well," replied Monday.

He rolled over a little, and got nearer to Harvey, to whom he communicated his plan, and soon his teeth were at work.

In ten minutes Harvey was free.

"Run Dick, for your life," whispered Jack; "and go zigzag, so that they won't be able to hit you if they fire. There is only Hunston who knows how to use a gun, and the lazy beggar is snoring."

"Aren't you coming too?" asked Harvey.

"No. Monday and I will stop. We can't all hope to get away."

"I can't leave you."

"But you must. Think how much you can do for me. There are arms in the boat, and you can come and rescue me. Whether you are successful or not, you must try to get away. I got you into this mess by asking you to stop to help me to carry off Emily from Hunston. Poor Emily!"

Jack sighed.

"If anything should go wrong with me, Dick," he continued, "promise me you'll be a brother to Emily. She mustn't marry Hunston."

"She shan't if I can help it."

"I may be a croaker by this time to-morrow; there's no telling."

"Well I'll go, in the hope of being of use to you," said Harvey. "Good-bye."

"Good-bye, old flick," replied Jack, trying to be jocular once more.

"God bless you!" said Harvey.

The next minute he was crawling on his stomach towards a dense jungle.

He had reached it, and was just about to plunge into it, when a Pisang saw him.

Uttering a fierce yell, he discharged the gun Hunston had given him.

So bad was his aim, that, instead of hitting Harvey, he shot a comrade who stood near him.

The native fell to the ground with a groan.

Hunston sprang up.

"You blundering fool!" he exclaimed. "What's the matter?"

The Pisang explained that one of the white chiefs had escaped.

"Which one?" cried Hunston.

He ran to the spot where he had left the prisoners.

Jack and Monday pretended to be fast asleep.

Kicking them in the ribs, he exclaimed, "Get up. Where's Harvey?"

"You needn't kick a fellow like that, in the middle of his first sleep," replied Jack, in a tone of remonstrance. "It's very hard a man can't have a nap for a few minutes."

He rubbed his eyes and yawned drowsily.

"Where's Harvey?" thundered Hunston.

"How should I know? Don't I tell you I've been nodding?" replied Jack.

Turning to the Pisangs, Hunston said—

"After him! I'll have all your lives, if you don't catch him."

By this time, however, the fugitive had got a good start, and, though the Pisangs ran hither and thither, they could not find him.

Hunston foamed at the mouth with rage.

"Now, that's what I call a shabby trick," remarked Jack. "He didn't appreciate your kindness at all. You were going to hang him to-morrow, and he's stepped it. Dick ought to be ashamed of himself!"

Jack's broad grin irritated Hunston.

"What do you want to work me up for?" he exclaimed. "I'll treat you as I did him, and make a cat scratch your back."

"Don't get wild. Dick's a very good fellow, but he shouldn't have taken his hook without saying he was going," replied Jack.

Hunston turned away, and assisted himself in the pursuit of Harvey.

It was fruitless, however.

He had got safely away.

Then the order to resume the march was given, and leaving the body of the dead Pisang, they continued their way to the town of Palembang, or, more strictly, what remained of it.

Hunston was more sullen than ever; but he comforted himself with the reflection that Jack and Monday were still in his power.

They reached the smoking ruins of the town about nightfall, weary and footsore.

The people had made themselves rude shelters of boughs and grass.

Loud were the lamentations over their burnt property, and their household utensils, for only a few had saved even the necessary implements of domestic use.

The fire occurring in the night time, had taken all by surprise.

Owing to the high wind prevailing, its progress had been very rapid.

Jack and Monday were placed in one of the few houses, which, owing to their isolated position, the flames had not reached.

The door was shut, and they were left to brood over their coming fate.

"Well, Mast' Jack," said Monday, "how um like it now?"

"Oh, tol lol; I'm pretty bobbish," replied Jack. "I think if I was going to be hanged in five minutes, I should sing my prayers instead of saying them."

"It what you call possum up um gum tree now, sare."

"And a very tall gum tree, too," said Jack.

"P'raps Mist' Mole come in night and walk into um Pisang."

"No such luck, I'm afraid."

There was a great noise outside, and looking through a crack in the wall, Jack saw the Pisang warriors beating back the crowd.

They had heard that Jack was the cause of the destruction of their city, and they wanted to get at him and tear him in pieces.

But Hunston reserved him for public execution, and the wild untamed mob was driven back.

"Want to lynch us," remarked Jack "Amiable beings, these Pisangs. I wish my hands ware not tied."

"Suppose Monday try um teeth, sare; and then you untie Monday when you free!"

"Stunning," said Jack. "Cut along, old chocolate and cream. You've got some sense in your noddle."

Monday set to work, as he had done in Harvey's case, resembling the mouse which liberated the lion, by gnawing the meshes of the net in which he was caught.

"Bravo!" cried Jack, springing up in a short time, and stretching himself.

"That all right, sare?" asked Monday.

"Ripping! I don't know if my grinders are so sharp as yours; but I'll have a go in."

By dint of biting and pulling, he contrived to liberate Monday.

"Now um fight, before they take us to die," said the black proudly.

Just then there was a crash, and something fell through the frail roof.

"Hallo!" said Jack, "who's chucking bricks?"

"What that, sare?" asked Monday.

"I don't know. It's so beastly dark I can't see; but it looks to me as if one of somebody's teeth had dropped out."

"Oh! Mast' Jack, how you make um poor Monday laugh! Why him do it, when there so much misery?" said Monday chuckling.

"That's the time to laugh, ugly mug," answered Jack, groping about in the dark.

Presently he stumbled upon a heavy stone.

"Lucky," he said, "that this little pebble didn't light on my nut. I know which is the hardest."

"Ah! de debble!" cried Monday, in a voice of pain.

"What's up now?" said Jack.

"Musquito bite him on the nose," answered Monday ruefully. "How um sting."

"Squash him, then," cried Jack. "I thought I heard one of the beggars buzzing about. I say, Monday, this stone didn't come here by accident."

"How him know that, sare?"

"Because I can feel a bit of paper tied to it."

"Paper?"

"Yes; and I shouldn't wonder if there was something written on it. Blow the darkness. It's no good asking you if you've got a match in your pocket, as one could in a civilised country; and as we're not cats, we can't see in the dark," said Jack.

"The moon him shine through that crack, sare."

"By Jove! That will do. There are more ways of killing a dog than hanging him, Monday," Jack said, in great glee.

He knelt down near the crack, and saw that the bit of paper, a very small one, had been written on with a pencil.

The writing was that of a woman.

"Emily, for a hundred!" he muttered.

With some difficulty he contrived to read.

" 'Dearest Jack——'

"Dearest!" he said. "I like that."

Then he went on.

" ' I took a walk near the coast to-day, and saw a quantity of boats lying off near the shore, hidden partly by the rock. They must be your friends the Limbians.

" ' Keep up your spirits. I was deeply grieved to hear you were recaptured; but I expect a night attack will be made, and if so, rest assured I will open the door of your prison before they can come and kill you.

" ' Ever your own loving
" ' EMILY.' "

"She's a brick!" said Jack, in great exultation.

"What that, sare?" asked Monday, who was all curiosity.

"A friend has sent this letter attached to a stone. The Limbians are off the island."

"My people. That jolly! Then they not hang um after all," said Monday, joyfully.

"I never thought they would, though it looked uncommonly black an hour ago. Hurrah, Monday! You weren't born to be hanged, you scoundrel!" said Jack.

"Mist' Mole come and fight like um tiger, sare. Monday like to see Mole fighting."

"I think Mole will be like the Yankee, who said to his men, 'Fight till all your powder is gone, and then run away; and as I'm rather lame, I'll start now, before the enemy comes up,' " said Jack laughing.

"Ha! ha! him brave man," exclaimed Monday, also laughing.

"Hunston will be sold this time."

The door suddenly opened, and a voice said, "Will he?"

It was Hunston.

"You're rather too fast, Harkaway; and you shouldn't talk so loud," he exclaimed. "These walls are not very thick, and you didn't think I was listening."

A diabolical smile played round the corners of Hunston's mouth in the moonlight.

Jack's heart fell within him; and Monday would have turned pale if his skin had permitted him.

Here was a disastrous interruption to their plan.

Their hopes were crushed in the bud.

CHAPTER LXII.

THE NIGHT ATTACK.

"So," continued Hunston, "the Limbian fleet is off our shore?"

"That can't be very pleasing intelligence to you," replied Jack, who began to recover himself.

"We have a traitor in the camp, it appears, and it is lucky for her she is a woman whom I love, or she should share your fate."

"Emily, you mean?"

"Yes; your correspondent. It was a clever idea to write you a letter, and fasten it to a stone. But you forget the old saying ' that walls have ears.' "

"I forgot that you were such a cad you wouldn't mind listening," answered Jack.

"You'll forget more than that soon,

for I mean to order you out for instant execution—instant death, you and your black friend here, do you understand that?"

"I've one comfort," replied Jack, "and that is, I'm not afraid to die. Don't you wish you could say the same thing?"

"Never mind. I meant to have had you tortured, but there isn't time for that. It will be torture enough to know that Emily is in my power."

Jack fretted inwardly, but outwardly he remained calm.

"Heaven will protect her," he said.

"Will it?" answered Hunston. "Why doesn't Heaven interfere for you?"

"Perhaps it may. I'm not dead yet; and while I have life there is hope, you know, old boy," Jack said cheerily.

"Not much hope for you. I could pistol you where you stand. I don't know why I shouldn't do it, and make sure of you. I wouldn't lose you for ten years of my life. Perhaps you are reckoning on your friends?"

Jack made no answer.

He had a faint hope that Mr. Mole might come up in time to save him.

Hunston saw this gleam of hope in his eyes.

"If they were at this door now, I'd shoot you through the head," he said.

"You're quite capable of it," was Jack's cool answer.

Suddenly there arose a great shouting outside.

Jack's heart leaped in his bosom.

Shots were fired, and then he knew that the Limbians had arrived.

A loud, clear voice was heard exclaiming—

"Fire away, my lads. No quarter. Give it them hot and strong."

Hunston turned pale.

He saw his prey escaping from his murderous clutches, just when it was within his grasp.

"Harvey's voice, by jingo!" cried Jack. "I must have a cut in."

He dashed his fist in Hunston's face, just being able to see him in the moonlight that streamed in through the open door.

Hunston stepped back, and the blow grazed his temple.

"Curse you," he cried; "I'll have one life at least."

Raising his pistol—the one he had taken from Harvey, he fired it point blank at Jack.

Our hero's days were nearly numbered.

Monday, however, saw the action, and quick as thought, jerked Hunston's arm so that the ball went through the roof, and the pistol fell from his hand.

"Touch and go," said Jack calmly.

Hunston turned and dashed through the open door, seeing that all was lost.

"After him, Monday," said Jack; "he's gone to Emily. Now's our time; we must save her."

But Hunston was too quick for him.

The ground outside was filled with frightened Pisangs.

They lost sight of him in the crowd, which was panic-stricken.

The night attack had taken them all by surprise, and they were ill able to cope with their well-armed assailants.

A dropping musketry fire continued at intervals, and Pisangs fell on every side.

At last they began to run.

Men, women, and children, helter skelter, sought the shelter of the woods.

Monday and Jack stood a chance of being shot by their own friends, and got separated in the confusion.

Dreadful cries arose on all sides.

It was not a defeat simply.

It was more than a rout for it became a massacre.

Jack ran he knew not whither, seeking for Emily and found her not.

No one took any notice of him, for all were intent upon securing their own safety.

At length Monday rested under a tree upon the outskirts of what had once been the thriving town of Palembang.

The moon which had been partially hidden by drifting clouds, now shone out brilliantly.

He heard groans, and was at a loss to know where the sounds came from.

Looking up, he saw a man perched on one of the lower branches of a tree.

"You come down out of that," exclaimed Monday, in his own language.

"Ah! my good Pisang," replied the trembling voice of Mr. Mole; "I mean you no harm. I was forced to take part in this expedition, much against my will."

Monday laughed quietly to himself, and determined to have some fun.

"I am a Pisang chief," he said; and I want the head of the Tuan Biza of the pale-faces."

"What a bother, I left my gun on the ground," Mr. Mole muttered. "That infernal arrow frightened me so when it grazed the calf of my leg, as I was leading the brave fellows to the battle, that I sought the friendly shelter of the first tree in a scamper."

"Will the white chief come down," continued Monday; "or must the Pisang warrior shoot him like a bird?"

"Don't shoot, my good Pisang; for Heaven's sake don't shoot!" said Mr. Mole in a terrified tone.

"Come down, then."

"I would gladly do so, if I could, but I fear I cannot. How on earth I contrived to get up here is a mystery to me."

"The white chief is a coward, and he must die," said Monday. "All the Limbians are conquered, and our young men are crying loudly for heads."

"What a fool I was to come here," said Mr. Mole to himself. "I wish I'd stayed with Ambonia and Alfura. This is out of the frying-pan into the fire. Dear me. I think I should have remained with the boats, if that impetuous boy Harvey had not suddenly joined us, and insisted upon my marching with him."

Taking up a stone, Monday threw it near Mr. Mole, causing a rustling in the leaves and a sharp hiss through the air.

"Is that an arrow?" cried Mr. Mole, in abject terror. "I say, you Pisang fellow, don't do that. I'll come down, at least I'll try. Oh, Lord! oh, Lord! why did my uncle die and leave me a tea-garden in China."

"Make haste! the Pisang wants the white chief's head."

"Won't anything else content you?" replied Mr. Mole. "My head isn't worth much, and I'm getting dreadfully bald. Oh! why did I leave England? Deuce take these beastly boughs; I can't get down."

Monday threw up another stone, and hit Mr. Mole on the leg.

"Oh, Lord!" exclaimed Mr. Mole; "I knew he'd do it. I'm wounded. Oh! my poor shin. The arrow's gone right through my leg. I can feel the pain up to my knee already."

In his fright he let go his hold, and tumbled rather ungracefully to the ground.

The distance was not great, so that the fall only shook him a little; but he lay quite still.

"I'll sham dead," he thought; "and then the bloodthirsty savage may let me alone."

Monday grinned, and altering his voice, as he spoke English, said—

"Mist' Mole not know um poor Monday."

The effect was magical upon Mr. Mole when he heard this speech.

He opened his eyes, took a look at the well-known features which he had been too much alarmed to notice closely before and sprang up.

His former terror vanished, and with his countenance radiant with delight, he said—

"You rascally black thief, if I wasn't so pleased, I do think I should be tempted to kick you!"

"Take care, sare. Pisang have um head."

"You musn't play those tricks with me. However, I forgive you. Yes, out of the generous emotions of my heart, which bubble up from—from—Confound it, I can't collect my ideas!"

"You have snug place up there, sare," said Monday, pointing to the tree.

"Ah! I crept up there to rest. See how I have been fighting. Seventeen Pisangs fell by my hand alone."

Monday looked as if he didn't believe him.

"You and I have always been good friends, Monday," said Mr. Mole; "and you must promise me one thing. That is, not to say anything about finding me up that tree."

"Not tell Mast' Jack, sare; not tell Mast' Harvey?"

"Precisely. They have an unfortunate habit of making fun of people, which they call chaffing. I detest and abominate the practice; and what I want to impress upon your uncultivated mind is that my courage is up to the average, I may say beyond it."

"Monday keep um secret."

"That's right. Mum's the word and you and I will be fast friends. I still hear the sound of firing, and the shrieks of the dying. Is it safe to venture far away?"

HIS ADVENTURES AFLOAT AND ASHORE.

"Monday have a lark with you, sare," replied the black. "Fighting nearly all over. Pisangs all beat; they fly 'way or dead."

"And Harkaway? I trust he is safe, and will thank me for the generous effort I have made to effect his liberation."

"Not know exactly, sare," replied Monday. "Mast' Jack him gone somewhere after Missy Em'ly."

"Ah! I have heard that he is much attached in that quarter. There's my gun; take it up, and mind, it is loaded. Walk in front; you shall have the post of honour. I will follow close behind you," exclaimed Mr. Mole.

"We go and find Mast' Jack, eh, sare?" replied Monday.

"We will endeavour to do so. I long to shake him by the hand, and receive his thanks; for I assure you, Monday, that I have risen in my own estimation by the prodigies of valour I have performed during this night's work; twenty-seven Pisangs did I kill."

"You say seventeen just now, sare?"

"Nonsense. I am like an old war-horse," cried Mr. Mole, after applying himself to the contents of a pocket-flask; "I smell the battle afar off."

"You great fighting man, sare."

"Rather, my young friend. I don't know how I did it, but my spirit carries me on. Seven and thirty Pisangs did I slay with my own hand."

"That ten more," muttered Monday.

"I laid about me with an old ship's cutlass, and the warriors fell before my prowess like leaves in autumn. Forty-seven Pisangs dead by my——"

Monday burst out laughing; he could not stand Mr. Mole's exaggeration any longer.

"Irreverent negro; I'll talk no more to you. When I again recount my exploits, you may tell me of it," exclaimed Mr. Mole, in high dudgeon.

"Come on, sare. This way. Quick march!" cried Monday, with military precision.

They walked cautiously towards the town, near which the sounds of the battle were dying away, though in the distance there was a noise as of furious pursuit.

The Limbian warriors were exacting a terrible account from their old enemies the Pisangs.

CHAPTER LXIII.

DEATH OF THE KING.

THE morning broke serene and cloudless, as it almost always did in those regions.

On the part of the Limbians, the loss was slight, for their guns had given them a great advantage over the surprised and terror-stricken enemy.

Harkaway had joined the pursuing party, but he could not contrive to find any trace of Hunston.

Nor was he more fortunate with regard to Emily.

Both of them had disappeared as completely as if the ground had opened and swallowed them up.

In the morning he returned, jaded and weary, to find Harvey, Mr. Mole, and Monday, preparing breakfast, by means of a fire they had kindled.

The Limbians were assembled in little parties, and all did their own foraging.

Great was the rejoicing of the friends at being together safe and sound.

"I owe my life," said Jack; "to you, Dick, and our faithful Monday."

"And me," continued Mr. Mole. "May I not claim some share in the good work?"

"Of course," answered Jack; "we haven't forgotten you, sir; and you shall have a medal or a statue, whichever takes your fancy most."

"I think I should prefer a medal," replied Mr. Mole, after a moment's reflection.

"What shall we put on it, sir?" asked Harvey.

"Let me see. Two natives fighting, and trying to kill a white man—myself——"

"Up a tree, sare?" put in Monday, with a grin.

Mr. Mole gave him a warning look.

"Behind one, if you like, firing at them, and underneath the words, 'In token of bravery and devotion;' while, on the reverse, you may put my portrait, and write, 'Isaac Mole, a tried friend, and a fierce soldier.'"

"It shall be done, sir," replied Jack, who could scarcely refrain from laughing at Mr. Mole's vanity.

Taking Harvey on one side, Jack informed him of his vain search for Emily.

"I too have looked for her," replied Harvey. "You know when I left you, I ran to the coast, and found the Limbians under Mole and the king landing?"

"Yes."

"They were delighted to see me, and I hurried their movements, because you were in danger. When we reached Palembang, I did all I could to discover you and Emily," continued Harvey.

"Hunston's got a hiding-place somewhere," said Jack thoughtfully.

"We'll unearth the fox."

"I fully intend to do so, but the task will be difficult. These islands abound with rocks, mountains, and caverns, to which the natives have taken themselves."

"So Monday's been telling me," replied Harvey.

"I mean to stop here, Dick, till I've found her," continued Jack.

"You won't get the Limbians to stay, I'm thinking."

"Never mind them. They've done their work, and they've beaten the enemy. So it is only natural that they should want to get back to their homes, and celebrate their rites and customs."

"I told them we'd have no head-hunting or eating captives," said Harvey.

"What did they say?"

"The king did not like it; but he gave orders that no prisoners were to be taken, so that has made the battle more bloody."

"I expect there are an awful lot of the poor Pisang beggars killed?"

"Awful! Over a hundred, I expect," replied Harvey.

"They won't get over this wollopping in a hurry," Jack said. "And now I'll tell you what we'll do. The Limbians may go home."

"Yes."

"We'll go and look out for a cave near the coast, so as to have an open front to prevent a surprise, if the disor-ganised band of Pisangs should try to have another go-in."

"And you and I, with Mole and Monday, form the garrison. I see," replied Harvey.

"Exactly. That's the ticket to a T," Jack answered.

"I've got stores in my boat; and Mole brought over a lot of grub, and powder, and things," continued Harvey.

"We shan't hurt. And now let's have some breakfast."

Mr. Mole's voice was heard exclaiming—

"Now, then, Harkaway, and you, Harvey, come and join me in a cup of tea. Who says bacon, and who'll have parrot?"

"I'll leave the cockatoo to you, sir, and go in for a slice of pig," replied Jack.

Monday handed some tea to his young masters, but in doing so stumbled, and let the calabash fall.

"Hold up!" cried Jack. "You're as awkward as a Newf'un'land pup; not half so clever, and twice as ugly."

Monday apologised, and the breakfast proceeded.

Presently an old chief named Madura came up, and beckoned to Jack, who went out to meet him.

"Anything happened?" asked Jack in the native language.

"Bad news for Matabella," replied Madura.

"Indeed!"

"During the battle, King Lanindyer received a wound, from which he has just died."

"Monday's father dead?" cried Jack. "By Jove, I'm sorry for that."

The old chief had wished to break the news gently to Monday, but Jack's loud exclamation reached his ears, and instantly stopped eating, he ran away to the camp.

Madura and Jack followed him.

They found him kneeling by the side of the dead body, which he kissed repeatedly, uttering wild lamentations the while.

The king had fallen fighting bravely, pierced through the heart by an arrow.

All the Limbians were profoundly grieved, and they talked together in whispers.

The ruined city was close by.

Great numbers of dead bodies lay on all sides, as yet unburied.

JACK'S ENEMY, HUNSTON, AFTER BEING TATTOED BY

"OH, JACK," SHE SAID, "CAN YOU EVER FORGIVE ME?"

The distant mountains, in which the defeated Pisangs had taken refuge, were lying like a blue cloud on the western horizon.

A dizzy light played over the surface of the land.

The sun looked like a shield of red-hot iron, and the hot earth scorched the feet.

Madura took Monday by the arm, and led him away, saying—

"You are called to the throne of your fathers; but though your destiny is high, remember that he who gazeth on the sky may stumble on the earth."

"Oh! my father!" replied Monday. "Why are you taken away from me?"

"Recollect," said Jack, "that you have plenty of friends, and you are now king."

"No, no!" cried Monday. "I will not be the Tuan Biza of my people. I will remain with you. Do not send me away. Monday will die if he be not with you."

Touched by the poor fellow's devotion, which was expressed by a piteous look, Jack replied—

"I like to have you with me; but who is to reign over Limbi?"

"My uncle Selim. O Madura, make Selim your king. He is a great chief. Let him reign."

"He who can neither save himself nor hunt his enemies?" replied Madura. "What is he but a broken spear, and a blunted sword?"

"Never mind," said Monday. "The man who has health, strength, and courage, has three parts that will not turn white in the fire."

"Stay with your people and rule over them, O Matabella!" said Madura sternly. "What are the white men, that they should rob us of our king? Has it not been said that the unpurposed man makes his meal of the clouds?"

"I will not leave my friends, the white men," answered Monday determinedly. "Call upon Selim, O Madura, he will make a wise and good king."

"Young man," replied Madura, angry at being baffled, "for six things is a fool known—Wrath without cause, change without reason, inquiries without object, putting trust in strangers, and wanting

the power to know a friend from a foe; and let me add, that long experience maketh large wit."

"I'm very sorry for you, Monday," said Jack; "very much so indeed. It is a great blow, and I thank you for wishing to stay with us. Think the matter over, Listen to this old swell."

"Monday go with you, Mast' Jack. Go anywhere—to end of the world."

"Don't be in a hurry to decide. I'll leave you to fight it out with your chief; and if you want my advice, give me a hail."

He walked away, and Harvey, with Mr. Mole, asked him what had happened.

"Monday's governor has burst up," exclaimed Jack.

"Done what?" said Mr. Mole, looking puzzled.

"Bust up. Croaked. Got knocked on the head in the scrimmage last night."

"'Bust' is not English, at least not grammatical English," said Mr. Mole, "and I did not understand you; though now I take your meaning. Is the young savage much affected?"

"Frightfully cut up," said Jack.

"Dear me! It is a bad job; but one savage the less is no loss to civilization. Finish your breakfast."

"I can't eat," said Jack. "I haven't had a wink all night. I'm more tired than an elephant at noon. So if one of you will kindly fan away the beastly flies, I'll seek the arms of—of——Who was that ancient swell whom they called the god of sleep?"

"I was never the cheese at classics," answered Harvey.

"You mean Morpheus," said Mr. Mole, "who, with Somnus——"

"Thank you, sir. Won't it keep till I wake up?" said Jack. "I know it was Morpheus, or one of the family."

Jack found a retired spot, and was soon asleep.

Harvey followed his example, and Mr. Mole, applying himself to his flask, said—

"What a wrong-headed creature is a boy. They waste their opportunities when young, and as they grow up they have neither time or inclination to learn."

CHAPTER LXIV.

BEN BLUNT THE BO'SUN.

MONDAY'S uncle Selim was very glad of the chance of becoming king of Limbi.

Being a wise and good chief, he was not unacceptable to, or unpopular with, the leaders of the little nation.

Still Madura was not willing that Monday should lose his right of succeeding to the throne.

A council was held.

It was decided that Monday should be able to assume the kingship whenever he liked, and that Selim should only reign in his absence.

"Oh, my son," said Madura, "never give up that which is within your grasp. The pearls in their beds are as thick as stars, but wishing never brought up one of them from the bottom of the sea!"

"Selim will make a better king than I should," replied Monday. "Matabella is young, but Selim has the wisdom of age."

"The wise men have said," answered Madura, "that the deer is swift on the plains, but a child leads him in the streets. You are young, and you must learn, and I would teach you, for the proverb is true which says—'The lamp may be made of diamonds, but it dies without oil.'"

Monday was glad when it was all settled, and Selim made king.

He could go away then, and mourn over his dead father, whom he loved dearly.

Selim at once assumed the position which the unanimous vote of the council gave him.

He decided that the Limbians should return immediately in their boats, and bury the late king with all the pomp usual on such occasions.

Monday said he would not leave his father's body till it was in the grave.

Therefore he returned with his followers.

"Good-bye, Monday," said Jack, when he heard what had been arranged. "I hope we shall see you again soon; but don't stand in your own light."

"Monday live and die with you, Mast' Jack," he replied. "If you live in Limbi with me, then I be king; if you go I go."

"Then we shall see you soon after the funeral?"

"I come back in boat."

"All right. I won't say how grieved I am at your heavy loss, Monday. You know what I feel," cried Jack.

He squeezed Monday's hand as he spoke, and the black returned the affectionate pressure.

"Give us your fist, Mon.," cried Harvey; "and here's fortune to you in a cup of cold tea—that is to say, half a cocoanutful."

Mr. Mole sidled up to Monday as he was going away.

"Monday, will you do me a favour?" he said.

"What that, Mist' Mole?" asked Monday.

"Tell my wives, I'm dead, will you?"

"Dead!"

"Killed in battle. Dead and buried."

In spite of his engrossing sorrow, Monday could not help grinning faintly.

"What! Tell um lie, sare? No; Monday never tell um lie," he answered.

"It won't hurt either Ambonia or Alfura; they'll marry again. Think of it, my good friend," urged Mr. Mole.

"No, sare! Monday have him conscience, and he not let him tell um lie," replied the black.

"Deuce take the beast," said Mr. Mole, as Monday walked away. "I suppose I shall have those beauties coming over here to take me home in a boat. A nice look-out that would be. Heigho!"

"What's that, sir?" asked Harvey, who had overheard the conversation.

"Oblige me be minding your own business, Harvey," said Mr. Mole.

"Didn't I hear you mention the names of Alfura and Ambonia, sir?"

"If I did, what then?"

"Nothing, sir. I thought you'd fret What is it Moore says—

> "I never loved a sweet gazelle.
> To glad me with its sweet blue eye,
> Than when it grew to be a swell,
> It always used to fight me shy;"

and married a market gardener——."

"How shamefully you misquote," cried Mr. Mole indignantly. "Moore is my favourite author, and you murder him."

"Very sorry, I'm sure, sir."

Jack called Harvey away to take a walk with him in the country.

They were well armed, and intended to look for a cave where they could locate themselves while they remained on the island.

They went to the sea-shore, and soon found what they wanted.

All their stores were removed into this harbour of refuge, and they returned for Mr. Mole.

"The Limbians have gone, my dear Harkaway," cried Mr. Mole; "and you have left me alone here at the mercy of the enemy, as I may say."

"You've got your gun, sir. Besides your reputation is so great, that no one would think of attacking you," replied Jack.

"Is it, indeed? Do you tnink that those benighted savages have heard of me?"

"I'm sure of it."

"What are we going to do?" continued Mr. Mole.

"Dwell in a cave, sir. Harvey and I have pitched upon a stunning place. Nice and dry—no snakes; not too big; close to the sea—and we have put our stores out of the boat there."

"This is foolhardy, Harkaway," said Mr. Mole gravely. "But you shall not say I deserted you. I will cast in my lot with you."

"What's wrong now, sir?"

"You are stopping here to rescue a chit of a girl, who would make Hunston as good a wife as she would you."

Jack ground his teeth.

"Don't excite me, sir," he said.

"Bless me! How like a Pisang you look," cried Mr. Mole. "I didn't know you were so deeply smitten."

"Jack's very hard hit, sir," said Harvey. "You don't know how spoony he is."

"I wish he had enjoyed my brief ex-perience of matrimony, that's all," replied Mr. Mole.

"Emily is not Ambonia or Alfura either," put in Jack. "And letting temper alone—though I'm sure she's the sweetest tempered darling in the world—wouldn't it be cowardly to leave her in that scoundrel Hunston's power, as long as we can lift a finger to get her out of it?"

"So it would, Harkaway," answered Mr. Mole. "You appeal to my feelings as an Englishman there. I feel them gushing and bubbling up from the fountain of my heart. You have touched a mine of sentiment in my breast, and you shall have my support."

"Thank you for nothing," said Jack who was getting angry.

Mr. Mole thought it prudent not to hear this remark.

The guns were presently shouldered, and they marched to their new home.

When they reached it, they found it very comfortable.

Leaves and grass made good beds, and they had such provisions as they stood in need of.

A watch was set, it being arranged that two should sleep while one watched.

Harvey and Mr. Mole entered the cavern, while Jack, who was almost always foremost when there was anything to be done, remained outside.

An oil lamp, such as we have previously described, was lighted.

Mr. Mole had his cocoa-nut shell and his whisky bottle.

He ate some dry bread, made of roughly-beaten unleavened maize flour, and began to imbibe.

"Now," said he, "this is what I call jolly. A sensible man ought to live in the present hour. What is ambition to me? I am happy now. Why should I disquiet myself about the future?"

"I wish you wouldn't disquiet me, sir. I want to go to sleep," said Harvey.

"Laziness—sheer laziness," answered Mr. Mole. "I had some hope of you boys at Pomona House, but——This whiskey is not bad; it has a grateful flavour."

Harvey closed his eyes, and let Mr. Mole have all the talking to himself.

He was ill and feverish.

The punishment Hunston had subjected him to, and the following excitement of attacking the Pisangs, had fatigued him dreadfully.

Mr. Mole filled his half cocoa-nut again, and emptied it.

"If I crook my elbow a little too much," he murmured, "it is excusable, under the circumstances. I have no respectability here to keep up, and I want to forget. I will seek oblivion in the flowing bowl. Let the landlord fill the bowl, until it does run over; for to-night I mean to be merry, and to-morrow I hope I shan't have a headache."

While Mr. Mole was amusing himself in his own peculiar fashion inside the cave, Jack was keeping a sharp look-out.

It was within an hour of sunset—a time when the dying away of nature in the tropics—if one may use the phrase—is most apt to attack and lull the senses.

His eyes almost closed.

He leaned against the entrance to the cave, and felt dreamy.

Suddenly a loud voice exclaimed—

"What cheer, my hearty!"

Jack started as if he had been shot.

A British voice!

A British sailor's voice in that lone island!

That such a thing could happen, at such a time, in such a place, he scarcely thought possible.

"Who goes there?" he cried.

"Who goes there?" repeated the voice.

"Why, who do you suppose but Ben Blunt the bo'sun?"

Jack looked up and saw a stranger before him.

But as he was unarmed apparently, he did not feel alarmed.

The stranger was dressed like a sailor, and had a bluff, hearty, good-natured face.

Was he friend or foe?"

That was the question.

CHAPTER LXV.

THE MUTINEERS.

THE new comer was unarmed, and did not seem to be in the least dangerous.

But Jack proceeded to act cautiously.

Raising his gun, he said—

"Don't come any nearer, until you have given an account of yourself."

"Right you are, cap'n," replied Ben Blunt. "I'm no sea lawyer, and shan't spin you any yarns."

"What's your ship?"

"Haven't got one, though this time yesterday I was first mate of as good a ship as ever sailed the sea."

"I thought you said just now you were a boatswain?" exclaimed Jack, suspiciously.

"Look 'ee here, my hearty, that's right enough. You see I was bo'sun on board the 'Rattlesnake' when I was in the R. N.; but I've left the navy and gone into the merchant service, I'm mate. Forge ahead. What are your next soundings?"

"Why have you left your vessel? Wrecked, eh?"

"No, I'm not wrecked either. It's this way," replied Ben Blunt, hitching up his trousers, and rolling his quid over in his mouth; "I shipped aboard the 'Seahorse' from London to Shanghai, and we were on the return voyage, when Sam Parsons—may the old un keelhaul him! —turned mutineer."

"A mutiny, eh?" exclaimed Jack, beginning to understand.

"May I never eat salt junk again, if I'm telling you a word of a lie, cap'n!"

"Go on!"

Jack was much interested in the recital.

"Well, you see, sir, they killed the skipper and all the officers, bar me. I was a bit of a favourite with the lads, you see, and they didn't make me go to Davy Jones. But when that mutinous dog, Sam Parsons, who's what we should call in the navy an A. B., asked me to join 'em, 'No,' says I; 'I'll see you jolly well hanged first, my hearty, and then I won't.'"

"Case of 'not to day, baker,'" remarked Jack, smiling.

"It was so, sir. 'Not to-day, baker; call to-morrow with a crusty cottage,'" answered Ben Blunt.

"You were quite right," said Jack; "and your experience of discipline in the navy did you good service."

"Well, look 'ee here, cap'n," continued Ben, "I'm Blunt by name and blunt by nature. You may dowse my daylights, but I'll stand true to my flag. So they talked among themselves, and then they shoved me into a boat and landed me on this here island."

"How long ago?"

"A matter of maybe two or three hours, and I've been boxing the compass, as ye may say, and taking an observation as to how to steer my course."

"The mutineers are in command of the ship, I suppose?" said Jack.

"Devil a doubt about that, cap'n! They've got her, and a beauty she is. Look! there she rides at anchor round that point."

Jack looked in the direction indicated, and saw a vessel, dimly visible, of about eight hundred tons register.

This was the "Sea-horse."

"I didn't think to meet an European, let alone a countryman on this outlandish bit o' ground," said Ben. "And now, sir, you've overhauled me, are my papers correct?"

"Quite. I'm satisfied, Ben; and I feel as if I'd known you for a score of years already," answered Jack.

His confidence was fully established in the man, who spoke with a genuineness that carried conviction with it.

"Thank you kindly, sir; and now, if so be as I may ask, how did you come to drop anchor in these parts?"

Jack told him how he had been wrecked with his friends; how the Pisangs had been defeated; and how he was stopping to rescue a beautiful young lady, a captive in the hands of Hunston, formerly a friend, and now an enemy.

"This Hunston's gone mutinous," remarked Ben Blunt. "String him up to the yard-arm, cap'n."

"I've got to catch him first," said Jack. "But what will your men with Sam Parsons do?"

"They daren't go back into our waters. They'll have to potter about these coasts, sir," replied Ben.

"I wish we could help you to get back the 'Sea-horse;' she'd take us all back to England," said Jack, thoughtfully.

"And that's a true saying," answered Ben. "What I'm thinking is, cap'n, that if you'll let me sail along of you, I'll sign articles, and go ahead this minute."

"You want to join us?"

"Heart and soul, sir. We'll get back the beautiful young lady of whom you was a-speaking. We'll hang our mutineers, or take 'em in irons to the first port where there's a British consul, and we'll sail her back to old England."

"A stunning idea. But there's a lot to be done first," answered Jack. "However, I gladly accept your offer of friendship, Ben. You shall be one of us."

"That's done me more good than I expected, when the muzzle of your gun brought me up all standing just now. Thank you kindly, cap'n. I'm true blue, and you wouldn't find a dog more faithful than Ben Blunt to those he takes to."

"We've got some stores inside the cave. Will you eat something?"

"I could stow away a chunk of beef and bread, cap'n, for my belly cries cupboard. But I say, sir."

"What?"

"Let's give one cheer for old England. I'm so happy I'm fit to bust, and all along of meeting you. Just now I thought I should die of starvation, or snakes, or tigers, or niggers, or some of the varmint that grows here, and now I'm up to the mast-head again. Just a little 'un for old England, sir."

"I'm with you," cried Jack. "Go it, my old sea-horse. Hurrah for Old England! Hurrah! Hurrah!"

Ben Blunt joined in, and their ringing cheers woke up the echoes in the island.

They did more.

They woke up Mr. Mole, who came out of the cave in a bad temper, to ascertain the cause of the disturbance.

"What is the meaning of this unseemly riot, Harkaway?" said Mr. Mole. "It is hard I cannot enjoy my natural rest. And who is this stranger?"

"Ben Blunt the bo'sun, sir, at your honour's service," replied that individual.

"I am in a fog. Explain the mystery to me, Harkaway."

Jack did so.

"You see, sir," added Ben, "I cut down the top hamper, and took in all sail under stress of weather; but I'm drifted into port after all."

"And we're going to recapture the ship, and hang the mutineers, sir," said Jack. "That's why we're cheering."

"Mind you are not cackling over an addled egg, my young friend," said Mr. Mole. "However, I'm glad to see our new friend Ben, and cheerfully hold out the hand of welcome."

"The more the merrier, sir."

"And now I'll turn in again," said Mr. Mole sleepily.

"Going to bye-bye again, sir? Don't do that. We're going to have a can of grog to celebrate Ben's arrival. Come and join us; don't be a hen, sir."

"A hen, Harkaway?"

"Yes, sir; be a cock for once."

"Grog is not to be lightly refused. You have put a different complexion on the case, and I will condescend to join you," replied Mr. Mole. "Arouse that lazy slumberer Harvey, with a poke in the ribs."

Going into the cave, which somewhat resembled the abode of the robbers in "Gil Blas," Jack woke up Harvey.

"Turn out, Dick," he replied.

"What for?" asked Harvey.

"There's a gentleman from England come to see you."

"Go on," Harvey exclaimed; "you're having larks."

"I'm not," answered Jack. "You go outside, and see."

Harvey did so, and was at once introduced to Mr. Benjamin Blunt, otherwise Ben Blunt the bo'sun.

He was much astonished at hearing his story, but, like Mr. Mole and Jack, delighted to have such an addition to their little party.

"Axing your pardon, sir," said Ben, pointing into the cave, "are there any more of them to come out?"

"No; that's the lot."

"Then I'll take this morsal of victuals we was speaking of, that is by your leave, cap'n," said Ben.

A dinner was hastily provided, and the cup that cheers passed round.

Ben became a favourite in less than no time.

He took his turn in watching and went out to scour the country with Jack to find some trace of Hunston, but in vain.

Days passed, and Jack grew sick at heart with his want of success.

They met isolated bands of Pisangs occasionally, but the poor fellows ran away like hunted hares.

Their city was burnt, the flower of their warriors killed, and they were no longer a great nation.

A week had elapsed, during which Jack's exertions on behalf of Emily had been unremitting.

"I'd give my life to save her," he kept on saying to himself.

One morning Ben the bo'sun was on the look-out.

Suddenly he exclaimed—

"Sail on the larboard bow, sir."

Jack was dozing under a tree, and thinking of Emily.

"Where away?" he asked, springing up.

Ben Blunt pointed it out, and Jack saw a small boat approaching.

Taking up a telescope he distinctly made out one man in her.

As she got nearer he recognised Monday.

"It's our native, whom we call Monday," said he by way of explanation. "The faithful fellow has kept his word, and is coming back."

In less than an hour, guided by a signal flag, Monday made the island, and was shaking hands in true British fashion with his young master.

"Well, Monday, what's the news?" asked Jack.

"Who that man?" inquired Monday, pointing to Ben.

Jack told him all about the new arrival but Monday did not seem to take kindly to him.

"You asked what news, sare," he continued. "Nothing much to tell. The funeral over and now all Limbi very gay celebrating victory. It all one big drink and war dance. You found Miss Em'ly?"

"No; I wish I had."

"Some one come for Mr. Mole soon," exclaimed Monday.

"What! his wives are coming?"

"That it, sare. Alfura and Ambonia tell me they sail over."

"We can't have them here. There is no room for a parcel of woman. He'll have to look out for a cave of his own."

"Mist' Mole not like that much, sare," replied Monday. Adding, "Oh, sare, here he is. He heard all we say."

Mr. Mole had indeed come out of the cave, and was looking the picture of blank despair.

"Harkaway," he said, in a sepulchral voice, "is this true?"

"What sir?"

"About my—ahem!—my wives coming over here!"

"Monday says so, sir."

Mr. Mole made a rush towards the sea and Jack becoming alarmed, ran after him.

"What are you going to do, sir?" he cried, as he held him back.

"Let me go!" replied Mr. Mole. "I will commit suicide. Let me go, I say! The awful prospect of Ambonia's presence is more than I can bear."

"Don't be silly, sir," Jack replied. "If they do come, we'll protect you. But perhaps we shall be gone away before that time."

Mr. Mole stepped on to dry land again, and heaved a deep sigh of relief.

"You have put new life into me, my young friend," he replied. "I will live. Oh, that I had the wings of a bird. I'd like to be a bird, Harkaway."

"Have a drink, sir, and pull yourself together. We can't spare you."

"What's that the gentleman says?" asked Ben Blunt.

"He's afraid his wives are coming to fetch him, Ben," replied Jack.

"There's only one enemy, sir, a sailor knocks under to, and that's woman. He's not a true sailor, if he doesn't strike his flag to a petticoat," replied Ben with a laugh.

"My good, amiable and worthy tar,"
replied Mr. Mole, "oblige me by not indulging your merriment at my expense. My domestic trouble's are my own."

"Belay sir! I'll put a stopper on my tongue, though there was no offence meant," answered Ben."

Mr. Mole retired into the cave, and was not seen again all day, though when Jack looked for him at night, he found him lying on his back snoring hard, with an empty bottle on each side.

When he was gone, Ben Blunt said—

"May I make bold to ask how many wives the gentleman has got, sir?"

"Only two," replied Jack.

"Oh, that's one for week days and an extra partner for Sundays; still, the ship's not short handed with two. I've got one at home, and stop my grog if she isn't one too many sometimes!"

Old Ben laughed heartily, and Jack, taking Monday with him, went out as usual to search for Emily.

They had not gone far before they saw a Pisang asleep under a bush.

"Look, sare, look!" he cried.

"Don't kill him, Monday; catch him alive," Jack replied, hastily. Creep up slowly. He may give us some valuable information."

Monday glided up through the long grass to where the sleeping Pisang lay.

The latter was unsuspicious of the presence of an enemy.

Jack looked on with his rifle at full cock, to be ready for any emergency.

CHAPTER LXVI.

THE BIRD HAS FLOWN.

"HOLD him tight, Monday," cried Jack.

This advice was not altogether unnecessary, for as soon as Monday fell upon the sleeping Pisang he awoke, and began to writhe and wriggle like an eel.

"You come help, sare," exclaimed Monday, out of breath. How um beast kick."

"He's as slippery as an eel," said Jack, coming up; "but we'll fix him. Soho! gently there. No kicking over the traces, my boy, or I shall have to take the curb up a hole or two."

In a few minutes the Pisang was sitting on the ground, with his hands tied behind him with a piece of rattan.

His face evinced the utmost astonishment, mixed with fear.

That he was doomed to lose his life in some cruel manner, he did not doubt for a single moment.

"I'm going to ask you some questions," said Jack.

The Pisang stared sullenly at him.

"If you answer truthfully I will spare your life; if you trifle with me, you'll have an ounce of lead showing the daylight the way into your ugly carcase. Will you speak the truth ?"

"Ya, ya, Tuan," answered the captive, his eyes brightening.

This was equivalent to "Yes, yes, chief," and it was clear that if he had any information to give he would not withold it.

"You know the Tuan Biza whom you call Hunstani. Where is he now ?"

"On the island still."

"Do you mean that he intends to go away ?"

"Ya, all go soon," replied the captive. "Several chiefs, with women and children, have gone already. We are not going to remain in Pisang, since you have burned the city and killed our best warriors."

"Where are you going to ?" asked Jack.

"Long, long way; to the city of the Golden Towers," answered the man.

Jack inquired where that was, but the fellow could not tell him.

All he knew was that it was a long way off, and that it was reached in boats which sailed across the sea.

"Have you seen a white woman, who was wrecked on your coast ?" continued Jack.

His voice trembled a little as he put this question, because it would let him know something about Emily's movements, if faithfully answered.

"Ya, Tuan."

"Is she with Hunstani ?"

"No," the Pisang answered; "she has gone away with the others to the city of the Golden Towers."

Something like a groan broke from Jack.

"Gone," he repeated. "Hunston has outwitted me again. Just when I think I have got him into a corner, he bests me."

He paced up and down impatiently.

"Any more thing to ask him, sare ?"

"No."

"Monday let um go ?"

"You may as well. I promised him his life, and I have no reason to think he has been humbugging me," said Jack.

Untying the rattan, Monday gave him a friendly kick to start him.

"You go 'long," he said; you no good, you can't fight. Go home to the old women, and say you've seen your master."

The Pisang did not stay to reply, he was too glad to get away; and running

with the speed of the wind, was soon lost to sight.

Jack lay down under a tree, which happened to be a palm, and fretted and fumed at the news he had just heard.

The sudden and unexpected emigration of the Pisangs was very annoying.

He had fancied that they could not get away, and that sooner or later he would discover the hiding-place where Hunston kept Emily.

Monday was thirsty, and wanted some cocoa-nuts, so, without thinking of his young master, he began to throw sticks up at the palm-tree.

For a time he was unsuccessful.

Then he cut off a large ripe cluster.

Jack at that moment started up, crying—

"It's a case of no thoroughfare. The way's blocked, and I'm floored, by Jove !"

He had scarcely spoken the words, than the cluster of cocoa-nuts hit him on the back, which was slightly bent, after grazing his head.

The force of the blow brought him on his knees, and looking round, he exclaimed—

"Bless your eyes, Monday, what foolishness are you up to now ?"

"Monday him dry, sare, and knock down nut."

"You needn't upset my apple-cart, if you are thirsty. I beg leave to observe that my head is not made of cast-iron."

Monday laughed, and began to suck a cocoa-nut.

"Halves !" continued Jack. "I think I deserve some of the milk."

When they had satisfied their thirst, they prepared to return to the cave.

"I am glad," said Jack, "I know what the Pisangs are doing, though I did not expect they would leave the island. That beggar told the truth, I suppose."

"Yes, sare," answered Monday; "him speak um truth safe enough. He too much funk to tell a lie."

"Did you ever hear of the city of the Golden Towers ?"

"Yes; Monday hear of him."

"Where is it ?" asked Jack.

"Great way off over the sea. Go in boat."

"Who lives there ?"

"Malay. All fierce, cruel Malay. They have ships, and go and take other ships, either kill all on board, or carry them home and make slave."

"You mean they are pirates."

"That it, sare," replied Monday, with a sagacious nod.

"Is the city made of gold, or is that only a tale of the natives?"

"Once a Limbi man was taken prisoner by the Malay he escape and come back, and tell us it one fine city full of towers and palaces, all made of gold."

"It must be a fine place, though I don't believe in its being all gold. That is a stretch beyond my imagination," said Jack, thoughtfully.

"Oh! it right enough, Mast' Jack, all built of gold! Very fine, grand city," exclaimed Monday.

"Well, we shall have a chance of judging soon, for I mean to go there."

"How go there, sare?"

"You have heard Ben Blunt speak of his ship the 'Sea-horse,' which the mutineers have got possession of?"

"Yes; Monday hear him talk of um."

"I mean to have that ship."

"That jolly, Mast' Jack. Fine thing to have ship of one's own, and sail 'bout anywhere," said Monday. "But how it to be done?"

"You leave that to me; we'll work it somehow," Jack answered confidently.

It was now noon, and the heat of the sun was so intense that they were glad to regain the cool precincts of the cave.

No one was to be seen outside, but when Jack whistled Mr. Mole came out.

"Don't think, Harkaway, that I am neglectful of my duty," said he; "I was on the alert."

"The guard should be outside, sir?" exclaimed Jack; "there are Pisangs about."

"Have you seen any?"

"Yes, we caught one; but what were you doing in the cave?" asked Jack.

"You'll laugh at me," replied Mr. Mole; but I fancy there is a Pisang concealed there."

"Nonsense, sir; what makes you think that?"

"You know that Harvey slung up some boards to the top of the cave, to make a sort of shelf to put things on?"

"Yes."

"Well," continued Mr. Mole, "I was sitting down under that shelf, when I heard a curious noise and rustling overhead, as if some heavy animal was moving about."

"I won't say that a Pisang wouldn't

be up to any low dodge," said Jack; "at all events we'll go and see what it is."

Monday and Jack entered the cave, which was only imperfectly lighted.

Having come out of the garish and blinding sunshine, it was some time before they could accustom their eyes to the semi-darkness of the cavern.

At length, looking up, Jack clearly saw a large mass of something overhead.

Gazing more carefully, he could distinguish yellow and black marks, like tortoiseshell.

"Oh, sare," cried Monday, "what um lark! It um big snake. Oh, my! such a whopper, sare!"

"You are right Mon. It is a snake, and as well as I make out, far and away the biggest I ever saw," said Jack.

As he continued to gaze the indistinct mass resolved itself into a huge serpent compactly coiled up into a kind of knot.

He could detect his head and his bright eyes in the very centre of its folds.

The sound which had alarmed and puzzled Mr. Mole was now explained.

During the night the snake must have crawled into the cave, and taken up a comfortable position on Harvey's shelf.

Perhaps the cave was its regular dwelling-place, and it had no idea of being turned out by the new-comers.

"What is to be done?" asked Jack.

He had tackled the python on board the vessel he came out in, but he did not care about another encounter of the same kind.

His voice aroused Harvey and Ben Blunt, who were equally alarmed.

Mr. Mole actually shook in his shoes.

"I can't stand them pesky varmint," said Ben Blunt. "Never could abide the critters."

"And I was just under him," cried Mr. Mole with a shudder. "It's a mercy he let me alone."

"Monday have um out!"

"You!" exclaimed Jack.

"Yes; me kill much big snake in our country. All you go out of the cave, and stand ready with guns and axes. Monday show how to do the trick."

Monday's instructions were obeyed, and he went to work immediately in a business-like manner.

He made a strong noose of rope, and taking up a long pole in his disengaged hand, began to poke at the snake.

The reptile began to slowly unfold itself.

By a clever throw, he got the noose over the reptile's head, and tightened it about it's body.

Then he began to drag it down.

The serpent resisted with all its might coiling round anything it could lay hold of.

Strong though Monday was, the snake gave him plenty of work to do.

First he got the advantage, then the serpent won a yard or two.

It was "pull devil, pull baker."

The boys laughed at the singular contest till the tears ran down their cheeks.

Monday jabbered away at the snake, and perspired at every pore.

"You black thief," cried Monday, "come out dat, or I'll give you some-thing. Oh, you beast; go in 'gain, will you? Come out that, I say, won't you? Then Monday have your head, you old villain."

"This is extremely comical," observed Mr. Mole, who being at a safe distance, had recovered his presence of mind.

"Haul on the rope, lad. Never let him cast anchor!" cried Ben Blunt, who enjoyed the scene as much as any one.

"Go it, Monday! I'll bet on Monday. Who'll take the odds?" exclaimed Jack.

"Done with you for a tanner," replied Harvey. "Just for the fun of the thing I'll lay the snake get's off through some hole or other."

"And I'll bet he don't," answered Jack.

They watched the varying contest with increased interest, and it was clear from the loudness of Monday's tone that he was loosing his temper.

CHAPTER LXVII.

HUNSTON'S NEW FRIENDS.

THE snake was certainly a formidable antagonist.

It was fully twelve feet long and very thick.

Such reptiles were common in these islands, and had been known to do much mischief, as they frequently swallowed a little child.

Suddenly Monday dropped the rope, and quick as lightning he caught hold of the creature's tail.

He ran out of the cave so quickly, still holding on, that the reptile seemed quite confounded, and did not know what to do.

"Look out, sare," cried Monday. "Now him come. Mist' Mole, mind um eye."

Directly he had dragged the snake out of the cave, Monday swung it round with all his strength, intending to knock its head against a tree.

Mr. Mole, however, was in the way.

The snake hit him on the head, and he fell down sprawling on the ground and howling dismally.

Monday was obliged to let go, and the reptile crept under the boat which had been drawn up near the cave.

It was difficult to say which was the most frightened, Mr. Mole or the snake.

"Poke um out, sare. Now we got him," cried Monday, who was fairly excited by this time.

Jack took up the pole which Monday had dropped and began to poke under the boat.

"There it goes! Tally ho! Stole away!" exclaimed Harvey, who saw the reptile gliding out at the other side.

Monday was after it like a shot.

He cleverly grasped its tail again, and with a quick jerk swung it round.

This time its head struck against a tree, and it fell confused and hurt to the ground.

Ben Blunt and Jack now fell upon it with hatchets, and it was quickly dispatched.

"That's the way we kill um snake,

"SEIZING MONDAY'S GUN, HARVEY FIRED TWICE QUICKLY."

sare," said Monday, standing in triumph over the quivering body.

"Bravo! You can do it," exclaimed Jack; adding, "Where's Mr. Mole?"

This gentleman had crept under a bush, and his voice was heard faintly exclaiming—

"Is it dead? Have you killed the brute?"

"Dead as a door-nail, sir," replied Jack.

Mr. Mole came out into the open air.

"I hope you did not think I was afraid," said he. "That would be a misconception I should be very sorry for you to put on my conduct."

"If you didn't hoist the white flag in token of surrender," observed Ben Blunt, "why, I never saw anything so much like it."

"Man," replied Mr. Mole, "it is unbecoming for a common seaman like you, to pass judgment upon me."

"On the likes of you," said Ben, with a hearty laugh. "We're all equal in the forecastle, mate. So tip us your flapper. There are no bones broke."

"I distinctly refuse to place myself on a footing of familiarity with you," answered Mr. Mole.

"Jack's as good as his master," remarked Ben. "But I don't want to run my ship where she's not required."

"Ben didn't mean any offence," said Jack. "It's only his way, sir."

"Then it's a very nasty, disagreeable habit, Harkaway," answered Mr. Mole. "I stopped the snake very cleverly. If it had not been for me, he might have crushed that poor black fellow to death. I don't like Mr. Blunt's jeers. I will not be mocked by him."

"Avast there, sir," said Ben. "I'll say you killed the varmint, if that will please you."

"It will not please me, because it would be untrue," Mr. Mole replied. "But I assert, and will maintain that without me the reptile would not have come to so sudden an end."

No one contradicting this assertion, Mr. Mole looked grandly around him, and went to examine the dead monster.

During the day Jack had the snake buried, as its remaining in the sun would have created an unpleasant smell so near the cave.

Then he took Harvey on one side, and told him what he had heard respecting Emily.

"She's gone, Dick, and what am I to do?" said Jack.

"I don't believe in this golden city," replied Harvey. "It is most likely a rich and luxurious place where the pirates live."

"So I think. It is a comfort to know that Emily is removed from Hunston, if only for a short time."

"Of course he means to join her as soon as possible, and imagines you will never find her."

"He's mistaken if he does," answered Jack, with his old look of determination. "I'll never rest till I have found her."

"It wouldn't be a bad dodge to capture Hunston and make him take us to her," said Harvey.

"If we could; but there is no telling where he is hiding. He's got a cave like ours, I expect; look how I've hunted for him."

"Let's have another try, shall we? Have you been round the coast?"

"No; inland chiefly."

"It's cool, now. Come for a stroll about the beach," continued Harvey. "I should think Hunston is more likely to be near the sea, so as to have access to his boats and be able to cut it, if hard pressed."

"You're right, by gum," said Jack. "I feel there is sense in what you say. Come on."

They took up their arms, saw that the caps were all right, and started on their journey.

After travelling about three or four miles, they saw a handsome ship not very far from land.

She lowered a boat, and a party of men got into her and pulled for the shore.

"I say, Dick, I'll bet a new hat that's the 'Sea-horse,'" exclaimed Jack.

"Ben Blunt's ship?"

"Yes; the one the mutineers have taken possession of, after murdering their officers."

"I shouldn't wonder," said Harvey. "But what a precious set of rascals they must be."

"This Sam Parsons, from all accounts, is a beauty. If all Ben says of him is true, he's a caution. What shall we do?"

"Perhaps," replied Jack, "they're coming on shore for water, or to have a spree. They don't expect to find white men here.

Let's get as close to where they are likely to land, as we can without being seen, and fog them."

"All right. Creep along behind these bushes they will hide us," said Harvey.

The boys made their way cautiously along, and whenever they looked up they could see that the boat was coming nearer.

At last they could hear the measured sound of the oars in the rowlocks.

"Let's pitch here," said Jack deeming it prudent to call a halt.

He pointed as he spoke to a clump of trees that afforded excellent shelter, at the same time giving them a capital view of the sandy shore.

There were fifteen men in the boat.

Two remained in her when she was beached, and the others landed.

Some carried small casks, so that it was evident that they were in search of water as Jack had surmised.

These started in various directions, and half-a-dozen stayed under a clump of trees, throwing themselves down and begining to smoke and drink.

Suddenly a form emerged from behind a rock, and advanced to the men.

All sprang to their feet and grasped their arms.

"Look, Dick, that's Hunston," whispered Jack.

"So it is. What's his game?"

"Stand close. We shall see directly," replied Jack.

Hunston, for it was he, stopped, and the leader of the sailors exclaimed—

"Who goes there?"

"A friend," replied Hunston.

"Are you alone?"

"Yes, with the exception of a few friendly natives. Who are you?"

"My name is Sam Parsons," was the answer; "and I'm the captain of that ship you see riding in the offing. Now, who and what are you?"

"I was wrecked on one of these islands with some companions, but we've had a split," replied Hunston.

"Where are the others?" asked Parsons.

"On this island, too. We've had a fight, and they've beaten us."

"Are they armed?"

"They are," answered Hunston; "but if you'd join me, we'd soon settle their hash."

"You seem a free and easy sort of chap," said Sam Parsons; "and if you like to turn pirate, you're welcome to a birth with us."

"Pirate?" repeated Hunston.

"Yes. Is there anything wonderful in that?" answered the mutineer. "We didn't like our officers, so we——"

He drew his hand significantly across his throat.

"Gave them a free passage to the other world, eh?" said Hunston, with a grim smile. "That's just my style, and if you'll have me, I'll cut and hang with the best of you."

"Well said, my hearty!" exclaimed Sam Parsons. "You're made of the right stuff, and a man of better kidney never sailed under the black flag, I can see. Come and join us in a glass of grog."

"That I'll do with pleasure, for I've tasted nothing stronger than water this many a long day," said Hunston.

The men dropped their arms, and they were soon pledging each other.

They seemed to consider Hunston an acquisition, and crowded round him to hear the story which he recounted.

"So you want to have a slap at your old friends?" said Sam Parsons.

"That's my pious intention. I wasn't strong enough without you, but with you we can easily do it."

"Where are they?"

"About four or five miles up along the coast. They've got a cave, and are well armed; still we might suprise them at night."

"How many are there of them?" continued the mutineer.

"Two youngsters, a middle aged man a native, and a sailor-looking sort of cove who has only just joined them," replied Hunston.

"How do you know this?"

"Because I watched them this morning, one of my natives having met them. He pretended to run away from them, but turned back and tracked them to their lair. He took me close to them afterwards, so I know it's all right."

"What's this sailor like?"

"He's a bluff sort of fellow, and they call him Ben Blunt," answered Hunston.

"Hang me if I didn't think so. It's Ben Blunt the bo'sun!" cried Sam Parsons.

" And who may he be ?"

" Why, he was in our ship's company, and being the only officer we liked, we spared his life and put him ashore here. So he's joined the enemy ?"

" Yes, that's the lot."

" Oh, by the Lord Harry," continued, the mutineer, " we must have a slap at Ben. He may get off the island with his new mates, and he knows enough to send a man-of-war after us, and get the lot of us strung up."

A savage smile lighted up Hunston's countenance.

" You're with me, then ?" he said. " Let us attack them in the grey dawn of to-morrow morning."

" Right you are my hearty ! What do you say, lads ?"

" Aye, aye," responded the mutineers, in answer to Sam Parsons' appeal.

Harvey grasped Jack's hand.

" It's lucky we came out," he said, in a low tone.

" Yes," replied Jack. " Now we're warned we shall be a match for them, though if they'd surprised us and killed our sentry, we should have been shot like parrots as we came out of the cave."

" Shall we go back now, and fortify ourselves."

" I think so. Those fellows who are out for water may see us if we stop," replied Jack.

With the same caution they had exercised in advancing, they beat a retreat.

They were disgusted with Hunston's constant enmity, and feared they would have no peace while he lived.

Mr. Mole and Monday had been preparing dinner, and having been successful in killing a hog that had escaped from its pen when Palembang was burnt, a very savoury smell of roast port greeted them as they approached.

" Come along, Harkaway," exclaimed Mr. Mole. " We've got a spread fit for a king."

" All right, sir ; pitch in," replied Jack. " I've got some startling news for you, but it shan't take away my appetite."

" Anything new," asked Ben Blunt.

" The 'Sea Horse' is anchored off the shore, a few miles away, and our old enemy Hunston, has met with and joined the mutineers."

" Is Sam Parsons ashore ?"

" That he is," replied Jack. " He and his confederates have hoisted the black flag, and they mean to attack us to-morrow morning."

" The deuce they do !" said Mr. Mole, who was in the act of conveying a savoury piece of pork to his mouth.

" The villains !" replied Ben Blunt. " It's all that Sam Parsons, though I could manage the rest of the crew, if it wasn't for him."

" It's you they want, Ben," continued Jack. " They are afraid of you since Hunston has told them you are with us. They say you can hang them."

" That's true enough ; but hanging at the yard-arm is too good for Sam Parsons."

" Never mind ; we won't give you up, Ben ; we'll fight for you."

" I'll tell you what I'll do," said Ben Blunt ; " I'll challenge Sam to fight me in single combat with cutlases, and let the best man win. That'll save bloodshed."

" Bravo !" cried Jack. " I like a fair stand-up fight."

" Will he consent ?" asked Mr. Mole.

" Oh, Sam's plucky enough. He'll fight."

" And you mean to propose that if you beat him they shall let us alone, and we won't interfere with him," said Jack.

" That's just the idea," answered Ben.

" I've got an amendment to propose," said Harvey.

" What's that ?" asked Jack.

" Only this :—When the fight is over, whichever way it goes, get up a big drink ; you and I will steal away, get into a boat and board the ship."

" They'll have men on guard," said Ben.

" Of course they will, but you forget that where there is no officers, there is no discipline. The men will be drunk or asleep. I know what sailors are well enough."

" Let me go with you, Harvey. I should like to share in that glorious enterprise," said Mr. Mole.

" More by token, the gentleman would not like to be left with Sam Parsons and his mutineers," replied Ben, with a grin.

" Silence, my good fellow," answered Mr. Mole. " My bravery has been tried often and often, in the hour of danger. We have got to see what you can do."

" Let us all go," said Jack.

"Better still," Mr. Mole continued. "If our friend, Ben, here is victorious, he will be of service, and when we have made friends with the mutineers, and they are all intoxicated, we will sail for the vessel."

"Monday know a plant which make um all sleep till this time next week," exclaimed the black.

"Do you propose to drug them ?"

"That it, Mist' Mole. Put something in one big stone bottle, that for them; put nothing but rum in another, that for us."

"Excellent ! The thanks of the meeting are, I think, due to Harvey and Monday for two excellent ideas. Eat up your pig, Monday, and go in search of the drug," said Mr. Mole.

"If it all comes off, it will be ripping," exclaimed Jack.

"We'll do our little worst, anyhow," remarked Harvey.

After dinner the cave was strengthened by the erection of some mounds of earth which protected the entrance.

Each defender could crouch behind one of those little hills, and fire at the enemy without being exposed himself.

Monday procured the herb he wanted, and put large quantities of it into a big bottle of rum.

The guns were all loaded.

Each member of the little board took up a position assigned him by Jack.

The oars were put in the boat, which was moored near the shore so as to be ready at a moment's notice.

Anxiously the moments glided by.

Each heart beat quickly, for the coming day was pregnant with events of importance.

CHAPTER LXVIII.

SENDING THE CHALLENGE.

THE excitement attendant upon the expected attack of the mutineers prevented any of the party from sleeping.

They sat outside the cave with their arms ready to their hands, and Monday walked up and down with a loaded rifle.

Mr. Mole had a bottle of rum, and dispensed the grog with a liberality which won the heart of Ben Blunt.

"You're a gentleman, every inch of you, sir," he exclaimed ; "I can see by the way you handle the liquor."

"No personal allusions, if you please, my worthy friend," replied Mr. Mole.

"I can't help it, cap'n. What I've got in my mind must come out. Now, if it isn't a rude question, what do you think it cost you to colour your nose ? It must have been a tidy sum, but you can make a rough guess."

It was a fact that Mr. Mole's nose had assumed a rosy hue of late, and shone like a fiery beacon on a dark night.

"Nonsense, my good fellow !" he exclaimed. "It's the hot sun of these infernal regions. You're mistaken when you ascribe the effect to intemperance.

It's nothing of the sort. Pass the bottle."

"Right, sir. B'ilers require water; quite nat'ral."

"Now, then," said Jack, "don't you two get sparring."

Mr. Mole had sprung up, as if he intended to correct Ben Blunt by striking him.

But Jack pushed him back again.

Putting one hand on his head and the other on Ben's, he said, in an unctuous voice like that of a clergyman—

"Bless you ! ber-less you, my children ! Kiss and be friends."

"Remove your hand from my head instantly, Harkaway !" cried Mr. Mole. "It's a liberty I allow no man to take !"

"Kiss and be friends, then," said Jack; "we can't have you fighting. Wait for the mutineers."

"You're becoming very impertinent," continued Mr. Mole. "Both you and Harvey seem to have lost the respect you ought to entertain for me. Don't take any more liberties with me, Harkaway, or you'll hear more of it."

"Hullo !" cried Jack. "What's the matter ? You're out of order, sir. Whose pills do you take ?"

"Never mind; I will keep my place as leader of this party and protector of you poor defenceless boys; you keep yours. It is my province to command, yours to obey."

Jack smiled and winked at Harvey.

"If so be as the gentleman wants a turn up on the grass, man to man, a fair field and no favour, I'm ready for him," remarked Ben Blunt.

"I do not fight," replied Mr. Mole. "Such low and blackguard practices may suit Whitechapel roughs."

"Hang me if I know how to take him. I'm game. I was never sick or sorry an hour in my life, and if he means fitting, why, I'll fit," said Ben.

"Don't you make any mistake, Ben," replied Jack. "Mr. Mole is as game as a pebble, and would come up fresh as a daisy after the fiftieth round. Don't you provoke him."

"What's he keep snacking at me for?"

"It is not for a boatswain, or whatever you call yourself, to insult a man of education like myself, understand that," exclaimed Mr. Mole, proudly.

"The likes of you! And what be I?"

"An indifferent cross, I should say between an idiot and a sea-cow," replied Mr. Mole, who was rapidly drinking more than he ought to.

Jack and Harvey roared with laughter at this sally.

Mr. Mole smiled blandly at this token of their approval.

"That's good. I flatter myself that's good, eh, Harkaway," he said.

"Stunning, sir. You've spotted him to a T."

"He asked my candid opinion, and I gave it him."

"Well, I'm blowed, gents," exclaimed Ben Blunt, getting as red as a turkey-cock. "He's a-giving it me a rum 'un all round the hoop and no kid. Cross atween a hidiot and a sea-cow. Blow me tight! That's a nice thing to say about a respectable cove, whose father fought with Nelson in the 'Victory,' and whose mother took in officers' washing at Portsmouth. I'll spoil his figure-head!"

"Harvey, hold that misguided man while I hit him on the head with a stick," exclaimed Mr. Mole, adding, in a whisper, "Harkaway, what shall I do?"

"Cheek it out, sir."

"Mutinous dog, forbear!" continued Mr. Mole. "You were the companion of mutineers. I will put you in chains, and convey you to your native land, there to await the judgment of your outraged countrymen."

Harvey had great difficulty in restraining Ben, who was speechless with rage and indignation.

"I think I've settled him," said Mr. Mole, with a hiccup. "What was it that broke the thingamy's back, Harkaway?"

"Straw, sir. Last straw broke the camel's back."

"Precisely. Turn to your natural histroy, and you find that the camel is a native of Bactria."

Mr. Mole took Ben's quiet attitude for cowardice.

His courage rose accordingly.

"You need not hold the poor wretch any longer, Harvey. Let him go," he said. "I think I have snuffed him out."

"He's in a mortal funk, sir. I don't know what it is, but there's something about you which knocks them all over," replied Harvey.

"It's my bearing, Harvey, my majestic bearing."

Suddenly Ben found his tongue, and sprang to his feet.

"I'll give him something!" he gasped, "when I've finished with him, he shall have a cock eye and a game leg. There won't be much what d'ye call—bearing about that. Sink me, if there will."

"My word, sir," whispered Jack; "his monkey's up. You'd better cut and run."

"Run, Harkaway! I'd scorn to. But do you really think he means it? I thought I'd cowed him."

"Cut into the cave, sir. I'll square it in two miuutes."

Ben Blunt was coming on at full speed, like an iron-clad ram with the steam full on.

Mr. Mole made a clean bolt into the cave, and began to barricade the entrance with some wood and bits of rock.

Jack stopped Ben Blunt, and exclaimed—

"Steady, Ben; steady!"

"Steady she is, sir," replied Ben, who was too good a sailor not to pull up when spoken to by one whom he considered his superior officer.

"Drop anchor, Ben."

"Lower away, my lads," replied Ben; adding, as he sat down—

"She's swung round to her moorings, sir."

"Right, Ben. Now listen to me. We make allowance for Mr. Mole. He is our senior, and we take no notice of what he says. He's privileged, Ben."

"That's all well enough, sir," cried Ben. "I'm no scholard, but it's hard to be called sea-cows and cussed hidiots, ain't it now?"

"All chaff, Ben. Nothing but empty chaff. I'll take my oath he didn't mean it. He's a good sort when you know him."

"Then may I be wrecked on a lee shore if I want to know him."

"Step aft, Ben, and say there's no bad blood between you. He's the bung on board this ship, and will stop your grog if you ain't civil."

"Will he 'pologise for the sea-cow, sir, think ye?" asked Ben, scratching his head dubiously.

"Avast there, Ben. He's your superior officer. Never strike your flag, Ben, but always doff your hat to the ward-room."

"You're right, sir. Tell him to come out. I won't hurt him," answered Ben Blunt, who was a good-natured fellow, and easily pacified.

Jack went to the cave and said—

"It's supper time, sir; come and join us."

"Is—is that wild sailor-fellow inclined to make peace, Harkaway?" asked Mr. Mole, looking cautiously through a hole in his barricade.

"He's like a lamb sir."

"Is he? Then I'll venture out. I don't like mutineers as a rule. Not that I am afraid of any man living, but directly I recollected he was a mutineer, I thought it best to get out of the dog's way," answered Mr. Mole.

"Now, then, Dick," cried Jack, "wake up! See what there is in the larder, and put on the feed."

"There's cold venison and some bird stuff or other—parrot I think," answered Harvey.

"All right; put it on. We'll make a night of it, and fight the enemy all the better when they come."

Mr. Mole emerged from the cave, and was induced to shake hands with Ben, who showed no further ill-feeling.

The "feed," as Jack called it, was put "on," and a very pleasant evening passed.

In a short time the daylight came and everybody was very valiant, especially Mr. Mole and Ben Blunt.

"Sam Parsons knows me well enough," exclaimed Ben, "and I don't believe that he'll show up."

"I've got an idea, Ben," said Jack.

"Bully for you, sir," replied the boatswain.

"Suppose you send Sam Parsons a challenge."

"I'm game to do that, sir, and fight him as long as I can stand, with cutlashes or pistols, or both."

"Very well; Monday shall take the challenge, but it must be written."

"I'm no scholard, sir, as I said before," answered Ben; "but if so be that your honour will write it out, I'll put my mark to it."

"I've got a pencil and a bit of paper," said Harvey.

"Fork it out, then," replied Jack.

Harvey gave him the pencil and paper, and Jack spread the latter out on his knee.

"What shall I say, Ben?" he asked.

Ben scratched his head, and looked up at the reddening sky, and then down upon the ground.

"It'll run somehow in this way," remarked Ben. "'I, Ben Blunt, late bo'sun of the "Sea-horse," bound from Shanghai to the port of London.' Got that, sir?"

"Yes; 'port of London.' Go ahead."

"'Challenge Sam Parsons, also of the "Sea-horse," and mutineer, to single combat.' Got that, sir?"

"All right; 'single combat.' Cut along."

"'And the said Ben Blunt will fight with cutlashes or pistols, and——'Got pistols, sir?"

"Yes; 'pistols.'"

"'And him as is whopped will have to bury the other, if so be as his lights is put out for ever.'"

"That's lovely! I like the last bit," observed Harvey.

"We'll avenge you, Ben, if you fall," said Jack.

"P'r'aps Mr. Mole will have a turn at him, sir, if so be as I'm beat," observed Ben.

"Do you think I'd condescend to fight your battle, you son of a sea-cook?" exclaimed Mr. Mole, angrily.

"Gents," said Ben, "he's at me again."

"Never mind him; it's his way," answered Jack. "It pleases him and don't hurt you."

"Right, sir," replied Ben. "I only clap on sail when there's a capful of wind; it's when I feel a tempest coming that I take in canvas,"

"Vulgar seaman!" said Mr. Mole.

"Well, sir?" inquired Ben.

"Peace, common fellow—peace?" continued Mr. Mole, waving his hand.

"Beg your honour's pardon," said Ben speaking to Jack; "is that in the articles of war?"

"Yes; hold your noise."

"But sea-cows, and sea-cooks, and vulgar seamans, and common fellows! Why, hang me, if I was a porpoise I couldn't stand it much longer.

"Polish off Sam Parsons first, and then you shall have a go at Mole."

"You promise me that, sir?"

"Religiously."

"Right. "I'm dumb as an oyster, and then he'd better batten down his hatch, or I'll walk into his hold," said Ben.

Jack got up and dispatched Monday, with a white flag, to seek out the mutineers.

"Give them this," he said, "and bring us their answer."

"All serene, Mast' Jack; Monday him do it," replied the black.

But he hadn't gone half-a-dozen yards before he ran back in a great state of agitation, crying—

"Here they come, sare—such a lot of 'em! Oh, my, Mast' Jack! look out sare!"

Each member of the party firmly grasped his weapon and stood on the defensive.

The mutineers of the 'Sea-horse" were advancing in force.

It was a critical moment.

CHAPTER LXIX.

THE SINGLE COMBAT.

"HARVEY," said Mr. Mole, "don't get behind me. Show yourself a man, as I mean to do."

Dick was only kneeling to load his extra rifle, and took no notice of the admonition.

"You, Harvey, are a fine specimen of the *vitulus Britannicus*," continued Mr. Mole.

"Who's he, sir, when he's at home?" answered Harvey, getting up when he had finished loading.

"The British calf. *Vitulus Brit——* oh! get out of my way Harvey. I will make for the cave. A bullet whistled past my head, and I thought there was only to be a single combat."

As Mr. Mole spoke a couple of shots hurtled past and buried themselves in the walls of the cave.

The mutineers had commenced the attack.

"This is getting hot," remarked Harvey.

"Getting hot," replied Jack; "it's boiling hot already. Monday, hoist the white flag, as a sign we want to parley with them."

Monday did so.

The white flag was simply a bit of an old shirt stuck on the end of a bamboo.

"Hold your fire, Sam Parsons," cried Jack. "Here's a letter I want to show you from an old messmate. Stay where you are. Don't advance another step or we fire."

Hunston at this moment came to the front.

"You haven't taken us by surprise, old fellow," continued Jack.

"Let them have it!" cried Hunston angrily.

"Hold hard, governor," said Sam Parsons. "If so be as my old shipmate Ben Blunt——"

"That's me," interposed Ben.

"I can see your old hull," continued Sam. "Well, as I was a-saying, if so be as Ben wants a bit of palaver, I ain't a-going to forget old times, and shan't say nary word against it."

"That's righteous, that is, Sam, and though we ain't cousins, blow me if I don't sort of admire your style!" answered Ben.

"Shoot them all down, you fool; you'll lose your chance!" exclaimed Hunston, more furious than ever.

"Belay, there! It's a truce, Ben, isn't it?" said Sam Parsons.

"Truce it is, Sam."

"Look here, Hunston," exclaimed Jack. "I know you to be a coward and a villain, and so I've covered you with my rifle. If——"

"You wouldn't break the truce?" said Hunston, hastily, fearing Jack meant to kill him.

"No, I shan't do that, but I shall keep my eye on the bead and my finger on the trigger and if you so much as move half an inch, or open your ugly mouth again, I take my Dick I'll pot you!"

Hunston turned ghastly pale.

But as he looked at Jack, he saw that he had his rifle to his shoulder, and that he could make " dead meat" of him in no time.

So he was obliged to be quiet.

"Ben!" exclaimed the mutineer.

"Here, lad," answered Ben.

"Where's this bit o' writin' you spoke about?"

"Monday!" said Jack.

"Yes, sare," replied the black.

"Deliver the challenge."

Monday advanced to Sam Parsons with the piece of paper on which the challenge was written, and Sam took it up, reading it with difficulty.

Some of his companions crowded round him and helped to make out its contents.

Turning to his lieutenant, Jimmy Clark, Sam said—

"What shall I do, Jim?"

"Do?" repeated Jimmy. "Why, fight him like a man. It's a fair challenge, and if he beats, we'll shake hands all round and let 'em alone."

"Well, if I beat?"

"Why, if you beats, we'll shake hands all round too, and after a good liquor-up, we'll up anchor and part friends," said Jimmy.

"Is that business, Jim?" asked Sam Parsons.

Jimmy had been a clerk somewhere, at some time or the other, and they called him the Sea Lawyer.

If anything difficult had to be decided, they always said—

"Go and ask Jimmy Clark; he's our sea lawyer, and be hanged to him!"

Thus it happened that Jimmy had great influence over his lawless companions.

A little learning is a dangerous thing, and Jimmy hadn't much, but what little he had he made do double duty.

"Of course it's business," replied Jimmy. "If Antony had sent a challenge to Cæsar, to meet him in the Campus Martius, wouldn't Cæsar have accepted it?"

"Then we must fight?"

"You and Ben must fight, that's about the size of it, and I'll bet a demi-quid on you, Sam.

"Right you are, Jimmy," said Sam Parsons. "I'm a plucked one."

"You have the choice of weapons, being the challenged party," continued Jimmy. "What will you have?"

"Cutlashes for me," exclaimed Ben.

"You dry up, old whale," exclaimed Jimmy. "It's for my man to choose. What do you want to spout for?"

"Well," said Sam, "cutlashes be it. I never liked to crab a pal, and if Ben Blunt says cutlashes, I'm on with cutlashes."

Two of the mutineers stepped forward, and gave each of the intending combatants a cutlass.

They took the weapons and faced one another.

Both sides made a circle round the principals.

Jack, however, did not lower his rifle, and never took his eye off Hunston.

The single combat was about to begin.

CHAPTER LXX.

THE RESULT OF THE FIGHT.

THE two old salts stood opposite one another and flourished their weapons, which glittered in the sunshine.

"Tip us your flapper, Ben," said Sam Parsons.

"Done with you, Sam," replied Ben Blunt; "I've no particular ill-will against you, though you didn't behave quite friendly."

"It's understood, lads," said Jimmy Clark, "that whoever licks we makes friends, and each party goes its own way."

Every one assented.

"We'll stand the liquor," remarked Harvey, "and all shall be agreeable as far as we can make it."

"All right," replied Jimmy; "I'll back up Sam, and that gentleman with the clerical mug on him will perhaps do the same for Ben.

He pointed to Mr. Mole.

"Did you allude to me?" asked Mr. Mole.

"You're the cove. Step out here and we'll see fair play."

"I can have no possible objection to seconding the champion of our party, but I strongly object to being called the cove with the clerical—what did you say?"

"Mug," replied Jimmy.

"I think I understand your meaning, though I must protest against the vulgarity of your language. However, let that pass. I will do my duty," replied Mr. Mole.

Jimmy Clark took his place behind Sam Parsons.

Mr. Mole took his behind Ben Blunt.

"Make ready," said Jimmy.

The cutlasses described circles in the air.

"At the word 'three,' strike," continued Jimmy.

There was a momentary pause.

Then Jimmy exclaimed—

"One, two, three!"

In an instant the blades crossed and struck fire.

Sam Parsons was a tall, active fellow, but Ben was the stronger of the two.

Perhaps he was not so active as his opponent, though he seemed to understand the sword exercise.

The spectators applauded their respective champions, taking the utmost interest in the contest.

"Lay on, Sam," cried the mutineers. "Stick to him, lad; let him have it!"

While Jack and Harvey said—

"Cut him down, Ben—that's your sort! Be careful, old man. Now you have him!"

Sam Parsons had the honour of dealing the first cut that drew blood.

It was an ugly blow on the left shoulder but it did not disable his opponent.

The pain it caused him made him more furious than ever.

Hunston looked on and gnashed his teeth, for this affair was so different to what he had anticipated.

He intended to have massacred all his own friends, and his plans were spoilt by the chivalrous combat that was taking place.

Of course he was safe with the mutineers, and did not fear being taken prisoner.

They would protect him.

At length, Ben, by a lucky stroke, brought Sam Parsons on one knee, having cut through the tendons of his left leg.

"Good again, Ben! Cut him down!" cried Jack.

"Curse the luck!" gasped the mutineer, still dealing blows with his cutlass.

Ben Blunt was excited, and encouraged by the cries of his party, rushed forward raised his weapon with both hands, and brought it down on the defenceless head of his enemy.

There was a groan.

Sam Parsons fell forward on his face, his head being cleft in two to the chin.

The mutineer's last hour had come.

There was a faint gurgle in his throat a sort of death-rattle, and he gave up the ghost.

With the utmost composure the mutineers removed the body out of sight.

Then Jimmy Clark went up to Ben, and said—

"I guess you're best man and Sammy's gone home."

"And you're cap'n of the 'Sea horse,'" replied Ben.

"That's right enough. However, we'll keep our compact. No more fighting. You've done the trick, Ben, and so we'll claim your promise. Bring out the liquor."

Jack was horrified at the careless indifference of those men at the loss of their companion.

A moment's reflection showed him that a ship's crew who had risen against and killed their officers were not likely to give way to tender emotions.

Nor had he any time to waste in a melting mood.

"Monday," he exclaimed.

"Yes, sare," replied the black.

"Bring out the stone bottle—you know which one," he added, in the native language, in a low tone.

Monday nodded his head in a significant manner, and entered the cave.

He returned with a large stone bottle containing rum.

The contents had been drugged with the peculiar herb of which he had spoken.

Harvey and Mr. Mole were attending to Ben Blunt's hurt, which they bound up.

"Now, my lads, bring yourselves to an anchor," exclaimed Jack. "We shan't charge you any more for sitting. Here are some cups, such as we use ourselves and here's the stuff."

With this he distributed some half cocoa-nut shells, which could not be set down until they were empty, the bottom being round.

The men began to pour out the liquor and Jack spoke to Hunston, saying—

"Are you going to join your new friends?"

"No, I'm not," replied Hunston. "I'm going to take my hook. The sight of you makes me feel ill."

"Does it?" answered Jack, with a sneer. "Then take that with you to remind you of me."

As he spoke he kicked him as hard as he could just as he turned his back.

"You dare——" cried Hunston, in a rage.

Jack levelled a pistol-barrel at him.

"Sheer off," he exclaimed, "or I'll settle accounts with you, and wipe out all I have got against you."

"A time will come," said Hunston, burning with rage.

The next instant he had darted away, and was lost to sight in the dense jungle.

Returning to the mutineers Jack saw that they had all drunk.

Then he gave the stone bottle to Monday, saying—

"This is empty; go and get another."

"Ah, that's right," exclaimed Jimmy; "you'll join us. I thought you weren't going to leave us all alone. When we've had this drinking bout out and the truce is over, we shall be at liberty to fight again."

"Oh, yes; I quite understand that," replied Jack.

"You know, we ain't going to let Ben Blunt crow over us."

"Of course not."

"We arranged that poor Sammy and Ben should fight it out, and that there should be a truce," continued Jimmy. "Now we're drinking to our noble selves; but when we leave you here and get out of sight, the war begins again."

"We're ready for you," said Jack.

Mr. Mole approached.

"I think, Harkaway, that I should not be showing the loving kindness of my nature if I did not drink the health of these fine fellows."

"Fire away, sir," answered Jack, handing him a cup full of rum.

Harvey, Ben, and Monday now came in for their share, and they all fraternized.

"Ben, you old lubber," said Jimmy, "come and join us, lad, and we'll make you our cap'n."

"Not if I know it, Jimmy," answered Ben.

"You won't? Then to-morrow will see you as low as poor Sam Parsons, and we shall have lost the two best men in our crew."

"I'll never be a mutineer," replied Ben. "Scuttle me first."

"Come, gentlemen," exclaimed Jack, fearing a quarrel, "let the merry jest go round. We're friends now, whatever we may be to-morrow."

"That's right," answered Jimmy. "Who'll favour us with a song? Will you, sir?"

This request was addressed to Mr. Mole.

"I—I sing?" said Mr. Mole, in sur-

"BURU FELL WITHOUT A SOUND."

prise. "I never did such a thing in my life. It is totally out of keeping with my character."

"Go on, sir," said Jack. "You can tip them a stave if you like."

"Harkaway, I protest."

"It's no use protesting, sir. You're knocked down for a song, and sing you must. It will be your call afterwards."

Harvey clapped his hands.

"Silence, gentlemen," he said, "silence, please, for Mr. Mole's song."

There was a dead silence, and everybody looked at Mr. Mole.

The unhappy gentleman bestowed a supplicating look upon Jack, who kept his eyes fixed on the ground.

"The penalty for not singing is being ducked in the sea, I believe," remarked Harvey.

Thus stimulated, Mr. Mole sighed, and said—

"If I must, I must, though I can only give you a dimly-remembered trifle of my childhood."

Clearing his throat he sang, in a cracked voice—

> " Did you ever, ever, ever see a whale?
> Did you ever, ever, ever see a whale?
> Did you——"

"Blarm me," interrupted Ben Blunt, "if I didn't once see a lovely spermaceti whale off the coast——"

"Order, Ben. Shut up," cried Jack. "You're interrupting the harmony."

"Beg pardon, sir. Thought he was speaking to me, acos he looked——"

"Will you dry up?"

Ben collapsed, and Mr. Mole continued—

> " Did you ever, ever, ever see a whale?
> No, I never, never, never;
> No, I never, never, never saw a whale,
> But I've often, often, often;
> But I've often, often, often seen a cow."

How much longer Mr. Mole might have gone on with his song it is difficult to say.

His voice, however, was drowned in a rude burst of loud laughter, in which every one joined.

This was followed by hurrahs and bravos, and it became quite a word afterwards with every one to say, "Did you ever see a whale?" and the reply would be, "No, but I've seen a cow."

Mr. Mole sat down and solaced himself with a little refreshment.

"I flatter myself I did that well, Harkaway," remarked Mr. Mole, "I was greeted with applause, and came off with flying colours."

"Certainly, sir," replied Jack. Adding, "Dick, did you ever see a whale?"

At this there was another roar, in which Mr. Mole joined.

"The fact is, Harkaway," continued Mr. Mole, "that it isn't everybody who could sing that song."

"So I should think, sir."

"The words are so simple——"

"Very simple, sir," said Jack, with a grin.

"So simple, I say," continued Mr. Mole, "that a great deal depends on the way it is sung."

Jack now remarked that some of the mutineers were lying on their sides.

The drug was beginning to take effect.

"Hullo! dowse my daylights!" exclaimed Jimmy Clark, "but this is a rummy go. I've come over wonderful sleepy all of a minute."

"Pitch on the ground, then," replied Ben Blunt. "Nobody won't eat you."

Unable to resist the influence of the drug that Monday had mixed with the liquor, the leader sank gently forward.

Directly afterwards he was fast asleep.

One by one the mutineers dropped off, and springing to his feet, Jack exclaimed—

"Now, my boys, are you all armed?"

There was a general chorus in the affirmative.

"Does the boat float, Monday?"

"Yes, sare; him float safe enough," replied Monday.

"Slip your cable then, and away to the 'Sea-horse.' She is ours if we do our duty."

"Hur——" began Harvey.

"Silence, Dick. No holloaing till we're out of the wood. That thief Hunston's slinking about somewhere. We've our work cut out for us yet," interrupted Jack.

They did not know how many men had been left on board the ship.

But their enterprise had succeeded so well as far as it had gone that they ran down the beach flushed with hope, and jumped into the boat.

When they were all seated the sail bellied to the breeze, and away they went.

CHAPTER LXX.

TAKING THE SHIP.

THEY had not gone far from the shore when Hunston, who had been hiding in the bushes, crept up to the scene of the late revelry.

The stillness that reigned where just before all had been noise and uproar alarmed him.

The sudden quietude boded no good.

When he saw the mutineers all extended on the ground, he thought they were dead.

But a glance assured him that they slept, and as their hearts beat, and they breathed easily, it was clear that they were not poisoned.

"They have been drugged," he muttered.

His next anxiety was to discover what had become of Jack and his companions.

He reached the cave, and found nobody.

Then he gazed out over the sea, and saw the boat sailing towards the ship.

"Fiend take them!" he cried. "This is Jack's plan, I'll bet a sovereign, and a good one it is too. There cannot be more than half-a-dozen men on board the 'Sea-horse,' and probably they are drunk and keeping no look-out."

He danced about with uncontrollable passion.

All at once he remembered that Sam Parsons had told him he had arranged a signal with those on board the ship.

This was to light a fire.

If the look-out on board the "Seahorse" saw a fire on the shore, he would know at once that there was danger in the wind.

"I'll try and foil Harkaway, at all hazards," he cried.

Hastily gathering together some sticks, he contrived to light a fire by striking two flints together over some dry grass.

Heaping what wood he could find on the top of it, he soon had a roaring fire.

A black column of smoke ascended high in the air and extended seaward.

"Those on board the ship must see the signal," he muttered.

If the ship was captured he knew that his dearest scheme would be frustrated.

Jack had learnt from the native he captured, that Emily had been sent to the pirates' stronghold.

This was called the city of the Golden Towers.

The ship would enable Jack to sail to the island, on which the famous city was situated, and the rescue of Emily would be comparatively easy.

Besides this, the vessel would take Jack back to England, while Hunston would be left alone amongst the savages.

"I could gnaw my heart out with vexation," he said, almost crying with rage.

He stood by the fire piling on wood, and watching the progress of the boat towards the ship.

The morning had broken clear and serene; not a cloud obscured the magnificent disc of the yellow sun.

A refreshing breeze carried the boat over the water like a thing of life.

In his impatience, Jack had sezied an oar, while Harvey had grasped another.

She flew through the water.

Monday looked after the sail, while Mr. Mole sat behind Ben Blunt, who handled the tiller.

The dangerous nature of the task they had undertaken prevented them from feeling any inclination to talk.

It seemed an age before they reached the ship, though the actual distance traversed was not more than five or six miles.

When they were within a few yards of the vessel, they saw dark forms on the deck.

"Ship ahoy!" cried a sailor.

"Lower your flag!" exclaimed Jack, dropping his oar and grasping his weapons.

"Who are you, and where do you hail from?" continued the mutineer.

"You know me, Bill Drake, don't you?" said Ben Blunt.

"Of course I do. What tack are you

on now, Ben?" returned the one addressed as Blake.

"Sam Parsons is dead, and I've come to summon you to lay down your arms."

"Never!" replied Drake. "There's something wrong, lads. I see the signal on the shore; it's a caution. Take your boat away," he added, "or, by——, we'll sink her!"

"Pour in a volley!" cried Jack. "Now, then, each of you cover your man and aim low. Are you ready? Fire!"

In a moment there was a succession of reports.

"Run her alongside, Ben, and then board her!" continued Jack.

"I'll stick to you," said Harvey to his friend.

"All right. Bet you a bob I'm on deck first, Dick," replied Jack.

Almost directly, the crew of the boat were clambering up the sides of the ship.

Whether the mutineers were disheartened or not, Jack did not know.

But they returned the fire in a half-hearted manner, which did not appear to do any damage.

With his pistols in his belt, and a knife between his teeth, Jack went up the ship's side as if he was walking upstairs into his father's drawing-room.

Harvey was after him in a trice.

They saw four men on deck, two having fallen at the first discharge.

Jack having fired his pistol at one, rushed at the other with his dirk and ran it through his body.

Harvey made short work with another, and the fourth fell on his knees and begged for mercy.

"Shall I settle him?" asked Harvey.

"No, let the beggar live. Take away his arms, though," replied Jack.

The mutineer gladly allowed himself to be disarmed, and then the victors looked round to see the extent of the damage.

By this time Monday had gained the deck, not being so active as the boys, who, of course, knew much better how to get on board a ship than he did.

"Oh, Mast' Jack!" cried Monday; "how him bleed!"

"Who?" asked Jack.

"You, sare; look, your face!"

Jack put up his hand and withdrew it covered with blood.

"By Jove!" he said; "I've copped it somehow, though I didn't feel I was wounded. Is it much, Dick?"

Harvey approached to examine and said—

"It isn't deep, but it's a neat enough cut over the cheek bone. It's a cutlass wound. I saw one of the fellows make a swipe at you as you boarded."

"Tie something round it, will you."

Taking a handkerchief off his neck, Harvey fastened it as well as he could round his friend's face.

"Hurrah," said Jack, "the ship's ours! Ben! Where's Ben?"

"Here, cap'en," replied the old sailor coming up the ship's side with difficulty. "I've got a bullet in the leg, but I wouldn't stop below."

"That's a pity, for we're short-handed already, and can't afford to let you go into the sick bay," said Jack.

Harvey had a look at the wound, and exclaimed—

"I'm surgeon's mate, Ben.

"Might have a worse, sir, and meaning no flattery to you," answered Ben.

The ball fortunately had not gone in very far, and Dick felt it by probing the wound with his finger.

"Can you plumb it, sir?" asked Ben.

"True as a die, Ben. Shut your mouth and keep still."

"Oh! That last poke seemed to touch up a muscle," cried Ben, wincing beneath the pain.

Harvey had one of those wonderful knives in his pocket, which are a corkscrew, penknife, stone-picker, bradawl, forceps, ect., all in one.

Opening the forceps, he, with great nerve and considerable skill, inserted the instrument in the wound, grappled the bullet, and drew it out.

"The Lord love you, sir," said Ben, joyfully. "Perhaps you've saved my life, leastways, my leg, which would have cankered without a doctor's help."

Harvey tore up part of his shirt and made bandages, which he tied round the wound.

"Now you lie still, my old sea-lion," he said. "You've got an uncommon bad leg, and we shall have you tied up in your hammock with a big shot at your feet, if you don't watch it."

Ben hobbled to the after-deck, and sat down on a carronade, knowing that Dick's advice was too good not to be followed.

The bodies of the mutineers were quickly thrown overboard by Monday, and the decks swabbed.

In a short time not even a blood-stain remained to show there had been an action.

Going up to Ben, Jack said—

"What's the name of the man whose life we spared? Will he join us?"

"Bouncer's his name, leastways, I never heard him called anything else," answered Ben; "and as to joining us, will a duck swim?"

"What do they call him Bouncer for?"

"'Cos he's the biggest out and outer at lying as ever had breath put into him," said Ben.

"Oh, that's it," exclaimed Jack, laughing.

"You mustn't believe anything that Bouncer tells you, 'cos he can't speak the truth even a little bit. He don't know how."

"Can we go to sea like this, Ben?" asked Jack.

"No, sir," answered the old sailor. "We couldn't work her if a storm came on. It would be a tempting of Providence, and I'd as soon sail on a Friday."

"Then what's the good of the vessel?" asked Jack in a tone of disappointment.

"Might man her with niggers, sir."

"Niggers? Natives you mean."

"Yes," replied Ben. "I've seen Lascers do their duty when they've been well larruped with a rope's end. But you can't do nothing with them with kindness."

"Are they lazy?"

"Ain't they?" said Ben. "I've seen 'em—a score or more—sleeping on deck of a night, cuddled up in each other's arms, all the world like monkey's, and that's what they'd like to do always—eat and drink and sleep; but these here niggers may be a chalk better."

"I'll consider what's to be done, Ben. Let Harvey help you below. Turn into your old bunk. You must take care of yourself."

"Thank'ee, sir. I shall know little rest though till I can take my place again by your side," answered the sailor.

"Where's Mole?" said Jack, as Harvey and Ben disappeared.

In the excitement of the moment he had forgotten all about Mr. Mole, and he now looked anxiously round for him.

The proprietor of a tea-garden in China was nowhere to be seen.

CHAPTER LXII.

HUNSTON IN DANGER.

THE delight of Harkaway at having so boldly and gallantly captured the beautiful little ship 'Sea-horse" was unbounded.

He had many difficulties yet to contend with; but having possession of the vessel gave him hopes of sailing to the mysterious city where Emily had been sent.

Then, having rescued her, he could up anchor and sail for England.

The very thought of his home and all his friends, who no doubt, for his long silence, were mourning him as dead, sent him wild with joy.

He forgot the pain of his wound, which was beginning to stiffen.

He forgot all the difficulties he had to encounter, and had it not been for his anxiety on Mr. Mole's account, he could have sunk into a charming reverie.

Monday came up at this moment, and he said—

"Have you seen Mr. Mole? I am afraid he is hurt, and I wouldn't lose Mole for the world. We should have no fun without him."

Monday grinned.

"Mist' Mole all right, sare," he replied.

"Is he? How do you know that?" asked Jack, much relieved.

"Monday saw him lower the sail in the boat, and creep under um, sare."

"He's in the boat, then?"

"Yes, sare."

Jack looked over the side, and saw the boat drifting astern.

"Drop into the water, and swim to her," he exclaimed, "or she'll get into a current and go in shore. He'll never work her himself."

Monday had no superfluous clothing, and quickly dropped into the sea, swimming like a fish towards the boat.

He looked under the sail, but saw no one.

"Him gone," he exclaimed.

"Gone! Pull the boat in, and make fast the painter to the ship," answered Jack whose presence of mind never failed him.

He had got into the habit now of giving orders, and commanded as if he had been born to it.

In a short time Monday worked the boat back, moored her, and came on deck, his dusky skin glistening in the sun after his immersion.

"Now, where's Mole?" said Jack.

"Monday saw him, sare, creep under the sail when we began to fire."

"Perhaps he's on board, and we have missed him. Come below."

Jack went down the hatch, and entered the captain's cabin.

Here to his surprise, was Mr. Mole.

On the floor lay a man, very much the worse for liquor, and Mr. Mole had put his foot on his neck.

Bottles of various kinds, containing spirits and wines, were displayed on the table.

Mr. Mole had been trying each of them, and held a glass of something red in his hand, which he was sipping with great gusto.

"How did you get here, sir?" asked Jack. "We thought you had come to grief."

"Harkaway," answered Mr. Mole, "I have subjugated this Philistine. Look at him!"

"I can see him, sir."

"Have I not put my foot on his neck?"

"But how did you get into this stateroom?" persisted Jack.

"You shall hear. First of all, try a glass of this liquor. I know not its name, but of a verity, Harkaway, it is comforting to the inner man."

"Don't mind if I do, sir. I got a nasty knock on the head, and don't feel over and above bobbish," replied Jack.

They drank, Mr. Mole raising his glass to his mouth with an unsteady hand, and saying—

"When the boat struck against the side of this goodly ship I saw a port-hole, Harkaway."

"Yes, sir."

"My first impulse was to follow you on deck, but on reflection, I decided not to do so. I crept through the port-hole, and entered this cabin."

"Where you found the liquor, sir," said Jack.

"No, Harkaway, not so," replied Mr. Mole. "Where I found this truculent mutineer. We fought for more than ten minutes, and at last I conquered him."

"You haven't got a scratch, sir. That's lucky, after a ten minutes' tussle."

"I don't show my wounds like some people. If I am thrust through the thigh with a murderous sort of knife, I don't go and proclaim it on the housetops, not I, Harkaway."

"Well, I'm glad to see you so well as you are, sir," replied Jack. "You'll excuse me for a time, as I have affairs to attend to."

"Can I help you? If so, command Isaac Mole."

"You can come on deck, sir. I must keep this cabin shut up."

"Shut up the cabin?" said Mr. Mole, in dismay.

"Yes; this is my den in the future. I'm captain, sir, and you shall be one of my lieutenants."

"This is reversing the order of things, Harkaway. Am I not entitled by my age and experience to be the leader? I will not quit this cabin at present, I protest against it; but I will drink your health nevertheless."

While he was speaking he slipped off his chair, and fell stretched on the floor.

"Let him be, sare," said Monday. "Him right enough now."

"You black beast!" exclaimed Mr. Mole. "I will teach you how to respect your pastors and masters when I am better. Just now I feel sleepy. My exertions in the battle have made me drowsy. You can go and play."

A benignant smile overspread his countenance, and Jack and Monday left the cabin.

Going on deck again, they met Harvey.

"Hullo, Jack!" said Harvey, "did you ever see a whale?"

"No, I never, never saw a whale, but I've just seen a Mole," replied Jack.

"Where?"

"In the cabin—tight."

"Well, he's happy. I thought he was potted. Shouldn't like to lose old Mole.

He isn't a bad sort, and taught our young ideas, you know."

"So he did. I like Mole. He keeps us alive."

"Well, what's the next move?" said Harvey.

"Blest if I know; I'm cornered," answered Jack. "I must have a little while to rest and think. There's Mole tight, Ben Blunt wounded, and I'm dead beat."

"You're wounded too."

"It isn't much, though I must own I wan't rest," said Jack.

"Have it then. Monday and I will keep watch. There are too small cannons on deck, which I suppose the crew had to protect them against the Malay pirates. We will keep them loaded, and if the mutineers wake up and try to board us, we will sink them."

"By the way, Monday," asked Jack, "how long will the fellows be before the drug works off?"

"They wide 'wake enough now, sare," replied Monday.

"How do you know?"

"You look, sare, See um all dance about; and, look, they got Mast' Hunston!"

"I'll be hanged if I can see them. Your eyes are sharper than mine," replied Jack.

"Get a glass, Monday?" siad Harvey. "We have one somewhere."

Monday saw one lying on the deck, and handed it to Jack.

He put the telescope to his eye, and took a steady view of the opposite shore.

"By Jove!" he said. "Monday's right, The fellows are all up, and bustling about like bees."

"Have they got Hunston?" asked Harvey.

"Yes; they are binding a fellow who looks like Hunston."

"Him Mast' Hunston, sure enough," said Monday. "Me never forget um face."

"What are they going to do with him?" continued Harvey.

"Jiggered if I know," answered Jack. "They've got him safe. There is something on, but what it is, I can't make out for the life of me."

"I expect he's had a row with the mutineers," said Harvey; "but he'll square it with them, no doubt. It isn't worth while bothering about him."

"Not much," replied Jack.

He dropped the glass, and as he did so, Bouncer who had been neglected in the confusion came up.

"Beg pardon, captain," he said.

"What do you want? Oh, you are the prisoner," replied Jack.

"Yes, sir, and I want to know what you're going to do with me."

"Look here, Mr. Bouncer," said Jack; "the ship is ours now, and we mean to take very good care she shall remain ours. If you like to become one of our crew, we'll take you to England with us, and say nothing about the mutiny."

"That's generous, sir," replied Bouncer; "though, to tell you the truth, I was dead against the rising from the first, and it was through me that Ben Blunt's life was saved."

Jack did not quite believe this, for he remembered what Ben had said about Bouncer's lying powers.

"You'll be short-handed, sir," continued Bouncer. "There's only yourselves, me, and Geary, who's been drunk in the captain's cabin for the last two days."

"You'll have to work double tides, then," said Jack; "but we mean to get some niggers to ship with us."

"From one of the islands?"

"Yes; say a dozen or so, and they can be brought to their homes by the next ship that comes out this way. I'll see about that."

"Then I'd better set about my duty, sir," exclaimed Bouncer; "for although I say it who shouldn't, there isn't a better fo'castle hand than I am."

"No treachery, mind, Mr. Bouncer," said Jack. "If I see the least symptom of an inclination on your part to join your old friends, I'll shoot you like a seagull."

"No fear, sir. I'm glad to be under a proper cap'n again. When do you sail?"

"Not yet. We must wait till that drunken hound in the cabin is sober, and Ben Blunt can get about and give us a hand. You, I, Harvey, and Monday, with Mr. Mole thrown in, are not sufficient to work the ship."

"That's the crew, is it, sir? Four men and a black—five all told."

"That's all—five men, if you like to call Harvey and I men."

"Ah, I could spin you a yarn, sir," said Bouncer, "of how I and another chap crossed the Atlantic, when we wasn't fourteen years old, in a cockle-shell of thirty tons. It isn't the years, it's the spirit that makes a man."

"There is something in that," replied Jack; "and now keep a good look-out. Those two small cannons are loaded. If the mutineers come near us in their boats depress the muzzles and fire low, and we shall sink the lot of them."

Having given some trifling orders to Harvey and Monday, Jack took up the glass again and reconnoitred the shore.

Hunston was certainly in trouble.

But what about?

CHAPTER LXXIII.

THE RAGE OF THE MUTINEERS.

To explain the peculiar position into which Hunston had fallen, we must return to the mutineers.

The drug which had been given them, though quick in its action, was not lasting in its effects.

In a few hours they had slept off the lethargy which had overtaken them.

Jimmy Clark, being a man of strong constitution, was the first to return to his senses.

He was followed by the rest of his companions, one by one.

They all awoke somewhat dizzy and drowsy, rubbing their eyes and stretching their limbs.

Hunston no sooner saw they were getting about again, than he left the signal fire and came towards them.

"What's the meaning of this, and where are your late friends?" asked Jimmy.

"They've been one too many for you, curse them!" replied Hunston.

"How's that; and why did you light the signal?"

"To give those on board warning that there was danger."

"What danger?" asked the mutineer.

"You've had some stuff put in your grog," said Hunston, "which sent you all off to sleep."

"Hang me, if I didn't think as much."

"While you slept, the party under Jack Harkaway sailed to the ship, attacked, and captured it. I heard the firing, and though I lighted the signal, it did not save the vessel."

The mutineers looked blankly at one another.

"Is this true?" cried Jimmy, fiercely.

"Judge for yourself," replied Hunston. "Look, they are lowering the black flag you hoisted, and running up the Union Jack.

"So they are. It's a case, and Ben Blunt has us in the palm of his hand. He'll send one of Her Majesty's cruisers after us, and we shall be shot or hanged."

The dismay of the mutineers increased.

"Death is better than being left on this island," said one.

Turning savagely to Hunston, and eyeing him suspiciously, Jimmy Clark exclaimed—

"It strikes me, my hearty, that you've had a hand in this."

"I?" repeated Hunston.

"Yes, you; they used to be your friends. How is it you were not drugged with the rest of us?"

"Because I wouldn't drink with them."

"That be blowed for a yarn. Catch an old sailor, refusing his allowance, when it's offered him," said Jimmy.

"Look here," replied Hunston, growing alarmed at the threatening looks which were bent upon him from all sides.

"Well?" said the mutineer, sullenly.

"If I'd stood in with them, shouldn't I have gone off in the boat with them, and not have stopped here with you?"

This argument did not convince Jimmy.

"Not you. There is some dodge on. You didn't expect us to wake up so soon, and meant to have joined them later. If they ain't waiting for you, why don't they set sail at once?"

"Look 'ee here," said a hairy, rough-looking mutineer, "you see the smoke from that fire's a-blowing right into the cave, ain't it?"

"Yes, it be so," replied Jimmy.

"Well, then, it's my idea he meant to

have dragged all our bodies in there and have suffocated us right off, only we come to a sight too quick for him."

This unlikely suggestion was eagerly caught at by the mutineers, and fully believed in.

Knives leaped from sheaths and flashed in the sunlight.

More than one pistol was levelled at Hunston's head, and his life with these ferocious men did not seem worth a minute's purchase.

Jimmy now interfered.

"Put up your shooting-irons, lads," he exclaimed. "There is one comfort, we've got the traitor."

"Kill him! kill him!" cried a chorus of voices.

"Not yet. Seize him and bind his arms, so as he shan't slip his cable."

A dozen willing hands fell upon Hunston, and securely bound his hands behind his back.

This was what Jack had observed from the deck of the "Sea-horse."

It was this confusion which had puzzled him.

"Now, my lads, let's have a bit of a palaver," said Jimmy.

The mutineers crowded round their leader in a circle.

Hunston was sitting on the ground, looking sullen and dejected.

"It was this chap," continued Jimmy, pointing to Hunston, "who got us to come here to attack Ben Blunt, wasn't it?"

"That's right enough."

"Well, Sam Parsons got killed, and I always thought there was foul play about that, which was all of a piece with the rest."

"Ben Blunt never could have beat Sam Parsons if there wasn't something quizzy a-going on," remarked a mutineer.

"So I say," remarked Jimmy; "and it's all bits of the same plot. Well, we gets drugged, doesn't us?"

"Sure," replied the men.

"Then, while we's asleep, Ben and his mates goes and takes our ship. Now what I say is that this Hunston is at the bottom of it all. He's helped his friends, and all what's happened is all along of him."

"Don't I tell you that I hate Harkaway and all his companions like poison?" exclaimed Hunston.

"What you say don't matter much. It ain't of no account," answered Jimmy.

"Won't you listen to reason?" continued Hunston. "A child, if he'd look at the facts fairly, could see that I've had nothing to do with it."

"Look here," said the mutineer, "you may jaw for a month, but you won't alter our opinion. We've dropped anchor at that idea, and we shall ride at it, shan't us, lads?"

There was a noisy chorus of assent.

"Now, you've done a deal for your pals, and they ought to do summat for you," persisted Jimmy.

"They won't do anything for me," replied Hunston, "so it is no use your thinking of it."

"We'll try them. I want that ship. We're treed so long as we ain't got our ship, and I don't know as we should do much good by attacking of her now she's well looked arter."

"Why not? You're four to one."

"Maybe; but Ben Blunt and his friends are wide awake, they are, not like our two scoundrels Bouncer and Geary, and the others, who must have got blazing drunk, and kept no watch."

"You've got two boats. Go and attack the ship. I'll lead the attack," Hunston suggested.

"No, thank you; I've got a better dodge than that. You'd go over to the enemy. I know you. Wanted to smother us all in the cave, didn't you?"

Hunston groaned at the pig-headed and ignorant obstinacy of the man.

"No, my lads," Jimmy went on; "we won't attack the ship to be sent to the bottom by the cannon, not us. We'll send a flag of truce, and tell whoever's captain of the 'Sea-horse' that if the ship isn't given up in twelve hours, we'll hang this Hunston on a tree in sight of his pals."

There was a roar of assent to this proposition.

"Jimmy can do it. He's a born lawyer all over," said one of the mutineers named Phillips.

"Are we sailing on the right tack?" asked Jimmy, much pleased with the applause he received.

"That's right," replied Phillips. "Let Hunston write a bit of a note—we've got pencil and paper among us—and then two of us will go in the boat with a flag of truce and let 'em think it over."

"It must be put strong and **simple** to them," said another mutineer.

"You leave that to me, and don't attempt to teach your betters," exclaimed Jimmy. "It's this way; they give up the ship in twelve hours, or we put a noose round their friend Hunston's neck, and hang him up to the nearest tree."

"But I'm not their friend," said Hunston.

"Go along, and tell that to the marines," replied Jimmy, derisively.

"We're enemies. We hate one another, and I've been trying to kill the whole of them this ever so long. My life doesn't matter a rush to them."

"It won't do, governor," said Jimmy. "We're able-bodied seamen, and it won't wash."

"All right; you're a parcel of fools, and must do as you like, I suppose," exclaimed Hunston, with a sigh of resignation.

He saw it was useless to talk to them.

They fancied he was a traitor to them, and a friend of Ben Blunt and Harkaway, which was quite enough for them.

Paper and pencil were produced, and handed to Hunston.

"Now, then, write for your life; that's what you've got to do."

Write to Harkaway to save his life!

What a strange turn events had taken since Jack was Hunston's captive in Palembang, and a high gallows had been erected especially for him.

Hunston had some spirit and pride left in him, and he hesitated before he put pencil to paper.

He felt it would be no use.

It would be an unnecessary humiliation.

Throwing the pencil down, he said—

"Write yourselves! I'll be hanged if I lower myself by writing to Jack, not even to beg my life."

The mutineers regarded him with astonishment.

CHAPTER LXXIV.

TWELVE HOURS ONLY.

THE scene was a striking one.

Hunston's arms had been unbound to permit him to write, and an empty biscuit cask had been rolled before him, upon which the sheet of rough paper was placed.

Around him were gathered the picturesquely-attired mutineers, with their savage faces sunburnt and swarthy.

On one side was a cave, situated at the base of a rocky ledge, which stretched for some distance along the shore.

Behind arose a vast forest, filled with all the luxuriant vegetation of the tropics.

In front a sandy plateau swept down to the blue, curly waves of the sea, which, agitated by a faint breeze swept in gently eddying circles, flecked with foam.

"Won't you write?" asked Jimmy Clark, angrily.

"No; I have told you I won't," replied Hunston.

"Perhaps we can find a way of persuading you, my bantam cock."

"What's the good of bullying me?" Hunston said. "Can't you write yourself? You seem to have some education."

"I can write, and read too, for that matter; not that either 'complishment's of much use to a sailor. But give us hold of the pencil, I don't want to be nasty," said Jimmy.

He took up the pencil, and hastily wrote—

"To Ben Blunt, and those on board the 'Sea-horse' with him.

"Look here, old mate, you've been and gone and done it, and we ain't a-going to stand it, that's flat.

"We've got your friend Hunston—leastaways he's a friend of the chap they calls Jack Harkaway, who's at the bottom of this fakement.

"Now this is the size of it.

"If so be as you don't part with the ship in twelve hours from the time of getting this writing, we shall string up Hunston.

"That means hanging of him.

"We give you twelve hours to think it over.

"Let us have our ship, and we'll shake hands and cry quits.

"Your lot, shall have this island, which we'll 'vacu—cu——"

"I say, how do you spell 'vacuate ?" asked Jimmy.

Hunston told him.

"There may be a ' e' at the end," said Jimmy; "I don't say there isn't, but blow me if there's one at the beginning, and blame me if I put one. It's 'vacuate, ain't it? Well, then, how can you put a ' e' at the top. Go on. It's foolishness. You'll tell me next I ain't been to school at all."

"Put it as you like," replied Hunston.

"Which will be ' 'vacuate the island,'" continued Jimmy, "' and say no more about it, though that drugging business was a dirty bit, and no flies. ·

"So give up the ship, and cry a go, or we'll hang this cur, Hunston.

"So no more from yours at present, and a hoping it leaves you.

"JIM CLARK."

"Will that do, lads?" said Jim, reading it out with conscious pride.

The mutineers said it was beautiful, and evidently regarded the composition as the higest style of art.

"Now, Phillips, my man, you and me will sail over to the old tub, and deliver this 'ere letter," continued Jimmy.

Hunston was again bound, and the mutineers, after seeing their companions start, began to busy themselves in preparing their breakfast.

In the cave they found a variety of articles, abandoned by Jack and his party, which came in very handy.

Hunston watched the boat sail off with a dogged look.

He did not expect any mercy from Jack, and thought that the attempt to get back the ship by threatening his own life, would be a failure.

On all occasions he had treated Harkaway and Harvey, too, so infamously that he fancied they would show more than Christian forgiveness if they raised a hand in his defence. ·

"I'm a bad lot," he muttered. "I'm a thorn in their side, and the sooner I'm dead and gone the better for them. What do they care for me?"

The mutineers left him to himself, taking no notice of him.

He could not escape; that was all they cared about.

Hunston evidently believed his end was approaching.

No wonder he was sullen and silent.

Meanwhile the boat was on its way to the "Sea-horse."

Jack saw it long before it came near, and seeing only two men in it, did not feel much alarmed.

He called Harvey to his side, and pointed it out.

"What shall we do?" he asked.

"Oh, we needn't funk," replied Harvey, "They've come to remonstrate with us, perhaps."

A white flag was run up to the top of the little mast, and Jack cried—

"Lay to !"

The mutineers hauled down their sail, and hove to.

"We're unarmed," cried Jimmy Clark; "and have brought you a letter, sir."

"Come on board then," replied Jac' "You, I mean the other fellow can st in the boat."

The mutineer approached near and in a few minutes Jimmy was deck.

"I'm the bearer of a letter, sir," he said; " and come with a flag of truce, so of course you won't do anything to me. More by token that we've got your friend hard and fast."

"What friend?"

"Him they call Hunston."

"He's no friend of ours, my good fellow," said Jack. "you never made a greater mistake in your life."

"I thought you would say so," exclaimed Jimmy. "Howsomever, read that bit of writing."

Jack took the scrawl, and with difficulty made himself master of its contents,

"Is this a dodge?" he asked.

"What do you mean, sir?" inquired Jimmy.

"Is this a dodge of 'Hunston's, or are you really going to hang him because you think he has betrayed you and is a friend of ours?"

"Wish I may die, cappen," answered Jimmy, "if every word of that letter isn't gospel truth."

"You mean to hang Hunston if we don't give up this ship in twelve hours?"

"That's it, sir."

"And you give me twelve hours to decide."

"MONDAY DREW A REVOLVER AND FIRED"

"Not a minute more. If we don't hear from you then, up he goes."

"Very well," said Jack. "I can't give you an answer off hand, but I'll think the matter over."

The mutineer inquired after his comrades, and declared that he was sorry Geary and Bouncer were alive as they deserved killing with the others, because they had kept such a bad look-out.

"You ought never to have had this ship," he said.

"But we've got it, my friend," answered Jack.

"I know that. Well, sir, we'll expect your answer, and if you'll give us a glass of grog——"

"Not a drop. You're a mutinous dog and I'll have nothing further to say to you," interrupted Jack.

"But sir——"

"Be off, or I'll help you," said Jack, who was indignant with the mutineers, and did not care to take the trouble to speak civilly to any of them.

Jimmy descended the side, and the sail of the boat was soon bellying to the breeze, as he returned to his companions.

"Dick!" cried Harkaway.

"Here!" replied Harvey, who had been standing at a respectful distance, and had not heard what passed.

"Come below; we must hold a council of war.

"All right. Lead on," said Harvey.

They went into the captain's cabin.

Monday remained on deck with Bouncer.

Ben Blunt was in a hammock.

Geary had been removed, and was trying to get sober, while Mr. Mole was drinking some fine Madeira he had found in a locker, and was nibbling a ship's biscuit.

"Ah! you have come at last, Harkaway," he said. "That is my lunch. Have some lunch."

"What is it, sir?"

"Merely a biscuit and a glass of wine. Excellent Madeira. Try a glass."

Both Harvey and Jack complied with his request, and had some lunch.

"Comfortable quarters these, Harkaway. When do we sail?" asked Mr. Mole.

"Not for a day or two, sir," replied Jack.

"Ah, well! I leave all those things to you. Of course you'll put me in the way of getting to China. I must see after my tea garden."

"Sell it, sir. We shall not get much further up the China Sea."

"I should like to see it. I must see my tea garden, and shan't die happy if I don't," exclaimed Mr. Mole.

"What are you going to do with your wives, sir?" inquired Harvey.

"Wives! ah! Great bother wives; but I've given them the slip, eh! Shouldn't mind Alfura so much, but Ambonia is—a—what shall I say?"

"A teazer sir."

"She's worse than that, Harvey. She's a millstone round a man's neck. What a lovely corpse she would make, to be sure."

"I'm ashamed of you, sir," said Jack. "You don't manage her rightly, but you'll have an opportunity of making up for your bad behaviour, as we are going to Limbi."

"Going—to—Limbi!" said Mr. Mole, in horrified amazement.

"Must go."

"What for?"

"Haven't got our full complement of hands. Want niggers to make up the crew," replied Jack.

"Let me work. Let me do the work of a common seaman. I will indeed; but don't for the love of Heaven, go to Limbi."

"Must," said Jack.

"Well, then, say I'm dead. Tell them I fell fighting bravely against the Pisangs. Tell them anything, only don't give me up to the furies," supplicated Mr. Mole.

"We'll see what can be done for you, sir," replied Jack. "By the way, did you hear the news Monday brought from Limbi?"

"That my wives meant to come after me?"

"No, not that. Mrs. Mole Number One expects to become a mother,"

"Oh, Lord!" cried Mole, pressing his hand to his head.

"And Mrs. Mole Number Two also has an expectation of the same sort, but isn't quite sure."

"The Lord be good to me! Two little Isaacs! Oh, Lord! what shall I do! Two little Isaac Moles, with a prospect of more," said the wretched man.

"It's nice to be a father, sir," remarked Harvey.

"Not when they're niggers; the children, I mean. No, Harvey, I cannot look forward to such a prospect with an equal mind."

"Poor little innocents. What have they done? If you don't like kids, sir——"

"Harvey, I beg of you to refrain from any indulgence in unseemly mirth on my account. I will not put up with it."

Harvey sang—

     "One little Isaac,
      Two little Isaacs,
      Three little Isaac Moles.

You can do it, sir. Perhaps Ambonia will have twins."

"Do you want to drive me mad?" asked Mr. Mole.

"Shut up, Dick; I want to talk about business!" cried Jack.

"Ah! business!" exclaimed Mr. Mole rubbing his hands, and taking another glass of wine. "That's more in my way. I hate and abominate chaff. What is the business may I ask?"

"The mutineers fancy Hunston has betrayed them, and mean to hang him in twelve hours if we don't give up the ship," replied Jack.

Both Harvey and Mr. Mole received this news without showing any signs of astonishment or regret.

They did not seem to care whether Hunston lived or died.

Possible of the two they would have perfered him dead.

—+·····+—

CHAPTER LXXV.

JACK'S GENEROSITY.

"LET them hang him," said Mr. Mole.

"So I say," remarked Harvey. "He's no good. It will save us the trouble of settling his hash some day."

"Give up the ship and these comfortable quarters, with the chance of getting to China or home again?" continued Mr. Mole. "We're not candidates for Colney Hatch lunatic asylum yet."

"Nor Hanwell either," replied Harvey. "What do you say, Jack?"

"I don't see the force of giving up the ship," answered Jack, "and yet I don't like to leave Hunston to his fate."

"Has he ever shown you any kindness?" said Harvey.

"Was he not always your determined enemy at school, and has he not been so since?" said Mr. Mole.

"That is true; but I shouldn't like to see an old schoolfellow hanged before my eyes, as I may say."

"The sentiment does more honour to your heart than head, Harkaway," Mr. Mole said. "If I were you I should not trouble about the scoundrel."

"But I shall, sir. You and I are two different people, and I won't leave Hunston in the hands of the mutineers."

"Dear, dear," said Mr. Mole. "This is an unfortunate determination of yours Here have we fought vailantly for the ship, and——"

"I'm not going to give up the ship."

"Oh! that's a different thing. What is it you propose to do, then?" Mr. Mole said, much relieved.

"I shall go ashore, and have a shy at the mutineers. By myself, if no one has the pluck to go with me."

"Really I must decline the challenge," Mr. Mole replied. "The fatigues of this morning's battle have been too much for me. It was mainly owing to me that the ship was captured. Had I not gone through the porthole, and settled the man down below, I verily believe he would have fired the magazine, and then what would have become of you who were struggling on deck?"

Jack looked at Harvey, who saw the glance and comprehended it, but he preserved silence.

"Won't you lend a hand, Dick, to save an old schoolfellow?" urged Jack.

"I'll tell you what it is," replied Harvey; "if it had been anybody but Hunston, I would not have hesitated a moment, but——"

He paused.

"Well, Dick?" said Jack, calmly.

"It seems to me to be folly to risk our own lives to save his."

"He's got friends, Dick. He's got a mother and father, and brothers and sisters. Won't they like to see him again, bad as he is. Think of his poor mother," said Jack.

"I wish you wouldn't be so eloquent," replied Harvey. "I shall have to give in, whether I like it or not, if you go on like that."

"He's young, Dick, not above a year or two older than we are, and he's led a wicked life, and done—what is it we say at church, Mr. Mole?"

"'Those things which we ought not to have done,' Harkaway. Is that what you mean?"

"That's it, sir. Well, Dick, he's got sins to repent, and you know he might turn out a decent fellow after all."

"Don't walk into my affections like that, Jack," said Harvey.

"But I must and will."

"What do you want me to do?"

"To come and save Hunston."

"How?"

"It's a time to forget his faults," said Jack. "We must put those on one side."

"I don't know at present. We've got twelve hours to do it in. Only twelve hours. Just one day. It doesn't seem long, though it's time enough to save a man's life in."

Still Harvey was irresolute.

"Would it look well to go home and see Mr. Crawcour, and Collinson, and Mr. Stonor, and all our own friends, and tell them that we left Hunston to be hanged before our eyes, when we might have raised a hand to save him? Dick, old boy, you're not showing your proper form, you're not, indeed."

"You've licked, Jack," cried Harvey, jumping up. "I didn't think anyone could have persuaded me to go across the street for Hunston, but you've done it."

"You'll come?"

"Rather. I'm with you, Jack, sink or swim. They shan't say we left an old schoolfellow in the lurch."

"He had me beaten with the bamboos," remarked Harvey, "till I thought my back was being skinned."

"And he tried to hang me twice over. Never mind," replied Jack, "we'll show them all that we've got some British pluck left, and we'll save him, or——"

He paused.

"Or what, my very impulsive young friend?" asked Mr. Mole, with a cynical smile.

"Turn up our toes, sir," replied Jack.

"What may that mean?"

"Croak, sir. Get ready for your six feet of polished elm or oak, if your family can afford the luxury."

"You should not joke about such subjects, Harkaway. It is wrong. I trust neither you nor Harvey will want a coffin; but, if you should, depend upon it, I will do the best I can, taking into consideration the slender resources of the country."

"Well," said Jack; "that's cool."

"I trust I am always cool in the hour of danger, Harkaway," replied Mr. Mole.

"Well, sir, laughing's better than crying, and I daresay we shall hit upon a dodge of rescuing Hunston without losing our lives."

"Let us hope so."

Jack was rather annoyed with Mr. Mole for the selfish way in which he spoke, and, rising, beckoned to Harvey.

"Come on deck, Dick," he said.

"Are you going?" asked Mr. Mole.

"Yes, we are going."

"You leave me with my friend," said Mr. Mole, playfully tapping the wine bottle.

"Take care of it, sir. It's the only friend you've got, and he won't turn out a real one," replied Jack.

Directly he had said this, he was sorry for it.

Mr. Mole got up, and running after Jack, caught him close to the entrance to the cabin.

He looked hurt, and really felt hurt, for it was the first time either of the boys had said anything unkind to him, or noticed his growing weakness for the bottle.

"Harkaway," he exclaimed, touching his shoulder.

"Well, sir," replied Jack.

"You said something, which I thought very unkind, a moment ago. Did you mean it?"

Jack's heart was in his mouth in a moment.

"No, sir, I didn't," he replied; "and I'm very sorry I said it. Will you forgive me?"

"Our lot," said Mr. Mole, "is cast in a foreign land, and we are in the midst of danger. I may have drunk too much, Harkaway; perhaps I have——"

"No, sir——"

"I'm not blind to my own faults, but it cuts me to the quick to be ridiculed by my own pupils, my dear friends, for I love you both as my own children."

"I believe you do, sir," replied Jack.

"You must not think I am a silly old man," continued Mr. Mole. "Out here I may indulge too much occasionally, but why shouldn't I? Look at the surrounding circumstances. What are they?"

"Niggers and sea, sir," replied Harvey.

"With occasional snakes and mutineers," said Mr. Mole. "But seriously, my dear boys, do not say anything rude to me again. I cannot bear it. Believe me, that however foolish I may seem to you occasionally, I do value your good opinion, most highly. I do, indeed."

"I beg your pardon, sir, I didn't mean anything. I didn't want to be cheeky," said Jack.

"And I'll say more, Harkaway, now I'm on the supject," Mr. Mole went on. "I admire the courage you have displayed under the most trying circumstances. It's been a source of pride and wonder to me."

"Don't butter me too much, sir; I can't lend you half-a-crown if you want it," replied Jack, smiling.

"No, no; you must not make fun of what I say. I do my best, but I cannot equal you. However, we are not of an age, and youth is always ardent."

"That's it, sir," exclaimed Jack. "Please accept my apology for hurting your feelings. I wouldn't have done it for a fiver. Will you forgive me?"

"Forgive you, Harkaway? There's my hand."

Jack took it, and grasped it heartily.

"Now we're friends, sir," he said.

"Yes, Harkaway."

"And you're perfectly satisfied."

"Perfectly. God bless you! No one shall say that Isaac Mole ever bore malice, but I wouldn't lose the esteem of you two boys for anything. Remember that, and if I do say anything foolish, try and think well of me."

"I assure you, Mr. Mole," said Jack, "that we have a strong regard for you, and if we leave you now it is because we have business to attend to."

With this assurance Mr. Mole rested satisfied, and the boys went on deck.

"Well, Jack," exclaimed Harvey "what's the little game now?"

"I don't know. I'm cornered," replied Jack.

"About Hunston, I mean."

"I know what you mean, well enough," Jack exclaimed. "But how to get him out of the hands of those blessed mutineers is more than your humble servant, Jack Harkaway, can tell."

Harvey looked puzzled, and they were both silent for some little time.

———◆———

CHAPTER LXXVI.

JACK DOES HIS BEST FOR HIS OLD ENEMY.

It was some time before Jack could hit upon a plan for being of service to Hunston.

That he should not die if he could help it, he determined.

At the same time he was equally firmly resolved that he would not give up the ship to the mutineers.

As the vessel was so short-handed, he could not take any one but Harvey with him.

We have already spoken of the two small cannon they had on board.

Looking at one of these, Jack said—

"I think I know how to do it, Dick."

"How?" asked Harvey, "I've had my thinking cap on for a long while, and can't hit upon any dodge which comes within a mile of the proper thing."

"Suppose we put one of these cannon on board the boat, load it up to the muzzle, take a slow match with us, sail in to the shore and when we get within range of the mutineers, let them have it, hot and strong."

"That will do, if they let us get near enough," said Harvey.

"The cannon," replied Jack, "will carry farther than their rifles, so that we shall not be in danger."

"What if Hunston is in the line of fire?"

"He isn't at present. I have been looking through the glass, and he is tied to a tree on the left. The tree, perhaps to which they mean to hang him."

What are the mutineers doing?"

"Just what might have been expected, drinking and gambling. They have one or two packs of cards and seem greatly excited. Shall we try the plan?"

"If you like. It's better than nothing," answered Harvey.

"At once, or wait for night?"

"Oh, at once. I hate waiting," said Harvey.

"All right. Send Bouncer aft, with Monday. We will sling the gun into the boat, and get ready," exclaimed Jack.

It did not take long to put the little gun in the bows.

They loaded it nearly up to the muzzle with bullets, slugs, and pieces of old iron.

With them they took a bag of similar ammunition, so as to be ready for a second discharge.

Over the gun they threw a bit of old bunting, to prevent the mutineers seeing it and having their suspisions aroused.

"Is it all ready?"

"Aye, aye, sir," replied Bouncer.

"Jump in, Dick."

Harvey took his place in the stern and Jack followed him.

"Going to give them pepper, sir?" said Bouncer, smiling grimly as he regarded these warlike preparations, which were intended for his old comrades.

"I think I'm justified in doing so," replied Jack. "They are murderers, for they killed the officers of their ship, and are consequently out of the pale of the law."

"That's right enough, sir."

"Therefore," continued Jack, "in dealing with them I need not follow the rules of civilized warfare. If I can shoot them like dogs, they deserve it, for they'd cut our throats without the least compunction, if they got the chance."

"So they would. I can't say much for them," replied Bouncer; "and I did all I could to stop the mutiny, though what is one against a dozen or more?"

"Shove her off, Dick," said Jack, who had not much faith in Bouncer's hypocritical assertions of innocence.

The boat by dint of successive tacks, made for the shore.

As they got nearer they clearly distinguished Hunston bound to a large palm tree on the left of the cave.

He looked very miserable.

The mutineers were gambling and quarrelling, but they desisted when they saw the boat.

They thought that Jack was coming to make terms with them, and did not apprehend an attack.

"Lie down in the bows, Dick, and get the match ready," whispered Jack.

Harvey did so, and Jack lowered the sail when they were within what he judged to be a proper distance.

Holding the tiller, he kept the nose of the boat well in front, so that Harvey might point the gun without any difficulty and in such a manner that it might do good execution.

"Ahoy, there! Ahoy," exclaimed Jimmy Clark, who was in the centre of his componions.

"What cheer?" replied Jack, putting his hand to his mouth to make a speaking trumpet.

"Are you come to give up the ship?"

"Speak louder; I can't hear," said Jack, pretending he could not distinguish what was said.

"Do you agree to our terms?" continued Jimmy.

Jack bent down.

"Are you ready, Dick?" he asked.

"Half a minute," replied Harvey.

"They're all in a heap. Cover them well, and fire as soon as you can. Remember, all depends upon the first fire. They will scatter and shelter if we don't chaw them up."

"I've got a message for you," said Jack, aloud.

"What is it? Let's have it," replied the mutineer.

"Look out then, it's coming. Now, Dick," he added, "aim low, and shoot straight."

The mutineers, numbering a dozen or fourteen, were grouped together.

They were not at all prepared for the sort of message Jack was going to send them.

Only a few of them thought it advisable to stand to their arms.

Suddenly a little tongue of flame shot up in the air, as Harvey applied the lighted match.

Then there was a puff of smoke and a sullen roar.

The next moment terrible shrieks rent the air, and more than half the number of the mutineers fell to the ground mortally wounded.

The others were so panic-stricken that they took to their heels, and ran for their lives.

Jack hoisted the sail, and saying, "Stand in," grasped the tiller again, and sent the boat rolling towards the land.

Harvey held a loaded rifle in his hand, and was prepared to pick off any of the survivors who showed themselves.

"Mind the boat as well as you can, Dick, and cover me while I go ashore," exclaimed Jack.

"Aye, aye!" replied Harvey.

Setting his teeth firmly together, Jack dashed into the sea as soon as the boat grounded.

In one hand he held a pistol, in the other a knife.

His intention was to cut Hunston loose.

Running across the sand, he soon gained the tree, and with a few vigorous cuts severed the cords which bound him.

Hunston was scarcely able to believe the evidence of his senses.

"How can I thank you?" he said, with tears in his eyes.

"Say nothing about it," replied Jack.

"I'd rather have owed my life to anybody else, but life is sweet, and if I can ever do you a good turn, Harkaway——"

"Never mind that. Take this pistol, and cut it to your friends the Pisangs as quick as you can."

"Won't you take me on board with you?"

"No; that's asking too much. Goodbye," said Jack.

He gave Hunston a friendly nod, and ran back to the boat.

At that moment Harvey's rifle was fired off with a sharp crack.

His quick eye had seen one of the escaped mutineers emerge from the cave where he had taken refuge.

He had levelled his rifle at Jack, but a leaden messenger of death cut short his career before he could pull the trigger.

Hunston was off like a shot.

He disappeared in the jungle, and the boys knew he was safe.

Jack put the boat about, and trembling with excitement, waited for the wind to catch her and send her out to sea.

Again Harvey's rifle was discharged, and again a mutineer fell to the ground.

"They shan't show a head," he exclaimed; "if they do I'm down on them like a beaver."

"Well done, Dick," replied Jack. "I think we deserve the Victoria Cross. Do you know, I am as pleased at saving Hunston as if I had escaped myself from a great danger."

"So am I," said Harvey, adding—

"Look at those fellows. What are they up to?"

Jack looked towards the shore, and saw five of the mutineers, who had emerged into the open from their temporary place of concealment.

They held their arms over their heads, as if to indicate that they surrendered and were defenceless.

"Ahoy!" cried one, who appeared to be the spokesman.

"What do you want?" inquired Jack.

"Take us to the ship, sir," answered the man. "We are the only ones left alive, and we must starve on this island."

"Serve you right; you should have thought of that before," replied Jack.

"Have mercy upon us, sir," continued the mutineer. "We surrender."

"But you have been guilty of mutiny on the high seas, and are murderers."

"We're very sorry. Take us prisoners, and convey us to Singapore in irons, if you like, sir, to take our trial," the man went on.

Jack hesitated.

"The fellows seem sorry enough, Dick," he remarked. "They're regularly licked. Shall we take them on board?"

"We're very short of men, and if we pardoned them they might turn out good men and true," answered Harvey.

"All our leaders are dead, sir. We had no hand in the mutiny. It was Sam Parsons and Jimmy Clark," said the mutineer.

"Come down to the beach, then," replied Jack, "and stand there unarmed. If you try any games on, I'll pistol the lot of you."

The mutineers did as they were directed.

Jack stood in shore and allowed them to come on board, making them sit down on the thwarts.

He held pistols in his hands in case of any treachery.

But the poor fellows were so cowed that there did not seem to be the smallest mutinous spirit left in them.

"If you'll try and look over it, sir, we'll work the ship like slaves for you," said the leader; "we will indeed."

"I can't promise you a pardon," answered Jack. "It depends in a great measure on your own conduct. If you behave yourselves I may be inclined to say nothing about the share you took in the mutiny, though you know well enough what the British consul would do to you."

"We were misled, sir, and acted on bad advice. All we want is to return to our duty, and get back to England. We're all—every one of us—married men, sir, and have wives and children, think of that!"

"I can't say any more than I have said," Jack exclaimed. "My conduct in the matter will depend upon your behaviour, though I've a good mind to have you lashed to a grating and give you a couple of dozen lashes apiece."

"Do that, and welcome, sir. We deserve it," replied the mutineers, in a body.

They spoke humbly enough, and in the end proved themselves very good men, and were of great use to Jack in the navigation of the ship.

He did ultimately pardon them, and did not have them flogged as he threatened.

They were grateful for his kindness, and it was clear that after the death of their leader they were pleased enough to return to their duty.

With this accession of strength, he hove up the anchor that afternoon and stood for Limbi to get a few natives to help make up the complement of his crew.

Mr. Mole was loud in his praises when he heard the successful result of Jack's expedition.

"A good action, Harkaway, is never thrown away," he said. "You will sleep all the better for it, and I'm sorry now that I tried to dissuade you from the enterprise. What did Hunston say?"

"We hadn't much time to talk, sir?" answered Jack; "the mutineers were popping away at me."

"Did he appear thankful?"

"Very much so. He was quite doubled up by his feelings. But that wouldn't last long. He wanted to join us, and be taken on board."

"Which you, of course refused?" replied Mr. Mole.

"I didn't see it, sir. A black sheep in the flock is not desirable."

"You put coals of fire on his head. Ah, well, it was a gallant action, and one you will never regret. And, now, whither away, may I ask?"

"Limbi is our destination, sir," answered Jack.

Mr. Mole trembled.

"My phrophetic soul," he exclaimed, "warns me that my wives will seek to annoy me. What am I to do?"

"Do the best you can, sir."

"Bad will be the best, I am afraid. However," replied Mr. Mole, with a groan, "I will hide myself, and trust to fortune."

Early next morning the "Sea-horse" was standing off Limbi.

They fired a gun to give notice of their arrival to the inhabitants of Tompano.

An hour afterwards several boats put off from the shore.

In one was the new king, Selim, who reigned in the stead of Monday's father, Lanindyer, and with him were several of the most prominent chiefs.

"Where's Mole?" asked Jack of Harvey.

"I don't know; he wasn't at breakfast. He's vanished into the coal bunk or somewhere," replied Harvey.

"Ain't there some women in that last boat?"

"Yes, I can see two."

"Mole's wives, for money!" said Jack. "I'll bet a pound to a pinch of snuff they are Mole's wives."

"Shouldn't wonder," replied Harvey.

In the meantime the little fleet of boats drew nearer.

CHAPTER LXXVII.

MR. MOLE BECOMES A BASE DECEIVER.

JUST as Harkaway was speaking he saw Monday with a sheet on his arm.

"Hi, you Monday! come here," he said.

"Can't stop, sare. Monday very busy," replied the black.

"What are you doing with that sheet?"

"That one secret, sare. Mist' Mole and me do business."

"Oh, Mole's in it, is he? What's the business you've got on?" asked Harvey.

"You not tell, Mast' Harvey?"

"Not I. Out with it."

"Mist' Mole, him sham dead."

"Do what?" cried Jack and Harvey in a breath.

"Sham dead, sare," replied Monday. "Him much 'fraid him wives come on board, so he sham dead. Monday go to lay him out and put the sheet on him. You not say a word."

"Where is he?"

"In the cabin, sare. Him lie stretched out on a table, and if Ambonia and Alfura come, I got to say he fight like a warrior and get kill."

"Oh, that's it. He's getting dodgy in his old age," remarked Jack. "Well, cut along, Monday. I shan't split."

Monday disappeared down the companion, and, turning to Harvey, Jack said—

"We must spoil old Mole somehow."

"I should like to," replied Harvey. "Fancy the beggar going to sham being dead!"

"How can we do it?"

"His sorrowing wives will weep over him," said Harvey. "Can't we stick a pin in his leg and wake him up?"

"He's a base deceiver. A pin might galvanise him, only, unfortunately, we haven't got one. There isn't such a thing to be had."

"I'll tell you what we can do," said Harvey.

"What?"

"Tell Ambonia it's the custom in our country, when a man dies, to pull out twelve hairs from each whisker and and twenty-four hairs from the head."

Jack laughed.

"You'll be the death of me, Dick," he said.

"And tell her," continued Harvey, "that to save trouble she can pull the hairs out in bunches, and count them afterwards."

"What is she to do with them?"

"Oh, wrap them up in a palm leaf and keep them as relics," said Harvey.

"That will do."

"We might add that the hairs from the head are to be pulled out behind, where it is most tender; and if Mole don't holloa out ten thousand murders, I'm a donkey."

"All right," said Jack; "I'll speak to her when she comes."

The boats approached nearer and nearer.

At last they came near enough for those in them to speak to those on board the vessel.

They were invited on board, and a grand banquet got ready for them.

Ambonia and Alfura were in the last boat, which was filled with fruit, with which they had intended to do a trade with the strangers.

When they heard that Jack and Harvey were the commanders, they freely made them a present of their cargo.

Their first inquiry, however, was after their husband.

"I'm afraid he is very ill, if not dead," replied Jack.

"Dead!" echoed Alfura and Ambonia.

"Yes, Monday is attending upon him, and he will tell you more about it; but will you come into the cabin and see?" replied Jack.

Both the ladies set up a most cruel yelling, and Jack put his fingers in his ears.

"Don't cry like that," he replied. "He may be all right, though I fear the worst. If he is dead, he fell fighting bravely."

"Let me see him," said Ambonia."

Alfura wept silently.

"It is our custom," continued Jack, "for the widow of a chief to pull out twelve hairs from each of the deceased's whiskers, and twenty-four hairs from the back of his head; you may pull them out in a bunch, if you like, and afterwards they are to be kept in your house to remind you of your husband. Mind you do this if he is dead."

"Call Matabella," said Ambonia."

Jack went to the companion, and called Monday.

He came up, and when he saw Mr. Mole's wives, told them, with a sorrowful face, that he was no more.

"He fell fighting, and has since died of his wounds," he exclaimed.

"When did he die?" asked Ambonia.

"This morning. He is scarcely cold."

"Oh, my poor husband! He was a great chief, and his child will be fatherless," said Ambonia.

Monday did what he could to prevent them going below, but the wives could not be persuaded to stop on deck.

So Monday led the way to the cabin, followed by Jack and Harvey.

When they entered the cabin, they found Mr. Mole stretched out on a table covered with a white sheet.

Their grief was about to burst forth again, when Jack whispered—

"Remember what I told you about our customs."

"Oh, yes! We will do that," replied Ambonia.

Removing the sheet from Mr. Mole's face, she took hold of a bunch of whiskers and gave it a sharp pull.

It did not come out.

Then she tugged again, and it yielded.

Mr. Mole gave the corner of his mouth a short comical twinge.

But he did not cry out.

"Take those hairs, and count them, Alfura," said Ambonia. "I will now try the other side of our dear husband's face."

Mr. Mole's whiskers were scanty, and there was not much hair left on the right side.

He suffered the most acute pain, but bore it like a stoic.

Setting her feet firmly on the floor of the cabin, Ambonia took another handful and pulled it vigorously.

The hair came out in a bunch like the other.

Something like a stifled curse escaped from the unhappy sufferer.

"Count them, Alfura," said Ambonia, handing her the second tuft.

Alfura proceeded to do so in dolorous silence, and she bathed the grizzly hairs with her tears.

Jack approached and whispered—

"Shall I hold up his head for you?"

Ambonia nodded, and went on with her duty of affection.

She twisted her knuckles firmly in the back hair of the supposed dead man, which was long and tangled.

There was a wrench.

Mr. Mole could bear no more—the pain was too great.

He sprang up and threw the sheet from him.

The resurrection of Lazarus could not have more surprised the beholders than this sudden coming to life.

Ambonia and Alfura darted back, and looked at the late corpse with undisguised terror.

"What the deuce do you mean?" cried Mr. Mole, rubbing the injured part savagely.

"Aren't you dead, sir?" asked Harvey stifled with laughter.

"This is your doing, Master Harvey," replied Mole. "I'll be one with you; and as for those furies, I'll be the death of one or both of them."

Jack and Harvey laughed immoderately.

The wives began to regain their courage, and advanced to their husband with a boldness which they had not shown at first.

He certainly was not dead.

If so, he had been playing them some trick.

Ambonia grew angry, and her yellow face glowed with passion.

CHAPTER LXXVIII

RUNNING A MUCK.

In his anger, Mr. Mole caught hold of Monday by the ear and shook him.

"You've betrayed me," he cried, "and I'll have it out of you."

"No, sare; not me, sare," replied Monday. "You let go um ear, sare."

"I'll give it you, you black swab," continued Mr. Mole.

Fortunately for Monday, Ambonia rushed up and pushed her husband away.

"Him dead man just now," remarked Monday, grinning with pain; adding, "Oh, golly how um pull um ear."

Mr. Mole grasped a chair, and brandishing it in the air, threatened to strike any one who came near him.

The women shrank back crying—

"Amok, amok."

This is a word of peculiar significance among all the Malay tribe.

If a man is unhappy with his wife, unsuccessful in business, and miserable in any manner, he does "amok."

That is to say, he runs into the street with a knife and stabs every one he can meet.

In return for this, the inhabitants raise the cry of "Amok!" and run after him with what ever weapon they can obtain.

Eventually he is killed like a mad dog.

It is the Malay mode of committing suicide.

The custom has become proverbial among Englishmen abroad, under the term of running a muck.

Even Monday got out of the way, thinking Mr. Mole was going to "amok."

Jack advanced to Mr. Mole, fearing from his wild appearance that he would do somebody some harm.

"I say, sir!" he said.

"Well, Harkaway, what is it? Keep off, I'm desperate," replied Mole.

"Turn it up, sir."

"I tell you I'm desperate. I tried a little plan of my own, and that black thief betrayed me; may his father, the devil, seize him."

"Are you going off your nut, sir?" asked Jack.

"Let me get at him! I'll pound him," cried Mr. Mole, making a dash at Monday.

"Amok! amok!" exclaimed the terrified women, fully believing that their liege lord and master had gone mad, and was about to run a muck; and, "Amok! amok!" cried Monday, who also thought the same thing.

The wives rushed up on deck, followed by Monday.

"Amok! amok!" rang through the ship.

The native chiefs heard the cry, and they, too, grew alarmed and sought the deck.

"Amok! amok!" cried everybody, with as much terror as we in England say "Mad dog! mad dog!"

The chiefs drew the dreaded creese, or curved knife, so common among the Malay tribes.

Every one stood on the defensive.

When they saw it was a white man who was "amoking," and that white man was Mr. Mole, the great Tuan Biza of the whites, they forbore to strike.

Jack ran on deck after him, and exclaimed in the native language—

"Don't touch him! He's all right."

"Am I all right?" replied Mr. Mole. hitting King Selim on the head with his chair.

Selim fell to the deck stunned.

"Dropped him like a bullock," continued Mr. Mole, with a ghastly grin. "Who is the next gentleman?"

Turning to Harvey, Jack said.

"Mole's cranky, and no humbug about it!"

Madura, the old chief, came up to remonstrate with the white man.

But Mr. Mole was ready for him.

"I'll floor you," he said, "if you come any nearer."

"Listen to the words of wisdom," replied Madura. "You have married our princesses, and you are dear to us as——"

"Bother the words of wisdom! Take that!" interrupted Mr. Mole.

"MONDAY JERKED HUNSTON'S ARM, SO THAT THE BALL WENT THROUGH THE ROOF."

Madura fell by the side of the king, and the Limbian chiefs began to get angry.

Knives flashed in the sun.

Again the ominous cry of "Amok! amok!" rose on the air.

Ambonia and Alfura now made their appearance on deck.

Alfura fell fainting into Monday's arms.

But Ambonia, being made of sterner stuff, ran to her husband.

"Put down that chair, and come home," she exclaimed.

"Never!" replied Mr. Mole; adding, "Mind your eye!"

He made a push at her with the chair, and struck her in the mouth with one of the wooden legs.

Ambonia began to cough and choke and fell on her back in strong convulsions.

"She's swallowed a tooth," said Jack.

"Ha, ha!" exclaimed Mr. Mole, with the light of insanity in his eye. "Who is the next? Will you kindly keep the ball rolling?"

Nobody seemed inclined to oblige him and the knives flashed more ominously than ever in the sunlight.

The Limbians were waiting for him to make a rush down the deck, where they were prepared to cut short his mortal career as quickly as possible.

But Ambonia was a woman of spirit.

She was one of those estimable women you don't knock down for nothing.

It is true she had swallowed a tooth, as Jack surmised.

But what then?

She was for the moment subdued, not conquered, and as soon as the tooth was properly down and she could breath again she was on her feet.

Advancing to Mr. Mole with the quickness of a canon-ball, she grasped the chair which he brandished on high, and a desperate struggle took place between them.

"Amok! amok!" cried the natives, advancing threateningly.

Wresting himself free from Ambonia's grasp, Mr. Mole sprang on the taffrail, and throwing up his arms exclaimed—

"Thus do I free myself from the strange women, and the house of bondage!"

With that he cast himself headlong into the sea and disappeared.

Jack was now fully assured that Mr. Mole had really gone out of his mind for a time.

"Man overboard!" cried Bouncer, who was standing near.

Jack had an idea that Mr. Mole could not swim, and was determined to save him at all hazards.

"Lower a boat and man her!" he exclaimed.

"Aye, aye, sir!" replied Bouncer. "We saved the lives of two hundred and fifty men off the coast of Africa, and——"

"Hang your yarns! Obey orders!" shouted Jack.

He caught sight of Harvey, who was taking off his jacket.

"Toss you who does it, Dick!" he exclaimed.

"All right," said Harvey; "I've got a coin in my pocket. First time. Man or woman?"

He put a small coin between his hands and Jack said—

"Man."

"Man it is; over you go," said Harvey.

The next moment Jack was diving like an otter after Mr. Mole.

He fortunately saw him as he rose to the surface, and grasping him by the arm held him up.

In a short time the boat which had been duly lowered under Harvey's superintendence came up.

It took them both on board.

Mr. Mole was insensible and raved incoherently, as if stricken with a fever.

They drew him on board, and put him to bed in what they call the sick bay or hospital.

Ben Blunt was still an inmate of this cabin, but he could get about a little, and readily undertook to nurse and look after Mr. Mole.

"I've seen many a fever, sir," he remarked, "and cured 'em too; they're common enough in these latitudes. The gentleman may be bad for a few weeks, but it'll do him good afterwards."

"He's very ill, Ben," replied Jack.

"Yes, sir; it's the mental excitement. He's been worked upon."

"So he has, Ben."

"And there's another thing, sir; he's had a good drop to drink lately, as I know of, and I shouldn't wonder if it wasn't no real fever after all."

Ben Blunt shook his head significantly as he spoke.

"No fever, Ben?" said Jack.

"No, sir. It's the delirium tremblings; that's what it is."

"Keep your eye on him, Ben, and say nothing to anybody. I must go on deck, and see to the women."

"Very well, sir," replied the boatswain.

"This affair has upset the banquet. We were going to put on a feed for the natives."

"Lor' love you, sir, they can allers eat," said Ben; "and they'll be none the worse for waiting. Though I may say as I did laugh that hearty as I was fit to bust, when I heard them a-crying 'amok, amok,' and saw the gentleman floor them beautiful."

Jack took leave of Ben, after exacting another assurance that he would look after his patient.

Then he went on deck.

Harvey had kept the women quiet, and was trying to explain matters to the chiefs.

The king and Madura were not much hurt, and under the soothing influence of a glass or two of good wine, which was handed round by Monday, speedily regained their good temper.

Ambonia begged to be taken to her husband.

Jack was obliged to refuse this request, though he told her she might see him later in the day.

It was soon understood that Tuan Biza Mole had been attacked by fever.

"He'll be all right in a short time," said Jack to the two wives; "and I know he really loves you both, though of the two I think he's rather more spooney on you, Ambonia."

The lady's eyes flashed at this announcement, which pleased her greatly.

"He's always talking about you," said Jack.

"Will he come on shore, and go to live with us at Tompano, when he gets better?" she asked.

"Of course he will; he's only too anxious."

"Bless him," said Ambonia, in her own language, "I could go and kiss every bit of him."

It was lucky Mr. Mole did not hear this expression of affection on the part of his biggest wife, or he might have died there and then.

Jack succeeded in assuring her that Mr. Mole had in the morning been attacked with a faintness, that Monday thought was death, and that no one had played any trick upon her.

After that, he gave her his arm, and led her into the chief cabin.

Harvey took Alfura in, and the chiefs followed in order of merit.

The banquet consisted of all the eatables and drinkables they could find in the ship.

Jack had arranged for the pardoned mutineers to wait at table, which they did with great steadiness.

The banquet passed off capitally. All the chiefs enjoyed themselves immensely, and some drank so much wine that they had to be carried out and put gently into their boats.

Alfura and Ambonia had a look at Mr. Mole before they went to shore.

This time they were satisfied that he was really ill, and said they would bring him some fruit in the morning.

Harvey gave Alfura a kiss on the sly, as he handed her over the ship's side, and she squeezed his hand in return.

Such are wives in Limbi.

King Selim readily lent Jack half a dozen of his subjects to help work the ship.

It was understood that they should be sent back again to their native land, and they were chosen by Monday from among his personal friends.

So popular were the white men, that they could have got a hundred men if they had wanted them.

Instead of the question being who should not go, there was a rush of men of all ages to get the chance.

When all was ready for sailing, Jack went ashore to return the complimentary visit of the Limbians.

He had also an object in going.

Madura was an old chief of great knowledge and experience.

He wished to ask him some questions about the City of the Golden Towers.

Who more likely than the venerable Madura to give him the information he sought?"

CHAPTER LXXIX.

AYOUB.

On arriving at Tompano, Jack sought Madura and explained, as briefly as he could, the object he had in view.

"I want," he said, "to recover this English girl, Emily, before I return to England."

"You say," said Madura, "that she has gone with the fugitive Pisangs to the City of the Golden Towers?"

"Yes. Do you know where it is?"

"I do. I have been there," replied Madura.

"Have you?" cried Jack, joyfully. "That's your sort, old man. That will do; tell us all about it."

"I cannot give you much information," replied Madura; "and for this reason——"

Jack's countenance fell again.

"I was very young when my father and I were out fishing, and the pirates captured us. My father died in the City of the Golden Towers, and I lived there some years."

"How did you get back here?"

"I escaped with some others in a boat, and can only dimly remember a great city, very rich, with many ships; and all the people pirates."

"That is a nice place indeed for my poor little Emily to be sent to," said Jack.

"Your Emily is young and beautiful," said Madura, "and they will guard her as carefully as they would a pearl of Sirendib."

"I hope so, I'm sure. But can't you tell us how to steer to get to this wonderful city of pirates?"

Madura shook his head.

"There is one amongst us who can if he will," he said, after a thoughtful pause; "and that is old Ayoub, the Arab. He is a great sailor, and was a pirate himself once, some say."

"Where is he to be found?" asked Jack.

"He has a house here in Tompano. You must have seen him, for he attends the council. It is now ten years since he came ashore in a boat and became friends with us, settling down and taking a Limbian woman to wife."

"Let us go to him. Is he very old?"

"No. Though his hair is tinged with grey, he is younger than he looks," replied Madura.

"Will he pilot us to this city?"

"Ask him. I dare say he will."

They walked to the house occupied by Ayoub, the Arab, who was sitting outside, with a little curly-haired child on his knee, that was just learning to call him father.

Madura, in a few words, explained to the venerable-looking man the object which Jack had in view.

"He has got a good ship, plenty of men, arms, ammunition, and provisions. All he now wants is to discover the City of the Golden Towers, rescue his beloved Emily, and return to his own land," concluded Madura.

Ayoub's eyes flashed with a keenness that showed he could remember the scene of his early days.

"Is it not written," he said, "that the bold man may be overthrown, and the wise man be confounded, but the patient man overcometh?"

"I'm not in a hurry, governor," replied Jack; "and am rather in favour of taking things easy."

"There are few nations and countries, my son, that I have not seen," continued Ayoub. "Most of my countrymen travel from the Bar-el-Sham to the Bar-el-Gemm" (really, Syria to Arabia Felix), "and say they have seen the world, but I ——"

"I'll tell you what I'll do," interrupted Jack, who saw that the Arab was a prosy old fellow, whatever else he might be.

"Speak. It is well to listen; so say all the men of understanding."

"I'll give you and your wife and kids a free passage to Arabia, if you will come on board and pilot us to this city of the pirates."

The old man's eyes sparkled.

"You have well said, O my son," he replied. "These old eyes yearn to behold my friends and relations once more. I would fain lay my bones with my fathers,"

"Do you accept my terms ?" said Jack.

"Yes, I will go with you," said Ayoub. "When I reached this land in a little boat, and all those who had sailed with me were dead and gone, I was received with kindness, which I have endeavoured to repay by lifting my voice in the council, but I thought to die here. You come to me, young man, like pleasant water to the traveller in the desert, and beheld, I find your speech good."

"Pack up your traps," exclaimed Jack. "as soon as you like. Say good-bye, and don't take more luggage than is absolutely necessary. By the way, is the missis agreeable ?"

"My wife obeyeth me in all things," replied the Arab. "For is it not written that 'a virtuous woman is a crown to her husband?'"

"You are sure that you can pilot us to the City of the Golden Towers," continued Jack.

An expression of lofty scorn sat on the old man's face.

"The dreams of the young," he said "are stronger than the realities of the old; but for many years I have steered the ships of the pirates in these China seas. So that they are become familiar to me as a well trodden path-way."

"How many days will it take us to get there !"

"When one moon shall have come and gone, then shall we behold the Towers of the Golden City," replied Ayoub.

"That means a month," replied Jack. "Time enough, too."

He returned to the ship, however, much pleased at having obtained a guide to the mysterious city.

The next day the ship sailed.

Ayoub took the post of pilot, and directed the vessel's course.

In a short time both Mr. Mole and Ben Blunt were well enough to get about again.

Mole's wives had been assured that their husband would return to them in a month or two.

They were desirous of accompanying him on the voyage, but this Jack could not permit.

Each hung a charm round his neck, to guard him from evil spirits.

Alfura's charm was a dried tree toad, and Ambonia's the tail of a snake also dried.

Whether they were efficacious or not, the fever left him in a few days, and he went about as usual.

As far as Jack could make out, Ayoub caused the ship to skirt the Malay peninsula, going towards Cape Pantani.

Everyone was well on board, and in high spirits.

Harvey did not like Ayoub.

He communicated his suspicions to Jack, who laughed at his fears.

"The old fellow talks to himself, and smiles when no one is looking, as he thinks, at him," said Harvey.

"He's all right enough," replied Jack, carelessly.

"I don't know so much about that," continued Harvey. "We are going amongst Malay pirates."

"Well ?"

"Well," said Harvey, "they are a daring and bloodthirsty race. This Ayoub has been amongst them."

"What then ?"

"He may intend to betray us. I don't say he will, still we should keep an eye on him," said Harvey.

This conversation produced a great impression on Jack.

He watched Ayoub narrowly, but did not for some time discover anything that would lend confirmation to the suspicions Harvey's remarks had excited in his mind.

CHAPTER LXXX.

H.M.S. " VICTOR."

AYOUB, the pilot, seemed a harmless, inoffensive man, and Jack could see no just ground for the suspicions in which Harvey indulged.

He had undertaken to guide him to the City of the Golden Towers, and he appeared to be keeping his word to the best of his ability.

How Jack longed to reach that mysterious nest of the Malay pirates, that hidden stronghold, where the defeated Pisangs had gone, and where Emily was a prisoner.

A slight incident occurred which tended to give some confirmation to Harvey's injurious remarks about Ayoub.

After they had been some days out, they sighted a large ship.

Ben Blunt was standing by Jack's side, and before a glass was brought to bear upon her, Ben said—

"I'm a Dutchman, sir, if that's not a man-of-war."

"Yankee?" asked Jack.

"No; she's not a Yankee either. That's one of Her Britannic Majesty's cruisers. I ought to know the shape of 'em if any one does, seeing I served aboard one for so many years."

"What's she doing out here, Ben?"

"After the pirates, maybe; or going from one station to another. Lor, sir, England's such a great power by land and sea that she's got ships and armies, leastways regiments, pretty nigh everywhere."

"Cut down below, Ben, and see that the cabin is all straight and shipshape," exclaimed Jack.

"Aye, aye, sir."

"If I've got to receive on board my ship one of the captains in the Royal Navy, I should not like him to go away with the impression that we are a set of lubbers. You know how to do it, and how things ought to be, Ben?"

"Do you think I'm a sucking porpoise, sir?" said Ben, in a tone of indignation.

He went below to execute his orders, and the two ships gradually neared each other.

It soon became clear enough that Ben's sharp eyes had not deceived him.

The approaching vessel was a man-of-war, and the mutineers whom Jack had taken on board getting wind of it, came aft.

"I ax your pardon, Captain Harkaway," said the foremost, "but here's one of the Queen's ships."

"What of that?" replied Jack.

"We've tried to do our duty, sir, and we're only poor fellows who were misled by others. You're not going to send us to Singapore, to be punished for the mutiny? Give us your word, sir, that's all, or we'd rather jump overboard."

"Go forward, and do your duty," answered Jack, "I shan't be hard on you."

"But, sir——"

"Do you hear when you are spoken to?" cried Jack, in a commanding tone he could assume when he liked. "Be off."

The men touched their hats and went forward, much comforted by the way in which Jack spoke to them, although they were not quite relieved from a fear of the consequences of their actions.

The man-of-war fired a gun as a signal that the "Sea-horse" was to lay to, which she did.

Then a boat was lowered and manned, pulling towards the merchantman.

Mr. Mole, who, like Ben Blunt, had recovered from his illness, heard the news and came on deck.

"Ah!" he exclaimed, "a ship, I perceive, Harkaway, a big ship. They tell me on H. M. S., which I presume you are aware is short for her majesty's service. They have lowered a boat. They propel it in man-of-war fashion through the waves and they near us perceptibly."

"They'll board us directly, sir," exclaimed Jack.

"And why so? Is not our ship private property, and why should they board us?"

"Nothing unfriendly about it, sir. There's opium smuggling going on, and pirates are about in these seas. They only want to see our papers, and know who we are."

"Ah, I apprehend I may be of service to you," said Mr. Mole. "My age, my manner, my position as a landowner in China, will give me weight with our visitors. They will treat me with more deference than they would bestow upon a mere boy."

"Mere boy as you call me," said Jack, biting his lips with annoyance, "I think I can manage my affairs better than any one can manage them for me."

"Listen to reason, Harkaway, I——"

"Mr. Mole," interrupted Jack, "without wishing to be in the least degree in the world discourteous to you, I must tell you, once for all, that you are only a passenger on board this ship and the sooner you recognise the fact the better it will be for all parties."

"Oh! as you please, as you please," replied Mr. Mole, shrugging his shoulders. "If you reject my well-meant offer of assistance, I can only regret your utter want of appreciation."

He walked away along the deck in high dudgeon.

In a short time the boat ran alongside, and an officer came on board.

He looked round him and stared, when Jack said—

"I am the captain of this ship, sir; anything you have to say I shall be happy to hear."

"You!" repeated the officer, who was a naval lieutenant about forty years of age, dressed in uniform, and who, from want of interest, had not been able to attain a higher rank.

"I have already had the honour to inform you that I am the captain of this vessel, and if you doubt my word I will give you satisfactory proof of the truth of what I say."

"I beg your pardon. You are so young that I trust you will forgive my momentary hesitation," said the officer.

"And who may I be talking to?" asked Jack.

"I am Lieutenant Skeffington, of H. M. S. 'Victor,' Commander Dacres, cruising in the China Sea in search of pirates, who have done a vast amount of mischief lately amongst the English and other merchantmen."

"Will you follow me into my cabin? We can talk more at our ease there," continued Jack.

The lieutenant bowed, and Jack, preceded by Ben Blunt, conducted his visitor into the cabin.

Directly Lieutenant Skeffington was seated and saw Ben, he said—

"I have seen you before, my man."

"Your honour's right," replied Ben. "I was bo'sun on board the 'Rattlesnake,' Captain Howard, nigh upon two years ago, and your honour was second luff."

"I remember you taking your discharge when we were paid off. I consider your presence on board this ship as a guarantee of the respectability of its captain," said Lieutenant Skeffington.

Ben bowed and scraped in true sailor fashion in recognition of the compliment, and retired outside the door, waiting within call.

Jack, in as few words as possible, explained to the lieutenant how he came to be in his present position, and why he was going to the pirates' stronghold.

"You have had some strange adventures, Mr. Harkaway," said the lieutenant. "Wrecked, cast on a desert island, nearly killed by savage head-hunters—you are quite a hero of romance, and will be the lion of the London drawing-rooms on your return to your own country."

"I have no wish to be a lion," replied Jack, laughing.

"Those who go down to the sea in ships, become acquainted with strange perils. However, I hope you will find, and rescue this young lady in whom you take such a laudable interest. We too are in search of this City of the Golden Towers."

"Do you know its position?"

"We do not, though we are told it is somewhere near here, on the coast of the Malay Peninsula. Has not the pilot, Ayoub of whom you speak, told you where it is situated?"

"No, he is very reserved. He says he will take me to the city, but he is not at all inclined to be communicative," said Dick.

"It is our intention to burn all the ships we can find, and then blow the town about the ears of the pirates. We might sail in consort."

"With pleasure. The 'Victor' would be an agreeable companion."

"Do you mind sending for this Ayoub? I will put some questions to him."

"Certainly."

Jack called Ben and despatched him for the pilot, with whom he presently returned.

The venerable Arab looked suspiciously at Lieutenant Skeffington, and asked what his pleasure was with him.

"What is the position of the pirates' stronghold, and how are we to steer to it?" said the lieutenant.

Ayoub's face assumed a sullen demeanour.

"I am not at liberty to make any disclosures," he answered.

"And why not?"

"Because you would go there in an unfriendly spirit. Those Malays, pirates though they be, were once my friends."

"That is as much as admitting that you were a pirate yourself."

Ayoub turned pale under his dusky skin.

"No," he said, "you do not speak the words of truth. I was not one of them, though they saved my life, and my lot was cast among them for many months."

"You have undertaken to conduct Captain Harkaway to the city?"

"I have, but he means no harm."

"What is to prevent us from following in your wake, and stringing you up to the yard-arm if you play us false," asked the lieutenant, fixing his clear grey eyes searchingly upon him.

"My poor life is of little value, and if an English officer thought fit to hang the poor Arab, he would be welcome to do so; yet would Ayoub, if he saw the British man-of-war following this merchantman, run her upon a rock, so that all should perish."

"The villanous old scoundrel!" muttered Skeffington, adding aloud, "you would destroy the ship and all on board of her."

"As surely as the water-logged and dismantled vessel, when caught by a swift current, rushes swiftly to her doom, so would Ayoub steer the 'Sea-horse,' to the waters of death."

"But reflect, Ayoub," said Jack; "those pirates are bloodthirsty villains; they murder people and sink ships; they are the robbers of the sea; do they not deserve death?"

"Ayoub has spoken."

"I am very much displeased with you. Return to your duty," exclaimed Jack, angrily.

The old man salaamed, and retired.

"He would be as good as his word, too," said the lieutenant. "Can you do without him?"

"Impossible. There is no one on board who knows where this mysterious city is but Ayoub, and I might wander up and down a dangerous coast, of which I have no chart, for months and never find it."

"I have heard that it is placed some miles up the mouth of a river. However, if you must have Ayoub's services, we cannot keep your company, that is evident."

"It is my loss."

"You are very good to say so," answered the lieutenant, politely. "I will make a favourable report of you to my captain, and I hope we shall not be long in finding out the town."

"I hope so, too."

"I have a word of advice to give you. Beware of that old man."

"Why? He is honest enough," said Jack.

"I don't think so," answered the lieutenant, shaking his head gravely. "He has a bad face. His eyes are full of deceit, and I fear he means to betray you."

"He will be clever if he does."

"His refusal to allow us to accompany you tells against him, but if you should be given up to the pirates——"

"By Ayoub?"

"Yes."

"We would fight to the last man, first," said Jack.

"Aye, aye, that is all very well, but you can't fight against treachery. Should you be a prisoner, will your friends, when we come to the city, and commence shelling it—for all things are possible—hoist a white flag over the house in which you are? and I will direct our gunners to spare that particular building."

Jack smiled incredulously.

"I hope, Lieutenant Skeffington," he replied, "that you are taking too gloomy a view of what may happen."

"I hope so, too. Promise me, nevertheless, that you will remember my undertaking."

"Certainly I will, and I thank you very much for the kindness you have shown in thinking so far ahead of the chances of war."

"And now farewell," said Skeffington.

"Can I offer you any refreshment?"

"Thanks, none at present. Is there anything we can send you? Medical stores, or things of that sort."

Jack declined the offer.

The lieutenant rose, and shook him heartily by the hand.

"I am very pleased to have made your acquaintance, Mr. Harkaway," he said; "you have displayed great tact and courage under very trying circumstances and you are an honour to the merchant service; I feel that the royal navy has suffered a heavy loss in not having you as one of its sons."

Jack uttered his thanks at this praise, and conducted the lieutenant to the side of the vessel.

As he was getting into his boat, he said—

"Once more, keep an eye on that villanous Arab."

"Never fear," replied Jack.

In less than a minute the oars fell into the water, and the measured sound of their rise and fall in the rowlocks fell upon the ear with that regularity which only a man-of-war's crew can produce.

"Now, my lads," said Jack, "give them a cheer. Don't be afraid of it. Three times three, and let it be a rouser."

Instantly the members of the crew, who had congregated on deck, gave a tremendous cheer in true British fashion.

The man-of-war's men acknowledged the compliment by raising their oars, and standing them upright in a row in the centre of the boat.

Then they fell with a splash, and the launch returned to H.M.S. "Victor," which looked the picture of beauty as she rode proudly on the rippling waves.

CHAPTER LXXXI.

THE CASTAWAY.

JACK was rather alarmed at the confirmation which Harvey's suspicions had received.

It was strange that Ayoub should show such a decided disinclination to have the "Victor" for a consort.

And yet, on consideration, Jack made excuses for his desire to save from fire and sword those amongst whom he had lived, and who had been kind to him.

However, he was sincere in his determination to find Emily, and nothing would have induced him to turn out of his course.

Harvey was anxious to know what had passed between him and the officer of the British vessel.

Jack repeated their conversation.

"What did I tell you?" said Harvey. "I knew that Arab was a bad lot."

"He won't do us any harm," replied Jack.

"I don't feel so sure about that. You are too easy going."

"My dear Dick, if one was always to fancy danger ahead, one would be worried into the grave. Time enough to face it when the peril comes," answered Jack.

"If I saw any indication of foul play I'd shoot him through the head, as a warning to others."

"So I will. He shall have a bullet through his head in double quick time," Jack said.

The man-of-war set her sails, and was soon lost to sight in the distance.

About midday the look-out reported an object in sight.

"Where away?" asked Jack.

"Abaft the beam," was the reply.

Jack gave orders to bear down upon it, and in about an hour, a small boat was clearly made out.

Whether there was anyone in it or not could not be distinguished.

But as the "Sea-horse" got nearer, the body of a human being was discovered lying down between the thwarts, apparently in the last stage of exhaustion.

Lowering a boat, Jack had the castaway brought on board.

He was laid on the deck, and seemed to be only just alive, if the spark of life wasn't already extinguished.

As Jack's eyes fell on his face, he uttered a cry of amazement.

"Dick," he exclaimed, "come here."

Harvey was by his side in a moment.

"What is it?" he asked.

"Don't you see?"

"See what?"

"The fellow's face. It is Hunston."

"Bless my soul! so it is; but how altered," replied Harvey. "He is pinched with hunger. Case of starvation. Poor beggar!"

"Poor beggar, indeed," said Jack, visibly annoyed. "I almost wish we hadn't seen him, and that the man-of-war had picked him up instead."

"You can't abandon him now."

"I don't mean to. But it looks as if he had done it on purpose."

Harvey could not help smiling at this view of the case.

"Have him put in a bunk," he said, "and attended to. Ben! Where's Ben Blunt?"

"Present, sir," replied Ben, coming up."

"Here is a man you have seen before. He was the friend and companion of your mutineers. Mr. Harkaway saved his life if you remember."

"They say a bad penny is sure to turn up, sir," remarked Ben.

"Have him taken below, please," returned Jack, "and pour some soup down his throat; he is in the last stage of exhaustion. Do what you can for him, Ben.

"Aye, aye, sir," answered the boatswain.

Hunston, pale, emaciated, scarcely breathing, was attended to with a care peculiar to sailors when cases of distress are brought before their notice.

"Monday brought a report a couple of hours later, that the sick man was progressing favourably.

"Him eat um soup, sare," he replied, "and him wink at it with um eyes."

"Is that a good sign, Monday?" asked Harvey.

"Always um good sign, sare, when um wink um eye," replied Monday.

"All right. Keep near him. He shan't say we are behind the age in civilization; we are not barbarians, and know how to behave ourselves even when an enemy comes amongst us."

"We've got two of them now, Dick," observed Jack.

"Two?"

"Yes; Hunston if he lives—and Ayoub, that is, if your suspicions are well founded."

Mr. Mole now came on deck with a book in his hand.

He had found a box of books in the captain's cabin, and he passed the principal part of his time lolling on a couch near an open port hole, smoking some good cigars, which he had also found and "requisitioned," and drinking brandy and water, which he called brandy pawnee.

"Fine thing, brandy pawnee," he said. "Stuff all Indian gentlemen drink; that is to say, all gentlemen—all English gentlemen—in India drink; for we can't call the native Mahomedans, Hindoos, and what not gentlemen."

"Well, sir, what's the time of day?" said Jack.

"You know very well, Harkaway," answered Mr. Mole, "that when I was in captivity among the Pisangs, the wretched Hunston stole my watch."

"Just like him, sir. He'd steal another if you'd got it."

"No, he wouldn't, my lad," replied Mr. Mole, with a knowing look; "Hunston is vegetating on his island."

"What will you bet about that, sir?" said Jack.

"Bet? I'd bet my—my tea-garden in China. It's a man-of-war to a fishing smack, or Homer to a boy's first Greek exercise."

"I'll take you, sir. If Hunston is now on board this ship, and I convince you of the fact, your tea-garden becomes mine?"

"Certainly," replied Mr. Mole, puzzled.

"Monday!" said Jack.

"Coming, sare," replied Monday, who was in the centre of a group of sailors, whom he was entertaining with an account of Hunston's villany.

"Isn't Hunston on board the 'Seahorse?'"

"For sartin, Mast' Jack; wuss luck, too. No good come to ship while villain Hunston on board of him," said Monday.

"Don't call names, Monday," replied Harvey.

"Is this a joke, Harkaway?" said Mr. Mole. "If so, it is a very bad one, and I will cudgel this black fellow for joining in it."

Monday grinned.

"Candidly, sir, it is no joke. We picked Hunston up this morning lying in an exhausted condition in a boat."

"All by himself?"

"Quite alone," replied Jack.

"Where is he now?"

"Monday will show you."

"Come, my coloured friend," said Mr. Mole, "I must behold him with my own eyes; seeing is believing. No offence to you, Harkaway. Lead on, Monday."

"Did you ever see a whale, Dick?" asked Jack.

Harvey put his tongue in his cheek, and Mr. Mole, turning sharply round, said—

"Harkaway, it is too bad of you to make fun of my poor attempt at a song. I will never oblige you again in a similar manner."

"Don't say that, sir," replied Jack, as he moved away. "Mole's awfully touchy about his song," he added to Harvey.

"Yes, he knows it's a bad one, and he would not have sung at all, if he had not been made, so he gets needled."

Presently Mr. Mole came back.

"Have you seen him, sir?" asked Jack.

"Yes, but what a wreck!"

"Are you satisfied?"

"I am not," replied Mr. Mole emphatically. "I look upon Hunston's presence in this ship as a fertile source of disaster. How do you suppose he came into that boat?"

"That's what the father asked about his son in Moliere's comedy—'How the deuce did he get into the boat?'" replied Jack.

"I think I can make a guess," cried Harvey. "He must have started with some Pisangs, for the City of the Golden Towers, a storm came on——"

"Or they had a free fight," put in Jack.

"That's probable at all events. The remainder of the crew were washed or thrown overboard, Hunston remained alone, and couldn't manage the boat by himself. Starvation ensued, as he lost his way in the pathless ocean."

"Don't become poetical, Dick," exclaimed Jack.

"Why shouldn't I, if I choose? You show me a road on the sea, and I'll never apply the epithet pathless to it again."

"Have a care, Harkaway, how you warm a viper in your bosom," said Mr. Mole.

"I am not in the habit, sir, of imparting artificial heat to vermin of that description," replied Jack.

"Nonsense! You know what I mean."

"I beg your pardon, sir, I do not."

"Then," said Mr Mole," you are more obtuse than I gave you the credit for being—I spoke figuratively. Mind that, if you are kind to Hunston, he does not, as he has done before, turn round upon you."

"I'll keep my weather eye open, sir. But you would not have had me turn the poor beast adrift in the state in which we found him," said Jack.

"Well, no; on consideration, decidedly no. There is something which beats under the fifth rib, Harkaway, which counsels a more humane course."

"The heart?" said Jack.

"Precisely; you have guessed rightly. We have hearts, we must be human. We are Christians, and must play the part of the good Samaritan. Will any of you boys come into the cabin and partake of pawnee?"

"Don't mind if I do so. Been reading?" said Jack.

"Yes, just a little go in at the higher mathematics, Harkaway. Having the advantage of books, one must keep one's hand in," replied Mr. Mole.

Harvey and Jack followed him into the cabin, to have some brandy pawnee, and Harvey whispered—

"The old humbug. Do you know what he has been reading? It's not mathematics at all. I looked at the book while he had it under his arm."

"What was it, then?"

"A French novel," answered Harvey laughing.

It must be confessed that Mr. Mole was a bit of a humbug,

"NO, I'M NOT WRECKED," REPLIED BEN BLUNT."

CHAPTER LXXXII.

THE STORM.

THE boys stayed in the cabin with Mr. Mole until that gentleman became very good tempered, and was more highly pleased than ever with his brandy pawnee.

Feeling an increased motion of the ship, Jack said the wind was rising.

"Let it rise," replied Mr. Mole grandly. "I trust we are superior to changes of the weather. In my young days, I knew the time when I was very glad to raise the wind."

"Uncle, sir?" said Harvey.

"Precisely so, but not for luxuries or superfluities. If I spent money, it was on my studies. Books, Harvey, were what I bought. I could live on a crust of bread and a draught of water for a week."

"You've changed a good bit since then, sir. Haven't you?" said Jack.

"Now, my dear boy, I am in the noon-tide of life, I have a tea-garden in China. Circumstances alter cases," replied Mr. Mole.

"If we get any rough weather I hope we shan't come to grief," Jack remarked.

"Ah," said Mr. Mole, "that's the worst of putting boys in men's places."

"What, sir?"

"It's the case of the square peg in the round hole, Harkaway."

"Am I a square peg?" asked Jack.

"Very square, and to use a vulgar expression, you may find yourself in a hole. You should have made good use of your time and have learnt navigation."

"I know a little enough for everyday use, sir," Jack said.

"It's my opinion there is only one man on board this ship who knows how to work it," Mr. Mole continued.

"Who's he?" said Harvey.

"Myself, Harvey. Isaac Mole, your humble servant."

Jack laughed.

"Do not laugh, my young, but still intelligent friend," Mr. Mole exclaimed; "it is not becoming to laugh at those older than yourself. I have an observant eye."

"Did you ever see a whale, sir?"

"That question shows a want of respect, and I shall devote my conversation to Harvey," answered Mr. Mole, in high dudgeon.

"Certainly, sir," Harvey said. "Curious creatures, whales, ain't they?"

"If you indulge also in the puerile amusement called chaff, I shall retire into myself, smoke the cigar of peace, and hold my peace," said Mr. Mole, mixing himself another pawnee.

Monday entered the cabin.

"Good morning, Monday," said Mr. Mole, forgetting that he had seen him before that day.

"It's not morning Monday, now, sir," remarked Jack.

"Eh?"

"It's Monday afternoon, sir," said Jack, perpetrating a joke, and adding— "What is it, Mon?"

"Um Ben Blunt want Mast' Jack. The weather, him getting very bad sare."

"Hang me if I didn't think so," replied Jack, rising with an uneasy expression of face.

"It all Mast' Hunston, sare; him like um Mother Carey's chicken. When him come on board, all go wrong," exclaimed Monday.

"I am not superstitious enough to believe that, though I don't like the look of things at all."

Suddenly the ship gave a lurch.

She was struck by a heavy squall, and had heeled a little on the left side.

The men were all at their stations, and touching his hat, Ben reported to Jack, as he hurried on deck, that the foresail was split.

"Bend another," replied Jack.

The crew set to work, unbent the split foresail and bent another.

For some hours the weather got worse.

They experienced a succession of heavy squalls, and shipped water.

At four o'clock a heavy sea burst into the main deck, sweeping water casks and loose gear overboard.

"Go forward, Dick, and ask Ben to

ascertain f the cargo has shifted," said Jack.

Harvey returned with Ben, who said he thought the first tier had shifted a little, but not to an extent of any consequence.

"What's the damage?" asked Jack.

"It's carried away the mainsheet," replied Ben, "and the peak halyards."

"Anything else?"

"Monday reports that the cabin windows are smashed in."

"Man the pumps," exclaimed Jack, "and at the same time secure cargo and repair damage."

"Aye, aye, sir," replied Ben, who liked to be commanded in this navy fashion.

If Jack had lost his head and said, "What are we to do?" perpaps the old boatswain would have lost his too, and the men would have followed suit.

Example is everything to men in a subordinate position.

The majority of men can obey, but they can't order.

Jack was as cool as a melon, and went about everywhere, encouraging the men with his presence.

At nine o'clock the pumps had hove out a quantity of water mixed with tea which had got loose in the hold.

There was a high cross sea.

Jack stowed foresail and jib, set close-reefed mainsail and hove the ship to, with her head north west.

The night passed without any change.

Mr. Mole was nowhere to be seen, though Monday hinted he was on his back, snoring loudly, under the mingled influence of fear and brandy pawnee.

In the morning the sea raged with dreadful fury.

Jack had not closed his eyes all night.

Ayoub still kept the helm, and stated that the coast was at times very stormy, and he knew they were not far from their destination.

"How many days' sail are we from the City of the Golden Towers?" asked Jack.

"Two, sahib," replied the Arab."

"Only two?"

"If we run before this wind, we shall make the land sooner, but we have to run some miles up a river," continued Ayoub.

"Then," thought Jack, "Lieutenant Skeffington was right in his suspicions.

This remarkable city does lie up a river, and there is more chance of H.M.S. "Victor" finding it out than I first thought there was."

While he was talking to Ayoub a sea swept the bowspit from the bollards and the foremast from the deck.

"Hullo! God help us," ejaculated Jack, who remembered his first wreck.

Another sea followed, and the mainmast snapped like a reed, three feet above the deck.

One man was hurt badly, and the cargo shifted.

The ship tossed, and swayed her spars with great violence.

Ben Blunt hastened to the helm.

He pushed Ayoub on one side saying—

"What's the blundering old ass about? He's no better than a woman at the wheel in a gale of wind."

"Wear her, Blunt, wear her;" cried Jack.

"Aye, aye, sir," replied the veteran.

Ayoub looked on with the passivity of an oriental.

"Steady, Blunt, for your life, steady," continued Jack. "She'll bilge and founder else."

"Aye, aye, sir," replied Ben, again, as the wheel flew round under his practised hands.

It was a great risk, but the ship answered to the helm, and she was brought to windward.

Jack now ordered the crew to cut away abaft, holding on forward.

In a short time she floated clear, but the once beautiful "Sea-horse" was a perfect wreck.

The storm was now at its height.

In a short time it began visibly to decline, and the immediate danger was over.

But Jack's heart grew sad when he thought of the irreparable damage that was done to the lovely ship he had hoped to reach England in, but which would now be useless.

Ben reported the rudder-head disabled and the wheel broken.

She was drifting at the mercy of the waves towards an unknown coast, the only inhabitants of which were a nest of pirates.

With difficulty the rudder was wedged, and damages again repaired in the best manner under the circumstances.

Finding the port anchor stock to be

the best elevation, Jack had a globular light placed upon it, during the night.

Then the wind went down and the gale abated, but not before it had swept away the storm drag, leaving the vessel a helpless wreck.

A small spar was stood by the stump of the mainmast, and secured as well as possible.

This formed a jury mast.

Two oars were clinched together for a yard and bent to a piece of canvas.

This set a sail, leg of mutton fashion.

With this curiously-rigged mast, and a signal of distress flying, the "Seahorse" drifted for two days.

Mr. Mole obstinately refused to move, and the boys took all the responsibility upon themselves.

Ben Blunt, who was an old sailor, gave Jack great credit for the way in which he had handled the ship.

"Under Providence, sir," he said, "you've saved this vessel, young as you are. I'm an old salt, and I know how things should be, though I couldn't have done as you did, and I doubt whether many a first luff in her majesty's service could have done better."

"I did my best, Ben," Jack answered.

"And a good 'best' it was, sir. We've saved our lives, and we may hope to make a port somewhere."

Jack and Ben Blunt were standing alone, Harvey was with Mr. Mole in the cabin, for Mr. Mole had not been at all well.

Either the brandy pawnee or the storm had not agreed with him.

In Jack's face could be discovered a trace of sadness and disappointment.

Jack had got to love the old ship.

She was to have borne him and Emily back to England, when he had rescued her from the pirates to whom the Pisangs had taken her.

How had his prospects altered in a few days!

The trimly-built "Sea-horse" was floating like a helpless log upon the water.

He did not think that his life or those of his companions were in danger.

There was a chance of making land, which Ayoub declared solemnly could not be far off.

All at once a pale, thin, skeleton figure crept up the main hatch.

It walked with difficulty, and, as it neared Jack, the latter exclaimed—

"Hunston!"

He had not gone near him or spoken to him while he was recovering from his privations, though he had caused every attention to be paid him, so that he wanted for nothing.

"Harkaway," Hunston said, in a hollow voice, "I am better now, and I have come to thank you for caring for me as you did."

"Don't say anything about that," exclaimed Jack.

"But I must. I have heard from Harvey how you picked me up and took me in."

"Glad of it," said Jack.

"No, you are not glad. I know you would much rather you had not met me, but you are a kind-hearted English fellow, and behaved as you thought you ought to."

"You might do as much for me some day," suggested Jack.

"Wrong again," replied Hunston. "If I had seen you adrift in a boat, I should not have stirred a finger to save you."

"You speak plainly, anyhow."

"I do, and I say what I mean. You have the advantage over me in generosity and good-nature, if that is any gratification to you."

"Yes; it is. I'd rather be thought a decent fellow than a brute," replied Jack.

"I don't care what people think of me. I've got over that weakness long ago."

"More's the pity."

"Perhaps; but if a man's hardened he can't be worried by scruples of conscience. I have just been snatched from the brink of the grave. I was at my last gasp."

"Yes."

"And I don't thank you for saving me," replied Hunston, whose malicious eyes twinkled with malignity as he spoke.

"I don't want you to," replied Jack.

"The fact is, Harkaway, I'm not a humbug, I never was. You can't accuse me of being a sham. I was always straightforward."

"I can't say that. You've done a lot of dirty things," answered Jack. "But you are ill and weak, and I would rather not argue with you while you are in that state."

"That be bothered. I should show the same spirit if I were dying," Hunston said. "Talk to me, or put me in my boat and cast me adrift once more."

Jack gazed at him with astonishment.

"Put me in the boat. I'm in your power," continued Hunston.

"No; I won't do that."

"Listen, then. I'm your enemy still, though I thank you for saving me. That's candid, isn't it?"

"Very much so," said Jack. "But look here, old fellow, if we can't be friends, the world is wide enough for both of us. I'll take care of you, and put you ashore wherever you like."

"You haven't much choice," said Hunston, with a sneer. "Your ship isn't the vessel it was when you stole it."

"Stole it," repeated Jack, indignantly.

"Yes."

"I only took it from the mutineers, and intend to return it to the owners."

"Oh, of course; your intentions are highly virtuous," said Hunston. "But while I am on board, am I to consider myself a prisoner?"

"No; you can do what you like."

"Then I shan't trouble you any more; and as soon as I can get away, I shall."

As he finished speaking, Hunston walked away and amused himself by talking to Ayoub, who was again at the wheel.

Something he said seemed to excite the Arab's attention, as they were soon engaged in earnest conversation.

"He's a beast," said Jack, half aloud.

"Who's a beast?" exclaimed a voice at his elbow.

CHAPTER LXXXIII.

JACK KEEPS HIS EYE ON AYOUB.

It was Harvey who spoke.

"Who's the beast?" repeated Jack. "Why, Hunston. He's not a bit thankful for being saved. I thought he would be. When I rescued him from the mutineers, he did say, 'thank you.'"

"Then," replied Harvey, "the fear of death was present to his mind. Now the case is different. He knows very well he's right, and can afford to be cheeky."

"What's he saying to Ayoub, I wonder?" asked Jack.

"There is some villany on, I'll bet."

"Lieutenant Skeffington warned me against Ayoub, and told me to keep my eye on him."

"Do it, then. It's my advice too," said Harvey.

"I wish I could hear what they are saying."

"So do I."

"Can't you fox them in some way?" said Jack.

"Not now," replied Harvey. "They would see me and stop talking. I'll tell you how to manage it, though."

"How?"

"I'll go up and stand close to Ayoub, ask him some questions and so on. Hunston will go away, and they'll meet again later, when we can watch."

"Good again, Dick; I always said you were a genius," said Jack.

Harvey went up the wheel, and, as he had expected, Hunston walked away, going down to his berth, from which he did not emerge till the evening.

It was with difficulty that Ayoub could, with the badly-broken rudder, keep the ship before the wind.

But he contrived to steer somehow, and ere nightfall land was discovered.

Great were the rejoicings of the crew, more especially when the mouth of the river was seen, and Ayoub declared that it was the very one they were in search of.

"In four-and-twenty hours, crippled as we are," said the pilot, "we shall be anchored near the City of the Golden Towers."

There was no further danger from the elements, for the storm had altogether subsided.

Harvey, who was worn out, went to his berth and slept soundly.

Jack, however, was watching Hunston.

Darkness had fallen and all was still, when he heard Hunston leave the cabin in which he was berthed, and go on deck.

He followed.

Ayoub was standing amidships, looking at the crescent moon, just rising in the heavens.

"Is it you, my son?" he exclaimed, as Hunston touched him on the shoulder.

"Did I not say I would meet you when the moon rose at this spot?" replied Hunston.

"You did."

"You hate these white men, and so do I; as far as that we agreed this morning. We were interrupted in our conversation."

"My son," replied the Arab, "I was formerly the most famous pirate in the City of the Golden Towers, but I was cast on the Island of Limbi, and seeing no means of getting back to my friends, unless I braved the perils of a voyage which was nearly fatal to you, I determined to wait."

"You settled on the island?"

"Yes; and when this boy, Harkaway, asked me to steer him to the Golden City, I was more than glad to do so. It was the wish of my heart. I have heard all about you, and I know that your friends, the Pisangs, have gone to the Malay pirates in large numbers."

"They have."

"With them they bore a lovely English maiden," continued Ayoub.

"You know that?" cried Hunston.

"And more than that, you love her. Harkaway loves her, and there is a hatred between you."

"You are right there," Hunston said, between his teeth. "The more he does for me, the more I seem to detest him. The reason I have come to speak to you is that I do not think you mean to keep faith with him."

"Can I trust you?" said Ayoub.

"I'll take any oath you like."

"What are oaths to men like you and I?" replied the Arab, contemptuously.

"You must have sense enough to know that you can trust me, and if I can give you a hand in any villany, I'm ready to do so."

"I don't know that you can do anything," replied Ayoub, "yet it is a relief to have some one to talk to, The ship is a wreck, and scarcely worthy of the pirates' attention."

"Are we near the pirates?" Hunston asked.

"Yes, they will be here soon. I shall hoist a red light at midnight, to show them there are friends on board."

"What then?"

"When they board the ship they will spare the lives of all who are near the red light, the rest they will slay."

"There will be an end of Harkaway then," said Hunston, with a savage smile.

"And all his friends," replied Ayoub.

Jack was listening intently to this conversation. "The fiends!" he muttered.

"You shall marry the white maiden, and be a great chief among the pirates," continued Ayoub.

"That will suit me exactly. I should like to be a pirate king.

"I held a high position among them," the Arab went on, "before I was wrecked off Limbi. Often have I longed to return to the scene of youth and manhood. But the voyage was too perilous to be undertaken alone."

"Are the pirates Malays?"

"Not all. They have men of all nations with them. French, English, Spanish and American. We are nearing the mouth of the river now. Cannot you see under the bluff headlands on the right some lights dancing like fireflies."

"Yes."

"Those are the lights of the pirates' praus riding at anchor. There is a safe anchorage there, and many ships remain there to guard the entrance to the river."

"There must be a lot of them from the number of lights," cried Hunston.

"Twice six, and full of armed men. What chance has this disabled ship of contending against the pirate fleet?"

"Have they seen us yet?"

"Not yet. We are hull down in the water," said Ayoub, who talked in the Limbian language, that being perfectly intelligible to Hunston.

"Have you got a red light ready?"

"I have."

"Will they recognise it?" continued Hunston.

"They will," replied Ayoub with a smile. "I used to go out in a boat on the look out for a passing ship, telling the captain I was a pilot, who would navigate his vessel through the dangerous channels with which the coast of the Malay peninsula abounds, and when I got them here, I showed the red light, which means blood.

Jack shuddered.

"They will say, 'Heaven is good to us,'" continued the Arab; "'our old friend Ayoub the mighty has come back again. Blood will run like water. Come, my brethren, let us go to Ayoub, and slay the disciples of the cross.'"

"You are sure they won't kill you and me by mistake," said Hunston.

"Our lives are safe in my hands; though, had you not spoken to me to-day, yours would have been sacrificed with the rest."

As he spoke, the infamous wretch who had been all along planning this massacre of the officers and crew of the "Sea-horse" took up a lamp he had concealed behind some spars.

He held it up in the air, saying, "Behold the signal."

The next moment Jack had levelled a pistol at his head, and crying—

"Rascally Arab, take that," he fired.

Ayoub, shot through the forehead, uttered the single word "Allah!" and fell forward at Hunston's feet.

There was another barrel in the pistol undischarged.

Jack played restlessly with the trigger.

"I'm a deuced good mind to give you the contents of number two, Mister Hunston," he said.

Hunston's eyes fell, and he trembled a little.

"Ha!" said Jack, noticing this. "Does the fear of death come upon you after all?"

"I am weak and ill. You forget what troubles I have gone through lately. It's the body that trembles, not the spirit," Hunston replied.

"Your companion revealed himself in his true colours at last, and he died the death of a traitor."

"Shoot away, if you are going to shoot," cried Hunston; "only don't stand jawing at me. You're as bad as the chaplain of a goal preaching a condemned sermon."

Jack's hand still held the pistol, and the least movement of his finger would have hurled Hunston into eternity.

He hesitated, however, to fire.

The recollections of the old days at school came over him.

CHAPTER LXXXIV.

ATTACKED BY PIRATES.

THE sudden death of Ayoub, and the consequent collapse of his treacherous plans, alarmed Hunston.

He saw that Harkaway was very angry, and he expected to be shot every moment.

"At least I will have a struggle for it," he muttered between his clenched teeth.

Rushing upon Jack, he endeavoured to wrench the pistol out of his hand.

Had he succeeded in doing so, he would undoubtedly have shot him.

But Jack would not release his hold.

They swayed backwards and forwards.

All at once the trigger of the pistol was accidentally pulled, and, as the muzzle happened to be presented against Hunston, he received the charge in his left arm.

The injured limb hung helplessly by his side.

He staggered against the bulwarks, pale as death, and cursing his ill luck.

"It was your own fault; you would have it," exclaimed Jack.

Ben Blunt, attracted by the firing, advanced, and examined the injured limb.

"It must come off," he said.

"What?" cried Hunston. "Lose my arm?"

"There is no help for it," replied Ben.

"Be a one-armed man all my life!"

The expression of Hunston's face, as he uttered these words, was fiendish in the extreme.

"You ought to think yourself lucky you have escaped with your life," remarked Harvey.

"I'll be revenged on you, Harkaway, for this," cried Hunston, writhing with pain.

Jack turned contemptuously from him.

"Wherever you are—in whatever quarter of the globe—I am more than ever your enemy, and I will find you out," continued Hunston.

He would have said more, but, faint from loss of blood and severe pain, he sank on the deck insensible.

"Take him below, Ben, and see to him," said Jack.

"Aye, aye, sir."

"And some of you fellows throw that carrion overboard," added Jack, pointing to the dead body of Ayoub.

His orders were obeyed, and Ben carried Hunston below.

Ben Blunt had a rough knowledge of surgery, having been in more than one action, and with Harvey's help, he amputated Hunston's arm just below the shoulder.

A sharp knife and a saw were all that was required, with a bit of silk for a tourniquet to take up the veins.

Bandaging it round afterwards, he left the wretched young man to go to sleep.

His thoughts were not pleasant.

For the remainder of his life Hunston would be a one-armed man.

His wickedness had been punished at last.

A good look-out was kept on board, and the best weapons that could be found were supplied to the crew.

Jack anticipated an attack from the pirates.

Nor was he mistaken.

About midnight they with difficulty made out half-a-dozen heavily manned boats rowing towards them.

"All hands forward to repel boarders," exclaimed Jack.

Directly he heard this order, Mr. Mole disappeared.

The remainder of those on board, however, evinced every inclination for the fight.

Steadily the pirates came on.

The movement of the oars in the rowlocks became more distinct.

Dividing into two parties, the pirates began the attack on each side simultaneously.

With their cruel sharp knives in their mouths they swarmed up the sides.

Volley after volley was fired at them.

Many fell back into the boats or the sea mortally wounded.

Others immediately took their places.

Jack fought valiantly.

A stalwart Malay singled him out, and after a few attempts succeeded in cutting him down.

Jack fell to the deck, badly wounded.

The fall of their leader damped the ardour of the English crew.

In vain Harvey strove to lead them forward.

They were overpowered by numbers, and surrendered at discretion.

Ben Blunt was stabbed to the heart, and his body stiffened in the moonlight.

Harvey had a flesh wound in the leg, and could only limp about.

When the fighting was over, the Malays ceased the work of slaughter.

It was the custom of the pirates to take as many prisoners as they could, in order to obtain ransom.

Monday had fought valiantly, and, strange to say, was unhurt.

Perhaps in the confusion the Malays, from his dark skin, mistook him for one of their own party.

The faithful fellow attended to his young masters and bound up their wounds.

He spoke to the pirates and told them they were great chiefs.

This made the Malays treat them with great consideration.

Mr. Mole was captured and fastened to Monday with a chain.

Jack and Harvey were conveyed below, and the latter did all that lay in his power for his old friend.

When the pirates had cleared the deck of the dead, they began to tow the ship to the mouth of the river.

All night long they continued to work and by morning the vessel was moored alongside a landing place, in the city of the Golden Towers.

Harvey was disappointed at the first view of the city.

It was like most oriental towns; an assemblage of narrow dirty streets.

In the centre rose a temple which had a dome, surrounded by twelve towers or minarets.

These were covered with gilding.

It was this temple that gave the pirates' stronghold the romantic and fascinating name of the City of the Golden Towers.

Ill as Hunston was, he contrived to speak to the pirate chiefs.

The result was that he was not classed with the other prisoners.

Probably he referred to the Pisang chiefs, who had left their own country and joined the pirates.

At all events he was treated with distinction, while Harkaway, Harvey, Monday and Mr. Mole were removed to a loathsome dungeon in the city.

Jack lay upon a heap of mouldy straw, Harvey by his side.

His wounds were very painful, and he was weak in the extreme.

"I shall never get home again, Dick!" he exclaimed, in a low voice.

"Yes, you will. Eat some of this rice, and drink some water," replied Harvey.

"I can't eat. Give me the water."

He drank copiously, for his blood was hot and feverish.

"They've done for me this time," he moaned.

"What's that you say, Harkaway?" exclaimed Mr. Mole. "Don't give way. Look at my position."

"You're not hurt, sir, as Harkaway is," rejoined Harvey.

"No; but I am suffering the intolerable indignity of being chained to a negro in this stifling vault."

Monday gave the chain a pull.

"Don't do that," cried Mr. Mole; "you'll wrench my leg off."

"Speak Monday civil," replied the black. "It's no good um grumble now. Monday pull um leg off if not quiet."

Mr. Mole groaned dismally.

"I wonder if they will spare our lives?" he said. "Perhaps owing to the way I fought, they will be extra savage against me."

No one took any notice of him, and he continued to grumble to himself.

The position of the little party was anything but agreeable.

Two of them were wounded, and they were confined in a hot, stifling vault; the only air and light they enjoyed penetrating through a little grated window high up in the wall.

Thus a week passed.

Food was brought them regularly every day, but they could glean no information from their gaoler, who refused to answer any questions.

Jack wanted quinine and fresh air to complete his cure, but there did not seem much hope of his obtaining them.

Their despair was at its height when they received a visit which put new life into them.

The gaoler one morning introduced a fairy-like vision, which Jack, from his straw bed, at once recognised.

He made an effort to rise, but was too weak to do so.

"Emily," he murmured, softly.

Her eyes, accustomed to the blinding sun, could not distinguish him in the semi-darkness.

Guided by his voice she ran to the side of the straw bed and sank on her knees.

Seizing his thin, transparent hand, she bedewed it with tears.

"Oh, Jack, dear!" she exclaimed. "It is so sad to see you like this; but I would rather meet you thus than not see you at all."

"Thank you, Emily," replied Jack. "I wanted to see you before I died. I can die happy now."

"Die! Are you hurt?"

"I was wounded with a creese when the pirates attacked us. How did you get in here?" he answered.

"I live in the palace of the pirate king, and he sent me to you to ask what ransom you could pay," replied Emily.

"Where is Hunston?"

"Very ill. He has had a bad attack of fever, and has been delirious for some days, which is lucky, as he might have done you some harm. All his Pisang friends are here, and he is being taken care of."

"Why have the pirates kept us here so long?" asked Jack.

"I cannot tell exactly, answered Emily. "But I have heard them say that one of Her Majesty's ships has been cruising about the mouth of the river."

"And that has occupied all their time?"

"Exactly."

A ray of hope lighted up Jack's face.

"Dick!" he exclaimed.

"Yes," replied Harvey.

"That ship they speak about must be the one we met, H. M. S. 'Victor,' Commander Dacres."

"I hope to goodness she is," replied Harvey.

"Well, Jack dear, what shall I say to the pirate king?"

"Tell him we've got lots of money at home, and we will ransom ourselves handsomely, as soon as we have means of communicating with our guardians," said Jack.

"Very well."

Suddenly a voice said—

"Young lady."

It was Mr. Mole who spoke.

"Who is that, Jack?" asked Emily.

"Only Mr. Mole."

"One of your friends?"

"The best, truest, and staunchest that Harkaway ever had, miss," replied Mr. Mole.

"Indeed, sir."

"I have shed my blood for him on innumerable occasions, and I will show my magnanimity now."

"That's right, sir," said Harvey.

"Monday," remarked Mr. Mole, "don't pull so hard on that confounded chain; do you hear? You gall my leg."

"Never mind um leg, sare," replied Monday, "go on with the magnanimimums."

"I, young lady, am the proprietor of a tea-garden in China," continued Mr. Mole.

"Yes," said Emily.

"Tell your pirate friends that I will make them a present of this lovely tea-garden, if they will give us our liberty and let us go."

"Bravo," cried Harvey. "Mole isn't such a bad sort after all."

"When you have occasion to allude to me, Harvey, you will please to address me as Mr. Mole."

"Beg pardon, sir."

"It is granted," replied Mr. Mole, grandly.

Emily spoke a few words to Jack in a low voice, begging him to keep up his spirits, and holding out hopes of speedy liberation.

Then she took her departure.

CHAPTER LXXXV.

SHELLING THE PIRATE CITY.

"ANGELS' visits are few and far between, and don't last long," said Jack, as if speaking to himself.

"Have I not behaved handsomely, Harkaway?" asked Mr. Mole.

Jack was thinking of Emily, and made no answer.

"Harvey, I appeal to you," continued Mr. Mole.

"You know, sir, that land is not like money. The pirates could never go and claim your land, because you could say who they were, and have them taken up," replied Harvey.

He had been thinking over Mr. Mole's apparent generosity, and the more he considered it, the less he believed in its reality.

Jack remembered what the lieutenant of Her Majesty's ship had told him when he overhauled the "Sea-horse."

Emily's remark about the pirates being worried by a vessel of war, raised his spirits considerably.

When Harvey damped the bandages with water and replaced them over his wounds, Jack said—

"I feel better, Dick."

"That's right, old man. Keep up your pluck," replied Harvey.

"It's so difficult to do that when you're ill. You don't know what a change illness makes in a fellow. It seems to take all the go out of him."

"I know it does. I was ill once—had a fever."

"But I feel different now. Emily has put new life into me."

"I thought she would, bless her!" said Harvey.

"And I don't believe we shall be prisoners much longer," continued Jack.

"Why not?"

"The 'Victor' has found the pirates out, and they will shell the city."

"It's an advantage, then, to be shut up in this vault."

"Well," said Jack, "so far as escaping the effects of the bombardment, it is. I know the British government have been trying for some time to exterminate the nest of pirates who have infested these seas so long."

While he was speaking, a loud booming was heard.

The whiz of a shell made itself distinctly audible as it flew over the devoted city.

There was a crash of falling masonry, and then for a minute all was still.

"By Jove, they're at it!" cried Harvey.

"Sooner than I expected," said Jack, with a quiet smile playing over his emaciated face.

Presently the sound was repeated, and it continued at intervals of half a minute.

The crashes were incessant.

It appeared that by morning there would not be one stone left standing on another in the famous City of the Golden Towers.

"That's splendid practice. How well they fire," said Jack, delightedly.

"Hurrah for the royal navy, and our rattling blue jackets!" exclaimed Harvey.

"What is all this hubbub?" asked Mr. Mole, trembling all over.

"The British fighting the pirates. They have found them out at last," replied Jack.

"How do you know?"

"I'm sure of it. We shall be free in a few hours, sir."

"That is good news. I hope this casement is shot-proof," said Mr. Mole, adding, "Monday."

"Sare," replied the black.

"Don't pull so confoundedly hard on that chain."

"Can't help um sare."

"You drag on it."

"Monday do um war dance, sare."

"Well, then, kindly postpone it, because it is painful to my feelings, and my skin is tender."

"All right, sare," replied Monday, "him stop um dance."

The bombardment had continued for four hours without a break.

Jack was anxious about Emily.

Suddenly he was relieved by seeing the door open, and his darling rush in, her hair dishevelled and showing signs of terror.

"Oh! Jack," she said, "I've had such an escape."

"From what, dear?" he asked.

"The city is on fire in a dozen places, and the pirates are leaving in crowds."

"Is it the 'Victor'?"

"I don't know the name of the ship, but it is a British man-of-war, and it is giving it the pirates finely."

"Hurrah!" cried Harvey.

"The pirate chief wanted to take me with him up the country somewhere, and make me his wife," she said.

"Beast!" ejaculated Jack.

"I escaped and ran through the burning city. How I missed being shot, or crushed by the falling masonry, or burnt, I don't know, but I thought it best to come to you."

"Did the guard let you in?"

"There are no guards; they have all run away. I merely slipped back the bolt, and here I am," she replied.

"Thank Heaven you are near me," rejoined Jack. "Sit down by my side, and let me hold your hand in mine, dear."

She did so.

Crash, crash, continued the shells.

H.M.S. "Victor" was in earnest this time.

The destruction is terrible when an unfortified town is bombarded by all the appliances of modern science.

At the expiration of about six hours, as well as the boys could guess, the firing ceased.

"Dick," said Jack, are you well enough to walk?"

"I can limp about a bit," answered Harvey.

"Go then to the riverside with something white, and let the English know that British prisoners are confined here."

"All right, I'll try."

"Shall I go with him?" asked Emily.

"No, my precious one," answered Jack, "I can't part with you; sit still where you are."

She pressed his hand affectionately.

Harvey was at a loss for something of a white colour.

He, as well as the rest of the party, had a handkerchief and a shirt.

These, however, had long ago ceased to bear any resemblance to white.

If any colour at all, they were black.

"To sally forth with such a thing, would be to hoist the black flag," as Harvey said, with a laugh.

Emily blushed.

"If you don't mind," she said, "you can have a bit of my petticoat. It is clean, for I washed it out myself yesterday."

"You, Emily?" exclaimed Jack.

"Yes; and I'm not ashamed of it. There are no laundresses here, for the best possible reason."

"What's that?"

"The people don't wear any clothes to speak about."

Everyone laughed at this answer.

"Now don't look at me and make fun," she went on.

"JACK, WITH HIS RIFLE, STOOD READY FOR ANY EMERGENCY."

"As if we could do such a thing," rejoined Harvey.

"Oh, I know what you boys are," she answered, smiling.

Turning round, she lifted up her dress and dexterously tore off a part of her petticoat, which she handed to Harvey.

"If you lose that, I'll kill you, Dick," said Jack. "It's more precious than cloth-of-gold."

"Don't be foolish, Jack," said Emily.

"I'll guard it with my life," answered Harvey, "and if I'm asked what flag it is, I shall say it's the flag of all nations."

"All nations?" repeated Emily.

"Yes; every man strikes his flag to a petticoat," said Harvey.

He had no difficulty in opening the door and going up the mouldy steps which led to the dungeon. He reached the open air.

A strange spectacle met his gaze.

The city, a few hours before proud and wealthy, was literally a heap of ruins.

Flames shot up into the air in different directions, and a thick pall of smoke obscured the sky.

No one was to be seen.

The city was deserted by its inhabitants.

He had not picked his way far between the *debris*, when a shot went by his ear and pinged against a wall.

"Hi!" he said. "Rule Britannia. Don't shoot a countryman."

He held up his strange flag.

The next moment he was face to face with a party of marines.

"Who are you, my lad?" asked the officer in command.

"British prisoner, sir; wounded in the leg, and taken out of a merchantman with others by the pirates."

"How many are there of you?"

"Five in all, and one's a lady," replied Harvey.

"In that case, I had better get you out of this and put you aboard. Lead on to the prison," said the officer; adding, "now, my lads, keep your weather eye open for an ambush. By your right, quick march!"

"Slow march, if you please, sir," said Harvey.

"Why?"

"Didn't I tell you I had a game leg? Give me an arm. It's uncommonly stiff, I can tell you."

"Ah, I forgot that; lean on me," said the officer. "Those creeses of the Malays give nasty wounds."

"That they do," exclaimed Harvey, limping along.

With a wildly beating heart he led the way to the dungeon.

Hope dawned in his breast once more.

Their troubles were nearly over.

CHAPTER LXXXVI.

ON BOARD H.M.S VICTOR.

IN less than an hour the prisoners were removed on board the "Victor."

Here the surgeon attended to Jack's wounds, and all was treated with the utmost kindness and consideration.

It was a pleasant and happy change.

A large quantity of valuable property was recovered from the burning city, and this put the sailors in a good temper, as they could look forward to prize money.

The pirates being thoroughly beaten and their city destroyed, the "Victor" dropped down the river.

It was the captain's intention to land the captives at Singapore.

His cruise was not yet over, and he could not leave the China Seas.

At Singapore no doubt a vessel would give them a passage to England.

Good food, fresh air, and excellent surgical attendance was all that Jack and Harvey required.

They soon recovered, and went about as usual.

Emily was the pet and darling of the whole ship's company, but she had only eyes for Jack.

There was one man on board Jack did not like.

He was tall and thin, with dark, flashing eyes.

His father was a merchant at Singapore, and a friend of the captain of the "Victor."

The young man, who was about nineteen, not being in very good health, had been received on board the ship as the guest of the captain, and taken for a cruise.

His name was Frank Davis.

He fell violently in love with Emily, and persecuted her with his attentions on all occasions.

Being an idle man, and having no duty to do on board the ship, he was able to roam about when and where he liked.

Emily did not encourage him, but she did not like to be rude.

Consequently Jack often saw them together and his face flushed as he saw Frank Davis bending over her.

Pointing him out to Harvey, Jack said—

"I shall punch that snob's head some day."

"I wouldn't," replied Harvey. "You are not strong, and we shall soon make Singapore, when we shall get rid of him."

"It's a nuisance to think I have got another fellow to worry me, just when Hunston is wiped out and we have made an end to all our troubles."

"Do you think Hunston is dead?"

"I fancy he must have died in the burning city. Ill as he was, he could scarcely escape," replied Jack.

"At all events, he is not on board this ship. That's one comfort," remarked Harvey.

Jack watched Mr. Davis carefully, and in spite of Harvey's advice, sought an opportunity to pick a quarrel with him.

Davis, however, was very civil to him and seemed to try to avoid a rupture.

Mr. Mole went about from one to another of the crew, and recounted his valiant exploits among the savages.

Monday caused the sailors great amusement.

He begged and borrowed from them a complete sailor's dress, and was very proud of it.

The "Victor" had to go out of her course to chase some pirate craft.

Sighting an island, a boat was lowered to go and obtain a supply of water.

Monday ran up to Jack in great excitement.

"Mast' Jack!" he exclaimed.

"Well," replied Jack.

"That's Limbi. That's my island. I know um well."

"Is it?"

"Yes. You ask the Tuan captain if he let you and me go and land with the sailor men."

"Would you like to see the island once more?" asked Jack.

"Very much like, sure," replied Monday.

"All right. I'll go and get permission."

Jack went to the captain, stated the case, and asked leave for himself and Monday to accompany the boat.

Leave was at once granted.

They embarked in the boat, and the Limbians came to receive them.

When they saw Jack and Monday they made a great feast in their honour, and would not allow the English sailors to do any work, but filled the casks with water for them.

They went up to the city, and Jack called upon Alfura and Ambonia.

He was asked a variety of questions about Mr. Mole, who he said had remained in the pirate city.

"Will he come back?" asked Ambonia.

"Oh, yes," replied Jack. "He is very anxious to see you again. Can I take him any message?"

"We have a surprise for him," said Alfura and Ambonia in a breath.

"What?"

"Two little babies; such beauties. Mine is a boy, we call Isaac, and Alfura's is a girl, named after her."

Jack whistled.

"Two kids," he exclaimed "Mr. Mole expected this."

"Did he?" asked Alfura.

"Yes; and he wants you to send the children to him. Cannot the nurse take them in a basket?"

"We should not like to part with them; but if it is their father's wish——"

"It is," rejoined Jack.

"Then the dear little innocents shall go," replied Ambonia.

She went into an adjoining room, and the nurse who had charge of them brought them in for Jack's inspection.

They were not quite so dusky as their mothers, but there was a half-caste tinge about their complexions.

"Bless 'em!" said Jack.

He kissed their foreheads.

This gracious act quite won the hearts of the mothers.

The infants were placed in a basket, covered over.

On the breast of one Jack put a piece of paper, on which he wrote "The gentle Isaac."

On the other he placed the inscription, "The lovely Alfura."

And on the top of the basket he wrote —"A present from Limbi, for a good Mole."

"Now, nurse," he said, "carry that down to the boat. You will come with us to take care of the precious babbies."

"Have they far to go ?" asked Alfura.

"Only a few days' voyage."

"And will Mr. Mole come soon?" sighed Ambonia.

"Before another moon has passed," replied Jack.

The mothers began to cry, and Jack cleared out, making for the boat, where the crew were waiting for him.

When the lieutenant in charge asked who the old woman was, Jack informed him that she was taking something on board for Mr. Mole, and it would be all right.

The children having been well fed, slept placidly.

At length the boat reached the ship, and the basket was taken up and placed on the quarter-deck.

"You stand back till you're wanted," said Jack to the nurse.

The captain and officers crowded round the basket.

The crew looked on at a distance.

Jack saluted the captain, and the captain saluted Jack.

"What's this, Mr. Harkaway ?" asked Captain Dacre.

"Present for Mr. Mole, sir," replied Jack.

"Pass the word for Mr. Mole," said the captain.

The word was passed, and Mr. Mole emerged from the captain's servant's cabin, where all the good things were kept.

He wiped his mouth as he came out, and he exhaled a smell of brandy.

"You did me the honour to send for me, sir," he said.

"Your former friends have sent you something," replied the captain.

"Ah! indeed. They remember my valorous feats. This is kind of them, and also proper."

"Will you open the basket now ?"

"I will, sir, with your permission."

Mr. Mole stooped down and untied the fastenings of the basket.

The cloth was thrown back, and the children revealed to view.

Mr. Mole staggered, and uttered a groan.

"The gentle Isaac and the lovely Alfura," he murmured.

The officers burst into a roar of laughter, and even Captain Dacre himself could not refrain from smiling.

Suddenly Mr. Mole's manner changed.

He grew furious.

"Who has done this ? Who has played me this base trick ?" he cried.

"They are your children, sir," replied Harkaway. "You know you married two wives in Limbi, and these children are the consequence of the rash act."

"I'll have none of them! Away with the reptiles; the vermin; the little black images !"

"I appeal to these gentlemen if the sleeping innocents are not the exact likeness of their father," said Jack.

"Into the sea with them," cried Mr. Mole.

He grasped the basket and would have cast them over the ship's side, had not the nurse run forward and seized him by the ear.

"Oh! my ear, my ear! The she-fiend; she'll wring it off," vociferated Mole, dropping the basket.

The children began to scream.

Leaving her hold of his ear, the nurse attended to the children.

Mole danced up and down like a madman.

"Mr. Harkaway," said the captain, "this may be a very good joke, but we cannot be burdened with this sort of live stock."

"Beg pardon, sir. Didn't wish to put you to any inconvenience," said Jack.

"Possibly not."

"Fact is, sir, I've got a feeling heart," said Jack.

"Every sailor ought to have one."

"Mr. Mole, sir, has deserted his wives, and the poor infants will be half orphans, if——"

"Yes, yes," said the captain, rather impatiently, as he detected a half twinkle in Jack's eye; "we know all about that; but you have given me the trouble of again lowering a boat to send these children and their nurse to the shore."

"Won't you have the half orphans, sir?"

"Not on board this ship; it is absurd to ask me. Any one would take you for their father, you are so anxious about them."

"I, sir? No, sir. Wouldn't do such things," answered Jack, with a broad grin.

"Go forward, Mr. Harkaway, if you please," said Captain Dacre, sternly. "We have had enough of this nonsense."

Jack retired, whistling—

"It's nice to be a father."

When Mr. Mole saw that the captain was going to send the gentle Isaac and his sister back, he recovered himself.

"Remove the brats at once, sailors," he said, "and you shall have a crown to drink my health."

A boat was soon lowered, and the nurse, with the precious tits," as Jack called them, put into it.

"This proper and decided act of the captain's has saved me the trouble and work of buying some vermin destroying powder," muttered Mr. Mole, "Ugh! the black beasts."

"They're yours, sir," whispered Jack, at his elbow.

"Harkaway, this is a painful joke," replied Mr. Mole.

"Bad for the poor half orphans, sir."

"You have exposed me to the ridicule of the officers and crew of the vessel."

"Never be ashamed of your own, sir," said Jack.

"The captain has behaved like a gentleman. Look at that boat conveying the vermin to the shore. It is a pleasant sight."

Mr. Mole sighed deeply.

"You're a gay deceiver, sir; but I shouldn't wonder if Ambonia followed you to England."

"If she does, I'll——"

Mr. Mole stopped abruptly.

It did not exactly occur to him what he could do in the event of such an unpleasant contingency.

Jack did not worry him any more, though he had many a laugh over the affair with Harvey.

The ship went on to Singapore, and there landed the little party.

Monday had made up his mind to go to England.

As Jack and Mr. Mole were the richest, they drew bills on England, and got them discounted to pay their expenses.

Before the "Victor" left, they made the captain a handsome present.

Jack took care of Emily, who, now her father and mother were dead, was a penniless orphan.

They all lodged at the same hotel.

Monday insisted on being Jack and Harvey's servant, but he would not do a thing for Mr. Mole.

"He one humbug, sare, that what Mist' Mole is," he used to say.

The boys secured a passage to England in a fast steamer, which was to sail in a few days after taking in cargo.

"Our worries are all over now, Dick," said Jack, gleefully.

"About time they were," replied Harvey.

CHAPTER LXXXVII.

JACK BECOMES JEALOUS.

WE have said that Emily was very grateful to Jack for all he had done for her.

Had it not been for him she might have endured an intolerable captivity among the pirates.

She might even have been compelled to become Hunston's wife.

It was not much she could do in return so she said.

But Jack thought it a great deal.

She could give him her heart, and promise to be his wife some day when he was a man.

"What shall I do, Jack dear," she said, "when I get back to England? I have no parents now—no home."

His eyes filled with tears.

"Stay with my father and mother, Emily," replied Jack. "They will make you happy for my sake."

"Oh, I don't like to do that. I'll go out as governess."

"You shall not," Jack said, emphatically. "I should like to see anyone bullying my darling. You'll stay with us."

"If you think your friends will let me——"

"I know they will; so don't fret about that, my pet."

"I have often thought lately, Jack," she exclaimed, "that it was very fortunate you were among the savages."

"We've had our trials, Emmy, but it doesn't matter so long as we've pulled through, does it?"

"No," she answered; "that is the great thing; and I am so happy to know that you love me."

Mr. Mole came in just then, and interrupted any further conversation of a private nature.

"I'm going home with you, Harkaway," he said.

"I always thought you were, sir."

"No; I had it in my mind to proceed to China, but I shall sell my tea garden."

"Sell it?" replied Jack.

"As soon as possible. I have had enough of savage life. I went forth 'strange countries for to see,' as the song has it, and I have seen enough of them."

"I think you have come to a wise determination, Mr. Mole," said Emily.

"I cannot doubt that I have, my dear, if you say so."

"As for Harvey and myself, we shall be glad to have you with us," said Jack.

"My idea," exclaimed Mr. Mole, "is to go to some university town.

"Indeed!"

"Yes; I am fond of teaching, and I shall establish myself as a private tutor."

"But you have an income?"

"I daresay when my tea garden is sold I shall have two or three hundred a year. Well with that and the proceeds of my teaching my life will glide calmly on."

"Capital sir," exclaimed Jack.

"Calmly on," continued Mr. Mole, "until I go over to the majority, which means the greater number, or those who have gone before to their everlasting home."

"You are becoming sentimental, Mr Mole," remarked Emily.

"I feel so, my dear young lady. When a man has come to a great determination, and settled a crisis in his life, he ought to feel happy."

The skipper of the homeward-bound sent word to say that his ship would not be ready to sail for at least three weeks.

He had a quantity of cargo to take on board, and this would delay his start.

There was nothing for it but to make themselves as comfortable as possible at their hotel.

When the "Victor" sailed, Frank Davis, of whom we have spoken as an admirer of Emily, remained behind.

His father was a rich merchant.

The sea air had done him good, and he was now able to stay on shore and resume his ordinary duties. Not that he did much work.

He would stroll down to the counting-house with a cigar in his mouth, stay for an hour or two, and then go away again.

Frank Davis had been born in England though most of his life had been passed in Singapore.

He had long, dark hair, regular features, and a keen, flashing eye.

Altogether he was not bad looking, though his face wore a conceited and haughty expression. Jack hated him.

Having made acquaintance with our little party on board ship, he thought himself privileged to visit them at their hotel, which he did very frequently.

He talked to Mr. Mole, and made himself very agreeable to Emily, but scarcely condescended to speak to Jack and Harvey.

One evening he had been for more than an hour turning over Emily's music while she sang and played.

Jack was biting his lips with vexation, for he really loved Emily, and did not like to see her encourage, as he thought, this comparative stranger.

At length she rose and went to the sofa.

Jack placed himself by the side of her immediately.

Davis walked up to Mr. Mole, and began to talk about the higher mathematics.

"Emily," said Jack, "do you find the society of that fellow Davis so very entertaining?"

"He praises my playing, and turns my music for me," answered Emily.

"Couldn't I do the same?"

"Of course; only you and Harvey get together and talk about old times, and never come near me. I must talk to some one. What am I to do?"

"I thought I wasn't wanted," said Jack.

"Nonsense!" she said, with a musical laugh. "You're not going to get jealous in your old age."

"I am jealous."

"You stupid old Jack. You deserve that I should scold you."

"But look here, haven't you been going on anyhow with that ugly brute Davis?" asked Jack.

"I'm sure he isn't ugly, and he knows how to make himself very agreeable to ladies," replied Emily, who, like all pretty women, was a tyrant, and wished to torment him a little.

"That is as much as to say I'm not."

"No, it isn't."

"And you like him best? Very well; I'm glad you've told me," said Jack, flushing angrily.

"Now, Jack, I shall be very cross with you indeed, if you run away with a mistaken idea like that," replied Emily.

"All right, you have said quite enough," said Jack, savagely.

He got up and walked away.

"Dick," exclaimed Emily, appealing to Harvey.

"What is it?" asked Dick.

"Do, please, go after Jack. He's in such a rage, and I'm afraid there will be a quarrel between him and—and Mr. Davis."

"Shouldn't wonder if there was," replied Harvey.

"Why?"

"If it had been me, I'd have punched his ugly head long ago."

"I haven't done anything wrong," replied Emily.

"I don't know about wrong," replied Harvey. "You've been carrying on anyhow with that fellow."

"I was only civil to him."

"I'm Jack's friend, you know, Miss Emily," continued Harvey, "and I don't like to see him made a fool of. He's awfully fond of you."

"So am I of him," she said.

"Well, you don't go the right way to show it," Harvey answered, bluntly.

"Never mind; I will explain all to Jack presently, only go after him, will you, please, and tell him how sorry I am. I don't want a quarrel. Mr. Davis might hurt him."

Harvey laughed scornfully.

"Hurt him? Hurt Jack!" he said, contemptuously.

"Yes."

"Why, Jack wouldn't make a mouthful of him. He's bigger than either of us, but I should be sorry if his face came against Jack's fist. Hurt Jack! Not much. Don't fret about that."

"Will you go and speak to Jack?" urged Emily.

"If you wish it, though I'd rather let them alone," replied Harvey. "Mr. Merchant's Son is sure to get a jolly good walloping."

"Very well," said Emily, leaning back; "I can see you are both against me."

"Let them alone, I tell you," replied Harvey. "I know what Jack's game is."

"What?"

"He is too much of the gentleman to have a row in his own room, with a fellow who is his guest."

"I hope so," said Emily; "but what will he do?"

"Oh, square him up somehow. Let them alone," replied Harvey.

Frank Davis now took his leave, the fact being that Mr. Mole rather bored him with cube roots and one thing and another.

Emily rather distantly wished him good-night.

She had not intended to encourage his advances, and wished to draw back as soon as she saw Harkaway was annoyed.

A little way from the hotel Davis met Jack, and said—

"Good night. I wondered where you had gone to."

"I came out here to speak to you," replied Jack.

"That is funny. I have spent the evening in your room, and you have had every opportunity of talking to me."

"I did not choose to talk to you upstairs."

"And I don't choose to talk to you in the street. That's the difference," exclaimed Davis, in his usual sneering manner.

"Excuse me; you cannot help yourself."

"Oh! but I can," replied Davis, walking on.

Jack ran forward, and placed himself before him.

"Really Mr. Harkaway, this is very strange behaviour," said Davis, finding himself stopped.

"Not at all."

"Perhaps you have lived so long amongst savages that you forget how to behave yourself amongst gentlemen."

This remark stung Jack.

"I simply want to tell you that I wish your visits to cease at my hotel," he said; "that's plain enough."

"I don't come to see you," said Davis, insolently.

"That is a remark which if you dare to repeat, I will knock you down for," cried Jack.

"I have no reason to say it again," replied Davis, "since you have heard it once, and seemed to appreciate the force of it."

Jack's fingers itched to strike him, but he restrained himself.

"Who do you come to see?" he asked.

"Use your eyes, and you will find out."

Jack felt inclined to spring upon him, but at that moment Monday came up.

"What do you want?" he asked.

"Mist' Harvey, him send me, sare," replied Monday; "him think you want me."

"So I do," replied Jack.

"What um for, sare?"

"Kick this fellow in front of me. I won't dirty my hands with him at present."

"Mist' Davis, sare? Kick um friend?" said Monday, in surprise.

"He's no friend of mine. Wire in!"

Davis looked alarmed.

"I warn you," he said, "that if this black fellow touches me, I will have him punished."

"You can do your little worst, my boy," answered Jack, adding, "go in, Monday; let him have it."

Monday did not hesitate any longer.

Jack's word was law to him.

He administered several hearty kicks and cuffs to Davis, who ran swiftly up the street, with Jack's derisive laughter ringing in his ears.

"Monday kick him well, sare?" asked the black.

"Beautiful!"

"Um proper kicks, sare?"

"Lovely, Monday. I'll buy you a new hat," replied Jack, still laughing heartily.

The way in which the dandified merchant's son ran away pleased him immensely.

Returning to his hotel, he found Emily had gone to bed, saying she had a bad headache.

Mr. Mole and Harvey were at supper.

Jack joined them, and told them how he had made Monday treat Davis.

"Impetuous as usual, Harkaway," said Mr. Mole. "Just like you."

"Why shouldn't I, sir? He tried to spoon on Emily," replied Jack.

"She should have snubbed him. You were wrong, and it is unfortunate just now."

"Why, sir?"

"Because we have been put up for election at the English club, of which Davis is a member. Two black balls in the ballot exclude, and he may so vote and influence his friends as to get us shut out."

"I didn't think of that."

"Of course you didn't. You bull-at-a-gate fellows never do think of consequences."

"I daresay we shall pull through, sir," remarked Harvey.

"We may; but it would not be pleasant during the short time we stay here to be shut out of the only club in the place, and for people to say that we were blackballed at the ballot. You really should think of these things, Harkaway."

"I'm not a bit sorry I made Monday kick him," Jack replied, obstinately.

"It would not have been so bad if you had kicked him yourself."

"I know that, and that's why I made the nigger do it," answered Jack.

"He has a revengeful face. I would rather have him as a friend than an enemy," said Mr. Mole.

"He can't hurt me."

"You don't know that. Never make an enemy. The mouse once helped the lion."

"That's a fable, sir," said Jack.

"It is, but we often see it exemplified in real life."

"Bother fables!" exclaimed Jack, yawning.

"That young man's father is one of the richest merchants in Singapore," continued Mr. Mole; "and he tells me that he is to be sent shortly to England."

"Indeed?" ejaculated Jack.

"Yes ; he is to go to a university to complete his education. His health is not good, and it is thought that the climate of England will do him a vast deal of service.

"We've enough scamps in England without him," replied Jack.

"Never mind. Take my advice, and don't make an enemy of the young man. This is only a half-civilised place after all, and you don't know what he might be capable of."

"I only know one thing, sir," said Jack.

"What's that ?"

"He won't stay here any more ; I've put the kibosh on that."

"My dear Harkaway——"

"My dear Mr. Mole. Good night. I'm not in the humour for a jaw, and I shall have a glass at the bar, and then turn in to my virtuous bug-walk."

"I should rather call it mosquito-run," added Mr. Mole, with a smile. "But good night, if you are off. Harvey and I will finish the wine over a game at crib. Eh, Harvey, what do you say ?"

"I am agreeable, sir," replied Harvey.

Jack left them to themselves, and they did not retire till nearly midnight.

CHAPTER LXXXVIII.

A SCENE AT THE ENGLISH CLUB.

THE English club was an unpretending building near the custom-house.

Its windows overlooked the water of the harbour, which flowed up to its walls.

All the Englishmen and the Americans in Singapore belonged to it ; and when our travellers were put up for election, it was considered as a compliment which the residents wished to pay them.

Captain Hammond, of the "Rangoon," the steamer in which they were to sail for England, which was now taking in cargo, had put them up.

They were influentially seconded.

On the morning after the fracas in the street between Frank Davis and Monday, Jack and Harvey walked down to the club to ascertain the result of the ballot.

They were ushered into the reading-room of the club, which was also the smoking-room.

Through the open window of the club they could see the shipping in the harbour, and the bright sunbeams danced gaily over the water.

Captain Hammond approached Jack, and said—

"I have much pleasure, Mr. Harkaway, in informing you that you and your friends were elected members of this club last evening. I was just coming to your hotel to bring you the news."

"Thank you very much for your kindness, which I shall not forget, and for which I thank you on behalf of myself and friends," replied Jack.

"Your friends were elected without opposition, and you had only one black ball."

"Indeed," said Jack. "I wonder who could have favoured me with that ? My stay here has been so short that I was not aware I had had time to make any enemies."

Suddenly he thought of Frank Davis.

"Is Mr. Davis a member of your club ?" he asked.

"Oh, yes. I remember that he came in last night just in time for the election," answered Captain Hammond.

"In that case, I know where to look for my enemy, though I care very little for the malice of a blackguard."

A slight cough arrested his attention.

Looking up, he saw Davis sitting on the ledge of one of the open windows, smoking a cigarette.

Had he known he was there, he would not have spoken so openly.

The attention of the few members in the club-room was called by this speech to Davis.

Looking very red in the face, the latter exclaimed—

"I think I heard my name mentioned ?"

"Yes," replied Jack, promptly. "By me."

"I wish you would say anything relating to me in my presence, and not attack me behind my back," answered Davis.

"I am perfectly willing to repeat what I said. My remark merely had reference to your attempt to keep me out of the club last night."

"If I choose to blackball you, I only exercised my right. I have no wish to associate myself with objectionable people. But was that all you said?"

"I called you a blackguard, if you particularly wish to know," exclaimed Jack, boldly.

"Gentlemen, gentleman," said Captain Hammond, "permit me to remind you that this is deplorably bad taste."

"Can't help it, my dear sir," replied Jack. "It is his doing."

Frank Davis grew very pale, and bit his lips.

"I have no wish to create a scene," he said; "but when I am grossly insulted by a man who has lived among savages, and makes a friend of a nigger, I really must protect myself."

"Certainly, certainly," observed some of Davis's friends.

Owing to his father's wealth and reputation, Davis was a great man with a certain set.

"Come outside, and have a dust up with fists," said Jack. "Give and take alike, and if you lick me, I'll shake hands."

"It is impossible, sir," answered Davis, "that I could so demean myself. If I fight, I use the weapons of a gentleman."

"What may they be?"

"Swords or pistols, either of which I place at your disposal," replied Davis.

"Gentlemen, gentlemen," again said Captain Hammond, "I really must beg that you will remember where you are."

"I decline your challenge. It is not the custom of Englishmen to fight duels. But I repeat, that if you want to see who is best man, I am ready for you with a bunch of fives," exclaimed Jack.

"Just what I might have expected from a man of your stamp," answered Davis, with one of his most offensive sneers.

"What do you mean?" asked Jack.

"Simply that, relying on your natural cowardice, you think you can insult a gentleman with impunity."

"Why, you ugly little whipper-snapper, you counter-jumping land lubber, I've a good mind to punch your head," said Jack, indignantly.

"Of course. Cowards are always bullies. But vulgar abuse only lowers you still more in my eyes; and let me tell you, my blustering friend, that I shall be under the painful necessity of horse-whipping you in public if you do not mind what you are saying."

Jack could bear this no longer.

He rushed across the room, regardless of clubs rules and etiquette.

Davis was still sitting in the open window, with his back to the water of the harbour.

Without giving him any notice, he struck him full in the face with his fist.

The blow caused the little dandy to lose his balance, and with a ludicrous cry of rage and fear, he toppled over, and fell with a splash in the water.

"Hullo!" exclaimed Harvey, as he disappeared, "where has he gone to?"

"Kingdom come, I hope," replied Jack, smiling grimly.

The members of the club rushed to the window in great excitement.

Davis was seen to rise to the surface, and shake his fist at Jack.

Then he swam away to a boat, climbed up the side, and was rowed, dripping wet, to the shore.

Jack laughed heartily; but Captain Hammond looked grave.

"This will have to be brought before the committee," he said.

"What will the result of that be?" asked Jack.

"I fear your election will be cancelled."

"That won't break my heart," answered Jack.

"I will try to avoid it, because that little wasp Davis will go about saying you were kicked out of the club for ungentlemanly conduct."

"Was it ungentlemanly?" inquired Jack, thinking the matter over for the first time.

Captain Hammond laughed.

"Ask yourself," he said. "That sort of thing would do very well on board ship, but in a club, my dear fellow, we allow no wrangling."

"Well, good morning. I am much obliged to you all the same," replied Jack.

He made a stiff bow to the gentlemen in the room, who regarded him coldly.

Some acknowledged his salutation, and others simply stared rudely at him.

As he passed out he heard such remarks as—

"Bull in a china shop." "Uncultivated boor." "Turn the club into a bear garden," &c.

"Come along, Dick," he exclaimed to Harvey. "It appears we're not good enough for this lot."

"They're no great loss," answered Harvey.

With a defiant air they left the club, and were just in time to see Frank Davis, covered with mud, wet through, and bare-headed, get into a carriage to be driven home.

His face wore the expression of a demon.

"I say, Jack," said Harvey, "mind that fellow doesn't knife you."

"Not he," replied Jack. "The beggar hasn't pluck enough to come within a mile of me."

The boys strolled about for some hours, visited several of the ships in harbour, and at length returned to the hotel to dinner.

"A note for you from the English club, Harkaway," exclaimed Mr. Mole.

"Read it, sir, if you please," replied Jack.

Mr. Mole did so.

"Dear me," he said. "It is a notice from the committee stating that, owing to your conduct this morning, the committee feel bound to censure you strongly; but on a vote being taken, it was decided to retain your name on the books by a majority of one."

"I'm glad of that," answered Jack; "because if I had been expelled, it would have been a triumph for that fellow Davis."

"What have you been doing?" asked Mr. Mole.

"Only punching, sir. Knocking this cove Davis into the sea for cheeking me."

"Ah! that is bad. What a pity you cannot keep your fighting propensities in check, but you always had too much of the bull-dog in you."

"Can't help it, sir," answered Jack. "It's the nature of the animal."

"You seem to have a great spite against Mr. Davis."

"It's his fault. Oh! here's Emily. First time I've seen her to-day," exclaimed Jack, "Emmy, dear, I'm sorry to say I've been slipping into your friend."

"What friend?" asked Emily.

"Mr. Frank Davis,"

"He's no friend of mine. I merely regarded him as an acquaintance of yours," she answered.

"Don't tell fibs, Emmy. You know you like him."

Emily began to cry.

"If you are going to treat me so cruelly," she sobbed, "I shall go upstairs again. I'm sure I did not put myself out of the way to be civil to him. You would not, I thought, like me to be rude to your guests."

Jack's heart melted in a moment.

Springing to her side, he kissed her tears away, and said—

"Don't cry, darling. Say you forgive me, and I'll never be naughty again."

"It's a great shame of you," she replied.

"So 'tis. I'm a beast, but that stuck-up sneering cad riled me. I couldn't stand it any longer, so I mauled him about a bit."

"I shouldn't care if—if you kil—killed him," Emily answered continuing to sob, "if—if you were not so unkind to me."

It was some time before Jack could make his peace with her, but at last he succeeded and they were better friends than ever.

Emily wiped away her tears. Dinner was brought up; they all sat down, and as if by common consent, Mr. Davis's name was never once mentioned, and no allusion was made to the disturbance at at the club.

After dinner the gentlemen lighted their cigarettes, and Emily took up a book to read.

Suddenly Monday burst into the room out of breath.

"What's up now, Monday?" cried Jack. "You'll bust up if you waste your wind like that."

"Take your hat off," said Harvey, removing his broad-bimmed Panama straw. "Why don't you learn decent manners?"

"I should think there was going to be a donkey race to-morrow," remarked Jack.

"Where?" asked Harvey.

"All round Monday's hat. Sold again. I had you then, Dick," replied Jack, laughing.

Monday now found his tongue.

"Oh! Mast' Jack," he exclaimed, "such um big fire down street."

"HALLO, SAID JACK, 'YOU ARE OUT OF ORDER, SIR!'"

"A fire!" cried the boys, jumping to their feet.

"Yes, a big one. All the houses crackle and burn ever much so. Come on, sare, and see um fun."

"By Jove! I'm in that," exclaimed Jack, putting on his hat.

His example was followed by Harvey.

"And I, too," said Mr. Mole. "I will accompany you to the scene of the conflagration. Perhaps with my usual bravery I may be instrumental in saving some poor creature's life."

Before he had finished speaking, the boys were out of the room.

They followed Monday down the street, and were soon in the midst of a great crowd.

Smoke rose in dense masses, and sparks fell around in all directions.

Some wooden buildings used as warehouses were in flames.

How they had caught fire no one knew.

The firemen had already brought up their hand-engines, and were busily engaged in laying the hose, and getting to work.

"Man the pumps," shouted Jack, pushing his way to the front.

He laid hold of the handle of the nearest engine, which was speedily manned.

Harvey seized the hose, and directed it against the burning building.

A plentiful supply of water was secured from the harbour, which was not far off.

The crowd took Jack and Harvey for British officers, owing to their uniforms, and having a great respect for the English, they let them do just as they liked.

A small tree grew near one of the houses, but sufficiently distant to be safe from the effects of the fire.

Mr. Mole espied this, and with difficulty climbed up, sitting astride one of the branches.

"This is capital," he said to himself, as he rubbed his hands. "I shall have a good view here, and be out of the crowd. Harkaway will not know where I am, and I can say I bore an active part in extinguishing this dreadful fire."

The houses, being made of wood, burnt fiercely, and in spite of the torrents of water poured upon them, they were speedily destroyed.

Fortunately, they were nearly empty at the time of the fire; had they been full of goods, the result would have been much more disastrous.

Jack worked at the pumps like a nigger, and at length left off from sheer fatigue.

The fire was nearly out now, and had been prevented from extending any further on either side.

Looking around him, Jack perceived Harvey guiding the hose as if he had been born a fireman.

"I say, Dick," he said, stretching his limbs, "you got a better birth than I did."

"Talent, sir, talent," replied Harvey.

"Hullo!" exclaimed Jack; "there's some one who has got a better birth than either of us."

"Who?"

"Old Mole."

"Where is he?" asked Harvey.

"Up that tree. Pump on him," said Jack.

Harvey looked round and saw Mr. Mole serenely perched up in the tree, and half hidden by the leaves.

In an instant he diverted the hose from the burning building.

It did not much matter now, as half-a-dozen engines were at work on it, and the fire was nearly over.

"Mind your eye, sir; the tree's on fire," shouted Harvey.

The next moment a shower of water fell like a deluge on Mr. Mole.

In his eyes, his mouth, knocking off his hat, in his stomach, filling his trousers and boots, came the unceasing stream.

"Wo!" he cried. "I say, Harvey, I am up in this tree"—splutter, splutter—"you'll choke me. I shall be drowned. Ho, ho! I say, stop that performance."

But Harvey continued to water him as if he was syringing a plant in a greenhouse.

"Go it, Dick. Give it him hot," said Jack.

"This is unseemly. Bother those boys!"—splutter, splutter—stammered Mr. Mole. "They'll be the death of me before they've done; I know they will. Ugh! I'm half full of water already, and nearly drowned."

The cascade played gracefully upon him.

Much amused, the crowd looked up and began to laugh.

Mr. Mole could bear it no longer, and toppled off the branch, falling on the heads of the crowd below.

This fortunately broke his fall, and he was only a little shaken.

Rushing up to Harvey, he shook his fist in his face.

"You scamp!" he exclaimed. "What do you mean by this?"

Harvey said—

"Sorry to knock you off your perch, sir. Mind your eye, again."

He lifted the hose, and sent another jet right into his face.

In vain Mr. Mole capered and danced, and tried to hit him.

The water drove him back, and he turned tail running away to his hotel.

"Well done, Dick. Wire in, old man," cried Jack.

Suddenly Monday touched Jack on the shoulder.

"Mast' Jack," he said, in a thrilling whisper, "you take care!"

"What of?" asked Jack.

"Mist' Davis close by. He speak to one man, and him a big scoundrel."

"What did he say?" inquired Jack.

Instead of answering, Monday turned rapidly round.

At the same moment a knife glided up Jack's arm, and he felt the hot blood slowly trickle down his sleeve.

CHAPTER LXXXIX.

THE HIDDEN HAND.

"I'M wounded!" cried Jack, clutching his arm, as a trickling sensation ran through it.

Turning round, he saw Monday struggling with an ugly-looking native, who, with a jerk of his leg, threw Monday off, and ran away, being speedily lost in the crowd.

Having heard Jack say he was stabbed Harvey came up at once.

"I hope you are not hurt?" he exclaimed, anxiously.

"Not much, I think," answered Jack. "though I believe the fellow tried to get at my heart with his bread-and-cheese cutter. Where's Monday?"

"Here him be, sare," said the faithful fellow.

"What does all this mean?" quickly inquired Jack.

"Monday him hear Mist' Davis point you out, sare, to that black thief, and just when I speak to you, him whip out um knife to stick with."

"Ah, I see; you turned the blow?"

"Monday seize him arm, sare, and turn him off. Don't know how he got away. Some twist him give with um leg."

"Perhaps you've saved my life," said Jack. "I didn't think Mr. Davis was one of that sort."

"But I did," answered Harvey. "Lean on me, and let us find a doctor. You must have your arm seen to."

With some difficulty they found a doctor, who happened to be an Englishman.

He examined the wound, and said—

"Where did you get this, young gentleman?"

Jack told him it was done in a scrimmage at the fire.

"Ah!" replied the doctor, "such things are not uncommon hereabouts; and if, sailor fashion, you will go in for free fights, you must take the consequences. My advice is, keep out of them."

"I will in future," answered Jack. "Is it anything serious?"

"No, it is not. I find it is merely a flesh wound; just a rip of the skin. You have had what we should have called a shave, when I was a medical student at Guy's."

"I'm the luckiest dog out," exclaimed Jack, joyfully. "Always drop on my legs, don't I Dick?"

"I must say you certainly do," answered Harvey.

When the wound was washed and strapped up, they went back to the hotel. Jack experienced nothing more than a slight weakness, with some smarting stiffness in the arm.

Mr. Mole was sitting before a big fire, huddled up in a thick dressing-gown.

A tumbler of steaming grog stood before him, and he had his feet in a pan of hot water.

"What on earth are you doing, sir?" said Jack.

"Enjoying the comforts of civilization, of which I have been deprived for some time," replied Mr. Mole.

"But a fire in the tropics, when it is hot enough to melt an iceberg in three minutes——"

"Is necessary for the preservation of my health. I have been shamefully treated, and already feel bronchitis fastening upon my chest.

"The ducking will cool you, sir," Jack said, laughing.

"It has done so. Can you find me a tallow candle, to tallow my nose with?"

"I don't suppose you'd get such a thing here, sir. Candles all melt. Try some soft soap."

"Harkaway, no joking; this is serious. Where's Harvey, the wretch? If I were not so ill, I would chastise him for his cruel joke."

"I am here, sir," answered Harvey. "Glad to see you're not dead yet."

"No thanks to you," said Mr. Mole, severely. "you see the wretched state you've reduced me to. Dreadful cold coming on—come on, in fact—and no candle to tallow my nose with. Awful!"

The boys could not help laughing.

Mr. Mole perceived that Harkaway carried his arm in a sling.

"What's the matter?" he inquired. "Nothing much, I hope."

"Oh, nothing half so bad as your cold, sir," answered Jack, carelessly; "only a stab in the arm."

"A stab? Dear me! Who did it?"

"Davis hired a fellow to knife me out of the way. It appears to be the custom out here. Nice sort of place to live in, isn't it, sir?"

"Dear me, how quietly you take it. Bless my soul, is there not some sort of justice here?"

"Perhaps, yes; perhaps, no. But where's Emily?"

"I don't know. She was not here when I came in, and I have been so much taken up with my cold that——"

"Bother your cold. Ring the bell, Dick," cried Jack.

"Impulsive youths," remarked Mr. Mole, "are like obstinate mules; they will have their own way."

Harvey rang the bell, and Jack questioned the servants about Emily.

One said he saw her go to the door to look at the fire, and while standing there a man came up and requested her to come to Mr. Harkaway, who wanted her."

Jack turned deadly pale.

"I never sent for her," he said.

"She went a little way down the street, sir, and then I saw her get into a carriage, which drove off at a rapid pace," continued the domestic.

Jack sank into a seat faint and ill.

"It's a trap," exclaimed Harvey.

"Brandy," cried Jack; "give me some brandy."

His request was complied with, and he freshened up a little.

"Who has done this base thing?" asked Mr. Mole. "Who can have carried off our little Emily, the life and soul of our party?"

"There is only one man in Singapore," replied Harvey, "who could have done it."

"And he is——"

"Frank Davis."

Jack was too agitated to speak.

"It is all part of a planned thing," continued Harvey. "Davis is in love with Emily—Jack insults him; he arranges to have Jack assassinated, and at the same time carry off Emily."

"I fear you are not far wrong," said Mr. Mole.

Jack got up and paced the room impatiently.

"Call Monday," he said.

Harvey went into the hall, and sent for the faithful Limbian.

When he entered the room he saw at a glance that something had happened.

"You taken worse, Mast' Jack?" he said.

"Look here, Monday, you must do me a service," said Jack.

"Monday lay down um life, sare. Can't say any more."

"I know that, and perhaps you will have to risk your life. Miss Emily has been carried off, we expect by Davis."

"Missey Emily gone, sare?"

"Yes; not an hour ago."

"Where she go to, sare?" asked Monday.

"That we can only guess. I have heard that Mr. Davis's father has a house a few miles inland, which he very seldom uses. Find out where that is; go there at once, and bring us what news you can."

"Monday him go now, sare. He find the Missey Emily."

"Take off those togs, and go about as if you were a native of this place. You will attract less attention," said Harvey.

"A good suggestion," remarked Mr. Mole. "I forgive you now for pumping upon me, Harvey, I do indeed, and pardon you freely, for your cleverness."

"I thank you, sir; I'll make a note of it," answered Harvey.

"Off you go, Monday," continued Jack, "and mind you don't come back without news of some sort."

Monday nodded, and started on his errand.

Turning to Harvey, Jack said—

"You and I will work the city. If I could only catch that cowardly hound Davis, I'd wring the secret out of him somehow."

"Perhaps," said Mr. Mole, "it is not Mr. Davis after all."

"Who else can it be?" replied Jack.

Puzzled at this question, Mr. Mole was unable to give any answer.

"If I were not so ill I would accompany you," he remarked. "You must take the wish for the deed."

Harvey was as much concerned as his friend, and he gladly accompanied him on his voyage of discovery.

"Let's go to the club first," said Dick. "We may see or hear something of Davis there."

A short walk brought them to the club, where they found several people they did not know talking about the fire.

In a small community like that of Singapore a fire is an event of importance.

Talking to some friends, Jack saw Frank Davis, who did not seem any the worse for his immersion.

With some difficulty he restrained himself from rushing up to him.

The folly of such a proceeding occurred to him, and he fortunately drove back the wild beast feeling that will take posession of all of us at times."

"Watch him," whispered Harvey. "We can always follow him when he attempts to go."

To Jack's intense surprise, Davis no sooner saw him than he walked up, and extending his hand before everybody, exclaimed—

"Will you shake hands with me, Mr. Harkaway?"

"With you?" replied Jack.

"Yes; I was a little hasty this morning, and provoked you. I am willing to forgive that disagreeable shove you gave me into the water, for I can't bear malice."

The members of the club were much interested in this scene.

"Capital fellow!" "Good heart!" "Always said so," and so on arose from various quarters.

"I would rather not make friends with you," said Jack.

"Come, come, don't cherish a nasty feeling. You a sailor, Harkaway, and treasure up a grudge!" exclaimed Captain Hammond in his cheery voice.

"I have my reasons," said Jack.

"I am sure they can't be very good ones."

"I'm the best judge of that," Jack exclaimed, dryly.

"Well, you must please yourself, Mr. Harkaway," continued Frank Davis, with an apparently open smile. "I have made the advance, which there was no occasion I should do, I'm sure; but we have been friends and travelled together, so that I can afford to put a little ill-feeling in my pocket. Have you hurt your arm—dear me! I did not notice that you wore it in a sling."

Jack was confounded at his cool impudence.

"I was stabbed in the crowd at the fire," he said, looking Davis straight in the face.

The latter did not quail or flinch in the least. He bore the scrutiny without so much as lowering his eyes.

"He's got the nerve of old Nick himself," thought Jack.

"Stabbed!" repeated Davis, incredulously. "Now you are drawing upon your imagination."

"I am telling the plain truth without any varnish," answered Jack.

Many gentlemen crowded round him, and pressed him with a dozen questions, to all of which Jack replied—

"Ask Mr. Davis. He pretends to be ignorant of an attack which was directed at my life, when he knows more about it than I do."

Eyes were turned inquiringly at Davis.

"Really, gentlemen," he exclaimed, "Mr. Harkaway is an enigma to me, and I am at a loss to understand his meaning."

"He insinuates that you tried to assassinate him," exclaimed one gentleman.

"No, I don't insinuate anything," answered Jack. "I say openly that he hired a man to kill me, and I can prove it."

"How?"

"By the testimony of my black servant who saw him in the crowd, and heard him point me out to the ruffian in his pay."

Frank Davis turned away with a laugh.

"Is he drunk?" he exclaimed.

"I'm as sober as you are, perhaps more so," replied Jack, furiously; "and, in spite of your sneers, I'll unmask you yet."

"Gentlemen," said Frank Davis, appealing to the members of the club, "I have tried to sooth the savage breast. What can I do more?"

"No, no; let him alone. Give him up," said his friends. "He must be mad."

What Jack would have said or done it is difficult to say, had not Captain Hammond seized him by the arm and drawn him towards the door.

"Let go my arm," said Jack, struggling.

"No, I will not. There will be a riot presently if you stop."

"What if there is?"

"Every man in the club except myself is against you. Come along," persisted Captain Hammond.

"I will not go, to let that fellow have the best of me," said Jack.

"You shall. Come, come, I am a man, and you are only a boy after all. I will have my own way in this instance," Captain Hammond, said goodnaturedly.

"That is right. Get him away. Our time will come," remarked Harvey.

He was not blinded with passion and a sense of wrong as Jack was, and he saw that it would be of no use to have a row in the club just then.

By the exercise of main force, Captain Hammond drew Jack out of the room.

Presently they stood in the street, Jack panting and glaring fiercely at his friend.

"Well," laughed the captain, "are you going to eat me?"

Jack said nothing.

"Come, that's better. I thought you were going to make a meal off me. Take a stroll and let us talk the matter over."

As Jack hesitated, Harvey said—

"Do, there's a good fellow. Captain Hammond's advice is sensible I feel sure."

Jack put his uninjured arm in that of the captain's.

Harvey took the other side, and they walked up the quay.

CHAPTER XC.

MONDAY AND THE BLOODHOUND.

It was not difficult for Monday to discover the locality in which Mr. Davis's country house was situated.

But when he heard that he possessed two, it was not easy to decide which to go to.

The idea which had struck Jack was that Frank Davis had carried off Emily to a country residence, where by threats and confinement he would try to induce her to marry him.

If he had succeeded in his attempt to assassinate Jack, his task would have been easier.

Mr. Mole would not have occupied himself much about Emily, and it was doubtful whether Harvey would have done more than communicate with the authorities about the affair.

When Monday, who thoroughly endorsed his master's idea, heard that one of Mr. Davis's houses was situated in a lonely place and seldom or ever inhabited he concluded that it was very likely Frank had caused her to be conveyed there.

It was late in the day when he had gathered all the information he wanted, but he did not hesitate to start at once and on foot, for the house.

The moon was shining brightly when he reached it, and saw a small one-storied pavilion-like house, surrounded with those verandahs so common in the east.

Gardens filled with lovely flowers and shrubs environed it, except at the back, where were built the stable and domestic offices.

Penetrating through the gardens, Monday cautiously advanced to the house.

A window in the Venetian style opened on to the lawn, and a light burning on a table enabled him to look inside.

Lying on a sofa, bathed in tears, with her hair hanging loosely over her shoulders he saw Emily, who was evidently plunged into the depths of despair, and overwhelmd with grief.

He was about to rush forward, when he found the window was carefully guarded with thick iron bars, which, while permitting the cool evening air to enter effectually prevented anyone going in or out.

Advancing cautiously to the bars, Monday said in a low voice—

"Missey Emily, Missey Emily."

The girl started, and rising, looked eagerly towards him.

"Is it you, Monday?" she cried. "Oh, I am so glad. Where am I?"

"You not know?" asked Monday, in surprise.

"No. I have not the remotest idea. All I am aware of is that I was induced to go down the street to meet Jack, thrust into a carriage, driven off at a gallop, taken here and put into this room, where I have only seen an old negress."

"This Mist' Davis's house," said Monday.

"Then it is he who has carried me off. Does Jack know this?"

"Him suspect it, Missey Emily, and he send me to find out."

"Where is he now?" she inquired.

"In Singapore; but he soon come take you out," answered Monday.

"Oh, pray lose no time, but go at once. I am so frightened."

"Monday go now, Missey Emily. Before to-morrow morning she get 'way."

Emily thanked him heartily.

"Keep up your pluck, missey; all be right soon," said Monday.

He retired as cautiously as he came, and reaching the extremity of the garden jumped over the wooden fence, alighting in the road.

He was much pleased with his success, and prepared for a sharp run home.

All at once the sound of horse's hoofs fell upon his ears, and by the moonlight he saw a man on horseback, followed by a big dog of the bloodhound species, approaching him.

His sharp eyes enabled him to recognise Frank Davis.

But the recognition was not mutual.

Stripped to the skin like an ordinary native, Monday appeared to Frank to be some prowling robber.

"Hillo, you black thief, what are you doing here at this time of night?" he exclaimed.

"Do? Nothing, sare," replied Monday. "Him as much right on the road as you."

"Have you, my good fellow, we'll see about that," answered Davis. "Here, Juno! Here, lass."

The dog looked up in its master's face and wagged its tail.

"After him, girl; fetch him down," continued Davis.

Monday took to his heels, having no fancy to be mangled and torn by the bloodthirsty hound.

His only weapon of defence was a long knife, which he had stuck in his girdle.

Although he could run fast, the hound could run faster, and sprang after him with huge bounds.

Hearing the painting brute just behind him, Monday turned, and drawing his knife, stood at bay.

Frank galloped up to see what he called fun.

A fight between his dog and a common nigger just suited his truculent and cruel disposition.

"Hi, at him! Stick to him! Hi, at him! Loo! Loo!" cried Davis.

Encouraged by her master's voice, Juno seized Monday by the arm, and drew him on his knees.

Then a terrible fight began.

Monday stabbed at the dog, and the dog tore his flesh in various places, always trying to get at his throat.

This Monday struggled to prevent, as he knew the beast would strangle him if she succeeded in doing so.

They rolled over and over in the dusty road.

Frank laughed immoderately at the sport, and kept on encouraging the dog.

At length Monday made a home thrust, which struck the heart of his enemy.

With a short yelp, the dog turned over on her back dead.

"Confound you," cried Davis angrily, "you've killed my best hound. If I had a pistol about me, I'd shoot you."

Monday rose with difficulty; he was streaming with blood, and was much exhausted.

Game to the last, however, he nerved himself for another encounter.

Rushing forward, he seized Davis by the right leg, and jerked him upwards.

Unprepared for such a novel assault, Davis was pitched off his horse, and felt half-stunned by the fall into the road.

The next moment Monday, with the agility of a deer, was in the saddle.

Turning the horse's head in the right direction, he kicked its sides with his heels and was off like the wind towards Singapore.

Frank Davis picked himself up with a rueful expression, and looked after his horse.

"That's what I call a clever nigger," he said with a laugh. "He's killed my best hound, and hooked it off with one of the fastest horses in the governor's stable. Well, I shan't holloa. He deserves it, hang me if he doesn't."

He shook the dust off his clothes, and walked along to the house.

"Now," he muttered, "for an interview with my little Emily. I wonder how she will receive me. It's a pity my fellow did not kill that infernal Harkaway right out, but I haven't done with him yet."

We must leave this amiable young gentleman to visit the bird in the cage, while we accompany Monday on his wild career to the city.

It was nearly midnight when he dismounted at the door of the hotel.

Jack and Harvey had just come in, after a long walk with Captain Hammond, which had cooled Jack's hot head.

Mr. Mole had gone to bed.

Bursting into the room, covered with blood and dust, Monday appeared to resemble some dreadful spectre.

"Why, Monday, what's come to you?" asked Jack.

"Him found Missey Emily, sare," said Monday.

"Have you? That's first rate. You're a trump, Monday; but you're hurt."

"Never mind um hurt, sare. Mist' Davis he set um dog on me."

"What! that bloodhound I have seen with him? What a beastly shame."

"Great big dog, big as a man, sare. Monday kill him with um knife, and come home on Mist' Davis' horse."

"Good again. You can do it," cried Harvey.

"But tell us all about it."

"No time lose, sir. Just tie up Monday's wounds," replied the black, "and order carriage and two horses; quick, tell um all on the road. Missey Emily and Mist' Davis all 'lone together."

"He's right," answered Jack. "Cut downstairs, Dick, and order the carriage while I tie up his bites; he's bleeding like a pig."

Harvey went downstairs, and Jack getting a sponge and a basin of water, wiped away the blood and dust, and then, tearing a shirt into strips, bound up the principal injuries which the black had sustained.

"Now um all right. Lose no more blood. That what um 'fraid of, sare," said Monday.

At the same time he tottered with weakness, and was obliged to lean against the table for support.

"Here, drink this," said Jack, pouring him out half a tumbler of brandy.

He did so, and it revived his drooping energies.

When the carriage was ready Monday directed the driver what road to take, and as they went along he related his adventures to his young master, who highly commended him for his cleverness and his courage.

"That must have been a nasty tussle with the pup," remarked Harvey.

"It would have been all up with Monday if he had not carried a knife. I know what those cross-bred Cuban hounds are," said Dick.

"Him think once it all up, sare," replied Monday. "The big brute him get me down and his face come close to my face. Ugh! It close shave."

They stopped the carriage at a little distance from the house, and told the driver to pull up by the side of the road and wait.

"Don't take the bridles off, or get down from your box, even," said Jack;

"we may want to bolt in a hurry. Let this case of pistols remain by your side, for I shall sit on the box, and we can't tell what will happen."

The man said he fully understood, and Monday led the way to the back of the house.

It would have been useless to go to the front, as it was impossible to get through the iron bars which guarded the windows.

A door stood open, through which they passed, walking on tiptoe.

The sound of voices guided them to a room at the end of a long corridor.

"Listen!" said Jack, holding up his hand as a signal for his companions to stop.

They did so.

It was Emily's voice.

"I tell you plainly, Mr. Davis," she said, "that I can never love you, and after this declaration, if you persist in annoying me, you are guilty of an outrage which no gentleman should be guilty of."

"Lovely Emily," replied the young man, "my love for you must be my excuse. I am passionately fond of you. With my wealth I can make you take a position that a princess might envy."

"All that I have heard before. I beg you to restore me to my friends."

"Your friends cannot help you. Believe me, you are entirely in my power."

"Not so much, perhaps, as you may think," Emily said.

"Do you defy me?" Davis asked. "If so, there is nothing before you but a long captivity. Who could find you in this lonely house?"

"Jack Harkaway would find me anywhere," she answered.

"Bravo, Emily!" muttered Jack.

"Do not rely upon him; he is a broken reed," said Davis.

"Am I?" muttered Jack, again. "I'll let you know, my tulip, in a minute or two."

"Mr. Davis," said Emily, "I have always believed you to be a gentleman. Why do you act in this extraordinary manner?"

"Because I love you, and mean to have a kiss," he replied.

"Sir," she exclaimed, "I am helpless and defenceless, yet I have the weapons nature gave me, and if you dare to touch me with your little finger even, I will bite and scratch!"

"Bravo, Emily!" whispered Jack, a second time.

"By Heaven!" replied Davis, "you are very lovely. I will have a kiss, if I die for it."

He helped himself to some wine— several decanters were standing on the table—and approached her with an amorous leer on his face.

"Help! help!" cried Emily, as his arm encircled her waist. "Help! Oh, Jack, why are you not here to protect me?"

There was a sound of feet in the passage.

A heavy body rushed towards Davis, a fist clenched so firmly that it resembled iron, was dashed into his face, and he fell on the floor stunned.

The next moment Jack held Emily in his arms, and was covering her lips with kisses.

"I thought you wouldn't come, Jack dear," she murmured.

"Just in time," replied Jack.

Harvey and Monday were busily engaged in tying Davis's hands and legs.

Having done this, Harvey exclaimed—

"What shall we do with him?"

"Have you tied him fast?" asked Jack.

"Yes."

"He can't wriggle out?"

"If he does, I'll forgive him," replied Harvey.

"Then chuck him under the sofa like a hundred of coals, and let him lie there for a bit. I've got a new idea for punishing him, but it will keep a little while. What have you got in those bottles?"

Harvey examined the bottles on the table, and replied—

"All sorts."

"Open some champagne; I'll have a lush of something to celebrate this victory," exclaimed Jack.

CHAPTER CXI.

TAR AND FEATHERS.

HARVEY contemptuously rolled Frank Davis under the sofa, where he lay as still as a mouse, either being really stunned by Jack's sledge-hammer blow or pretending to be so.

Not a sound escaped him in reality.

"It was fortunate you came when you did," said Emily. "I can't tell you how thankful I am."

"You must thank Monday," replied Jack.

Monday was grinning with delight.

He presented a singular sight, covered with white bandages as he was.

"Is he hurt, or are his clothes torn?" asked Emily.

"It isn't clothes; it's bandages," replied Jack. "Tell the lady all about it. What are you grinning at, you old mummy?"

Monday complied with this request, and Emily thanked him very much for his bravery.

Suddenly Jack jumped up from the sofa with a yell.

"What's the row?" said Harvey.

"Something's bitten me in the calf of the leg, and made its teeth meet," replied Jack. "Have you any dogs here, Emily?"

"I have seen none," she answered.

He looked under the sofa and found that Davis had rolled over, and so been able to bite him.

"You brute," exclaimed Jack. "If you weren't bound hard and fast, upon my word I could kick you in the face. Why didn't you fasten him up better, Dick?"

"I thought I had," replied Harvey. "It was my impression he couldn't wriggle a little bit."

"Bring him out, and put him in the middle of the room," exclaimed Jack.

Harvey hauled him out, and Davis looked up in Harkaway's eyes with a malicious expression of gratified malignity.

"I shouldn't care if I had been bitten by a decent sort of man," said Jack. "This cad may poison the flesh or some-thing. Perhaps he's been eating mouldy victuals."

Harvey laughed.

"He's not so bad as that," he said.

"When are we to go home?" asked Emily.

"Presently, my dear," answered Jack. "I have a carriage waiting outside. But first of all I must settle accounts with this cur here."

"What are you going to do with him?"

"You'll see if you live long enough," said Jack; adding, "Monday."

"Yes, sare," replied the black.

"Go into the yard, and see if you can find a barrel of tar."

"Tar?" exclaimed Emily. "What's that for?"

"Don't ask questions," answered Jack. "Be a good girl, and you'll see what you will see."

"There generally is tar about a country place to do up the palings with," said Harvey.

"Of course," answered Jack. "When you have found it, bring it in here."

"Yes, sare," replied Monday.

"What am I to do?" asked Harvey.

"Go into the yard and kill a couple of geese or half-a-dozen fowls, and bring them here."

"Are you going to have a feed?"

"Never mind; do as I tell you. Off you go—both of you," said Jack.

Monday and Harvey started together, and were gone nearly half-an-hour.

Jack put his arm round Emily's waist, and looking at Davis, said—

"You wanted a kiss, just now, from the best girl that ever lived?"

Davis made no answer.

Jack got up and kicked him in the ribs.

"Answer when you are spoken to, or it will be the worse for you," he exclaimed.

"If I did what then?" asked Davis, with some of his old independent manner.

"Just this; see me kiss her. That's all, old boy. That's you share."

Jack drew Emily to him as he spoke, and she let her head fall on his breast while he bent down and kissed her as he liked.

When he had done, he said—

"How do you like that? Nice isn't it, Mr. Cowardly Davis?"

Davis groaned.

If he could have got at Jack he would have killed him then and there, regardless of consequences.

Harvey came in first with two fine geese, a turkey, and three hens, which he had surprised in the hen house, and killed by wringing their necks.

"There they are," he said.

"Chuck them down," replied Jack.

"What am I to do?" inquired Emily, with a smile.

"Help Harvey to pluck them, and throw the feathers in a heap on the floor."

"Oh! what a mess it will make on this beautiful carpet," she exclaimed.

"Never mind that. I think I shall burn the house down before I go."

"Oh, Jack?"

"You needn't say 'Oh, Jack!' as if I were going to jump down your throat," said Jack laughing. "Get to work instantly, miss."

Presently Monday returned, lugging a small barrel of tar with him.

Jack went to Davis, and putting him on a chair, took a knife out of his pocket and stood over him.

"Don't kill me," whined Davis, who thought his last hour had come.

"No fear," answered Jack; "I know a trick worth two of killing you."

He began to cut away his clothes until he was naked to the waist.

"What are you going to do with me?" asked Davis, who was puzzled at all these preparations.

"You'll know all in good time," answered Jack; who added—"Monday, as I tar him you throw feathers on him."

Monday grinned all over his face.

Jack took up a turkey's wing, and dipping it in the tar, smeared Davis all over with the sticky stuff.

Monday threw handful after handful of feathers over him, and he began gradually to take the appearance of a feathered creature.

Jack left his face unsmeared, so that people might know him; but he feathered his hair, and covered him in a most artistic manner.

Frank Davis' rage knew no bounds.

He swore, raved, and threatened them all with the severest penalties of the law.

"Don't you talk about law, my hearty," returned Jack. "You have carried off a young lady, tried to have me stabbed, and endeavoured to worry with your dog a poor inoffensive fellow you saw on the road. Law, indeed! I'll give you enough law, if you want it."

When he was thoroughly tarred and feathered Jack said—

"Now we are ready to start. Come along, Emily; take my arm. Dick, see to the bird."

Harvey touched Davis on the leg, and exclaimed—

"Get up."

Davis refused to move.

"Won't budge," said Harvey.

"Won't he?" replied Jack. "Emily, give me a pin."

She handed him one, which Jack stuck into Frank Davis' thigh.

He sprang up in a moment with a cry of pain.

"Found your legs, have you, old fellow? Thought you would," laughed Jack.

Davis had his legs untied, and walked by Harvey's side, his arms being fastened behind his back.

They all went to the carriage, which was waiting for them in the road, and getting in were driven to the city.

Davis was made to sit by himself on the front seat, Harvey standing over him.

Monday got on the box, and Jack and Emily sat side by side.

When they reached Singapore it was early morning.

Under the tropics people get up early and sleep in the middle of the day when the sun is fiercest.

Consequently the city was astir.

When the principal street was reached Jack stopped the carriage near the market place, and told Davis to get out.

"Get out here?" he exclaimed, with horror.

"Yes; out you go—immediately, if not sooner. Stir your stumps," answered Jack.

Reluctantly Davis descended the steps and stood in the street.

He presented a strange spectacle.

Half man, half bird,

"JACK HAVING FIRED HIS PISTOL AT ONE, RAN AT THE OTHER WITH HIS DIRK."

When the people in the street saw him they set up a great shout.

"Go on," said Jack; "cut along, or I shall stick a pin into you again."

Davis knew the locality very well, and his father's offices were not far off, so that he decided to run as fast as he could through the streets.

He made a start, but could not go very quickly owing to his hands being tied behind his back.

"Men, women, and children howled at him and threw any object that came nandiest, and it was only when bruised and exhausted that he reached a haven of refuge.

"That will teach him a lesson," said Jack, laughing heartily.

"I should think so," replied Harvey. "He will be a week getting the tar and feathers off."

"Mind one thing, Emily," exclaimed Jack; "don't you be humbugged again."

"I will take very good care I am not," replied Emily; "and believe me, dear Jack, and you, too, Monday, that I shall never, never forget your kindness."

"What have I done," said Harvey, "that I should not be thought of?"

"Oh, you're nobody; you can go and play," replied Jack.

When they reached the hotel, they inquired for Mr. Mole.

The servant said that he had called him, but he refused to get up.

"Look here," said Jack, "perhaps Mole's taken worse; he said he had a cold. I will go and see to him."

"All right," said Harvey, "I will see Monday looked after. His wounds are getting stiff."

Harvey and Monday went away together, and Jack saw Emily to her bedroom, gave her a kiss, and went to Mr. Mole.

"How do, sir?" said Jack. "We've got back the lost dove."

"Glad to hear it, Harkaway; it is more than you deserve." answered Mr. Mole, who was wrapped up in bed, as if he had a severe attack of influenza, and lived in Kamschatka.

He wore a nightcap, which culminated in a most ludicrous tassel.

"Get up, sir," said Jack, "and take a turn with me in the fresh morning air."

"No, Harkaway, I distinctly refuse," answered Mr. Mole. "I have been very badly treated, and I shall not move from this bed for a month."

"What, sir, sleep for a month?" cried Jack.

"I did not say sleep, but I shall not get out of this bed for a month, and during that time you cannot play me any tricks. I have been pumped upon, and the result is a severe cold, which only the most careful nursing will cure."

"You've got a tile off, sir," replied Jack.

"Cease, if you please, to make vulgar allusions to the state of my mind, and leave me," said Mr. Mole.

"As you like, sir," replied Jack. "Hope you will be in a better temper when I see you again."

Mr. Mole pulled his nightcap over his eyes, and settled himself down for a second sleep.

Jack was tired and turned in, marvelling at the peculiar state of mind in which he had found Mr. Mole.

CHAPTER XCII.

MR. MOLE GOES TO BED FOR A MONTH.

THE boys did not breakfast till late.

Both were worn out with the fatigue and excitement of the previous night.

Monday's wounds, though not dangerous, were exceedingly painful, and the doctor who had been called in advised him not to move out of his bed for a day or two.

When Harvey and Jack met over their coffee, the former said—

"Where's Mole?"

"Gone to bed for a month," replied Jack.

"Go on!" said Harvey. "What's the use of chaffing me?"

"I'm not chaffing. He swore last night

he would not move. He is sulky because we pumped upon him."

"Does he mean it?"

"I believe he does."

"Oh, I can't live without old Mole," replied Harvey.

"Why?"

"He's such fun. We must have him out."

"It's all very well to say, have him out," answered Jack. "But how are you going to do it?"

"Easy enough," replied Harvey. "Look at those fellows in the street."

Jack looked out of the window, and saw some jugglers, who were performing with snakes, which they twined round their necks and even allowed to bite them.

"Well," said Jack, "what have those men to do with Mole?"

"I'll show you," replied Harvey.

He went downstairs, and talked to one of the jugglers for a few minutes, and when he came back, he carried something with him in a small basket.

"What have you got there?" asked Jack, curiously.

"A fine young cobra," replied Harvey. "It isn't dangerous, so don't start; besides it can't get out, unless I open the basket."

"Isn't it poisonous?"

"It was once upon a time; but my juggling friend told me that they had drawn his poison fangs, and that if the thing did bite now, it wouldn't do any harm."

"I see," exclaimed Jack. "Still I don't like snakes, whether they are harmless or not."

"I don't suppose Mole does either. Don't you think he would jump, if he found a thing of this sort in his bed?"

"By Jove!" cried Jack, laughing; "he'd have a fit."

"Sorry for him, but he will have to make acquaintance with this new sort of bedfellow."

"When and how is the nameless deed to be done?"

"Presently he will get up to have his bed made, and then I shall introduce the snake. It will be all a lark."

"You're improving," said Jack, patting him on his back.

"It's being so much with you," replied Harvey. "Evil communications corrupt good manners. Come up to Mole's room."

They ascended the stairs together, and found Mr. Mole sitting in his dressing-gown, with a cotton nightcap on his head, looking out of the window, through which a cool breeze entered.

The servant was just finishing making the bed.

Jack went up and spoke to Mr. Mole, and, when the servant departed, Harvey opened the basket, and allowed the serpent to glide into the bed.

Then he, too, went up, and talked to Mr. Mole.

"Going to turn in again, sir," he said; "or have you thought better of it?"

"No," replied Mr. Mole, "I intend to keep my bed until we sail for England. You boys shall not play me any more tricks, I promise you, for I will keep out of your way."

"What shall we do without you, sir?" said Jack.

"You should have thought of that before. I am sure the deprivation of my society must be a great blow to you."

"You're sulking, sir. Don't sulk; it's childish," exclaimed Jack.

"I am the best judge of my own actions, and I tell you flatly, once for all, that I have gone to bed for a month, and no persuasion on your part shall get me out."

"Won't anything induce you to change your mind?"

"No power on earth will do it, Harkaway," answered Mr. Mole, firmly.

He threw off his dressing-gown and stood in his night-shirt, looking very comical with his old-fashioned nightcap on his head.

"In my bed I am at peace," he murmured.

Turning the clothes down a little way, he crept in, and a smile of placid satisfaction stole over his features.

All at once the placid expression vanished.

He fidgeted in bed, and seemed ill at ease.

"What's the matter, sir?" asked Jack.

"The slut who made this bed has left something in it. I can feel something about my legs. What the deuce is it?" exclaimed Mr. Mole, uneasily.

"Better have a look, sir. Perhaps it is a dead dog."

"Drat it!" continued Mole. "It's something alive. It keeps on moving."

He rose up and threw down the bed-clothes.

The snake had been making itself a nest to go to sleep in, and was annoyed at being disturbed in the midst of its preparations.

It coiled its tail, and sat upright, darting its forked tongue in and out, and emitting a sharp hiss.

"The Lord be good to me!" cried Mole, in dire terror.

"Why, it's a snake," said Harvey. "How on earth could it get there?"

"It's a deadly cobra," continued Mole. "A venomous serpent. Oh, Lord! oh, Lord! I wish I was well home again Strike it, Harvey. Take it by the neck and throw it out of window."

"Thank you, sir; I'd rather not, if it is the same to you," replied Harvey, coldly.

"Harkaway," pleaded Mr. Mole, "you are a brave boy."

"Hope so, sir."

"For goodness sake, seize the snake! It will spring upon me. Already it is fixing me with its awful eyes. Save me, Harkaway; all my worldly goods shall be yours. Save me—save me!"

"Nasty things snakes, sir; don't like to handle them," said Jack.

Mr. Mole's terror increased every moment.

The snake did not attempt to fly at him.

It had been more than two years with the jugglers, and was used to human beings, and expected to be taken up and put through its performance.

"Look," cried Mr. Mole, white with fear, "look at the venomous creature. It will dart at me, fix its fangs in my flesh, and in half an hour, I, Isaac Mole, will have ceased to exist. Oh, Lord! oh Lord!"

"Neither Harvey nor I dare touch it, sir," said Jack.

"What am I to do?" asked Mole.

"If I were you, sir, I'd bolt. Perhaps there are more in the room. There is generally a nest where you see one."

Finding that Mr. Mole did not attempt to handle it, the snake, which was inclined to be tame, thought it would commence the performance by itself.

It put itself in motion, gliding along Mr. Mole's leg, and causing him to utter the most awful yells.

Then it wound round his arm, and reaching his neck, coiled itself in two folds, and bringing its head to a level with Mr. Mole's nose, looked in a half affectionate manner at him.

Jack and Harvey laughed immoderately.

They had never seen anything so funny.

"It wants to kiss you, sir. Stroke it," said Jack.

For a moment Mr. Mole had been paralyzed with fear.

Recovering himself, he sprang out of bed, and in his night-gown and cap, descended the stairs six at a time, cleared the hall at a few bounds, dashed into the street and ran for his life.

He uttered incoherent cries, and the crowd in the street thinking he was mad, ran after him, hooting and yelling like demons.

The snake clung fast, evidently regarding this as a new performance.

Mr. Mole had only one idea, and that was to throw himself headlong into the water of the harbour, which was at the bottom of the street.

He thought that land snakes could not live in water.

But just as he reached the quay, a rough grasp seized his arm and forced him on his knees.

The jerk threw off the snake, which glided away, looking for its basket.

Unfortunately for it, some boys in the crowd saw it, and speedily dispatched it with stones.

The person who had stopped Mr. Mole's wild career was Captain Hammond.

"A madman," shouted the throng.

"Who are you," asked the captain, "and what are you doing?"

Mr. Mole put up his hand, and finding the snake was gone, breathed again.

At the same moment he looked up and recognised Captain Hammond.

"Do you not know me?" he said.

"No; hang me if I do," replied the captain.

"I am Mr. Mole."

"Harkaway's Mole?" asked the skipper.

"If you choose to put it so. I am anybody's Mole. Take me back to the hotel; the danger is over now."

"What danger?"

"Snakes."

"Snakes?" repeated the captain. "Humbug. They don't come into this city.

"Don't they! There was one in my bed. But take me back. I fear, from the tittering of the crowd, that I present a singular not to say a ludicrous appearance."

The captain gave him his arm, and in a very tottering state, Mr. Mole was conducted back to his hotel.

Nothing would induce him to go into his bedroom again; he was afraid of more snakes, and throwing himself into an armchair, he sighed deeply and shivered.

"If ever I am caught out of England again," he exclaimed, "I'll buy a stick and beat myself."

Harvey took Captain Hammond on one side and let him into the joke, at which he laughed.

Mr. Mole, however, did not suspect Harvey's share in the matter.

He thought the snake had crept into the house through the window.

In fact, his mind was so perturbed, that he could scarcely think at all.

"Heaven has been good to me," he said. "I will make a vow—in olden times, people, after a great mercy had been vouchsafed to them, used to go on a pilgrimage or a crusade. I can't go about like a pilgrim or a crusader. What shall I do Harkaway?"

"Go to bed again, sir."

"No!" replied Mr. Mole, with a shudder. "No more bed for me in Singapore. I shall sleep on a sofa during the remainder of our stay here."

"About this vow, sir?"

"Ah! What shall I do to show my gratitude for my preservation from that poisonous reptile? I will never pass a blind man without giving him sixpence. There, Harkaway, what do you think of that?"

"Make it a bob, sir; a tanner's mean, and will look shabby."

"A shilling be it then. But what are you duing there?" said Mr. Mole.

"Opening a case of wine, sir."

"Wine?"

"Yes. It has just come. It is directed to 'Mr. Harkaway, with Captain Hammond's compliments.'"

"Ah! Something very choice, I dare say," said Mr. Mole, smacking his lips. "Just what I want to revive me after my trials. Pour me out a tumbler full. I will taste it, Harkaway."

"All right," said Jack. "You shall have the first swig."

He drew out a bottle from the case, and removing the cork, poured out a tumbler full, which he handed to Mr. Mole.

The latter drank it at a draught.

"What do you think of it?" asked Jack.

"Not bad—not bad, by any means; but it's funny tasting stuff, and has a burning in the mouth," replied Mr. Mole.

"Your mouth's out of taste, sir."

"What's that?" inquired Captain Hammond, who had just finished listening to Harvey's relation of the trick of which Mr. Mole was the victim.

"We have tapped your wine, captain," said Jack.

"My wine?" repeated Hammond in surprise.

"Yes! the wine you sent me just now, and for which I have not had an opportunity to thank you before now."

"My dear fellow, there must be some mistake!" said Captain Hammond.

"How?" inquired Jack.

"I sent you no wine."

"Look at the direction on the case," said Jack. "Here it is, as plain as a pike-staff: 'Mr. Harkaway, with Captain Hammond's compliments.'"

The captain looked carefully at the label.

"Yes; you are right so far," he said. "But still I'll swear I sent you no wine, neither is that direction in my handwriting."

Jack had refilled Mr. Mole's tumbler, and was going to drink, when the captain said—

"Don't touch it, my lad. There is something wrong here."

Jack regarded him with astonishment, in which both Harvey and Mr. Mole shared.

What new danger or mystery threatened them?

CHAPTER XCIII.

MORE TREACHERY.

THE captain was positive that he had not sent the boys the wine, and Mr. Mole became alarmed at having drunk it.

"It seems to me," said the captain, "that this direction on the case is in Mr. Davis's writing."

"My enemy," remarked Jack.

"Yes, indeed. We have heard at the club all about your tarring and feathering him, and then turning him up in the market-place, more like a bird than a human being. He is the laughing-stock of the town."

"Why then should he become civil, and send me some wine?" asked Jack.

"Perhaps it is poisoned. Let us procure a dog, and try the experiment on him."

"No need to do that," said Jack; "Mr. Mole has drunk half a tumbler—Hullo! what's the matter with him?"

Mr. Mole had fallen into a chair, and was putting both hands to his stomach as if in pain.

"Got the mullygrubs, sir?" said Jack.

"I'm very bad. I was taken all at once," replied Mr. Mole, groaning. "Send for a doctor. Get a stomach-pump."

"Good idea, stomach-pump," said Jack. "Run, Dick, and fetch a sawbones. I should like to see Mole pumped."

Mr. Mole sank from the chair to the floor and writhed in sinuous contortions, while Harvey went for the doctor.

"I'm poisoned," he said. "It's very hard to be poisoned. Oh, Lord! what a time they are getting that pump!"

The captain and Jack were much alarmed at the symptoms displayed by Mr. Mole.

There was no doubt that the wine had been poisoned, and that Frank Davis had hoped by these means to kill the whole party.

It was a great relief when at last the doctor arrived with the strange apparatus called the stomach-pump, which was immediately applied.

Instead of feeling any relief, and getting better, Mr. Mole's limbs contracted, and he appeared to be sinking into a state of stupor.

"He is not going to croak, is he?" said Jack.

"I cannot tell," said the doctor. "It is a serious case."

He put his hand on his breast.

There was no movement.

"I fear," he added, "that the unfortunate gentleman is gone."

"I'll have it out of that Davis," cried Jack.

"Poor old Mole," said Harvey.

"Well," continued Jack; "I wouldn't have lost Mole for anything. Is there nothing you can do, doctor?"

"He is beyond human aid. Allow me to give you the card of an undertaker. In this climate, the body must be buried to-morrow morning."

"I'm flummoxed," said Jack. "This is getting severe. It's cut me up more than anything."

Seeing he could do no more, the doctor retired.

Jack had Mr. Mole put on his bed, and covered with a sheet.

The captain went to communicate with the police of the town, who said that the evidence against Mr. Davis was not strong enough to warrant his arrest.

In fact Davis's father was so great a man in the town, that they were afraid of attacking him.

Both Harkaway and Harvey were much shocked, and Emily joined in their grief.

They had narrowly escaped a sudden death themselves.

"It's an awful grief, just now," remarked Jack, "when our troubles are nearly over."

"He wasn't a bad sort," said Harvey, "and it makes me mad to think that the poor beggar, who had done nothing, should suffer through our rows."

"I've a good mind to have him embalmed, and take him back to England in a glass case," said Jack.

"Better bury him. You be chief mourner," replied Harvey.

"No. I should like to have him mummified. There are always embalmers in these countries; we must inquire for one," persisted Jack.

Emily laughed.

"I am ashamed of you, Emmy," said Jack, putting on a severe look. "Come here and give me a kiss, by way of doing penance, at once."

"If you want one, you can come and take it," she answered coquettishly, adding—

"I know it is a very dreadful thing to laugh at a time like this, but the idea of poor dear Mr. Mole being made into a mummy, is so funny."

"So it is when you come to think of it," observed Harvey.

"I don't see it," replied Jack. "Mole, in a glass case, looking as large as life, with a suitable epitaph, would be highly edifying. "Suppose we were to say—

"This is the mummified Mole,
Who was a jolly old soul."

"Give us another ryhme, Dick."

"Let the bell toll for poor old Mole,"
replied Harvey.

"That's better. Go on," exclaimed Jack, encouragingly.

"He wasn't worth a farden,
Till he got his tea-garden,"

"That's bad. You began well, as you generally do, but you always fall off," Jack exclaimed.

"If you can't make a better epitaph than that, you ought to give up the attempt," said Emily; "and I think your trying to do so is much more disgraceful than my laughing."

"We don't mean anything, Emmy," replied Jack. "If I wasn't to talk and chaff a little, I should cry. You don't know how this has cut me."

"I can say ditto to that," remarked Harvey. "It's entirely crabbed any pleasure I feel in going back to England."

They became grave after this, and it soon was time to retire to rest.

Early the next morning they were astir, and the first visitor at the hotel was the undertaker, who was a Dutchman, unable to speak a word of English.

Jack looked at his card, and read "Mynheer Van Clootz," and seeing the word "undertaker" in English, divined the motive of his visit, and sadly led the way upstairs.

An assistant followed with a coffin, which was placed on the floor.

Mr. Mole was then perfectly rigid and motionless, and taking him up in his arms, Mynheer Van Clootz laid him down in the coffin.

As it happened he did not quite fit.

It was necessary to bend the legs a little, to make them come in, and this Mynheer Van Clootz proceeded to do with some force.

Jack had turned to the window, and was wiping away the tears as they chased one another down his face.

Suddenly he heard a noise, and Mynheer Van Clootz, uttering strange cries in his own sweet native tongue, ran past him.

Turning to the coffin, Jack saw Mr. Mole sitting up, and looking curiously around him.

"Harkaway," said Mr. Mole, "I have overslept myself, and the bed feels hard. What have you got for breakfast? My stomach is strangely empty."

Jack could understand this when he recolled how the doctor had worked the pump the night before.

His surprise at seeing Mr. Mole alive was immense, but his joy equalled his astonishment.

The Dutchman and his assistant were so frightened that they did not stop until they reached their place of business, for they thought they had seen a ghost.

"Where am I?" continued Mr. Mole, looking round him; "and what have I been doing?"

His mind was so confused that he could not recollect anything.

"You have been on a visit to another land, sir, and I'm very glad they let you come back again," said Jack.

"Let me see; I drank that wine—I was ill—the doctor came—I got worse, and I suppose you thought me dead."

"That we did, sir."

"I must have fallen into a trance. The stomach-pump saved my life, but the effect of the poison was to send me into a deep sleep. What is this? A coffin? Bless my soul! I have had a narrower escape than I thought."

"You would have been screwed down in another five minutes, sir," said Jack. "The cold meat box was ready, and things won't keep in this climate."

A shudder ran through Mr. Mole as he extricated himself from the coffin and threw off the ghastly cerements of the grave.

"I say, sir," exclaimed Jack, "have a lark with Harvey."

"In what way, may I ask?"

"Go into our sitting-room, and frighten him into fits. If Emily is there, I will prepare her for your resurrection."

"Upon my word, Harkaway, I do not think I ought to lend myself to such an imposture," replied Mr. Mole, with a grim smile.

"Just for fun, sir,"

"And moreover, I am physically incompetent. I am consumed with a raging thirst, and my unhappy stomach is as empty as a drum."

"It shall be filled, sir, without delay. Tog yourself up a bit, and in ten minutes come downstairs. I will order a cold collation—champagne and cold fowl, or something; and if we don't give Dick fits, I'm not all there."

"Very well. On that understanding, I fall in with your views, but I will first offer up a thanksgiving for my deliverance from the grave."

"Perhaps you are reserved for a different fate, sir. Water won't drown you, poison don't hurt you, savages won't eat you, snakes won't bite you, and two wives only make you grow fat and saucy."

"Do you mean to imply that I was born to be hanged, Harkaway?" asked Mr. Mole.

"No, sir, we won't say that; we will say that you were born to be elevated. Don't rile, sir. Don't shy your coffin at me. I'm not strong, and mother says I'm not to be hurt," exclaimed Jack, laughing, as he ran from the room.

"What a boy that is," remarked Mr. Mole, as he poured some water into the basin and washed his face and hands. "But I do think he is pleased to see me alive. What an escape I have had, to be sure?"

Jack's first care was to order the banquet, as he called it, and to see the best spread that could be got ready at a moment's notice was sent upstairs.

The food and Jack entered the room together, and Harvey exclaimed—

"What, grubbing again? You have only just had your breakfast. What a fellow you are to gorge! Have you seen the decent thing done by poor old Mole?'

"Yes; he's screwed down as tight as wax."

"How did he look?"

"Fine. I never felt so queer in my life as when I took my last look at him," said Jack.

"I couldn't do it," exclaimed Harvey. "I tried to screw my courage up, but it was no good at all. You've more pluck than I have."

"Of course. You're not in the hunt with me."

Harvey wiped his eyes with his sleeve.

"Hullo!" replied Jack; "why those weeps? You're doing the briny, old woman."

"And I'm not ashamed of it. If any one would bring old Mole to life, I'd——"

Harvey hesitated.

"What would you do?" asked Jack.

"I'd stand on my head in a corner till dinner time, hang me if I wouldn't," replied Harvey at a loss how to express the gratitude he would feel in the event of such an improbable occurrence taking place.

Jack smiled quietly, and drawing Emily on one side, whispered to her—

"Don't be frightened. Mole isn't dead. It was only a trance. I want to startle Dick; do you twig?"

Emily looked astonished and made no reply, though she intimated by a significant look that she understood him.

Going back to the table Jack drank some iced water and exclaimed—

"Perhaps Mole's ghost will favour you with a visit some of these fine nights, Master Dick."

"And if it did do you think I should care? I've seen too many things in my time to be frightened easily," replied Dick.

"Wouldn't anything frighten you?"

"No. I don't believe any mortal thing would, after the course of Pisang I have been put though," replied Harvey, boldly.

At this moment Mole entered the room.

He looked gravely, almost threateningly at Harvey, who trembled violently, and showed symptoms of being startled, if not really frightened.

"It—it's Mole!" he stammed.

Mr. Mole raised his arm, and Harvey shrank back into a corner.

"Jack," he cried, "what is it?"

"What's what?" replied Jack, rather ungrammatically.

"Why this—this thing."

"I can't see anything," answered Jack.

"Not see anything? Then it's a ghost. It's Mole's spirit! What shall I do?"

"Get under the table," suggested Jack.

Thoroughly terrified, Harvey crept under the table and laid still, until a hearty laugh fell upon his ears.

He got out of his undignified position and beheld Mr. Mole eating a salmon steak, done to a turn, as fast as he could.

"Ghosts don't eat!" he exclaimed.

"Any fool knows that," replied Jack.

"Then it's no ghost."

"Touch him, and see. He's tucking in a good un," continued Jack. "Thought you said nothing could frighten you, eh, Dick?"

Harvey looked crestfallen; but he was not yet satisfied, and walking up to Mr. Mole, said—

"Is it really you, sir?"

"Yes, Harvey, I am the sleeper awakened. Pour some of that iced hock into the silver goblet," replied Mr. Mole; "you may be my cup bearer."

Harvey did so, and remarked—

"I am delighted to see you again, sir; but I must admit I was considerably knocked off my perch at first, although I wasn't really frightened."

"Now, Dick, that won't do. It's a clumsy get off," exclaimed Jack, laughing.

"No more I was."

"You know you were in a dismal fright."

"I wasn't. It was only a slight shock, that's all. I knew it was Mole all along."

Emily approached Jack, and said in a low tone—

"I fancy I can see some one listening at the half-open door."

"Nonsense!" replied Jack.

"I'm almost certain," she persisted.

"Hold hard," replied Jack; "I'll soon unearth the fox. Wonder who it is?"

He approached the door on tiptoe.

"Oh, be careful, Jack!" said Emily.

He nodded, and prepared himself for a struggle.

CHAPTER XCIV.

FRANK DAVIS HAS HIS EAR NAILED TO THE DOOR.

THE next minute Jack bounded over the threshold.

A man who was in reality listening at the door, tried to escape.

Jack seized him in his powerful grasp.

There was a short, sharp struggle.

Presently he reappeared, dragging the listener in triumph into the room.

A glance sufficed to show that he had captured his enemy, Frank Davis, though how he came in his peculiar position, or what his motive was, he had yet to find out.

"So Mr. Davis, you add listening at doors to your other accomplishments," said Jack, holding him down.

Davis looked sheepishly around.

"I came to pay you a visit," he said, "to explain, or rather, to demand an explanation."

"Why did you not send your name up like a gentleman?"

"I did not consider it necessary."

"You were anxious, I suppose, to know if we were all dead, but you see we are alive and kicking," said Jack.

"I have heard something about some poisoned wine being sent to you. Though why you should accuse me of the crime, I don't know."

"We have our reasons."

"Ever since you have been in Singapore," cried Davis, "you have persecuted me. First of all, you knock me into the harbour; then you break into my house, and cover me with tar and feathers; now you assault me, in an infamous manner. What is the reason of it?"

"It's all very well to put on a face of injured innocence," replied Jack; "but, as I said, we have our reasons."

"What are they?"

"Did you not insult me?"

"Not that I am aware of," replied Davis. "Let me get up, please."

"Get up, if you like, but if you stir

without my permission, when you are on your pins, it will not be well for you."

Davis rose, and shook himself.

"Now answer my question," continued Jack. "Did you not hire a man to stab me?"

"Certainly not."

"Did you, or did you not carry off Emily?"

"I was wrong there, I admit, but I offer a most handsome apology to the young lady," replied Davis, sheepishly.

"Did you not send me a present of poisoned wine, which might have killed the lot of us, and very nearly settled Mr. Mole's goose as it was?"

"No, I deny that."

"Were you not listening at the door to hear what our suspicions about you were?" pursued Jack.

"I repeat," replied Davis, "that I came to demand an explanation of your conduct, which I hold that I have a right to do."

"It will be the best for you to clear out of Singapore as soon as you can, or I shall insist upon the authorites arresting you," replied Jack.

"That you can do as you like about," said Davis, with his accustomed insolence. "Do you still refuse me an explanation?"

"You cowardly humbug!" cried Jack, "you will see directly what I will do with you, Dick, go and get me a hammer and a long nail."

Harvey ran downstairs at once, and soon returned with what he had been sent for.

"Now," cried Jack, "hold this cur up against the door."

Harvey seized the unfortunate Davis, and pushed him up against the edge of the door.

Jack approached with the nail and hammer.

"In Heaven's name, what new outrage am I to be subjected to?" cried Davis.

He was watching the preparations with dismay.

"You needn't howl before you're hurt," replied Jack.

"Miss Emily," pleaded Davis, "you are a lady; intercede for me."

Emily remained silent.

"Mr. Mole," exclaimed Davis.

"Sir to you," replied Mr. Mole, with his mouth full.

"Save me from this treatment; I am a gentleman."

"Pity you don't behave as such," answered Mr. Mole. "I cannot help you. People who send other people poisoned wine, and subject them to the exhaustive action of the stomach-pump, deserve no mercy at my hands."

"Hold him tight, Dick," exclaimed Jack.

When Davis' right ear was close to the door Jack put the nail against it.

A sharp blow from the hammer forced the nail through the cartilage, another sent the iron into the door, a third made it fast; and Davis had his ear nailed to the woodwork.

A sharp cry of mingled pain and rage broke from him.

"You shall repent this!" he screamed.

"That is how we serve fellows that listen at doors," remarked Jack, surveying him complacently.

"It just serves him right," observed Harvey; adding, "what a fool he looks."

"So you would look a fool, under the circs.," replied Jack.

"Don't keep him long like that," replied Emily, whose tender heart felt for him.

"I shall," answered Jack. "We are all going out for a walk when Mr. Mole's done pitching in, and he will have to stop where he is till somebody finds him, unless he likes to bolt and leave his ear behind him."

"I am just getting my second wind," said Mr. Mole, attacking a larded capon.

"Don't hurry, sir; the performance is not yet over. Come here, Emily."

"What for, Jack?"

"To stick pins into him. Come along. Stick them in anywhere soft, and make him holloa again, like the cur he is."

"This behaviour is worthy only of savages," protested Davis.

"How about the poisoned wine and abduction?" asked Jack. "Is that civilised?"

"I am sure Miss Emily is too much of a lady to torture me," continued Davis.

"She will have to do what she is told. You come and prick him Emily, or there will be a row in the house."

Emily hesitated.

"Let him off, Jack dear; you have punished him enough," she said.

"This is mutiny in the camp; but I suppose I must, if you ask me, my pet," replied Jack. "Put on your sun hat, and let us go out. I can't breathe while I am in the room with this fellow."

Davis presented at once a painful and a ridiculous figure, nailed by the ear, as he was, to the door post.

His face was distorted with rage.

"Look here, Mr. Harkaway," he exclaimed.

"What now?" asked Jack.

"You sail in a day or two for England, and you may think that you will escape me."

"I ain't afraid of you. Now I know what you are and what your game is, I shall be on my guard."

"Never mind; listen to what I have to say. I, too, am going to England to complete my education at a university."

"I daresay it requires it," sneered Jack.

"Mark my words, we shall meet again."

"I hope not."

"But I say we shall," replied Davis.

"Well, there is one comfort, England isn't Singapore; and if you try any of your poisoning dodges on there, you will find yourself in the wrong box."

"You hope to marry Emily," continued Davis.

"That's my business," replied Jack, flushing.

"I tell you, she shall never be your wife. Never, never; as long as I live."

Jack stared at him in amazement.

"You're a nice sort of fellow," he said. "What do you mean by threatening me?"

"I speak the truth, and you will find that making an enemy of me was the worst day's work you ever did," answered Davis, vindictively.

Suddenly a gust of wind blew the door to with great violence.

A horrible cry broke from Davis, who was forced outside.

Dismal yells were heard in the corridor.

"By Jove!" said Harvey, "he's left his ear behind him."

"Has he? I didn't mean that," exclaimed Jack.

He opened the door, and there, on the post, was the unfortunate man's ear, literally torn from his head.

They could see nothing of Davis.

The fact was that, mad with pain and rage, he had run away, holding his handkerchief to his head, to seek for medical assistance.

"Blow me tight," said Jack, "that's a funny thing. He's a settled member now. I am sorry for it though."

"You have two enemies, Hunston and Davis," said Harvey. "The first is one-armed, and the second one-eared."

"Can't help spotting them in a crowd then."

"Not much."

"I didn't mean to wrench his ear off," observed Jack; "though he deserves it, for what he has done to us."

"What's that?" asked Mr. Mole, throwing himself back in his chair with a sigh of satisfaction.

"Mr. Davis has bolted, sir, and left his ear behind him."

"Left his ear! Ha, ha! You're joking."

"I'm not. There it is on the doorpost," replied Jack.

"Dear, dear! What a strange proceeding. Poor fellow! Well, I had no hand in it, that's one comfort, though I hope you won't get into trouble for pulling people's ears off."

"It was an accident. I nailed him up, but I didn't make the door blow to."

"It came as a punishment to him. He was cursing like a pagan," observed Harvey.

"Can't be helped," said Jack. "Have you fed, sir?"

"Well, Harkaway, very well," answered Mr. Mole; "the inner man is comforted, and Isaac's himself once more. I shall now be glad to join you in a drive—say a drive, for walk I cannot, with all the luggage I have taken on board."

"We must not let Emily see this," replied Jack. "I'll undo the ear, and you can swab the claret with the table cloth, Dick."

The blood was quickly wiped up, and Jack unfastened the ear, which he wrapped in a piece of paper with ghastly precision.

"What shall we do with the lug?" he asked.

A waiter solved the difficulty by coming in and saying—

"Mr. Davis has sent for his ear, sir."

In spite of the horror of the whole thing, Jack could not helping smiling.

"Here it is; in the paper," he replied. "Give it his messenger with my compliments."

The servant, who was an American, and who had seen a little shooting and

"YOU GIVE ME TWELVE HOURS TO DECIDE,' SAID JACK."

bowie knifing, did not seem in the least surprised.

One man had gouged another's eye out in a bar and then thrown it at him, so that acts of violence were nothing new to his experience.

"That's done with," said Harvey. "Wonder if they can stick it on?"

"Not they," replied Jack.

"Funny idea, a cove sending for his ear."

"Very. Wasn't my answer studiously polite?" asked Jack.

"Quite O. K. He's nothing to grumble at," replied Harvey.

They went for a drive, and Jack could not help wondering if he should meet with Frank Davis in England.

If Hunston made his way back, and Davis really went to England, he would have two determined enemies to contend with.

"I don't care," he muttered, in his dare-devil way; "one's only got one arm, and the other's minus an ear. What is the good of a man with one ear? Let them rip, they can't hurt me."

During the remainder of their stay at Singapore, which was very brief, they neither saw nor heard anything more of Frank Davis.

When word was brought them that the steamer was ready to sail for Europe, they were all delighted, especially Emily and Mr. Mole.

While he was residing in Singapore, Jack had made a wonderful collection of savage guns, bows, spears, and all sorts of things he thought would be interesting to the good folks at home.

Six boxes, or rather packing cases, were filled with curiosities of savage and tropical life.

He had enough to start a museum.

And with all this he had a supply of live stock, including monkeys, parrots, and even a snake or two.

When he wrote home, he spoke in the most affectionate and loving terms of Emily.

He wanted to make sure of a welcome for the poor orphan whom he loved so fondly.

She had no one but him to look to now.

He was her only hope.

Her only friend.

CHAPTER XCV.

HOME AGAIN.

LUGGAGE was not a consideration to our travellers.

All they possessed they had bought at Singapore.

Monday had attired himself in canvas shirt, trousers, and jacket, with a straw hat.

Harvey said he looked a very intelligent and decent nigger indeed.

They went on board of the steamer, and made a rapid passage to London, without encountering any accident.

"This was a wonder," Jack remarked, considering he was on board.

Harvey went to his father's house in the suburbs.

Mr. Mole took up his abode at an hotel.

Jack and Emily, with Monday, went by train to Mr. Bedington's house.

They were not unexpected, because the boys had telegraphed from Singapore, informing them of their safety and their probable speedy arrival.

It was a lovely evening in autumn, as the fly drove up to the house.

Emily's heart beat quicker than Jack's.

"If your friends should not be kind to me," she said, "I shall die."

Jack pressed her hand.

"Do not fear on that account," he said softly.

In a few minutes he was shaking his father by the hand, and being kissed by his mother.

"My boy, my darling!" exclaimed Mrs. Bedington, "we never expected to see you again. What perils you must have gone through."

"A few, mother," replied Jack. "I shall astonish you when I tell you some stories."

"So you have had enough of the sea, John?" observed his father.

"Enough, and to spare," answered Jack.

Emily remained timidly in the background.

"But," replied Mrs. Bedington, "where is little Emily, of whom you spoke in your letter which came overland from Aden?"

"Emmy, where are you?" cried Jack.

Emily stepped forward.

"My dear child," continued Mrs. Bedington, "in future you are to be my daughter. We are not strangers, you know, for we have met before."

Emily sobbed on her shoulder.

"Bless me! what's this?" exclaimed Mr. Bedington.

He saw something black, with white gleaming teeth, in the passage.

"That's my tame nigger," said Jack.

"Your what?" said his mother.

"Only Monday. It's the cheese where I've been to start a private nigger."

"Step forward, Monday, and let's have a look at you," said Mr. Bedington.

Monday came forward, bowing profoundly.

"He saved my life, mother, more than once," remarked Jack.

"That is enough, dear, to secure him a home beneath this roof.

"Monday, mum, do um work for Mast' Jack, but he no wait 'pon other peoples," said the black, drawing himself up.

"He's a king in his own country, and gave up a throne to stick to me," said Jack.

"What a wonderful instance of fidelity!" replied Mrs. Bedington.

"It's true, mother. I'm not cramming you."

"I didn't say you were, John. Have you anything else?"

"Yes; lots of things."

"Any monkeys, parrots, vegetable productions; all the Fauna and Flora of the distant land you have visited?"

"I think you will find I have a very neat collection indeed, mother," replied Jack.

Monday was sent to the servants' hall, and was as much an object of amusement to the inmates as they were to him.

Mrs. Bedington and Emily retired upstairs to talk at their ease, while Mr. Bedington and Jack took a turn arm-in-arm in the garden.

It may be readily imagined that some wonderful stories were related that night.

Jack and Emily were the lion and lioness of the evening.

In a few days, friends came from all parts to see them.

Mr. Crawcour and his masters were among the visitors.

Everyone listened breathlessly to tales of Limbians and Pisangs, of desert islands and volcanoes, of pirates and dungeons.

All concurred in detestation of Hunston.

It was hoped that he had perished in the pirate city. Jack had his doubts.

When questioned upon the subject he would say—

"The begger has nine lives. I daresay he'll turn up again some day."

For a fortnight the time passed very pleasantly.

He rode his father's best horse, and drove Emily out in his mother's pony carriage.

Monday accompanied them on all occasions, as groom or personal attendant.

After a while Mr. Bedington called Jack into his study.

"Have you had enough of sea," he asked, "or do you still want to follow it as a profession?"

"No," replied Jack; "I don't."

"Now, the question is, what would you like to be?"

"A soldier," replied Jack. "Buy me a commission in the army."

"I have no objection to that, but don't you think you would be all the better for a year or two at an university?" replied Mr. Bedington.

"Just what I should like."

"We wish to study your happiness," answered Mr. Bedington. "Now which university would you like to go to?"

"Oxford; it is more swell than Cambridge," replied Jack.

Mr. Bedington smiled.

"Very well, to Oxford you shall go."

"Thank you very much," replied Jack. "May I ask you another favour?"

"Certainly."

"You are well off."

"Yes."

"My friend Harvey's parents are poor. He was my friend during my troubles with the savages, and he has often told me it would make a man of him if he could go to Oxford."

"Well?" replied Mr. Bedington.

"Will you pay for him too? I should so like to have him up at Oxford with me."

"Yes," replied Mr. Bedington.

Jack was overjoyed at this concession.

It was settled that he and Harvey should go to Oxford.

Emily went away to Paris to finish her education.

Jack and Harvey had a private tutor at Mr. Bedington's, who in a short time prepared them for their examination.

This they passed with flying colours.

At the commencement of term they were to take up their residence at college.

We shall now introduce to our readers the career of Jack Harkaway at Oxford.

We trust they will follow him with as much interest, and may we hope, pleasure as they have hitherto been kind enough to do.

Life at Oxford presents temptations and trials, adventures and triumphs, of all of which it will be found that our old friend Jack Harkaway had his full share, and bore himself bravely through everything.

End of Jack Harkaway After Schooldays.

NOTICE.—Now ready, JACK HARKAWAY AT OXFORD. At all Booksellers.